Jack leaned for ___ going on with that st___ do you call them? The sticks with the skulls on them?"

"That—that's a looooong story." Abe gusted another cloud of smoke.

"We've got time."

"Yeah. Well, there's somethin' about this place. How good are you at believing crazy stories?"

Jack's eyebrows arched. "Try me. I believed the marine recruiter."

"Hah. I bet you did. All right, well... There's somethin' in the bottom of that valley."

"You mean the stone where you found me? Is that what you're talking about?"

"No, that's the Isaac Stone. It's only halfway down the valley side. You didn't make it all the way down. This thing is somethin' different." The old man looked ill at ease.

"What is it?"

"Somethin' evil. Somethin' we call the Fountain."

The Fountain

by

Christopher Farris

The Fountain

Cover Art by *Kristian Norris*

The Wild Rose Press, Inc.
PO Box 708
Adams Basin, NY 14410-0708
Visit us at www.thewildrosepress.com

Publishing History
First Black Rose Edition, 2021
Trade Paperback ISBN 978-1-5092-3383-0
Digital ISBN 978-1-5092-3384-7

Published in the United States of America

Dedication

For Arianna, who saved my life.
For Deede who stood by me.
For Greg who lent me his imagination.

Prelude

1980: The Boston Mountains, Arkansas

The wind cut hard across the mountaintop cemetery. It sent skirling leaves and the season's first flurry of icy snow over the weathered gravestones. Abe stood holding his hat, his hands clenched, rawboned and knotty. The old man's lean shoulders were stooped, his long white beard combed and spread across his chest. His suit was clean but too large and shiny at the elbows and knees—old, like Abe.

Father Preddy laid his hand on Abe's shoulder. He was rewarded with a scowl and a refusal to meet his eyes. Preddy's mouth moved as if to speak but then stilled. He squinted into the wind instead. Clouds rolled across the rounded mountain peaks. He ran a hand under his eyes and walked away.

"Why'd you do it, Sam?" Abe's voice grated with unshed tears and smothered anger.

The freshly filled hole was an obscene wound in the soft flesh of the earth, another old man returned to the soil, Abe's only friend for years. More than a friend, his best friend, a teacher, a confidant, a source of strength and, most importantly, the second to the last of the Wall's defenders. A man who had always known what to do, until, one day, he hadn't. Until now.

"Jesus, what am I gonna do now?" He could feel

the Wall in the back of his mind, strong at the moment, still solid, but weakening, already weakening. He didn't know if he was strong enough, smart enough, or wise enough to keep the barrier going. He was old and so, so tired; he was the last of the faithful.

A wave of fury and fear rolled through him. "You coward. You dirty, dirty coward." He spat. "Why? Why did you do this? You know I can't do the work on my own. People are going to start hurting themselves, hurting others. People are going to die, Sam! You knew! You knew!" The yell sounded flat in the dead air. It disappeared, unheard, unnoticed. He staggered as another gust of wind tried to push him away, adjusted his crooked tie for the fiftieth time, and wiped away a tear. He licked his dry lips.

"You left me alone." Abe dropped to his knees in the cold, careless of his suit pants, and placed his leathery hand palm down on the upturned earth. He bent his head. His lips moved, a whispered prayer, an invocation, a pledge. He closed his fingers on the dirt, gripped the powdery soil in his fist, and rose haltingly back to his feet. He inspected the handful. Later, he'd cast the soil at the base of the big oak on his property and, in this way, keep some part of Sam's spirit as a ward against the encroaching evil. He looked at the darkening sky, put the earth into his pocket, and walked away.

The Wall was fading, always fading, and now there was only Abe to do what needed to be done. God willing, he'd find a way.

Chapter 1
Jack

1987: LaFayette, Arkansas

Suicide or sobriety? Jack wavered after exiting the midnight Greyhound from San Diego to LaFayette. He slept in a park the first night and surfed an oxycodone high, then decided to live a little longer. On day two, he found a dishwashing job at a greasy spoon called the White Spot. He found the name ominous, but it was a normal diner, nothing special. The job was nothing special either.

The nights were cool, and there were cicadas and lightning bugs. Mountains loomed nearby, old and rounded, hazed and mysterious some days, clear and tempting others. They called to him.

He took the last of his pills on day three. *Sayonara to that.*

On day four, the junk left his system. He found his nose running, stomach knotting up, and joints aching. It hurt to move, but he had a difficult time staying put. He wandered all night and was jittery at the job, dropped some dishes and got yelled at. That night he drank too much and passed out in a park.

The next morning, he couldn't make it into the White Spot. He had a terrible hangover and nasty flu symptoms. He spent the day curled on a park bench and wished that God would fix one of his mistakes by killing him on the spot. That didn't happen. In desperation, Jack looked for a rehab. They had warm beds and square meals. He pooled his few remaining quarters and made some phone calls. He found one.

The Army of God was a low brick structure with fast-food wrappers blowing in the parking lot. A ten-foot-tall cross glowed over the steel entrance door. It glared and beckoned in the early morning dark while Jack kicked his heels on the pavement trying to decide whether to go in. Sick and hungry as he was, he still had his doubts. The cross mocked him. He made his way over the street anyway. He felt like he was checking himself into prison.

The induction room was small and tiled with orange industrial linoleum. The receptionist's desk hid behind a sheet of thick Plexiglas. The room was empty. He waved at the CCTV camera and sat on the couch to wait. His knees jumped and quivered.

An older man walked past the desk behind the window, noticed Jack and stopped. "You checking in?" He leaned on the desk, and his gray ponytail fell over his shoulder. His eyes looked kind.

"Maybe. What's it all about?" Jack sniffled and ran his sleeve across his running nose.

"Just a place to get clean, man. But you gotta be twenty-four hours sober first. You got twenty-four?"

"Yeah. More like forty-eight." Jack didn't figure alcohol counted.

"Yeah?"

"Yeah."

The man took in Jack's wind-burned face and sun-faded, stained work shirt and shrugged. "I have things

I've got to do right now. We're not technically open for induction yet. Take this flyer." He slid it through the slot under the glass. "Read it and see if you're still interested."

Jack flipped it open, then closed.

"Don't go busting the place up," the man said. "You hear me? You need a bathroom, we've got port-a-potties out back. Someone will be with you in about..." He checked his watch. "I guess about two hours. Even if you're not interested in staying, you can have breakfast, at least. Sound good?"

Jack nodded.

"I'm Robert. I'm a counselor here. I hope you stay." He smiled and walked away.

Jack sat on the couch and read through the pamphlet and then again. He was having a hard time tracking the words. His hands shook. The pamphlet was full of God and Christ, sinners and salvation, but it didn't look cultish, no mention of space aliens or gurus. He could fake his way through. He hung on while his body jittered and sweated. He cursed these people who left a sick man suffering for two hours. Later, a woman with brassy hair and linebacker's shoulders arrived. She frowned at him and made him wait while she got coffee. She wasted more time flipping through a manila folder with DIVORCE written on the front. Eventually, she explained the program to him.

Salvation, Jennifer told him, wasn't a requirement. Patients were expected to attend church services and to work in the thrift store. He'd have to deal with therapy sessions and obey a curfew. Free room and board if he could follow the rules. She wasn't selling it to him. In fact, she was pissing him off. She didn't look him in the eye during her recitation, spending her attention on touching up her fingernails and moving papers around. As far as Jack could tell, she didn't give a shit whether he checked in or dropped dead. At the end, she asked: "So you stayin' or what?"

He almost didn't do it. He let the minutes go by while he considered.

"Take it or leave it, buddy," she said. "It's no skin off my nose. We're the only free game in town."

He smothered a flash of rage. The thought of a warm bed won out.

He signed in.

****

Forty-seven days later, Jack was pill free. He still wanted them, every day, but he'd found a way to keep things manageable. He'd snuck out to the corner liquor store one night. He'd been sneaking drinks ever since. No one had noticed or cared.

Not yet, anyway.

Chapter 2
Jill

1982: Arkansas

The Little Rock airport smelled of damp. Jill stood at the end of the jet way, crossing one unlaced patent leather combat boot over the other. She tugged at her ponytail, adjusted her hoop earrings, and tried to blend in with these Midwesterners. California seemed a long way away.

Abe approached from the crowd. His skin was tanned and spotted with the sun. She gave him a tentative hug. He smelled of pipe smoke and sweat. He returned it as if he didn't know how. Her stomach fell. Jill was nineteen and hadn't seen her grandfather in ten years. She hadn't expected to feel like a stranger.

Abe eyed her mountain of baggage, scowled, hitched up his overalls and helped her drag the stuff out to his battered pickup. She climbed into the dusty passenger seat and searched for her seatbelt. Abe noticed. "Ain't no seatbelts. She's too old. Don't worry, I'll get you there alive."

She gripped the door handle and braced herself with her feet as Abe swayed the farm truck through Little Rock's evening traffic. This wasn't her daddy's Mercedes. She felt naked without the retaining belt.

The city looked tired, older, and dustier than Los

Angeles or Anaheim. The skies were lowering and dark, the air thick with humidity. Abe and Jill exchanged few words as Abe drove north and west into the mountains. The tired, low concrete buildings and gravelly overpasses gave way to trees and hills, rivers and farms. Abe seemed to relax.

He smiled shyly and patted her hand, his palm like a leather glove, seamed and hot. The gesture was loving and brought a tear to her eye. She couldn't remember the last time her father had touched her in passing. He lit his pipe. The smell of vanilla and old spices filled the truck with a feeling of reassurance, and Jill began to relax, too. Maybe choosing to attend college in Arkansas would be okay after all.

The miles rolled by.

****

Jill learned to love Abe by small steps. Abe, like Jill's father, was taciturn, though unlike her father, Abe was present and interested in her life. The old man did not speak his love; he showed it. The next time he picked her up, his truck had new seatbelts. Abe paid attention; it was how he loved people.

He lived in a rundown motel on the side of a scenic highway that twisted its way over the tallest mountain in the Boston Mountain range. The place was called the Moondust Motor Inn and had few visitors. One of the buildings was falling down, the second peeling and dusty, and the third was taken up by office and Abe's living space. The neon sign out front glowed fitfully at night. She suspected that many travelers thought the place abandoned.

There was a pattern to Abe's bachelor life, and though happy to interrupt it for her, it was a struggle to get him to share. Jill's grandmother Sarah had died years before, his best friend after. He had been living in silence since. Jill concluded that the best way to connect with Abe was to work with him. She began to look for things that they could do together.

It worked. When painting the motel's fascia boards or planting flowers, Abe was a little less laconic than normal. He was a natural teacher and loved to touch her hands, to guide her in her work. He took pride in showing her the correct way to do things. Better, her grandfather dropped hints about her grandmother in-between offering instructions. "Zinnias were your grandma's favorite flower," he might say. "You gotta plant them about six inches apart. Like this, see?"

Jill grew used to the look of Abe's hands, cracked and dirty from working on his land. Her initial impression, fostered by his falling-down motel, of a careless and backward country bumpkin, was pushed aside as she saw how hard he worked at all of his pursuits. Jill began to notice the care that he took with his tools and the fine quality of his work.

Hummingbird feeders proliferated on his property; deer feeders hid in the edge of the forest. Rabbits darted around the corners of the buildings, and a sleepy, ambling skunk had startled Jill more than once. She was convinced that the little black and white animal lived in the building with the falling roof.

Abe was kind to his sheep in a gruff manner and was fond of his chickens, though not so much his rooster. "Ain't nothin' but a rapist in pretty feathers."

The old bird had done its best to spur Jill the first time she'd entered the hen house. He was a big red-and-black bastard named Scratch, and she hated him. She'd danced around it the next few times she'd visited.

Abe noticed and pulled her aside. "You can't be puttin' up with an ornery rooster." He placed a hand on her shoulder, then strode toward the bird. It scooted away from him, squawking its outrage. Abe stopped with his hands on his hips. "You come on in this here yard, and when he goes for you, you grab hold of him, and you hold him tight against your side. Get some gloves on first. You got that?"

She nodded.

"I'd grab him myself," he continued, "but I done it before, and it won't teach him no respect for you, if you don't do it yerself. You understand? Put on some long sleeves too; he's gonna try and cut you."

Jill kept her eye on the rooster when she returned. Scratch danced in place, his head low and wings extended. His beady, hate-filled eyes fixed on her. She took a deep breath and hesitated.

"Well," Abe said, "it ain't gonna get no better, you just standing there. Sometimes, you gotta go forward in life, grab things, and wrestle them. It's seldom pleasant, but that's the way of it."

Jill's stomach churned with fear. *It's a bird. It's just a bird.*

Abe crossed his arms and shifted from one foot to the other, waiting.

She squared her shoulders and walked toward Scratch. The rooster launched itself at her with a raucous clatter, and then, somehow, it was under her arm. She wasn't certain how she'd managed to grab it, let alone hold it, but there it was between forearm and torso, struggling like mad, wild-eyed, and squawking over the injustice. "What—what do I do now,

Grandpa?"

"Well." He sounded more surprised than Jill wanted to hear. "You done it. Look at that. Now you gotta hold onto it for a while. Just walk around with it. He'll settle soon, soon's he figures you're the boss. But also...just to drive her home. Turn to face the north." He pointed. "Close your eyes."

Jill frowned.

"Close your eyes, I said."

She did.

"Now," Abe continued, "say this prayer: Lord God, give me power over this here spirit of the air."

Jill peeked between her lashes, looking to see if Abe was making fun of her.

"Well? What you waiting for?"

"Lord God," she said, still waiting for the old man to laugh. "Please, uh, give me power over—over..."

"This spirit of the air," he said.

"Please give me power over this spirit of the air." Scratch settled down. The rooster molded itself to her side. Surprised, she almost released the bird.

"Don't let him go just yet," Abe said. "Sometimes, they play possum like that. You gotta do the whole thing, prayer and hold him. It's all part of it."

"Part of what, Grandpa?" Scratch gazed up at her with its insane, but calm, eyes.

"Just some stuff we do back here in the hills."

She carried the rooster for the next fifteen minutes, as instructed, and, when she put it down, it settled with a meek flumpf. When she walked away, the rooster sprang to its feet and followed her like a happy puppy.

"Well," said Abe. "I ain't never seen that before. I mean, well, I never." He gave her a long measuring

11

look and that night, over fried chicken—not Scratch—he'd taken her into his confidence. He'd told her about witchery then and white witchery, which he'd called witchmastering.

She'd sat through his tall tales and explanations. She was curious but a little weirded out. He'd explained that witches gave their souls to the devil, and that he didn't believe in that kind of thing; he didn't, in fact, believe that that kind of practice even worked, but that witchmasters, well, that was a whole other thing.

"What's the difference?" she'd asked.

He'd pushed himself back from the table, loaded his pipe, and puffed until he got a smooth draw. "Well," he drawled. "It's like…" He paused. "Witches are all tied up with Satan worship and doing evil to people and what not. Witchmasters are…well, they're mostly helpful. They used to do a lot of removin' of curses and such. They just knowed things, you know? Like how to chase off haunts and tell weather and…well, some of it was silly, like love charms and such. But it's other stuff, too. Like…well, like what you did with Scratch out there."

"Hugging a chicken, Grandpa?" She gave him a dubious look.

"No, missy. Not hugging no chicken. What you did was *turn* that rooster. Stronger than I ever seen it done. Most people try that, they get a rooster that leaves them alone. You got a—I dunno what you got, a pet maybe? Tell me you didn't feel something when you was saying that prayer?"

"Well." She thought hard what to say next. She *had* felt something. "I felt…sort of an outrushing."

"Yeah? Hmmm." He puffed on his pipe for a

moment. "Well, we all feel it just a little different. Myself, it feels like rolling a marble around in my brain."

"You're talking about magic, seriously, magic?"

"Well, yeah." He smiled. "Course I am."

She sat, quiet for a moment, wrestling with herself. She didn't want to hurt Abe's feelings. "I don't... I don't really believe in magic, Grandpa. I'm sorry, I don't mean to be rude. It's just—I just don't."

"Yeah. You don't now?" He puffed away at the pipe, arms crossed across his chest. "That feeling you got? That rushin' feeling? That don't mean nothing to you?"

"Adrenaline rush? Relief? I don't know, some reaction to stress, I expect."

Abe rolled his eyes to the kitchen ceiling. "You kids," he said. "It started with your daddy's generation. You un's can't understand nothing 'cause you're too busy knowing everything."

"I'm sorry. It doesn't make any sense to me."

"Look, just—just come with me a second." He opened the kitchen door, led her out to his small patio. "All right, just have a seat in that chair over there." He pointed at the steel table and chair set. She took a seat. Abe gave her a thimble-sized hummingbird feeder. "Hold that."

"What are we—"

"Just hush up a minute, will you?"

Abe screwed his eyes closed, and raised his palms flat into the dusky spring sky. Darkness descended over the valley below them. West to east it crept out of the stones and trees like a nervous cat. Jill was embarrassed for the old man. She held the miniature feeder and looked at her feet. She glanced back at him. His lips were moving.

From the still twilight, a diminutive shape zoomed into sight, hovered over the table. The hummingbird was tiny, machinelike in its jeweled precision. It flashed forward, back, side to side. It made its dainty, jerking approach to the feeder in her hand. Jill held her breath as it lowered its tiny beak into the cup and drew some nectar. The air fanned her fingers as the creature's toy-like wings battered the air. Seconds later, a second, third, fourth arrived. Abe was behind her now, humming a low gravelly drone that rose and fell. More and still more hummingbirds parked themselves in the air above the old metal table. A gentle buzzing encircled her, and flashes of ruby, sapphire, and topaz swam through the air. The first bird was no longer feeding. It regarded her with its tiny eyes, helicoptering in front of her. They were all looking at her. A great cloud of tiny and beautiful fairy creatures, floating in the twilight.

Abe's pitch changed; it went higher, and the birds began to circle in great swirls around her, faster and faster. The beautiful avians choreographed a flickering dance in the dusk until suddenly Abe whistled, and the flock exploded like a firework. Their jeweled bodies scattered across the face of the mountain.

Jill sat, the feeder grasped in trembling fingers. *What the hell was that?*

Abe was silent.

"Grandpa—"

"One more thing." He made a rapid shooing hand, his fingers flexing and then curling, and from the still night, a rush of icy wind curled across the table and blasted over Jill. "There," he said and fell into the chair across from her. "I ain't as strong as I used to be. That's about all I could come up with on the spot, and I don't like doin' that to the hummingbirds, takes a lot of energy out of 'em. But..." He shrugged. "You believe me now?"

"Yes." She grinned. "I want to learn."

Abe winked and took out his pipe, started filling it.

"Will you teach me?" she asked.

He puffed until clouds of smoke separated them and then drifted away. He was quiet for a while, tapping the pipe against his teeth and looking out over the valley. Finally, he smiled. "I expect I will."

For four years, Jill majored in journalism at the university and Witchmastering on her grandfather's mountain. She got good at both.

Chapter 3
Soft Robert

1987: West Port, Arkansas

Something was wrong with Robert. He'd been more temperamental lately. He'd found himself crying for no reason or holding back sudden spurts of liquid rage. It was inexplicable. He had a new batch of men at the Army of God, and most of them, with the exception of Jack, were doing well. He had a lovely wife, a good home, money in the bank. He couldn't figure it out.

Robert's TV remote and slippers were waiting on the footstool when he returned home from work. It was a joke. His wife and he had laughed over the attention that 1950s TV husbands got from their spouses.

She'd grinned. "I bet his wife's got Stockholm Syndrome."

"Nah, he's amazing in bed."

And here was the remote, laid in the lap of a wide-eyed stuffed animal. Both remote and stuffed fox nestled between the points of his slippers. Robert flipped his ponytail over his shoulder and grinned.

He called out to his wife, "Donna, I'm home." Robert's friends complained of empty nests, of wives they hardly knew, but not Robert. Life hadn't always been easy, they'd had their fair share of knocks, marital and otherwise; but now, with the children grown and the arrival of their first grandchild, Robert took a growing pride and enjoyment in Donna. He found her wittier than he remembered, gentler, more graciously beautiful. She proceeded through his life like slow molasses.

"I'm making master's dinner." Her voice lilted from the kitchen.

Robert found her stirring a pot, dressed incongruously in her ragged gardening overalls, dirt stained at the knees and cuffs. Her hair rayed around her face, escaping its restraining clips. Static lifted graying strands to float in the air. She smiled at him with a mischievous eye and turned her back to attend to the stove. "How was your day, dear?"

"Better now that I've—" He enveloped her in a hug.

She jerked, and a great dollop of boiling sauce splashed from her mixing spoon to Robert's cheek and neck. He screamed and struck her with a vicious and savage fist. She was hammered to her knees. Her forehead met the lip of the stove on the way down. The spoon splattered red sauce on the tile.

She wept, sprawled on the cold surface, fearful eyes on her husband's face. Her lovely mouth was whited with shock. A huge red bruise bloomed on her cheekbone and brow.

Blood, oh blood. It trickled from her forehead. He stood with pudgy fist raised and tried to frame apologies, groped for words to explain, for a reason that he could not find.

Chapter 4
Jack

1987: LaFayette, Arkansas

Jack called his counselor "Soft" Robert. He was earnest, wore cardigans, had a graying ponytail, a propensity for weeping while telling a story, and a soft-spoken voice. Jack had to lean in closer and closer to hear him when he spoke. It was irritating as hell. Robert enjoyed asking questions like…"What is your truth today?" and "Have you accepted that you're powerless?" and, the one that made Jack's eyes roll, "Have you asked the Lord Jesus to take away your addiction, son?" He made Jack crazy.

Today, an old man sat on the ragged chair parked outside of Soft Robert's office. Jack looked the guy over. The man returned his inspection with washed-out blue eyes. His hair was thin and white, his face age-spotted and wrinkled, and his beard long. He looked like a man who'd spent a lot of his life outdoors. He wore bib overalls and rough worker's boots, a plaid shirt buttoned all the way up, even though it was summer. He had an unlit pipe clenched between his teeth. The man didn't say anything. His eyes bored into Jack as he walked into Soft Robert's office for his noon counseling session.

Jack ignored him. The vodka sat in his belly like a

banked fire. He'd drunk too much this morning. He planned to speak little and listen politely to Soft Robert's whispered advice. After, he'd take a couple more shots and then climb into his bunk for a good afternoon's nap. He'd take it easier on the booze tomorrow.

Robert didn't look his normal welcoming self. The counselor's eyes were red-lined, and when he wiped his hand across his fleshy lips, his knuckles were blued with fresh bruises.

Strange. Jack took the chair across from him.

Robert tapped a pencil on his pad and frowned. His glare was ruined by his smudged glasses. "Well, Johnathon." He insisted on calling Jack by his *whole* birth name. "It looks like we're going to be parting ways. I must say I'm very disappointed in you, I ha—"

"What do you mean, parting ways?" Jack leaned forward to hear him.

"As I was saying." Robert's chair creaked as he leaned away. "I am very disappointed in your progress. I am afraid you had some of us quite fooled." He sniffed. "It seemed you were getting very close to sobriety and, I might add, a real relationship with the Lord Jesus." The capital L and J dropped into place. Soft Robert loved to roll Jesus' name around in his mouth for a while. He couldn't pop the words out like a regular guy.

"I'm sorry, I couldn't quite hear—"

"You heard me fine!" Robert's face flushed. He fiddled with the gold-plated Nails of Christ displayed on his desk. "You've been drinking. You're either drunk or on the way to it right now. Did I say that loudly enough?"

19

Jack sat back. "So…what now? You caught me. What do I have to do to get right? I'm sorry. I'm sure that Jesus—"

"Oh, please! I've heard enough about Jesus out of you. You don't believe in Jesus. Stop trying to play me."

"All right, all right." Jack raised his hands. "I got it. You're right…but surely you're not just going to kick me out."

"Johnathon," Robert said, his voice hitching. "Of course, I don't *want* to kick you out, but you've brought alcohol into—into an institution filled with men who are sincerely trying to get sober. Maybe you don't care about their sobriety; maybe you don't care about your own. Maybe you just don't have what it takes. Whatever, you—"

"I kicked the pills, Goddammit. I can kick the booze."

"Watch your mouth! You don't have any respect for our beliefs, you've made that clear, but if you have a single grain of gratitude in you at all, have a care for the words you use. We are sending you out because you are a danger to the other men—"

"What—"

"A danger." Robert overrode him. "A danger to their sobriety, to their faith, and to their sincere desire to get well. You don't care. I understand. Some of *them* really, really do. You've done this to yourself." His voice had risen higher than Jack had ever heard it.

Jack twisted in his chair. "All right. I guess I'll go back and live on the streets. Not very Christian of you to throw a man to the elements, not what I've heard that good Christians do, but you do it your way, Robert." He cursed under his breath. He had made it through the US Marines Officer Candidate School, faced combat, and brought his men back alive, damn near raised himself, but now, now he couldn't manage to pass muster in this backwater religious institute.

"As it happens, Johnathon, I'm not feeling like a particularly good Christian right now." Slow tears tracked down the counselor's face. He inspected his knuckles, smeared with bruises, yellow and purple, blue and brown. The counselor pulled his hands back and placed them in his lap. A fat tear dropped onto his shirt front.

"Are you okay?" Jack asked.

"We don't normally do this." Robert ignored him. "Father Preddy knows a man who is looking for some help at his motel. You remember the good father from Tuesday night's Bible study?"

Jack nodded.

Robert wiped his eyes again, sniffled a little. "The man who's hiring is sitting outside right this instant. You probably noticed him on the way in. He says he'll give you a place to live and provide you with a living. He knows you're an alcoholic. He says he was one too. It appears he has a soft spot for men like you. I personally think it's a mistake, but..." Robert let the words hang there for a moment. "Are you willing to hear him out? One way or another, you cannot stay here, Johnathon."

Jack didn't have anywhere to go. He gave a short, sharp nod.

"Very well. I had higher hopes for you than this. You are a sincere disappointment. Let me say, Johnathon, that I hope the Lord truly breaks your heart, because—"

Jack leapt from his chair and yanked the office door open. "Hey, mister," he said to the man outside. "You the one hiring?"

Robert gaped at him.

The old man looked at Jack. "Yep."

Jack pointed at Robert and growled. "Give us the office, Robert." Jack turned to the old man. "Mister…" He waited for his future employer to give him his last name but got silence. "Me and…this gentleman need to talk. I'll be out of your hair shortly, Robert."

The counselor frowned.

Jack snarled.

"There's no smoking in here," Robert told the old man hurriedly.

The fellow blinked at him, unlit pipe dangling between his lips.

Robert gathered his dignity and evacuated the office.

Chapter 5
Abe

1987: Army of God Rehab, LaFayette, Arkansas

This Jack kid was tall, lean, too thin maybe, but broad-shouldered. Mid-twenties. His hair was long and sandy blonde. He had a memorable face, all sharp lines and angles with a proud, eagle-like nose. Not a bad-looking fellow, even with the scar that ran from the edge of his right eye down his cheek. He didn't look friendly, though. Not right now, his face flushed with alcohol and anger. There was something in his eyes, like a scared child crouched in a corner and ready to lash out.

Abe didn't want to know the kid that well. He needed someone that he could use. He slumped in Robert's chair, lit his pipe, and sent a cloud of smoke whirling through the room. "You lookin' for a place to stay?"

Jack didn't react to the smoke, even when it curled around his face. "Maybe. What do you have?"

"Motel. Up in the mountains." He waved south. "Town called Windsor."

"Big town?"

"Nope."

"What do you need me to do? What's the job?" The anger was draining from his face.

"Odd labor."

"What's your name? I'm Jack. Jack Diaz."

Abe nodded. He knew who Jack was. "Abe." He drew on his pipe. "Just general work. I got a motel. Old 'un. Built in the fifties. She ain't in great shape. Don't get much visitors no more. But she still gotta be took care of. Fixed up. That's the job."

"I'm not a carpenter, or plumber, or whatever."

"Can't afford a carpenter or plumber. You know how to clear brush? Chop wood? Cut grass? Ever use a hammer or saw before?"

"Yeah. Of course."

Abe shrugged. Problem solved. Question answered.

"What's the pay?"

"Place to sleep. Three squares. You eat what I eat. Fifty bucks a week."

"Jesus, man. Fifty bucks? You've gotta be kidding me!"

"Nope."

"Look, man, I ain't working for slave wages."

"Didn't know slaves got paid nothin'. Live an' learn I guess. You're a drunk, right?"

Jack's face flushed. "Yeah. I'm a drunk."

Abe had expected the kid to bluster. To his credit; he didn't. "You off the drugs?"

"Yeah." Jack cleared his throat. "Yeah."

"I don't care if you drink. I make my own shine. I been told it's pretty good. I don't drink the stuff myself. You can have as much as you want as part of your pay. I ain't got no regular hours and won't hold you to none neither. I just expect you to get your work done. Don't care if you do it at six in the mornin' or six at night. If you get hurt, that's on your own watch. I ain't here to take you under my wing or to babysit you. Ain't gonna be my problem if you get yourself killed. Clear?"

Jack nodded, his face drawn. "What happened to the last guy?"

"Died."

"Yeah?"

"Yep. He was pretty old. No great loss." *Only my last friend.*

"Well…"

"You in or out, kid?"

"I'm in, I guess."

"All right." Abe extended his right hand. "I like to shake on deals."

Jack had a powerful grip but didn't squeeze and there was no tremor. He had more inner strength than Abe had expected. It gave him a moment's pause. He worried that he might have underestimated him. He chewed on his pipe stem and considered reneging on his offer. *I shook on it.* He'd have to make the best of it. Once the kid hit the bottle, he didn't expect he'd be much to worry about in the brains department. "Get your stuff. I'm in the Ford outside. Let's get movin'. I got stuff to do."

****

Jack

Abe stopped at an Army/Navy store, gave Jack twenty bucks, and told him to get some good boots. "Those sneakers ain't gonna do it. You can take it outta your first week's pay."

Jack bought used combat boots and a Ka-Bar knife. The boots went on like a hug and felt like coming home. The knife, well, he had tossed his last blade before leaving San Diego. It was good to be armed again.

Abe's sixties model Ford pickup rattled as it climbed into the mountains. The scenic highway out of LaFayette curled its way over the hills and through dense forest. Great, green trees met and intertwined over the roof of the vehicle. A winding waterway shared the road's route. Jack saw whitewater, then placid stretches, fallen logs, overgrown banks. Men in floppy hats cast and reeled in from the shore. Twenty minutes later, they came to a small valley town, nestled in the enshrouding arms of the mountains. The sign read West Port, Gateway to your Dreams. The houses were small, most clapboard, some native stone, dressed and undressed. Small shops and a fancy coffee shop graced the downtown; a small grocery and a greasy spoon lurked on the mountain highway. It wasn't a rich town. It was tidy.

Abe drove straight through, took the bridge over the Grey River. Teens climbed the river's high rock face and leapt into the water. Children waded the shallows. It reminded Jack of the childhood he wished he'd had. Abe pointed the truck farther south, deeper into the mountains, and West Port disappeared in the truck's rear window.

"How far are we going?" Jack asked.

" 'Bout another twenty minutes."

Jack looked back wistfully.

The road climbed in earnest now. Longer, higher hills followed by shorter drops. It curved and curved back on itself. The river winked at the bottom of the right shoulder. It fell away, lower and lower, as the road rose higher.

"How far up are we going?" Jack shaded his eyes against the sunlight, trying and failing to see the peak of the mountain.

"To the top."

"To the top? Figured…" And strangely enough, he had. West Port, the cliff and river, each corner, each hill, felt less like a discovery than an uncovered memory. Jack was experiencing a moment-by-moment déjà vu that grew stronger the farther south they traveled. It was troubling and, yet, comforting.

The windows of the Moondust Motor Inn winked in the sunlight like old men's eyes. Three long low buildings, cinder block, and half overgrown, awaited Jack and Abe. The main building was in good repair. Someone had touched up the trim, a vibrant red slapped over peeling paint that shone leprously in the sunlight. Freshly planted flowers stretched for sunlight in the shade of the great oak that spread its arms over the courtyard. There were other signs of improvement about the place, though nothing big, a few touches that told Jack that someone was trying.

"All this painting and stuff," Jack asked. "You do this stuff or the last guy?"

"What do you care?" Abe climbed out of the truck.

Jack hurried to catch up with him. "What do you mean, what do I care?"

"Just what I said." Abe slammed the office door behind him.

Jack grabbed his duffle, cursing under his breath. He stopped to take a pull from a hip flask, then banged open the half-glass door. Abe sat puffing his pipe behind an ancient desk. The old man ignored him, rifled through a pile of mail on the desk in front of him. John

Wayne strutted in proud black-and-white across an old Bakelite television screen in the corner.

Jack dropped his duffle. "Look, man, I'm here, you've gotta tell me *something*. You barely said two words all the way up here, then I ask you a perfectly polite question, and you bite my head off. What gives?"

Abe took the pipe from his mouth, shrugged, then replaced it.

Jack gritted his teeth. "What am I doing? Where am I staying? You want me to just pick a room? What's next?"

"You can start by shuttin' up. I got stuff to do." The innkeeper opened and closed desk drawers, checked the contents of the small cash box, wrote in his ledger book with a broken pencil. He mumbled, "Must be crazy, he thinks I'm puttin' a lousy drunk in a motel room."

Jack fought his temper. He yanked up an orange vinyl chair and slumped into it. Arms crossed, he took out the flask and sat waiting and drinking, drinking and waiting. The highway was silent. He looked out of the office's watery windowpanes, saw the riot of green outside, the high blue sky above, the pearlescent clouds wandering sheep-like across the face of the sun. *Berto would have loved this place.* A hawk cruised through his vision, its eyes fixed on the ground for prey. A sudden bleakness settled on him. It was a heavy weight. *The world is a turd and so am I. He don't wanna work, well neither do I. So bottoms up; here's mud in your eye.* He fished around in his duffle bag for a big plastic booze bottle and, confident that even if the old man cared, he did not; Jack got down to some serious drinking.

Chapter 6
Jennifer

1987: Windsor, Arkansas

The toilet was clogged again. Jennifer took it in stride. It happened a lot. What had once been frustrating had grown commonplace. "Old house, old plumbing," she liked to say. At least it was *her* house, bought and paid for by her work as the induction specialist at the Army of God. Only the Universe knew how challenging it was to put up with all of those losers. Each new patient was more annoying than the last. She'd loved her job at the beginning, but that was back when she thought she could help. Lately, everyone pissed her off. Didn't they know she had problems of her own? Like this damn toilet?

Her real problem wasn't a recalcitrant commode but how to explain to her mother, politely, that it was none of the old woman's business who Jennifer saw or when. Maybe in the old days couples stayed together forever, but Jennifer wasn't going to be trapped that way. Now, having fought so hard for the divorce, she wasn't about to be penned up as a divorcée. Her mother's outmoded mores, she thought, as she unrolled a complete roll of toilet paper into a growing white mound and reached for another, were fine and good, but they didn't apply anymore.

Men in Jennifer's life hadn't proven to be as loyal and generous, as kind as her father had been. She finished the second and third rolls. The white feathery sheets spilled over the bathroom floor. She added crumpled pages of the *West Port Partisan*. Maybe if Gene had been a little kinder or hadn't gotten so boring so quickly. Maybe if the sex had been any damn good.

She hadn't told her mother that. *Imagine what she'd think. Talk about conniption.*

She bent and lit the pile with her cigarette lighter. It flared with a burst of curling black flakes. The decorative, cotton shower curtain caught, and the hungry, orange petals of flame climbed in huge leaps, lapping against the ceiling.

Now that she had the house, she was free to find the right man or, heck, maybe no man at all. She tossed a towel onto the growing fire. It caught. She added another two and nodded with satisfaction, tossed the bottle of lighter fluid on top and closed the bathroom door. She straightened the pillows on the couch, opened the front door and walked outside, and ambled to the end of her sidewalk. Billows of black smoke rose from her rooftop. Jennifer lit a cigarette, crossed her arms, and smiled in satisfaction. "Now, isn't that better?"

A small line appeared between her brows. A frown grew on her face, and her eyes opened wide. Her hands fell, the cigarette dangled from her open mouth, and Jennifer screamed as she realized what she'd done.

Chapter 7
Jack

1987: Moondust Motor Inn, Windsor, Arkansas

Jack's clothes hung heavy with dew and sweat. His eyelids felt filled with glue and gravel. His tongue tasted like it had been boiled with garbage jelly. He lay under the motel's great oak. The sun shone in his eyes. He remembered leaving Abe's office and sitting/falling on the grass under the tree. He must have passed out here.

"Aaaauuuggghhh." Jack's stomach lurched as he raised himself on an elbow. Wavering there, gasping and choking, he had an impression of a line of pale sand outlining his body. It reminded him of a corpse's chalk outline. He glared at it blearily, blinking the sleep from his eyes. He couldn't quite focus. His gorge rose, and last night's vodka emptied itself all over the morning dew-wet grass. He crawled to his feet and lurched back to the motel. He sat on the small shade porch in front of the office and half-heartedly wished to die.

"Gonna live?" Abe spoke through the storm door.

"Unfortunately." He rubbed the sides of his forehead, pinched the bridge of his nose. He could smell coffee, hot grease, maybe toast. His stomach echoed like an empty drum.

"Y'ain't a violent drunk, are you? But you're a

pretty good one. You always tuck it away that fast or just 'cause I peeved you?"

Jack stifled a burp. "I guess you could say I'm a natural. Inherited it from my momma and probably my daddy. I never knew him. Some people get money or property from their parents, I got this. Hardly seems fair."

Abe snorted. "Got breakfast. Want some?"

"Got milk?"

"Yeah." The ghost of a smile walked across Abe's face. "Got bacon, too, if you want. Fresh aigs, just gathered 'em myself. Still warm from the henhouse."

"Good God, no. Uuuurpp." A violent belch drove itself between Jack's teeth. Eggs, or aigs, came from the grocery store in his world, not fresh plucked from a chicken's butt. He hung his head between his legs and thought hard about making himself throw up again.

"Come on through to the kitchen when you're ready."

Jack nodded, heaved himself to his feet, followed the old man through the office, and into the small kitchen. The room reminded him of one of the foster homes he'd been in as a kid, green Formica, green linoleum floor. The bacon smell made his tender stomach roil. Abe got him a glass of milk and a glass of water. Jack gulped the cold white liquid down. Abe refilled it and set it in front of a plate. Jack sat. He glanced at Abe and pointed at the toast.

"Help yourself," Abe said. "I done ate. You want coffee?"

Jack nodded.

"So you go on eatin' while I talk." Abe poured Jack a mug of black coffee. Didn't offer cream or sugar.

"That all right?"

"Yeah." Jack eyed the scrambled eggs. The toast had settled the acid in his belly. A powerful hunger had replaced the nausea. He glanced at Abe again and then helped himself with the big tin spoon the old man had left lying half in, half out of the eggs.

"Well, I'll just say this short then. We ain't gonna be friends, kid. I'm old, and I'm set in my ways. You need a job, I need some stuff done, that's all there is to it."

Jack frowned, his mouth full of the yellow stuff. The old man was blunt, he'd give him that.

Abe took the frying pan from the stove and flipped a couple of pieces of bacon on to Jack's plate. "The other thing is you got a powerful thirst on you." He waved a placatory hand at Jack. "I don't mean you're a bad guy or nothin', I'm just sayin' that drunks ain't real reliable. I had to give it up myself. The booze, I mean. It was as hard as anything I ever done, so I understand." He scratched his chin. "I guess I'm just sayin' I ain't expectin' nothin' from you but to do your work. I'll give you your space, and you give me mine. We'll keep this all businesslike." He placed the frying pan back on the stove. "I ain't plannin' on wasting *my* time tryin' to get you sober. I don't wanna get to liking you just to watch you drink yerself to death. So, I'll just be your boss. You do your work, you and me are gonna be okay. You good with that?"

Jack shrugged. He was used to going it alone. The only friend he had left in the world was Ray, if he could still call Ray a friend, and he hadn't talked to the sergeant in months. Jack nodded, then turned his attention back to his breakfast.

"All right," continued Abe. "I got one rule, and it's an easy one. No cussin'. My dead wife didn't like it, and now she's gone, I can't abide it neither. You okay with that?"

"Yeah."

"There's a couple churches around here. You see that little gray chapel two, three miles down the road when we was driving in?"

"Our Lady of the Mountains?"

"Yep. That's her. Father Preddy's the priest. She's the closest church. She's Catholic. Since Preddy told me about you, I thought you might be, too." The old man searched Jack's face for agreement; Jack shook his head no.

"Well." Abe sighed. "I reckon they'd be happy to have you, anyway. To be honest, Preddy and I don't see eye to eye, but it ain't none of my business how you worship. If that ain't what you need, there's a Methodist church off downtown Windsor and a Primitive Baptist down toward the south a ways. You'll need a ride to get to them. I can do that for you if you give me some warning. I don't agree with those pastors neither, but I ain't standing between a man and God. You do a good job round here; I may loan you the truck." He frowned at Jack. "Depends on how you drink, I guess. I don't want nobody around here gettin' killed by a drunkard on my watch."

Jack's face burned. His resentment began to climb. "I'm not Catholic or Methodist or—or, whatever Baptist you said, so you don't have to worry about me driving drunk. I don't believe in God."

"Well, more the fool you. A fellow who don't believe in God ain't got much in the way of brains, if you ask me."

"I didn't."

"Well, you mind your beliefs, and I'll mind mine."

"Yeah, let's do that." Jack scraped his fork across his plate and spilled some of the eggs in his lap. "Shi…" Jack caught the word on his tongue. He pushed back from the table, and the eggs fell to the linoleum floor. He winced.

Abe tsked and tossed him a wet rag.

"You said downtown," Jack said to change the subject. "When are we going there? I'd like to see it."

"You saw it yesterday, kid. Down where the gas station was."

"Seriously? I saw West Port. I didn't see Windsor. Wait…you mean that crossroads by the railroad tracks? That's it?"

"Pretty much, they's some old buildings a little off the road there, back behind the trees, in a short draw. There used to be businesses back when I was a kid, but all the buildings, they got people livin' in them now. The town of Windsor… Well, it used to be bigger, but most of her got burned down. That's a long story though." He paused. "A weird one, too, but for another time, maybe." Abe frowned and ran a hand across his nose. "You sure about the churches?"

"Jesus, old man. I thought we were going to stay out of each other's way on that stuff."

"Language. What did I just say? Language."

Jack started to snap back. He didn't let people push him around like that, but, unlike Soft Robert, Abe looked like a man whose anger sparked and burned. He had a hard core to him. Jack let it pass unanswered.

"I asked," Abe continued, "because they're pretty

much the only social thing you can do around here. Period. Even I go to Preddy's fish fries occasionally. Even though I don't like the man, or his fish for that matter. Somethin' to do and, even if you don't particularly want to see people, bein' neighborly is necessary in a place like this. It may save your life someday." The old man paused. "Maybe you oughtn't to be socializing after all." He cleared his throat and continued. "They's an old barn behind the second building." He pointed vaguely out the back door of the kitchen. "You'll find the usual lawn stuff in there. You can start with cuttin' the grass, trimming the bushes and such. Only trick to that is the slope on the backside. Don't go rolling my tractor down into the holler. You're gonna have to push mow back there. I keep the shine back in the shed. I use it to power the tractor and a few other things round here, so you're gonna wanna cut it with water. It ain't gonna poison you or make you go blind as long as you do, but I tell you again: You hurt yourself; you're a long way from any hospital. Something to consider on when you're thinking about driving that tractor drunk. I can fix a broke wheel, but you roll that big sucker on yourself or chop your leg with a chainsaw, you might as well pick out a nice spot for me to bury you." He waited until Jack nodded to show that he understood. "Do what you can to keep me in wood. Chopping extra is always good for the winter." He pointed out the window again. "They's an old camper trailer back by the shed. That's where you'll be staying. There ain't no room in the motel for me to be housing nobody. The rooms are for the guests. Before you ask, we don't get many. When we do, you'll be responsible for carryin' luggage. If they ask, that is.

Some of the older folks do. Otherwise, you'll kindly stay outta their way. I don't want no drunkard pesterin' visitors."

"All right."

Last thing. Don't go messing around back in the holler." The old man pointed down into the valley. "You'll know you gone too far if you get past the pond. Even the sheep don't go past the pond. You hear me?"

"Yeah, sure." Jack shrugged. It was a weird prohibition, but he didn't see any reason to go wandering down there anyway. "Whatever you say."

"We lost a guy back there a couple years ago," Abe continued. "City fellows, like you, don't have any business—"

"I was a marine. I'm not a stranger to the field. I know how to do land nav—"

"I don't care. It's a rule. You got a problem with it? If you do, I'll take you out of here right…" Abe gasped, and his face went gray. He pushed his left hand into the side of his belly and leaned uncertainly against the kitchen counter. Jack started to rise. Abe waved him away.

"All right. All right." Jack eyed his boss. He was drawing his breath through clenched teeth. "You okay?"

"I'm fine." The old man grunted and forced himself upright. "Stay outta that holler."

Chapter 8
Abe

1987: Moondust Motor Inn, Windsor, Arkansas

The kid was looking at him funny. Abe did his best to crack a grin. "Just wind." He lied. "Aigs give me gas somethin' fierce." He lifted his chin, pointing Jack out of the kitchen door. "Go on, get busy."

Jack gave him a dubious look but left the kitchen, pausing at the door to look back. He looked concerned. Abe cursed himself, then mentally apologized to his dead wife. He couldn't afford for the kid to get any ideas. He dropped into a chair. The pain was getting worse. It didn't help that last night's new moon had been in Cancer. His momma had always told him that when Cancer was high in the sky, it caused more stomach troubles. He couldn't help but wonder if these waves of pain and the temporary weakness that washed over him, maybe they were at the bottom of the Fountain's sudden strength. *If only Sam hadn't killed himself.*

In the end, his friend hadn't been able to help himself. He'd taken a short cut out of the problem. Abe had started down that path himself. Only for him, it'd been the booze. If it hadn't been for his wife and Sam, he'd probably be in the ground, too. That was the hell of it. Sam had helped drag Abe back from the cliff only to throw himself over. He flirted with the idea that Jack might help him with the Wall the way Sam once had but discarded the idea. The kid was no Sam. He was too fancy by far, too city, too spoiled. He wasn't violent, though. That was good and…puzzling.

Abe had tested the kid last night, been rude to him, pushed him. He'd wanted to see how the kid acted when provoked. With the Fountain kicking up, he'd expected Jack to push back, but he hadn't. He'd seemed normal. Abe hadn't seen that before. Even *he* had more difficulty holding his temper these days. This close to the source, and drunk to boot, Jack should have been raving. Instead, the kid had passed out. Abe had surrounded him with a sawdust circle then, protection magic.

He needed Jack. He grimaced when he thought of why he was keeping the kid around. He didn't like it, but what else was he going to do? *I know you wouldn't approve, Sam, but you left me alone. I gotta do the best I can with what I got.* He felt a moment's uncertainty at the justification but pushed it aside. *At least the Fountain hasn't started drawing in outsiders yet….*

The pain in his side returned as a solid mass of knotted agony that doubled, then redoubled and left him gasping. He rested his cheek on the cool surface of the table. "Gotta do the best I can, Sam." The pain surged again, and he slipped from the chair, fell to his knees and prayed. Prayed that God still listened to men like him.

Chapter 9
Ronnie

1987: Highway 71, Boston Mountains, Arkansas

There were three men in the sports car. Ronnie, the leader, small and mercurial; Barry child-like and huge; and Chuck, a tall, thin redhead whose sole talent was surviving Ronnie's temper tantrums. Together, they made up the disillusioned remains of the Plains Tornados, a garage band that should have stayed in the garage.

Their dreams of big-time stardom had met with the reality of small-town Texas honky-tonks. The Plains Tornados weren't any good, and drunken Texans weren't shy about telling them so. Inevitably, Ronnie's drug-fueled bad temper got the worst of him. Small words led to big bar fights, which led to expulsions and forfeited paychecks. Soon, the word was out, and the Tornados stopped getting gigs.

Somewhere in north Texas, the men put the last of their remaining funds into a half tank of gas and tried to figure out what to do next. After the gas pump clicked off, Ronnie slipped his daddy's sawed-off shotgun into his duster and walked into the quick stop. Barry and Chuck followed him inside. Ronnie robbed the place while the other two froze in panic.

After the robbery, Ronnie told them that, since they

hadn't stopped him, the cops would figure they were in on it, and that they'd go to jail the same as him. Especially, he pointed out, since they'd helped themselves to a couple of cartons of cigarettes while he'd cleaned out the register. Barry and Chuck, used to knuckling under to Ronnie, grimaced and agreed. Ronnie found it easy to talk them into another score.

They drifted. Small town Texas became small town Oklahoma, and things cruised right along. Robbery, robbery, robbery. Threaten the guy behind the register, pop the till, grab the cash, collect some food and cigs, and then get back on the road. It all went well, until they came to Zeb. Zeb, Oklahoma, population 497, so small that it only had one quick stop. And one fine, fine lady with a pretty blue car.

But that was yesterday. Today, Ronnie was flying high and wide, and the baby blue sports car was eating the pavement in front of the Tornados like the road was all one great, sliding feast. "Eatin' cement and shittin' smoke" was what his daddy used to say. The mountains were Ronnie's launch pad to heaven, the big blue sky open above him, the dark valleys falling behind, and all of it, all of it so crystal fine, so cocaine clear and sharp. He didn't know why he'd turned off the highway. He'd planned on heading down to Little Rock, hiding out for a while, surveying the land. That had been the plan, but something was calling to him. Some subtle hook had pierced his mind, had drawn him to these unknown mountains. *Probably best to get off the big roads. It ain't like a stolen baby-blue Camaro stands out or nothin'.*

Ronnie was going to have to dump the car, but he didn't want to yet. She was so sweet, fast, and polished and had a nice throaty cough when you put your foot in her and gave her some of "the old motion-lotion." Motion-lotion, that was another one of his daddy's sayings. The blue car reminded him of its previous owner. He smiled. He gave it some "motion lotion" now, and the convertible jumped and squealed around the next tight hill road. Higher and higher. Some instinct told him to go higher. Higher until there wasn't any higher to go.

"Jesus, Ronnie, slow down, man," Chuck said. His greasy, red hair streamed in the wind. "You're gonna get us killed or arrested, you keep up that shit."

Ronnie sneered. "There ain't no cops out here, Chuck. That's the beauty of my plan."

"What plan, Ronnie?" a small voice from the large man in the back seat asked.

"It's all in my head, boys. You don't have nothing to worry about."

"Shiiiiit. He ain't got no plan, Barry. He's running away," Chuck said.

"Course I got a plan. Shut your mouth, Chuck. You want me to kick your ass over the edge?"

Chuck looked out of the window where the narrow two-lane highway fell away into the deep valley below. He eyed the sheer drop. "Hell, no."

"Good. Then shut up." Ronnie laughed, a short, sharp bark.

"Dude," Barry said. "You oughtn't to have done what you did to that Zeb lady."

Chuck grimaced, waiting for the explosion. They didn't get one. Ronnie was feeling too good.

"Yeah," Ronnie drawled. "Probably not. I'll give you that. But you know, man, she was pure askin' for it.

Y'all saw how she was dressed. Probably, if it hadn't been for your big greasy self, Barry, she'd have been into it. You ever want any chicks, you're gonna have to lose some weight, lard-ass."

"The cops ain't never gonna stop chasing us though. We goin' away for that one."

"No," said Chuck. "They're gonna fry our asses."

"Why? Didn't nobody see us." Ronnie said. "They ain't gonna find her nowhere, and by the time they do, you think anybody gonna come lookin' for us? Hell, she probably ain't even from around there. This look like the car of somebody that lives in Zeb? Hell, no."

"Yeah, man, but the quick shop guy—" Chuck said.

"Yeah, that was unfortunate, I'll give you that, but..." Ronnie cocked his head and gave his best John Wayne impression. "I won't be wronged. I won't be insulted. I won't be laid a hand on." Ronnie's mouth opened in a wild peal of laughter, and he gave the Camaro more gas. The car pounced ahead, twisted its tail with a squeal, and continued to climb the mountain.

Chapter 10
Jill

1987: Windsor, Arkansas

"Who's that guy chopping wood, Grandpa?" Jill looked out of the window over the kitchen sink at the tall, blond man. He had his long hair in a loose ponytail. He lifted the axe into the sun and dropped it into log after log with a solid chunk. The light shone on his arms and shoulders. He was slicked with sweat. Jill took a sip of her tea without taking her eyes off him. Abe fried bacon on the stove. She was up for the weekend. She'd taken over the local newspaper, *The Westport Partisan*, after graduating college. She liked to spend a couple days a month working on her grandfather's motel. Her boyfriend, Leon, didn't like it, but lately, she didn't much care.

"Who?" Her grandfather's voice was a tad too casual, and he'd stopped scraping the grease off the griddle.

Jill smiled to herself. The sudden quiet was a dead giveaway. Abe was smart, but not good at dissembling. "That tall guy out back. He looks good with that axe. I mean, he looks like he knows what he's doing with it."

"Oh." Abe went back to scraping. "He's a guy I hired. Ain't nothin' worth worryin' about." He didn't make eye contact.

It made her curious. "Don't worry, Grandpa." She laughed. "I'm not interested in him like that. Strange to see a new guy out here. What's he doing? How long's he staying?"

Abe looked at her for a few moments, chewing and thinking.

Trying to decide what to tell me.

"Name's Jack," he said. "Gonna be with us for a while, 'nother week or so anyway. Just a drifter."

"Ooh, a drifter. You make it sound like he's stepped out of a detective novel or something. The Moondust Drifter starring Jack." She laughed again as her grandfather's face flushed.

"Jill, you want to take this serious. That kid ain't all right. You hear what I'm sayin'? Make me happy and give him some space. All right?" His voice grew rough.

Surprised, Jill inspected his face. She didn't think he was angry with her. He almost looked afraid or…embarrassed. She began to wonder about this Jack character: Was he threatening her grandfather? Abe was tough, she didn't think it likely, but…he was getting older. Maybe something was going on here, something questionable. She resolved to keep a close eye on the situation. "I told you, Grandpa, you don't need to worry. I've got a boyfriend." She shrugged. "Sort of."

She watched Jack, framed against the early morning sky. He *did* look picturesque, but Abe's words had had a greater effect than he knew. She was interested in Jack now, interested in whether he could be trusted. She filed it away for future thought. "I'm going to redecorate number four today. Are you okay with that?"

"I really wish you'd stop doin' that stuff; nobody stays here 'cause it looks nice."

"I know, Grandpa, and nobody's going to want to until it does." An old fight, Abe's stubbornness reminded her of her father. Her dad still refused to see Abe when he flew in to visit Jill. He was father enough to want to stay in touch with her, but that didn't mean the great David Woodley was going to extend a hand to his own father. To be fair, Abe didn't reach out to his son, either.

"All right." Abe sighed. "You can redecorate it and all, but let me look at what you're gonna do first. All that red paint you put up in the spring is gonna come back down, 'cause you didn't do no scraping before you put it up there."

"I told you I was going to paint the building."

"I know, I know." He smiled. "I didn't think you were serious. I shoulda known better. I shoulda helped then."

"What're you smiling at, old man?"

"Nothin'. Just thinkin' you're a lot like me, only prettier."

Jill grinned. He didn't say stuff like that often. She loved it when he did. She crossed her arms and tapped her foot. "About that paint? Can't we charm it up there? Like, make it stay up there longer or get...fresher or something?"

"You know it don't work that way, girl, and I ain't never had that strong a power no how. Nobody has since your great-grandma and maybe some of the older ones. Maybe you." He used a rag to remove the splattered bacon grease from the surface of the stove. "Besides, *she* wouldn't have done it anyhow. She'd have told you to get out there and fix your mistake. Ain't no sense in wasting the magic on something you can do with your own two hands." He threw the rag in the sink. "You, uh, you ain't been using it for that kind a thing, have you? Like, simple around the house stuff?" Abe's voice betrayed his anxiety. "It ain't good to lean on magic when your own hands'll do, you know." His nose wrinkled. "That'd be kind of…I dunno, unholy or somethin'."

"No, Grandpa, you told me not to."

"Good girl."

The office door slammed, and the broken night bell *clunked* as someone pounded their fist on it. Abe frowned at the interruption. "Guests, I guess." He stopped at the kitchen door and said: "Stay away from Jack."

Jill wanted to laugh but didn't. Abe's jaw was thrust forward, his eyes bleak. She nodded instead. The old man went to see about his guests.

Chapter 11
Abe

1987: Windsor, Arkansas

There were three of them. Abe's blood took a chill at the sight of the little guy standing on the other side of the desk. He was dressed like a cowboy, slouch hat, duster, and cowboy boots. He smelled like he hadn't bathed in a week. His shirt and pants were stained. He looked hungry, but not for food. Abe had seen his kind before, hopped up on drugs, traveling the back roads of the mountains, looking for escape, release, thrills, something. The blue sports car parked out front looked expensive. He had the feeling this crew ran to mayhem. He put his right hand on the heavy hickory stick he had hidden under the desk. He wished Jill hadn't talked him into putting his shotgun in the closet.

"I'm afraid we're all full up," he said with a grimace intended to be a smile.

"All full up?" Ronnie blinked. "There ain't no cars out there. How you all full up?"

Abe thought fast. "Convention," he lied. "They're all at their convention."

"Convention?"

Abe shrugged and clamped down on his pipe. Better to see the lie through.

"You gotta be kiddin' me, man. You hear that,

Chuck?"

"I heard him, Ronnie."

"You're gonna have to do better than that, old man," Ronnie said.

There was a crash, the sound of dishes falling over, from the kitchen. Abe couldn't help himself. He glanced in that direction.

"I heard," Ronnie said, "you talking to someone back there. Maybe, they wanna rent me a room if you don't? Huh?"

"I wasn't talking to nobody. Just the radio." Abe tightened his grip on the stick. This wasn't going to end well. A prayer of blessing started rolling through his mind, prepared to slip across his tongue.

"Is that the radio smashin' your dishes in there? Sounded like you was talking to a girl to me."

Abe measured Ronnie's eyes and knew what came next. He yanked the club from behind the desk.

Ronnie danced back, his rundown boots clocking across the wood floor. His sawed-off shotgun popped out from under his duster, and the hammers clicked as he thumbed them back. He giggled and pointed the barrel at the old man. "Get hold of him, Barry!"

The fat man lumbered forward with a growl. Abe swung the hickory stick at Barry. It landed with a crack. Barry groaned and enveloped him in a sweaty embrace. The kitchen door swung open, and Jill poked her head through.

Ronnie licked his lips and smiled. He gestured to Chuck.

Chuck grabbed her by the forearm and yanked her into the front office. She cried out as he rushed her forward and slammed her across the reception desk.

Her head hit the desktop hard. It made a sound like a coconut being split with a hammer. She lay still.

Abe groaned and struggled to break free, to get to Jill. Barry pushed the old man into the corner and kept squeezing. Chuck stood over the unconscious girl panting, his face a blur of fear and desire.

"Good God, old man," Ronnie crowed. "You are one terr-uh-bul liar." He laughed at Abe, pinned against the wall by the elephantine Barry. Abe grunted and struggled, crushed under the weight of the big man's gut.

"I knew, I really, really, really knew, it was a great idea coming here!" shouted Ronnie. "I don't know why, I don't know why, but I feel like I'm gonna live for a thousand years all the sudden. I am full. Of. My. Self!" He slapped his knee. "You hear that old man? I ain't—I ain't. Never. Gonna be insulted by the likes of you! You got that?"

Abe didn't respond. The world began to go dark, and his knees buckled. He fought to stay conscious.

Ronnie stroked the back of Jill's bare thigh. Something dark entered his face, his voice deepened and roughened. He looked bigger, nastier, toothier. "Hold her, Chuck." He undid his belt and set his daddy's shotgun to the side.

Chapter 12
Jack

1987: Moondust Motor Inn, Windsor, Arkansas

The motel office smelled of sweat, rage, and madness. A red-haired man held Abe's granddaughter facedown across the registration desk, his back turned to Jack. An obese man held Abe in the back corner. The third man, a little cowboy dude with greasy hair, had his blue jeans around his knees. He was fumbling to pull down the struggling girl's underwear. She wasn't making it easy; she was coming around, thrashing and kicking at her attacker. The cowboy's face was obscured by a deep shadow, a strange darkness hovered over him.

"Hold her, Chuck!" the cowboy growled, and his voice vibrated the darkness.

"I'm trying, Ronnie! She's strong!"

The fat man holding Abe stared at the attempted rape in progress. His lips hung slack, his eyes hungry.

Jack crossed the office low and fast. The office door crashed closed behind him, scattering shivered glass across the floor. His heart pounded in his ears, beat in his chest. The flat of his axe caught Chuck under the chin. His head snapped back with a sharp cracking noise, and he collapsed bonelessly to the floor.

The young woman, her hands freed, raised herself

from the desk with a scream of rage. She lashed back at her would-be rapist with an elbow that caught him across the brow and sent him staggering. Dazed and furious, she fell away from the desk.

The fat man lumbered away from the wall with a bellow. Jack managed to slide his gripping arm, got behind him and put the huge man between himself and Ronnie's double-barreled shotgun. The gun roared. Ronnie's double-barreled shot, intended for Jack, sent the fat man's brains, blood and bone spraying across the room.

Jack moved, axe in hand to close the distance to the shotgun. He leapt over the fat man's falling body in a single stride. Ronnie pulled the trigger again. Nothing. He shrieked, and the crotch of his blue jeans went dark and wet as his bladder released. He chucked the spent shotgun at Jack and darted out of the office, slipping and sliding on the glass. Jack leapt after the man, slipped in the fat man's blood, and fell with a crash. The Camaro's engine roared to life. Its tires screamed, and before Jack could regain his feet, Ronnie was gone. The other two men lay on the office floor like so much meat.

The pounding in Jack's ears receded. A voice caught his attention, a high whisper, repeating the same rhythmic words. The young woman knelt at the end of the desk, arms crossed, eyes closed. She rocked back and forth, forming sibilant words that slithered between her small white teeth. He moved to offer comfort, certain that she was in shock, but as his boot crunched the glass underfoot, she opened her eyes wide. His brown eyes stared into her green orbs, and he was shaken. This woman was not in shock. She was furious.

She was not self-comforting; she was committing…something.

Jack stopped, raised his hands to let her know that he meant no harm. She stared at him with a frightening intensity. Abe coughed and climbed to his feet. The old man hesitated, rubbed his neck, and tried to clear his throat. She rocked herself to a stop, her tongue, teeth, and lips slowing as well. Abe reached out to touch her, to lay his hands on her shoulders, but as her hot eyes turned upon him, the old man froze. She shouted the final words. "There the evildoers lie fallen; they are thrust down, unable to rise!" Her verse hung in the air and echoed in Jack's memory as silence returned to the room. She closed her eyes, then snapped her head back and screamed, a shriek of pure rage that went on and on. A sudden pulse ripped through the air. It flowed through his chest, his limbs, as it bloomed outwards, outwards, rippling the walls, the glass of the windows, across the property, out into the mountains. He took a step back. Abe grunted.

Jack couldn't look away from her, the source of this wave of power, as she stood to regard him. *What the hell was that? What the hell have I gotten into?*

Chapter 13
Ronnie

1987: Windsor, Arkansas

Ronnie scrubbed tears of rage and humiliation from his cheeks and pounded on the steering wheel. He'd lost his friends, the only two friends he'd ever had, and he'd lost his shotgun, the only thing his daddy ever gave him. He punched the car's windshield, felt the pain in his knuckles, punched again and again till his fist was bloody.

Everything had been going so well and now this. He'd been feeling powerful, strong and certain. He had been riding a wave of savagery, and everything, everything was going how he wanted it to go. Finding the little motel had felt preordained. The valley below had seemed to sing to him. The clash with that crankcase motel owner, the chance to teach that fine, little lady something about loving—it all…flowed. He'd thought that nothing could stop him.

He hit the brakes as he came to a sharp turn of the mountain road. The car's tires protested with a squeal, and the back end slewed out, then snapped back as he regained control on the far side of the curve.

But something *had* stopped him. Someone had broken that smooth, smooth flow. First that tall, eagle-nosed asshole had broken in the door and smashed

Chuck in the face. Even then, Ronnie'd been certain he could handle it, but then that bitch had started whispering and, the power, the wonder had…drained out of him. Everything had gone to hell. He'd shot Barry, pissed his pants. He'd been terrified. He was ashamed that he'd run. *I'll go back. I'll go back. I'm going to make that dude pay, and when I'm done with him I'm gonna really give it to that chick, and when I'm done doing that, I'm gonna make her so there ain't nobody ever gonna want her again. I might carve her tits off for her. Feed them to that old fart. See if he likes it.* Ronnie looked in the rearview mirror. No sign of pursuit. *Yeah, I'll lay low for a while. Then I'm going back.*

Ronnie's grin popped out again, tear tracks drying on his face, and he gave the blue sports car some more motion lotion. The Camaro downshifted and powered into a long steep curve with a silent drop on the right. *Hell yeah, I'm coming back.*

The air rippled like a mirage, and the racing engine of the car hiccupped. The front right tire went with a whistling pop as Ronnie entered the apex of the curve. The car ducked and swerved, and he was struggling to hold it from going over the drop when the other three tires went in rapid succession. Bang. Bang. Bang.

And then, he was into a flat spin, and the vehicle shot out over the valley, its pristine blue paint sparkling in the sun, then dropped and began tumbling down the slope. Ronnie's screams echoed up the walls of the valley and then, abruptly, stopped.

Chapter 14
Jack

1987: Moondust Motor Inn, Windsor, Arkansas

Jack sat on the kitchen stoop staring at his bloodied fist. The sun slanted in from the west and cast the shadow of the motel and its great oaks over him. He shuddered at the memory of the blackness in the motel office and ran through the events in his head again. He was still missing pieces.

A detective had Abe and Jill in the kitchen. His deputy had been assigned to shadow Jack. Other deputies had come and gone; a forensics team had taped off the front office, doing what they could to make sense of the gruesome mess. It had been a long day. Jack licked his lips and looked at his quivering hands, thought of the booze he had hidden away in his camper. It had been a long dry day.

Abe's granddaughter's name, Jill, had been a surprise, an unwelcome one. Jack hadn't been ready for another Jill in his life. As numbed and shocked as he was feeling, he wondered if there was some significance in the fact that Abe's granddaughter and his ex-wife shared a name. He couldn't find a connection, but the coincidence worked to strengthen his feeling of the surreal. He told himself to wake up; he was feeling the aftereffects of stress and fear. The coincidence didn't mean anything.

As to the rescue itself, he wasn't as certain that he'd done the rescuing as he'd initially thought, or at least not all of it. Something else was going on here. Something...weird. That woman had done *something*. When her hard, green eyes had stared into his, he'd felt a chill he'd never experienced before, in or out of combat. He'd found himself frightened of her.

The door to the kitchen opened. The detective stepped outside. He was shorter than Jack, maybe a couple inches under six foot, compact and muscular, built like a bullet. He spoke fast, and when he spoke it was obvious who was in charge. Jack knew his kind, always certain, always suspicious, always on your ass.

The detective spoke back into the kitchen. "You oughta have a gun up here, Abe. I can't imagine what a guy like you was thinking going defenseless like that."

"Yeahhh," Jack heard Abe reply. "Yeah. I'll keep that in mind, Detective Fratelli."

There was something in Abe's voice. The old man didn't like the detective. Jack would have bet money on it.

"Seriously, Abe, living out here so far from anybody, it's irresponsible."

"Leon." Jill sounded exasperated. "He put his shotgun away at my request, okay? Lesson learned on my part. Just leave it alone. Okay?"

"Yeah. Yeah, of course, honey." The detective's tone had turned from nagging to sugary sweetness. "Sorry about that, Abe. I didn't realize my girlfriend had been at work on you. This is what all that liberal theory gets you, Jill."

Jack couldn't see Jill's face, but the long silence

was informative.

"All right," Leon said. "You sure y'all don't want to go to the hospital? You're pretty bruised up, Abe."

Abe must have waved the suggestion away as he had waved away the paramedics when they'd asked.

"All right, all right, but if you change your mind." He shrugged and pointed at Jack. "I'm gonna catch up with your man here."

Leon's demeanor changed when he turned to Jack. "Come on," he snapped. He led Jack down the mountainside, found an old concrete bench under a maple tree. The two men sat for a moment in silence, an uncomfortable one for Jack. He knew Leon was letting the moment stretch to make him nervous. He resolved that he wouldn't let it work.

The view was breathtaking, a deep rift valley unfolded before them, a steep mountainside climbed in the distance. Under the late afternoon sun, they could see the glint of a small river flowing far down amongst the trees. "Looks pretty, doesn't it?" Leon asked.

"Yes."

"Mostly marshland at the bottom, I hear. Legend was that hunters used to go in there every now and again. Some of them never came out again. It's strange, but nobody has been hunting down there in my lifetime. I don't think so, anyway. It's pretty swampy down there according to Fish and Game. I don't know, I've never been in, myself. Hell, I don't even know that Fish and Game have been. Not for years."

"Abe said they lost a guy," Jack said. "Maybe he said a couple of guys, I don't recall. Recently, he said. He warned me to stay out."

"Did he? Huh. Well, Abe's always saying

something."

And now, Jack could tell that Leon didn't like Abe, either.

"What's your name?" Leon asked.

"Jack. Jack Diaz."

"Johnathon?" Leon's notepad had come out. The pad was cheap, ring bound with wrinkled pages.

Jack snarled. This wasn't a friendly fact-finding interview. "Yeah."

"Middle name?"

"R."

"R? R is short for what?"

"Just R, Detective. It's the name my momma gave me."

"Seriously?"

"She said it was all she could remember about my daddy. His name began with R." Jack delivered the lie deadpan. He didn't like being pushed.

Leon frowned at him. "All right, R..." He wrote in his notebook, circled it several times with his pen, drew a large question mark beside the circled initial. "I'm Leon Fratelli. Don't laugh at the name, Jack. I'll have to run you in." He chuckled and loosened his already loose necktie, a sloppy silk thing, purple and pink paisley. He pulled out some cigarettes, offered one to Jack. They smoked in silence for a few moments.

Jack's eyes drooped. He was bone weary, and his head hurt. He needed a drink. He caught Leon inspecting his hands. He put them between his knees to stop them from shaking.

"You okay, Jack?" There might have been sympathy in the man's voice, but Jack didn't think so.

A sudden wave of hopelessness rolled through him,

left him feeling useless and so, so tired. He considered standing, running down the slope until he started to roll. Once he started to roll, it would turn into a tumble. At some point, he'd hit something hard, something that would smash his head wide open as he'd smashed Chuck's.

"Where you from, Jack?"

"New York."

"Address?"

Jack wrestled with how much truth to tell. "Garden City."

"All right, Garden City, now, how about you answer the question. Address?"

"Marine Barracks, 1st Division, Alpha Company. Third room on the left by the latrine. Just short of the water fountain if you're coming in…let's see." He pointed. "If you come in from the…south."

Leon sighed, wrote something down. "Marine?"

"Yeah."

"What kind of marine?"

"A pretty damn good one, I think."

"Don't give me shit. What was your job? I'm not asking again."

"Just a ground-pounder."

"Does that mean infantry, or do you jarheads have a different definition?"

"Infantry."

"You AWOL? Discharged? They boot you out? You a discipline problem, Jack?"

"Aw shucks, detective." Jack made a show of patting his pockets, eyes wide and guileless. "I don't have my discharge papers on me. You know us Jarheads ain't good at 'membering stuff like that. What the hell, man? I did what I could to help Jill, and you're gonna give me grief?"

"All right, asshole. I've had enough." Leon's face was brick red. He looked like he was chewing on a piece of meat, grinding out the words. "Don't get smart. Getting smart wouldn't be a real good idea. All I know about you is that you're a drunk, a drifter, and that you're giving me grief. I'm trying to figure whether I should take you in on vagrancy—"

"I've got a job."

"Sure you have, sure you have, but that's just for the moment, and I can always book you on suspicion. How long do you think it will take Abe to replace you if you're sitting in jail? And I gotta tell you, man, it's not hard to make suspicion stick on a guy like you. And once I have that on you, I can hold you, and then I can keep bringing you in for every little thing we have going on the street. Mugging? Hell, let's look at ol' Jack. He's a suspicious vagrant type. Rape? Jack's probably the guy. I can make you regret ever stepping across the state line. Hell, man, I can push you right back out of the state if you piss me off enough. There's nobody..." Leon paused to let the word sink in. "Nobody, Jack, that gives a shit about you, man. You're not from here, and I'm betting if I put the word out to a couple of states something will turn up." He slapped Jack's knee. "I mean, we've got your fingerprints, man. Did you think of that? I'm betting a guy like you has a record somewhere. Am I right?"

Jack returned the detective's stare with a blank look. Inside he was thinking hard about a crack house in California and a drug dealer turned inside out. He did his best to keep that from his voice, his face. "Whatever you want to do, man."

"Detective Fratelli," the man corrected him.

"Whatever, Detective Fratelli."

They sat in a sour silence. Jack stubbed out his cigarette on the bottom of his boot.

"You took those guys." Leon gestured over his shoulder with his chin. "To pieces, Jack, and that's got me real worried, man. I mean, you used an axe, brother. You smashed that dude's face to pulp. You shattered his teeth and drove the front of his skull into his brain. Dead from one hit. One hit, you hear?"

Jack nodded. It'd been a shock to realize he'd killed the man. He hadn't meant to. He blinked, embarrassed to realize that he was trying to hold back tears.

"Are you going to make me feel better about any of this?" Leon asked. "Seriously, Jack, you'd better say something, or you're gonna spend the night in jail, and I'm gonna make sure I never see your narrow ass around here again." Leon's face hardened until Jack knew he'd run out of time. The detective started to rise from the bench.

"Got scared," Jack blurted out. "I saw what was happening; saw them hurting the girl—Jill. They were—they were…" He ordered his thoughts. "I got back from Beirut twenty-four months ago. It was bad over there. Real bad. I got out of the marines when I got home. I needed a change. I thought maybe here. I'd never been here before and don't know anybody. I know that may seem suspicious, but I don't have any people, and I didn't have anywhere to go. This seemed as good a place as any." Jack watched Leon taking notes. "That cowboy dude was about to rape that woman. I wasn't going to let that happen, and I didn't think about it. I had the axe in hand because I was chopping wood, and when I went through that door, I didn't mean to kill anyone." He cleared his throat. "Truth is...I'm hating myself really hard right now, and I didn't like myself much before I killed that man tonight. I can't seem to—I don't... Just—I didn't mean to do that, and I'm seriously considering checking out, man; I don't know how to live with it...all of it." Jack flushed, embarrassed that he'd revealed so much. Once he'd gotten started, the words had forced their way out. He'd never been half as honest with Soft Robert. He wondered if the cop believed him or whether he thought it was more junkie lies.

"Would you do it again?"

"Hell, yeah. With or without your approval." Jack jerked to his feet. "Arrest me, or leave me be. If you want to know what happened from my perspective, ask. I'll tell you what I can remember, but know this, I didn't hurt Jill, I didn't hurt Abe, and I'm not going to. One more thing, and don't you forget it; I hit the fellow with the flat of the blade, I could've used the edge and didn't. Those two little shits got what was coming to them, and I'll do the same to the little weasel that got away, if he ever shows his face around here again."

"All right, Jack. Now we're talking. That sounds like honesty to me. Good God, I do love it when people are honest." He offered Jack another cigarette. Jack waved it away. "He's not coming back," Leon said. "The rapist. We found his car, well...I say his. He and his buddies stole it from a college girl over in Oklahoma. They raped her and, looks like, tortured her before wrapping her in a tarp and dumping her in a ditch. Dumbasses left their van right outside of town. Parked down a dirt road."

"Yeah?" *People really are animals.*

"Yeah."

"And why's he not coming back? You guys catch him?"

"No, we didn't catch him. He lost control of the car a little way down the road, couldn't have made it more than four or five miles after he left here. Spun right off and into that damned valley." He pointed down in the rift, now dark as the angling sun shot over the top of the forested gulch. "They're winching the car up now or they're going to try to. They may end up having to leave it there. It's tissue paper, rolled up like a ball with snot inside. There's no way he survived."

"They find the body?"

"I'm sure, by now. If not, he's down there somewhere, that was a steep drop."

"Good." Jack remembered Jill's eyes, beautiful and angry green, remembered her whispering and drawing a circle on the floor. Remembered the power flowing out of her.

Leon flicked his cigarette out into the gathering dark. "I guess I'd better be going. Abe told me there was gonna be a big storm tonight." He scanned the clear dusk sky. "Doesn't look like it to me, but he said he saw Jill's rooster standing and fluffing its feathers on a woodpile." He chuckled. "Don't ever let anything these people believe surprise you, Jack. There's some craaaazy folks out in these hills." He put his hands on his hips. "She's a pretty girl, isn't she, Jack?"

"Who?" Jack looked away.

"Jill. She's a beauty, I say. There is nothing in this

world like a blonde surfer girl. I tell you, Jack, I feel like the luckiest S.O.B in all of Arkansas."

"You two together?"

"Yep."

"Well, congratulations then." *Message delivered.*

"One last question, Jack?"

"Shoot."

"How'd you get to town?"

"Hitchhiked." The lie fell right off of Jack's tongue.

"All right."

The night grew quiet again. A heavy breeze moved through, rustling the leaves over their heads. Leon let the silence lengthen. "Well, I'd best be going," he said. He stood one more moment, and Jack could feel him staring at the back of his head. The detective cleared his throat and sighed. "Mind what I said."

Leon moved up the hill and entered the motel. The kitchen door slammed behind him. Jack heard voices raised in argument, sounded like one of them was a young woman's.

He smiled.

Chapter 15
Jack

1987: Moondust Motor Inn, Windsor, Arkansas

The midnight storm lashed Jack's camper trailer.
Rain spattered through the louvered windows. Thunder
echoed and dopplered up the mountainsides like the
wails of the damned. Discarded Milk of Magnesia
bottles scattered the floor. When they were full, they
had held Abe's shine. Jack howled with the gusts and
screamed at the lightning.

He staggered to the small trailer's door. The wind
tore the door from his grasp and ripped a deep gash
across his palm. He gaped at the blood running down
his arm.

He staggered down the folding steps and fell to his
knees in the mud. Rain plastered his briefs to his thighs.
He regained his feet, steadied himself against the blast
and wove his way past the chicken coops. No sign of
the birds, they'd hunkered down for the storm. The
kitchen door was locked. He tugged again, then again.
Frustrated, he slammed his hand on the screen panel,
then again. The screen snapped back on him and
smashed his bleeding hand. He lacerated his fingers
clawing the wire mesh out of the frame.

The kitchen door opened. Jack fell forward and
landed hard on his knees. He looked up, bemused, and

saw a pair of green eyes. Beautiful and angry. "What are you doing?" Jill asked. "It's the middle of the night. Are you okay?"

"Just—jusss…" But he couldn't remember what he was doing. Couldn't remember why it had been so important to get into the kitchen.

"You're drunk." She frowned. "You need bread and Tylenol, and you need to go to bed." She yanked him into the kitchen.

Jack found himself in a chair at the table with no real idea of how that'd happened. Jill placed a large plastic tumbler on the table in front of him and a peanut butter sandwich sliced into four quarters. "Grandpa said you had a problem with the booze."

"Don'—don't have a problem with it. Got problems *without* it."

"What? What did you say?" She wore a nightdress, clean and white, that jumped out of the night when lightning flashed. She smelled of flowers and sleep. Something relaxed inside of him.

"You're slurring a lot," she said. "I can't understand."

He wanted to reach out and take her hand. He did reach out, a little, but stopped and slowly, deliberately placed his hand flat on the surface, and splayed his fingers.

"You're bleeding." She took his hand and cradled it in hers. "A lot. Wait here." She wrapped a dishrag around his palm and left the kitchen.

Jack sat looking at the lumpen cloth. He took a bite from the sandwich, chewed speculatively. He wanted to put his head down on the table, fall asleep. Jill returned with bandages, a white plastic bottle. She was beautiful in her bare feet, moved with grace and poise. "Let me see that." She reached for his hand again.

He gave it to her willingly.

"Can I ask you a question?" she asked.

Jack nodded in reply; her fingers were cool against the back of his hand.

"Did you lie to Leon?" She flashed her eyes at him. "He thinks you did."

Jack started to answer, then shrugged and looked away.

"He's gonna check with the airlines, train stations, things like that. He thinks you're hiding something."

Jack laughed. "Don't care, don't care...he finds out."

"Finds what out? What's he going to find out?" There was a long silence. She'd stopped with the bandaging, was examining his face.

Jack didn't answer. He had lost his train of thought, lost it in inspecting her lips, the slope of her nose. He was lost in the wanting of her, and a life that would never be his. His self-loathing coiled in his throat. He'd seen too much, done too much. Life, for him, wasn't a place that made sense. He'd stumbled through it and hurt a lot of people, been hurt by some, too. He'd been so certain that he knew everything. The relationships had crashed down; the hopes disappeared. He was lonely and afraid.

"Jack." She shook his hand, squeezed. He grimaced. "What's he going to find, Jack?"

"Had a friend, once. Once..." Hot tears crawled down his cheeks. He put his head down, embarrassed. It occurred to him that his aloneness, his great separation was his own fault. Grief fell on his shoulders, like a harness, snug, a burden that he'd made with his own hands. *The problem is me. I'm the guy that drives people away.* Sadness overwhelmed him. Shame drove him from the room. She called after him, but he ignored her.

He staggered out into the storm leaving his sandwich and the girl behind. The pounding of the water and the cracking of the wind shattered his senses.

He went down the hill, into the valley.

Chapter 16
Abe

1987: Moondust Motor Inn, Windsor, Arkansas

"Grandpa, wake up." Jill shook Abe in the darkness. "Jack's in trouble."

The old man rolled over, ran a hand over his eyes, looked at the clock. "What kinda trouble?"

"He's really drunk and—"

"I told you, girl, he's a drunk. It's what drunks do; some say it's what they're best at."

"Yes, I know, but he was talking crazy. Like, I don't know. Like he might hurt himself. He was... I don't want to... He was crying. He seems really upset about something, maybe it's the whole, you know, thing that happened yesterday, but I don't know. He seems like he's breaking down, like...I don't know."

"Yeah, that's the other thing drunks do. They're good at making you feel sorry for 'em. They all got a sob story. I should know. Why you suddenly worried?" He looked at her with muzzy suspicion. "How you know he's feelin' down anyway? What're you doin' up?"

"He was trying to get into the kitchen. He could barely stand. I made him a sandwich, but he got upset and ran out into the storm. Look, if you won't go, I'll go myself."

"Jill, you gotta listen to me, now. You can't be around him when he gets all liquored up. I don't know him that good, but he's a guy and you're in nothin' but a nightgown. You don't know what he might get up to when he's drunk. It ain't safe."

"I can take care of myself."

"Didn't yesterday teach you any—"

"Leon tries to push me around, and I don't let him. I won't let you either." She offered him a nervous smile. "I love you for worrying, though."

"Ah, well. Enough said. Go back to bed. I'll check on him in the morning. He's probably passed out in his trailer by now, anyway."

"I don't think so. He was heading downhill. Toward the valley."

Abe sat up straight in the bed, his thin white hair floating on the air. He clicked on the lamp, threw the blankets back. "Stay here."

"What? I'll go—"

"Listen, Jill," he snapped. "Don't argue, just this once, don't argue. I know I'm old-fashioned, but please don't argue. I gotta go get him. Quick."

"…Okay."

"Make some coffee and pray. I'll be back soon." He stepped into his worn boots. He didn't bother to put anything on over his pajamas.

"I tried to tell you…"

"I know you did. I know you did, now."

He opened the nightstand drawer. He hesitated, his hand hovering over a .38 revolver and a flashlight. He grabbed the flashlight. "I'm an old fool. I'll be back soon."

****

The storm shattered on Abe's head. *Somethin's wrong. These storms don't last this long. The sky ain't happy, or...it's fightin' the Fountain. Or it's trying to claim him. The Fountain is trying to claim him. Oh, God, let it not be.*

Bloodshed made the Wall thinner. He should have remembered that. He'd been exhausted after the attempted rape and the beating he'd taken. The pain in his guts had returned as well. Hiding it from Jill, from everyone, had been eating away at his reserves all day. *Oh God, I can't afford to lose him.* He groaned. *Please God. I need his blood.* He shaded his eyes and strode down the hill. *Please God*, he prayed, *don't let him find the Isaac Stone.*

Chapter 17
Jack

1987: The Isaac Stone

Something told Jack to go down, down the mountain, and he followed its direction. He looped out and around the chicken coops, then the sheepfold, then followed the path that went down the mountainside and to the stock tank. The forest deepened as he descended, and he had to stop to get his bearings once the foliage closed over his head. The path was darker now, more menacing. The rain, which had been torrential on the open mountainside, shattered through the intertwined sheltering branches and leaves. Jack didn't notice. He had a mission. He must get down, down the side of the mountain. There was something down there that he needed. Drunk, he couldn't remember what, exactly, but something was drawing him on, promising things. He walked the forest path in the darkness. He followed it down.

He fell twice. The second time over a piece of abandoned farm machinery that tore a great gash across his arm and chest. The blood trickled down his belly, washed away by the rain. The darkness and the storm confused him. The trail he followed stopped at Abe's stock tank. He remembered Abe's admonition to go no farther and almost turned back, but on the far side of the pond, he found a narrow metal gate camouflaged by a pile of brush. He ignored the old man's warning, forced the gate, and found the path continued on the other side.

Jack howled his pleasure, tilting his head back to the sky. He felt savage and fierce, strong and wolf-like. The downward draw, the pressure to go, circled in his chest like a whirl of blackbirds. He howled and howled and continued down.

Chapter 18
Abe

1987: The Isaac Stone

Abe realized his worst fears in a glance. The rain had washed out Jack's tracks, but the hidden gate behind the stock tank stood open. Jack had found the path to the Isaac Stone.

Abe rushed to follow, slipped in the mud, and slid down the hill. A flailing hand caught the metal gate and stopped his careening body, bruised but otherwise unharmed. He felt around in the mud for his flashlight. Gone. He climbed to his feet and worked his way down the secret path, a hundred feet, farther, until it opened again onto the Isaac Stone's plateau. Wild things thrashed in the limbs beyond the clearing. Something gibbered in the night. *I'm not thinking right.* His gut was aching again. He drew a hand across his brow to clear the water and mud from his vision. A fence made of piled bones ringed the small, round clearing. Ancient animal bones mostly, but somewhere in the pile, lurked the bones of men. *Things come and go in circles. Crimes, big and small, they do come back around.* His grandmother had called it a spirit fence. She said that it kept malign spirits like the Fountain's at bay.

In the center of the small clearing stood a rust-colored stone. The Isaac Stone. Someone in the distant past had squared the rock with chisel and hammer. Three feet high and six feet square, it resembled a table or altar. Ancient symbols had been carved into the top of the altar. Symbols that meant nothing to Abe, had meant nothing to his grandmother.

Between the stone and the spirit fence were five wooden totems, each capped with a skull. Rabbit, sheep, wolf, and bear skulls capped four of the poles; their bare eye sockets streamed rain like tears. An ancient human skull grinned from the tallest of the poles. Cardinal, woodpecker, raven, owl, and eagle feathers had been attached up and down the totems with rawhide cords. They twisted in the wind. The fluttering feathers, the glistening skulls, Abe shuddered. The totems looked like they were breathing.They looked like they were watching.

Jack lay naked and facedown across the top of the Isaac Stone. His arms and legs spread in a great hug. His pale skin flashed in the lightning. He looked dead or unconscious.

Abe groaned and dashed the water from his eyes.

Jack raised his head to look into the forest on the other side of the spirit fence. The darkness condensed there. A shape, troglodytic in the darkness, hunched and long-limbed, stood in the dripping trees. It could have been a trick of the mind, an extension of fear and exhaustion, but Abe knew better. The man-shaped shadow stared at Jack. He looked right back at it.

The Fountain. Abe felt a sudden savage stab of fear. *Oh, God it can't be that strong. Is it too late?*

The shadowy manifestation beckoned and pulled at the air. Jack jerked like a marionette, twitched, and flopped on the stone. He tried to rise to his hands and feet, tried to go to the shadowman. Lightning struck around the ring of the clearing. Abe's vision went white. Tree limbs fell crashing into the undergrowth.

Abe's sight returned. Jack stood square in the center of the Isaac Stone, his white body straight and true in the fury of the storm. Crimson blood streaked down his belly, trickled down the outside of his thighs, pooled under his bare feet on the stone. He had taken a wicked cut to his upper chest and arm. But it was Jack's hand, his tight-clenched right hand, that drew Abe's eyes. Scarlet lifeblood dripped between the man's knotted knuckles as if squeezed from a pumping heart. It streamed onto the stone at Jack's feet, filled the ancient runes.

Jack took a step forward, toward the darkness, and Abe was certain that he was losing him, losing his one chance to restore the Wall. He cast about in the darkness and found a jagged rock, large as a softball. He hefted it in his right hand and lumbered toward the kid. *It's too soon. The alignment is only starting. I'm not ready. You can't die yet, Jack. Oh, God, please tell me what to do.* "Jack!" He called out.

The young man didn't respond, didn't appear to hear him at all. The shadow-thing beckoned, and Jack took another step forward, another step into the Valley.

It'll have to be close enough. God help me. Let this work. God, God help me. Help us. Abe lurched forward again, the jagged stone raised in his hand, a grimace of despair on his face. He didn't want to do what he was doing, but God's ways were not man's ways.

Jack stopped at the edge of Isaac Stone, oblivious to Abe's slow approach. The young man raised his arms to the howling sky; the blood slicked his forearm, streaked over his bicep, curved around his taut shoulder. He turned his face to the storm, opened his mouth, and drank in the rain. A savage and pure smile sprang to his lips, and he laughed once, loud and free. Abe froze, frightened. Lightning struck.

Electricity danced around the clearing, arched over the valley in a great dome, traced the invisible Wall that contained the Fountain far below. The sky turned a crackling volcanic white, hot with energy and vibration. Abe was thrown from his feet. The shadow creature, so solid-seeming only moments ago, was gone in the flash as if shattered by the hot stroke of electricity. Jack stood like some pagan sorcerer. St. Elmo's Fire danced around his limbs. His long hair floated on tendrils of electricity. He laughed, carefree, like a child. Thunder rumbled across the landscape. The storm reached for the young man. Crackling bolts of lightning stabbed out of the lowering clouds and impaled Jack's body.

Abe shrieked as he saw the kid consumed in a flash of super-heated fire. Surely, Jack was vaporized. But no, the lightning kept falling, over and over on the same spot, striking Jack. Striking but not destroying. He was still in there, and the silvery, jangling voltage was dancing across his extended fingertips. He was molding it, playing with it, shaping it into streamers. He turned to Abe with a grin on his face, his features lit by clean power. His lips and cheeks jumped with the deadly voltage. Jack laughed in simple glee and extended a hand to Abe. Silver electricity arced between his fingers, snapped, and popped.

Abe shrank back from this elemental creature. Disappointment crossed Jack's face, then uncertainty, and, finally, disbelief and sudden doubt. The stream of voltage closed with a pummeling jerk. Jack's back whiplashed, and Abe was certain the tall man's spine had snapped. Jack was thrown punishingly onto the Isaac Stone. He lay there unmoving. Tendrils of smoke rose from his hair, limbs, and the stone itself.

The rain stopped; the lightning gone as quickly as it arrived. Drops made small splashes as they fell from bent tree limbs. The sudden silence left Abe with roaring ears, a crippling fear. The tempest had died without fading. It had stopped when Jack fell. Abe crawled toward the stone, certain of what he would find. Certain that Jack had died with the storm.

Chapter 19
Jack

1987: Moondust Motor Inn, Windsor, Arkansas

The sunlight slanted warm through the latticed windows of the wood-paneled room. It caught dust particles in its syrupy light. The outdoor sounds, a cycling lawnmower, a lone big rig hectoring down the road, mechanical and distant, made the silence feel oppressive. Jack lay under a single sheet, his eyes open, trying to get his bearings. *Must be one of the motel rooms, one that Jill fixed up. Damned hot in here.*

His body ached from scalp to toes, especially his joints. They felt like they'd been pulled apart and then allowed to snap back. He checked himself over, found that he was clean, albeit sweaty, hair washed, dried, and combed back. He wore a fresh pair of boxers under the sweat-soaked bedsheet, nothing else. He didn't recognize them. Fresh scars decorated his tanned chest and shoulders. He had a vague memory of tearing his hand open on the trailer door. He examined his palm; a V-shaped scar nestled in the center of the tender white flesh. He was pretty sure that he'd seen Jill after and that she'd tried to help him. Maybe? He couldn't put the scene together in his mind.

Oh God, please God, don't let me have done anything stupid. He inspected his palm again. *How long have I been out? This thing is completely healed.* He sat up and groaned. His stomach muscles complained. *What the hell did I get up to?*

He hoped he hadn't broken into the motel room. He swung his legs out of the bed and propped himself on the edge of the mattress. A shadow darkened the latticed windows, and the door handle turned with a grating squeak. Jack started to rise, remembered his state of undress, and jerked the sheet across his midriff, covering his lap. He dug his fingers into the mattress and gritted his teeth. *Here we go.*

Jill peeked around the door and smiled on seeing him awake. Jack's stomach muscles unclenched a little and he let out a sigh of relief. Whatever was going on, she wasn't upset with him, which meant, probably, that Abe wasn't either. She carried a tray in her hands. One of Abe's ubiquitous blue shine bottles stood on one side of the tray beside a plate of bacon and pancakes, a jug of water, and two glasses, one full of orange juice, the other empty.

"You're awake," she said and put the tray on the small table by the window. "Wow, it's hot in here, but Abe said you'd need it hot, to sweat it—you know, to sweat it out. How are you feeling? Hungover?"

Jack shrugged, nonplussed, and offered an embarrassed smile.

"Do you mind if I turn on the AC?" she asked.

"Ple—" He had to stop and clear his throat. "Please."

"Grandpa said you might not be hungry but that you really need to eat."

"Yeah?" The sight of the blue bottle brought a wave of helpless heat that poured through his limbs. He

81

tried to hide his trembling hands under the sheet. He grunted with self-loathing and desire. A memory rose like a shower of crystals in his brain. He remembered standing on a great carved stone, under some sort of pagan totems, naked against a hell-spawned storm, his arms outstretched to grasp the clouds, and...lightning, power, power, power running through him like a river of hot pleasure. He remembered the liquid electrical current sizzling in his blood, pouring from his hands and the cuts on his body, the curling snaps that flowed from the end of his fingers, the jolting amperage that jumped and pumped down through his legs and into the pregnant earth of the mountain. The muscles across his chest, arms, and shoulders crawled and convulsed with chaotic, rippling power. The moment lasted but a second and was gone; Jack slumped again on the edge of the bed.

"Are you all right?" Jill studied his eyes.

"Yeah...yes." He looked at the shine bottle. He needed a drink, but he didn't want one. "Could—could you get that blue bottle out of here?"

"Abe said he thought you might need it." Something that looked like hope danced in her eyes.

"Hah, he's righter than you know, but...I don't—don't want to do that anymore." His voice, rusty and worn, jumped in his mouth as his body fought against his new-found determination.

"You're shaking."

"Yeah."

"You really want to quit?"

He looked down at his bare knees, saw fresh scars there as well. "Yes."

"All right, I'll be right back. Try not to eat

anything if you can. It'll be better if you wait." She took the blue bottle and the empty glass in hand and darted out of the motel room without looking back.

Jack took the opportunity to strip the sheet from the bed and wrap it around his waist. He took a big draft from the water bottle. It tasted sweet on his dry and swollen tongue. His belly clenched in protest. His body didn't want water. It wanted liquor.

Jill returned with glass in hand. There was something in it, something...questionable. It smelled like pepper sauce and industrial cleaner. "Look," she said, "this is going to look disgusting, believe me, and it's probably not going to taste any better, but I looked it up and the old books say it fixes the problem. Abe says it doesn't, but well, he doesn't know everything, and this was usually a woman's thing, anyway."

Jack took it in his hand. He smelled shine and fish. The concoction was red. Two small raw egg yolks floated on the top of the liquid, and something gray slithered around the bottom of the glass, appearing and disappearing as the liquid swirled. The liquor smell caught in the back of his nose and made him curl his nostrils. His stomach clenched again. "I don't want any booze."

"There's less than a tablespoon in there, but it's mixed in with some stuff that's supposed to cure..." Her face flushed. "Well, it's supposed to help you stop drinking."

"What stuff?"

"Look, do you trust me? I'll tell you after, just— just drink it. Just trust me."

"Trust you? I hardly know you." Hurt walked across her face. "Did you put me in this bed? Clean me up and all?"

"Yes." She blushed but didn't turn her eyes away.

He liked that. A lot. "Then I guess you know *me* pretty well by now." Her blush went from red to nuclear. He chuckled. "Here's to blushing innocence." He downed the potion in a single glugging passage. It wrenched his belly, like he'd swilled garbage mixed with rocket fuel. Something crunched between his teeth. "Oh, God," he gasped.

Jill plucked the glass from his hands.

Jack coughed and pounded on his chest. "Oh God, that was truly, truly awful."

"Do you want a drink now? Alcohol, I mean?" She rested her hand on his bare shoulder, bent to search his tearing eyes. "Do you want a drink?"

"Good God, no." He choked. "What was in that?"

"Are you sure you want to know?"

"Yeah, I'm an old hand at collecting hangover cures."

"That's not a..." She searched for the right words. "Look, that's supposed to be a cure for alcoholism, not a—a remedy for hangovers."

"Okay." He considered telling her how well addiction cures worked but decided it didn't matter. "So. What's in it?"

"Umm. Grandpa's shine."

"I got that much."

"Yes, it has to have some of what the person drinks. Can't be, you know, random alcohol. It has to be the alcohol they actually drink, so I went with Grandpa's stuff, because I know that you like to drink it."

She tilted her head. "You know, it's interesting that

it has to have that personal connection, I'm not sure—"

"Stop stalling. What else is in it?"

"Two owl eggs, umm, a minnow, but I didn't have one so I used an anchovy, some frogs' eggs that I whipped up with a fork and kind of mashed up so you wouldn't—well, the texture, you know. I would have whipped up the owl's eggs, too, but the book was specific. Tabasco, apple cider vinegar, rendered beef fat, pork fat, and salt and pepper, for taste. You don't think the anchovies messed it up, do you?" She gave him a concerned look. "Are you still okay? You're not wanting another drink are you?"

"Whoa. Whoa. That..." He smothered a liquid burp. "No, I definitely don't want another drink." He fought to keep it down, succeeded. "How, uh, how long have I been out?"

"Since last night, it's eight o'clock now...at night, I mean. You slept all day."

He frowned. "No, wait. Last night? That's impossible." He looked at his healed hand. *No way that heals in twenty-four hours.*

"Yes."

"Just, yes?"

"It's true." She tilted her head, gave him a small smile. "It's only been a day. And yes, it seems impossible that you're all healed up, but that's the way it is. Abe doesn't understand it either, or at least he says he doesn't."

"All right, well..." He made a helpless gesture. "How did I get here? The room I mean? And where are my clothes?"

"Yeah." She looked at the ceiling. "You, uh, you weren't wearing any when Grandpa brought you up."

Jack remembered lashing rain and cold stone against his bare back. He rubbed his hand across his eyes, trying and failing to remember more.

"You remembered something, didn't you?" She crouched in front of him and took his right hand in hers. Cradled it. The ghost of the electric current returned, radiated out from where her fingers cupped his hand. He felt each individual fingertip, her nails in his skin. He was acutely aware of her touch, her nearness. The air felt close, and the scent of her was everywhere. "You were down the side of the mountain. Abe brought you up with his tractor, but he won't tell me what happened. He's trying to *protect* me, I guess." She looked at him, a question.

Jack watched her lips as she spoke. He didn't realize that he was staring. Her eyes were green like ferns uncurling in a private forest. Secrets hid in those shadowed glades. She became aware of his inspection and released his hand, rose and took a chair beside his half-forgotten breakfast. "You remembered something."

It was Jack's turn to blush and look away. "Yes."

"Yes, what? Just yes?"

He shrugged and smiled. "Just yes."

She froze, mouth open. "Dammit, Jack!"

"Hey, if Abe doesn't want you to know, far be it from—"

"Great! What is it with you men and your patriarchal bullshit?" She leapt to her feet. "Eat your damned breakfast or dinner, or whatever it is. I'll get your clothes." She jerked the door open. He worried that he'd broken their momentary connection. She paused to look back at him through the cloud of her blonde hair.

Maybe, he thought, and took a chance. "To be honest… I don't know what happened. I'm—well, I remember flashes, and I've got—I've got some serious questions for Abe. Let me talk to him first? I don't understand a lot of what I'm remembering. It doesn't—it doesn't make sense. Once I talk to him, I'll tell you anything you want to know." He took a chance. "If you take a walk with me later. I'd really like to take a walk with you."

The setting sun shone behind Jill, and he could not tell if her blush had returned. He thought it might have.

"Okay," she said.

Chapter 20
Abe

1987: Moondust Motor Inn, Windsor, Arkansas

Abe was tired, bone weary from the storm-wracked night and from clambering around the mountain, first following Jack down and then hauling the big man back up to safety. He was also relieved. A great invisible burden had been lifted from his shoulders, and with the weight lifted, his horizons had opened. The world looked fresh and new. *No blood on my hands, thank God, no blood on my hands.* Everything looked possible now, assuming he could figure out what to tell Jack. If the kid had any recall, he was sure to have some pointed questions.

Abe needed him now more than ever, and his one worry this fine late-summer evening was that, having found Jack, he might now lose him. That hadn't been a concern when Jack was a means to an end, but now that Jack was able to strengthen the wall and to do…whatever else he was able to do, Abe had to find a way to keep him near. He needed the kid's strange power.

Jill was upset with Abe for his refusal to answer questions. She was a reporter and not good at taking silence for an answer. He'd been avoiding her until he could figure out what to do and what to tell her. Better to leave her to take care of Jack. *No matter what, she can't know. She's gotta stay out of this.*

Abe pushed the mower into his weather-grayed barn and headed uphill for the final time. It was time to see how the kid was doing, time to find some things out, and maybe, share some of the burden.

****

Jack looked wild around the eyes; his hands had a quiver to them that Abe recognized. The kid sat on the edge of the bed with the bedsheet wrapped around him and vibrated.

"She didn't bring you your drink?"

"She did," Jack replied. "Then she brought me a different one."

"You turned down the shine?"

"Yeah, yeah. I did." Jack's voice sounded incredulous.

"She have you drink that booger drink with the eggs and such?" Abe sank into the chunky wooden chair by the motel room table.

"Yes. It was…" He burped and grimaced. "It just *was*, let's leave it at that."

"Yeah, my Sarah, my wife I mean, tried it on me once 'pon a time when I was still drinkin'. I don't reckon it did nothing for me, but…" His shrug was suggestive of the many things that he'd done for love. "You wantin' a drink?"

"No." Jack's voice was solid, no bravado. He'd demolished his breakfast as well, a good sign.

Abe liked that. "You still hungry, kid?"

"A little, maybe."

"How are you feeling? Without the booze, I mean?"

Jack cocked his head. "Like my body is hollowed out. Like I'm going to, I don't know, jump out of my skin or something. It's like there's this…fishhook in my belly, pulling. I feel kind of…frantic, you know? To do something, or take something, break something, make something, drink something. Anything really. Eating helped for a while. I don't know. Maybe it was keeping me distracted."

"You decide to stop drinking before or after drinking Jill's witch brew?"

Jack put his chin in his hand and rubbed. The stubble rasped under his fingers. "Before."

"Yeah. That's the way it was for me, too. I dunno. Maybe that stuff works, but I think it's gotta be something else. Maybe it helps. I know I didn't wanna drink nothing for some little while after drinking that potion, but that had more to do with the taste than anything else." Abe shuddered. "Is it as bad as I remember?"

Jack grimaced. "Yeah. I feel like that anchovy's trying to fight its way out."

"She used an anchovy? 'Sposed to be a—"

"Minnow. I know, she told me. Don't remind me. Anchovy is bad enough."

"Why do I even have anchovies? I never remember buyin' stuff like that. Hmm, well. Like I said. No harm. It ain't the drink that got me sober, no how."

"What got you sober?" Jack's knuckles were white. "What's going to get me sober?"

"I don't know for you. Heck fire, I don't even know if you really mean to *stay* sober yet. We'll find that out, I suppose."

Jack's closed his eyes. A shudder passed over his

face.

Abe waited until Jack mastered himself. "For me," he continued. "I needed a little self-knowin'. You know what I mean? Just a moment of, of... It felt like waking up. That's all. That's how I got sober. Or got started on bein' sober, at least." Abe sighed. "I reckon I hated myself and what I was and what I'd done and everything else. Hated everything. I was right on the edge of killing myself. I was so full up of anger and—and judgment. I was sitting judgment on everybody and everything. Myself worst of all. I'd done things...Well, that's another-time story." He frowned. "Let's say this; somethin' had to change, and God gave me that moment. That vision into myself. He let me see myself, and when I saw what I really was and what a mess I was making, I—I give it all up and then, gave it right back to Him. Finally figured I didn't know what I was doing. That's how I stopped."

"So. It's a God thing. Somehow it's always a fu—a freaking God thing."

"Was for me. Don't mean it's gotta be for you, I guess. I dunno. You asked how I did it."

Jack looked at his hands, turned them palm up, ran his pointer finger over the deep V scar on his palm.

Abe could see the memory of power in the kid's eyes. "And I drank Sarah's potion, too. Can't forget that. For the first couple weeks."

"Weeks? You mean I gotta take that stuff for weeks?"

"Well, we'll see whether Jill's as stubborn as her grandmother. Also, you ain't married to her, so I don't reckon you have to worry about hurtin' her feelings or nothing."

"I have to ask you, Abe. If you're an alcoholic like me, why are you making moonshine? I don't understand why you'd tempt yourself like that. And why are you giving it out to other alcoholics like me? I mean, come on, man, you know what it's like. You know. Doesn't that make it kind of your responsibility?"

"I use the stuff to run the tractor and genny. You know that. I ain't got pots of money layin' around. And *temptation*, well, I got a little of that every now and then, I don't wanna pretend otherwise, but...I either don't gotta drink or I do, if you see? I mean, if I want booze, all I gotta do is run down to the gas station, and if they're closed, well, they's 'plenty of other guys around here makin' shine. It ain't just me."

"But what about giving it to me, how is that okay?"

"I dunno." Abe refused to tell Jack that his survival hadn't been important until now. "It might be a bad thing, might not. I really don't know. I figure people are gonna do what they're gonna do. Somebody gets ready to stop drinking, they'll stop."

Jack frowned. "I'll tell you this," Abe hurried on. "When I wanted to drink, ain't nobody could stop me from doin' it. Heck, I walked three, four miles in a snowstorm to get some booze once. I figure it's something a person's gotta come to on their own. Maybe I'm wrong, I dunno." He fished his pipe out of his overalls, packed and lit it. The air conditioner rattled in the window. A vehicle whooshed by on the highway, coming from somewhere, going somewhere else. The motel room door opened with a rattle.

Jill poked her head in. "Everyone decent?" She carried a handful of laundered and folded clothing.

Abe sighed, grateful for the interruption.

Chapter 21
Jack

1987: Moondust Motor Inn, Windsor, Arkansas

Jack wrestled to pull up his worn blue jeans after Jill delivered his clothes and Abe chased her away. He found himself at a loss. He needed answers but didn't know how to start. His memories couldn't be true. He'd simply had too much to drink. But Abe sat there, looking at him with expectation in his eyes, like he wanted to be asked, like he needed to be. Jack threw a question into the silence. "What's going on?"

"What do you mean?" Abe puffed at his pipe. The light of the setting sun tinged the smoke orange.

"You know what I mean." He waved a hand to encompass everything; it sent Abe's smoke swirling in the dying light. "What Jill did to that—that guy. I'm pretty sure she killed him, but I don't have any idea how and last night, man. I don't even know where to start. I just remember—What the hell happened to me, Abe? And why were you there? And what was all of that...shit that I was looking at? The stone and the bones and—and..."

"I told you about cussing."

"I know, I know! Can you answer me please? We can worry about my language later."

"Well, that's a lot of questions."

"So help me, are you going to tell me or not?"

"Yeah, I don't know."

Jack jerked to his feet. "Abe, I'm freaking out. I'm trying not to drink, and I feel like I'm going to jump out of my skin. You playing mysterious isn't helping. If you don't tell me, as God is my witness, I'm leaving."

"Whoa. Whoa. I'm gonna tell you. I'm tryin' to figure out how. Where to start kind of thing."

"Start with Jill. What the hell happened there? What did she do?"

"Well, Jill. Well. I really oughta let her tell you herself…"

"Abe," Jack warned.

"She can give you the details, but—but I think I know what you wanna know. She's, uh, she's what we call a witchmaster, Jack." Abe gave him a measuring look. "We both are, actually."

"What? A witch? Seriously? You're expecting me to believe that?"

"No, not a witch." He made slowing motions with his gnarled hands. "I never said witch. I said witchmaster, witchmaster. It ain't the same thing, ain't the same thing at all. See, see, a witch. Well, a witch has truck with the Devil and all that stuff. I ain't never even met a witch. Witchmastering ain't like that. Witchmastering is more like, just, tweakin' things. And mostly the only doings witchmasters ever have with witches, if they do anything 'round witches at all, is to chase 'em off, remove the hexes they've been puttin' on people and whatnot. Witchmastering ain't witchin'. It's mostly, well, it's just…greasin' the skids every now and then. Making life a little easier. Know what I mean?"

"No, Abe, I've got no idea what you're talking about."

"Don't know how to explain it better than that. We got these old verses that we use. Spells, I guess, and we can kinda feel things inside of us. Some say they feel it in their heads, like in their thoughts. You see? Others claim it's a heart thing. I don't know. Sometimes we say verses to make things happen and, you know, God kinda adjusts things for us, sometimes we can kinda make things happen on our own, and sometimes—sometimes it's a mix of the two. I wish my old buddy Sam was still around. He paid better attention to the old folks than I did. He was a big one for the old-timers' books, too." Abe sighed. "Anyway, sometimes we can do things. Like tellin' an animal what to do. Silent-like, you know? Or we can kind of twist fortune, sometimes to the good, sometimes to the bad. That's what Jill did to that little cowboy. We can do other stuff, too. Some important, some silly. Some are stronger at it than others. Jill... Well, she's real strong. Strong as I've known."

"You don't know what she did? You can't tell? I mean, if you're one of these witch—witch..."

"Witchmasters."

"Right. Shouldn't you know what she did, if you're one of those?"

"Nope. Each of us do things a little different. Sometimes it's of our own power. Sometimes it's of God's. Hard to tell, even for another witchmaster."

It sounded like madness or lies, but Jack didn't think Abe was a liar. The jury was out on madman. *Still, I saw something. I definitely saw something.*

"With that cowboy fellow," Abe continued. "I

think she laid out a bad luck thing and then... Well, she put some oomph behind it, you know? Like she put something of herself into it. She was pretty het up, and she had good reason to be. No knowin' how powerful that'd be in a spell. Old folk used to call that the evil eye, or the jinx, lots of things." He frowned. "Gotta be careful with that kinda thing. Witchmastering can be used for bad the same as witchin'. In fact, I don't really believe in them witches, but I seen a few witchmasters go bad in my time."

"So she killed him?"

Abe took a few mighty pulls on his pipe. "I don't know. I don't think so, least not directly. I think she made him a gift of bad luck. A lot of it, all at once, and something went wrong at the wrong place, and he went over the edge of the road. Bad luck, see? I don't know she even knew how much hexing she was sending out." He made a helpless gesture. "I'll say this. I ain't losin' no sleep over that little guy. You done a fair amount of killing yourself."

"Yes. I did. I don't think..." He put his head in his hands, exasperated with his inability to express himself. "How do I say this? I'm not upset that he's dead, and if anybody had a right to take him out, Jill did. I just... Well, I want to understand what happened and what I'm dealing with. I guess—I guess I want to know whether I'm dealing with the good guys or the bad guys."

"Ain't no such thing," Abe growled. "They's just people. Some do good, some do bad. Those that do bad, they get in the habit of it. It's hard to kick that kind of habit. Sometimes doing bad feels like the right thing to do, and sometimes they become what they do. At the end, they's all still people." The old man's voice grew earnest. "Jill does good mostly. Don't mean she don't get angry, don't mean she don't make mistakes, don't mean she ain't selfish sometimes; it *does* mean she don't do stuff like that to people who ain't got it coming. It also means that she's real upset about that little guy dying, but she's her daddy's daughter and my granddaughter, and she's doing a mighty fine job of hiding it. That answer your question?"

"Yes. I think it does." Jack bent to pull on his combat boots. "What happened to me last night?"

"What do you remember?"

"Enough. Just tell me what happened? No games."

Abe sat for a moment, knocked his pipe out in a stolen Ramada Inn ashtray. Repacked it and went through the laborious process of relighting. The black tobacco stained his thumb and forefinger, sprinkled across the lap of his overalls. The pipe lit and sent a fresh bloom of smoke out into the room. "I don't know."

"You don't know?"

"Yep. I don't know."

"All right, all right." Jack fought back frustration. "What do you think happened?"

"I don't know. I reckon you got something I ain't never seen before. Jill can't do nothing like what you did. Neither can I. Ain't nobody I ever knew could do that with the lightning and all. You're all healed up, too, ain't you?"

Jack nodded, showed his palm.

Abe grunted. "You had a real good cut on your chest and arm, too." The old man pointed at the fresh scars. "There was legends about what you did. Legends that I got from my momma and granddaddy, but I ain't never seen it, didn't think it was possible. It ain't Witchmastering; I'll tell you that. More of an Indian thing, though that don't make sense."

Jack sighed, ran a hand over his brow. He didn't know whether to believe the man or not. He had never felt any sort of power before. Last night, what he remembered of it, felt like a fever dream, like a hallucination of power, and yet, something had happened. He knew it in a way that pushed aside his uncertainty. "What do I do about it?"

Abe smiled. "Don't play in the rain, maybe?"

"Funny." Jack snorted. "You've gotta know more than that."

"I don't, I sure don't. Maybe one of my books might have something. I don't."

"Books?"

"Yep. You can borrow 'em, long as you take care of them. They's mighty old, some are handwritten."

Jack nodded. If there were books, maybe there were answers. If not answers, at least pointers. He'd learned in the marines; sometimes a little knowledge could overcome a big problem.

"I ain't never been able to read most of them." Abe knocked his knuckles against his skull. "I ain't a reader, and the old stuff, some of it ain't even in English. Spanish, I think, but it's handwritten and real hard to cipher. And, you know, I don't know Spanish so good."

Jack knew Spanish well. His mother had given him few gifts, but a second language was one of them. "And I can read them?"

"Sure. I reckon you can try."

Jack leaned forward, elbows on knees. "What's going on with that stone down there and those... What do you call them? The sticks with the skulls on them?"

"That—that's a looooong story." Abe gusted another cloud of smoke.

"We've got time."

"Yeah. Well, there's somethin' about this place. How good are you at believing crazy stories?"

Jack's eyebrows arched. "Try me. I believed the marine recruiter."

"Hah. I bet you did. All right, well… There's somethin' in the bottom of that valley."

"You mean the stone where you found me? Is that what you're talking about?"

"No, that's the Isaac Stone. It's only halfway down the valley-side. You didn't make it all the way down. This thing is somethin' different." The old man looked ill at ease.

"What is it?"

"Somethin' evil. Somethin' we call the Fountain."

Chapter 22
Ronnie

1987: Night of the Storm: In the Valley of the Fountain

Ronnie awoke in a sharp-edged world of pain. His vision was blurred. He wiped his eyes and his fingers came away red. He blinked and blinked until the mountainside came into a dim focus. He lay crumpled on a half-buried stone littered with pine needles and broken branches. Each breath brought a stabbing pain from his right shoulder and chest. His calf burned with a snapped icicle cold, and his left foot was a hot ball of pain. He tasted iron in his mouth. *I'm fucked up. I'm bleeding. Truly, truly fucked up.*

An angular blue blob in the distance resolved itself into a shape that he recognized. The Camaro lay on its side fifty feet away, cradled between two fraternal oaks on the steep valley wall. It had come to rest a long way below the highway's drop-off. *Must have been thrown free. Daddy always said seatbelts was killers.*

He levered himself into a sitting position using his good arm and looked down the length of his body. The toe of his boot was pointing in the wrong direction. Seeing it sent waves of darkness through his vision and made him feel like he couldn't get enough air. *I gotta straighten that, shouldn't oughta look like that.* He grunted and leaned forward to pull his leg toward him. His calf shifted with the pressure, and the bones inside grated and rasped. His vision went black. He fell back coughing and gasping for breath. The deeper he breathed, the more his chest hurt. Blood ran down his chin. *I'm dying. Oh, Daddy, I'm dying. I'm dying. Please don't let me die.* Bile rose in his stomach like an acidic slug. He vomited and passed out.

Night had come when Ronnie came to. Far above him, over the valley rim, blue and red lights flashed. They were a long way up, but he knew what they meant. The cops and, probably, the paramedics were up there and looking for him. He was saved.

In that moment, he was transported back to his childhood when he'd been certain that his daddy could fix anything, his toys, his wounds, his tears. *Only Daddy never fixed any of that shit, did he?* He'd only told Ronnie to get over it, to suck it up, to get out of his damn way. His daddy had hard fists. *Daddy did it to make me tough, and he wouldn't be feeling sorry for me if I let them catch me. Hell, they're gonna lock me up if they find me. No, no, they're probably going to kill old Ronnie, the bastards. They've always had it out for me, ever since the beginning. They're gonna put me in the electric chair. I'd rather die free than in a damn prison. I gotta get out of here.*

Ronnie made it to his knees, graying in and out. Black dots swam into the edge of his vision as the pain rolled in waves from his blasted chest to his crushed foot and rebounded back again. He dug into his pocket, fished out the little baggie of cocaine and took a snort. The blast woke him up, gave him the energy he needed to continue, and better, it made the pain recede. He blinked away tears and lowered himself down the side of the rock, deeper into the valley. *Only one way to go. Gotta go down.*

As if answering his thought, a strange voice spoke in his head. He ignored it at first, chalked it up to the pain and the fear, but it grew stronger, more insistent. Something called to him; something promised him things, an end to the pain, freedom, life.

I want to go home.

Come on, the voice in his head replied, *home is down here. Healing is down here.*

The descent was terrible, and Ronnie lost consciousness several times. Before his blackout periods, as the black motes swam up to overwhelm him, he had the feeling that he was being watched. A dark shape, something man-shaped, hovered in the corner of his pain-smeared eye, something following him and, maybe, helping him.

****

Later, deep in the valley's darkness, long after the sun had set and the day's heat had receded, Ronnie reached the valley floor. He didn't notice until, coming out of yet another swoon, he realized that he no longer rolled down the hill while trying to rise to his elbows and knees. He grasped a sapling and tried to get his bearings. The dark made it difficult, but he focused his weary eyes and tried to remember what he was doing, where he was going.

Far above him, a flash of lightning lit the sky, and rain poured through the trees. A great roaring wind took the treetops and shattered them against each other. The violence sent Ronnie back to his knees as a lightning bolt crashed and blazed overhead. He glimpsed the shadowman again in the sudden flash of light. The rumbling thunder vibrated the valley floor and falling leaves plummeted down to land on his head and shoulders. The shape came closer. The storm, the injuries, the exhaustion, it was too much. Ronnie tilted his good shoulder against a stunted tree and sank to his flanks, sat uncaring in the swampy dirt. *I'm done, Daddy. If you was ever gonna fix anything for me, this'd be the time to do it.* A pair of black arms wrapped around him and jerked him away from the sapling. Ronnie shrieked. The dark shape that had been following him, now carried him. Ronnie fought. He twisted and hollered, but the crushing pain built into a crescendo that sent him back into the darkness once more.

When he awoke, the storm still pounded down. Ronnie lay in a clearing across from a cave. A pool of water that splashed and distorted with the storm's heavy rainfall lapped the cave entrance. Great oaks ringed the clearing. The pool offered a faint glow like the phosphorescence of a million fireflies. *Where am I? What happened?* Another great stroke of electricity split the night and flashed across the water. The cave flashed into relief. Ronnie saw a great beaming eye, an opening at the top of the roof that lit with the lightning. He screamed, convinced that some single-eyed monster had risen from the pool to kill him, to eat him. The pain, the fear, the exhaustion, and now this; something broke in Ronnie's mind. With madness came peace. He stopped screaming.

Ronnie rolled to his side, grunting with the pain. Lightning flashed, and he saw the shadowman again, standing in the mouth of the cave. It beckoned to him as if to say, *Come, come home.*

"Is that you, Daddy?" Ronnie shouted into the storm. "I can't, Daddy, I can't go no farther." The lightning splintered across his vision again. The shape was gone. "Oh, Daddy. Don't leave me, Daddy. I'm comin', Daddy. I'm coming home." He rolled once more to his knees, made to stand, but his shattered calf betrayed him. He stumbled and fell full-length into the lambent pool. The storm threw another arc of electric light into the mountainside. Ronnie lay facedown in the rain-dimpled water, streamers of blood from his many wounds turning the waters around him red. The fountain bloomed with a sudden blue light that reflected from the leaves of the overarching trees. His body twitched once, twice. He drank the water for a long time, raising his chin to take great gasping breaths. It burned on the way down, like good whiskey, and his limbs unkinked, his skin stretched taut, almost as if new. He drank until he could hold no more.

Sated, he rose to his feet and inspected himself in wonder. His shattered leg was whole; his many small wounds closed.

The shadowman beckoned again from the cave entrance, and this time Ronnie was able to follow. He splashed around the shallow pool, coming closer to the cave mouth, closer to the shadowman. He knew that he should be frightened, but he was not. As he entered the cave, the spirit wrapped its arms around him. The embrace, now insubstantial, was warm.

Ronnie began to cry. The fears and the disappointment, the rage and the humiliation streamed down his cheeks. The shadowman's touch was intimate, all consuming, and its voice spoke directly into his brain. It offered words of commiseration, of assurance, of peace, and most of all, of revenge. Ronnie's tears dried as he nodded along. The spirit was right, everything he heard was right. He had been mistreated; he had been abused and neglected. The creature told him how to solve his problems, how to build his strength.

Ronnie didn't fight when the spirit slipped into his mind. He was happy. He'd found a friend. He'd found a new home.

He'd found the Fountain.

Chapter 23
Jack

1987: Moondust Motor Inn, Windsor, Arkansas

"I don't really know if it's a real fountain or what." Abe sat by the motel room window and rolled his pipe around in his hands. The smell of tobacco lingered in the air. "I never been down there." He pulled a leather tobacco pouch from his overalls and dropped a little of the ribbon-cut leaf in his lap as he began repacking the briar bowl for yet another smoke. "It does something to people, the Fountain, sometimes animals, too. Makes them, kinda crazy-like, angry, more—more, well, het up is how my grandma said it. It gets stronger the closer you get. People can get real crazy, they get too close. Some of the old-timers told stories of the Fountain taking people for itself. My grandma said it ate men's souls, and when it was through with them, they were left as nothing but…pure evil, I guess. Bodies walking around and doing harm. Killing and rapin' and all kinds of horrible stuff. It can get bad. Real, real bad." Abe shrugged. He looked embarrassed. "From a distance though, say down in West Port, even LaFayette when it gets real strong, what it does—it makes it so normal folks with normal lives act out. Jealousy, envy, rage, all that stuff the Bible talks about. The Fountain kinda focuses all that in a person, makes them more jealous, more envious, and so on." He puffed on his pipe for a moment. "Some folks are more susceptible to it than others. Just like… Well, like an allergy. You get stung by a bee, it's gonna hurt, but if you're allergic, it's gonna do lots more than that. Like your counselor, Robert, you remember him?"

Jack nodded, uncertain where Abe was going with this.

"That day we met, I saw the shadow of the Fountain on him as strong as I ever seen it. Scary thing when the Fountain reaches that far. For most, at that distance, with the Wall in place, it ain't no big deal. Just like a bee sting, but for folks like Robert, it's a big deal even when it's a weak influence. Some folks are more sensitive, I guess. I ain't saying Robert done nothin' bad. I'm just saying I could see it workin' on him." He waved away the mention of Robert and sent his smoke swirling through the room. "Anyway, the Fountain makes people act their worst. That's what it does to innocent folks, like just fer instance, let's say there's this insurance salesman fellow. Not a real guy, just an example. You with me?"

Jack nodded.

"So this insurance fellow, this guy's always been honest, but, then one day, the Fountain's kickin' up real hard, or the Wall is real weak, or maybe both are happening at the same time. Well, our insurance fellow, he's a Sunday school teacher and law-abiding citizen and all. Suddenly, he up and decides to steal from his company and run off to Mexico or something. You see? Or let's say there's a truck driver. Been drivin' trucks his whole life, can't wait to get home to his wife and kids and such. Maybe he ain't even from here. Maybe he's drivin' from Kansas City to Little Rock and passes right down that highway out there." Abe pointed with a long, wrinkled finger. "Maybe the Fountain gets under his skin since he's so near to it. Then later, down the road a ways, some fellow cuts him off on the road or something. Next thing you know, that happy truck driver plows right into that guy's car in a fit of rage. He don't even know why he did it. That's what it does to regular folks, you see?" Abe puffed on his pipe. Used a stick to aerate the tobacco. "It's a lot worse when the Fountain gets hold of folks who are in the habit of thinkin' bad already, folks that already like to do bad. Folks like that little cowboy. Fountain plays with their minds long enough... Well, it makes them so they ain't nothing *but* bad. It's kinda like it takes the worst of a person and...boils it down, I guess, or...or, I don't know. Just makes things all het up."

"Het up," Jack repeated.

"Just like Grandma said. Het up. Rageful, vengeful, lustful, angry, dishonest, and just—het up. Sometimes it causes good stuff, too, I guess, or not so bad stuff, anyway. People tend to marry quick around here. That's an example of the not bad side. When people get a shine for each other round here, it goes right quick. It kinda concentrates..." Abe's mouth moved as he tried to find the right word.

"Passion?"

"Yeah, yeah, that's it. Passion. You see?" Abe slapped his knee and gave a triumphant grin.

"What does that have to do with the stone?"

"I'm getting to that." Abe stopped to fiddle with his pipe. "Anyway, back in, oh, I guess it musta been the 1800s or so, my folks settled out here. They was all part of this same church you see? There was lots of Spanish and French folks in north and south Arkansas, and they was mostly Catholics. My folks were part of a Protestant group, from Scotland. I'm talking 'bout my grandfathers' grandfathers, you know. I wasn't there, of course." Abe snorted. "Though I feel like I'm that old. Some days."

Jack smiled dutifully.

"Anyway," Abe continued. "My folks come up into these mountains looking for a place to make their own and to avoid the Spanish. Back in those days, the Spanish fellows weren't real happy about a bunch of Americans moving in, you know? Back then, the Spanish and the French still thought this part of the country belonged to them, or so I been told."

"Abe, tell me about the stone, man. I don't need a history lesson."

"I'll decide what you need. You wanna know what's goin' on? I'm telling you. Now just listen."

Jack clenched his fists in frustration, noticed that the shakes had passed. Maybe Jill's concoction worked after all.

"So," Abe continued, "my ancestors settled in right across that valley, and everything was going good for a while. They'd run into some Indians every now and again, mostly the Osage who used to do their huntin' over here. They tried to stay out the Indians' way, and the Indians mostly left them alone, too. Everything was going okay. But somehow, and I ain't real clear on this, the pastor of the group, kind of the mayor and the leader of the congregation at the same time, if you get my meaning...?"

Jack nodded.

"Well, he run into this tribe that was different from the Osage. I don't know, they may not have even been a tribe, they may have been a special kind of Osage. Sam said they wasn't, though. Sam thought these Indians was a whole 'nother tribe. He was probably right. He knew lots of stuff. The books said they was all from the same family. I ain't sure. Anyway, turns out these fellows was camped on every mountain peak around the valley, and they was doing something. Some kind of rituals." He tapped his pipe on his chin. "Isaiah, that was the Protestant folks' leader's name, Isaiah Walker, he sees them doing their pagan rituals, and he decides they need converting, and so, he takes a few of the settler menfolks, and they go out to, you know, spread the gospel and all. Only, it didn't work out that way, not so much.

"What happened is that Isaiah and his folks got told about the Fountain and what she does to people. Isaiah didn't believe none of that, of course. He chalked it up to savage thinking, but then them Indians give them some proof of some sort. The books don't say what, and my grandma, she didn't know neither. What I think is, they let the Wall down. I think they showed 'em what happens when the rituals ain't being done. There's a story that one of the settlers killed her baby and herself around that time. Set the little one on fire and then cut her own throat. I figure that had to be Fountain work. Anyway, the settlers went out there to convert the natives and ended up getting converted themselves."

Jack leaned back against the headboard. Abe paused and gave him a questioning look. Jack gestured for him to continue.

"So, the settlers learned about what them Indians

was doing, and then they kind of made the rituals their own. But they tried to make it Christian, you know? That's what Sam said, that they didn't wanna do it the Indian way 'cause it was pagan. I think it was 'cause the settlers *couldn't* do it the native way. Didn't have the power, see?" Abe crossed his arms. "Whether that's true or not, it don't matter. The settlers did it a lot different, took some of their ideas straight outta the Bible. My grandma told me the Indians didn't have to use blood at all…"

"Blood?"

"Yeah. It ain't what it sounds like, but there's some sacrificin' involved. I'm talking about sheep and such, like slaughterin' for the dinner table. I'll get to that in a minute. Anyway, them Indians, they didn't do any of that. Grandma said they didn't need to. She said the sacrificin' was a white man thing, something that we brought to the rituals. My ancestors and the Indians actually worked together for a while, but that didn't last." He frowned. "Things weren't always so good out here if you were an Indian. My ancestors weren't no better than the rest of the white folk running around the country, especially when it came to taking the Indians' property and such. I ain't proud of that. Ain't a fair way to behave, but that's the way it was. There's some pretty grim stories I could tell you about those days, but I won't." He sighed. " Anyway, those Indians that used to work with the family either died off, got locked up, or driven away."

"My momma said most of her people were driven out of Arkansas."

"You got native in you?" Abe's eyebrows rose.

"Yeah, I guess so. I don't know. Momma always

said so."

"She never tol' you nothin' about your family?"

"Just a little here and there. She said my grandpa was from up this way, but that he and his folks had been chased off their land years ago. I don't know what happened. Hard to believe anything she said. She, uh…" He shrugged. "She wasn't around much. She was an addict. The courts kept putting me in foster homes."

"Hm." Abe drew on his pipe.

"So the settlers took over the rituals completely?"

"Yep. It ended up being six families, descendants of the original church group, that did the rituals to keep the Wall strong." Abe made a circling motion around the valley. "They settled all 'round the valley. They did the sacrifices as they'd worked 'em out, and they passed on the old ways and traditions, including the Witchmastering and the Goomer Doctoring, which is mostly a different kind of Witchmastering. The healin' kind, you know? Together, they kept the Wall going."

"I haven't seen any wall."

"It ain't a wall you can see, of course. It's like a…well, it's a spiritual Wall, I guess. Keeps things safe for us. Keeps the influence of the Fountain in check. Only…" A note of sadness crept into Abe's voice. "The old families died off or stopped believing. Some moved away. The Great Depression was mighty hard on this area. People hear a lot about the Okies, but there was a lot of Arkies on the road goin' west, too. That's when things started to fail, I think. When Sam was around, there was two of us left, and that was barely enough. I thought I'd pass it on to my son, but he runned off when he was a teenager. Went off to school, got himself a law degree, and lives out in California. He's Jill's daddy. Smart fellow in some ways, in others..." The old man shrugged. "Anyway, I wasn't happy about that, but there was still a couple of old-timers kicking around back then, and I always hoped Sam might get married and have some kids of his own. Thought we'd at least keep a small group going, but the old-timers died off, Sam never married, I only had the one boy, and he left."

"Then Sam died?

"Yeah." The innkeeper traced a fly buzzing around the single-paned window. "Yeah. Sam died. Now there's only me, and I'm the only one doin' the rituals and trying to keep the Wall up." Abe puffed on his pipe for a while. Tears gathered at the corner of his eye. He dashed them away quickly.

Jack looked away, embarrassed. In Abe's day, men didn't cry.

"Lately"—Abe hurried on—"it's been getting stronger, and my rituals, well...they ain't been working that great. Seemed like the Wall was getting thinner every day. You don't know it, 'cause you ain't from here, but things been getting real bad. We've had some fires, lots of fights, even a couple of deaths, murders, maybe, and then...well, sometimes the Fountain, she seems to call people to her, and that ain't good. I don't know what'd happen if anybody ever got the whole way down there. It'd be bad, I guess. Anyway, when things are getting real out of control, it kinda draws bad folks, or folks with lots of...feeling. I think that may be what happened with that little cowboy and his crew."

"Is there a way to tell?"

"Nah, but the Wall has been pretty weak, lately, so might be. I been doing my best to keep it strong..." He shrugged. "It ain't working."

"But how are you doing it?"

Abe looked at his boots. "Sacrificin'. Praying, other stuff. Like I done told you."

"What's this—this sacrificing…ritual look like?"

"Well, it's—it's about the blood, I guess." Abe clenched his pipe between his teeth. "Kind of like the old Jewish rituals, except theirs were forgiveness rituals; ours, well, ours is to keep the Wall going. My ancestor Isaiah tried to model the ritual on what the Israelites did. That's why the sacrifice stone." Abe shrugged. "I didn't used to do real sacrifices like you're thinking. I mostly used the stone when I was slaughtering my sheep or chickens. When you're a farmer, and you wanna eat, you gotta do some slaughtering. Might as well do it at the stone. Sam did the same. It seemed to work." Abe's face fell. "That's the way it used to be, anyway." He gestured down the valley. "The Wall was real strong when I was a kid, but as the old-timers died off and the families moved away, it got weaker." Abe humphed. "Still, as long as Sam and me kept doing our part, it stayed strong. Then when Sam went…"

Jack's brow furrowed. "What did you do then?"

Abe refused to meet Jack's eyes. "I, uh, I tried some bigger stuff, cows and pigs and stuff, some, uh, some dogs 'cause I thought, you know, they was smarter, and they's so humanlike, you know." He searched Jack's face, then rushed on. "I did it more often, too. Tried doing the sacrifices on the Holy Days as well as the reg'lar days. Tried holy water I stole from Preddy's chapel. Tried lots of stuff. It mighta helped a little but not enough. I been losin' ground."

Jack cleared his throat. "So what are you going to

do about it now?"

"'Bout what?"

"The Wall. You said things were going to get worse."

"I did." The old man gave a sharp nod, and new excitement entered his creased face. The innkeeper leaned forward in his seat and fixed his washed-out eyes on Jack's. "Things ain't bad no more. Not right now."

"What changed?"

"I dunno, kid." Jack could hear the wonder in the old man's voice. "But *you* did it. I don't know how, I don't know what to tell you, but I ain't seen the Wall this strong in years, not since *I* was a kid, and there was a bunch of us working together. Strong as it is right now, I reckon it's good for a while. I don't know how, I don't know why, but it was somethin' you did."

"Something I did?" Jack looked over Abe's shoulder. A slim shadow lay across the glass of the motel room window. The shadow moved, a little. Jack smiled to himself. *Jill.*

"What're you looking at?" Abe turned to see.

"Nothing. Just, uh, just the tree out front. You know, just watching, you know…"

"Wasn't Jill, was it? She can't know about any of this." Abe opened the motel room door. No one there, the great oak in the center of the drive waved its branches in a gentle wind.

"Just a tree, Abe. Just the tree."

Abe scowled suspiciously.

Jack changed the subject. "Where is this wall anyway? I don't remember seeing anything or hearing anything."

"Really?" Abe mused. "It's always there for me, like a hum in the back of my throat. Hard to describe." He pointed down the valley. "It runs around the valley, just below the Isaac Stone." He shook his head. "Anyway, it don't matter that you can't feel it. Trust me, you done something, and the Wall's strong again and that means, no more people acting up, and nobody trying to go down there and mess with the Fountain." He grinned and clapped his hands together, like a delighted toddler.

Jack leaned forward. "What happens if I go down to the Fountain right now? Try to go through the Wall. Will it stop me? Am I going to get turned around? Or— or bound somehow?"

"It's hard to say. I dunno whether it'll effect you like others. It should, but I ain't real certain. I'd have to stop you tryin', though." Abe's jaw clenched. "I don't need you going crazy."

Jack shrugged. "All right, well…"

"So are you willin' to stay and help me? I'll teach you everything I can, if you're willing. I really need the help, kid."

"I don't know. I'm not sure I believe in any of this."

"What's not to believe?"

"Seriously, Abe? Would you believe, if you were in my shoes?"

"Of course, I would." Abe glared. "It's the truth!"

"I'll think about it, okay?"

"Don't think about it, Jack. I need you. You gotta—" Abe was interrupted by the rattle and grind of the motel room door opening.

"What are you two talking about?" Jill glanced at

Abe, then gave Jack a small smile.

Jack grinned. *She knows exactly what we were talking about.*

Abe looked back and forth between them suspiciously.

Chapter 24
Jack

1987: Highway 71, Windsor, Arkansas

Jack and Jill walked the side of the mountain highway in the early evening dark. He was prepared to keep his promise, to tell her what Abe had told him. The old man hadn't forced any promises from him, and he figured if she was willing to believe in magic, hell, if she was trying to *practice* magic, she'd be unlikely to think his supposed powers too incredible to accept. He still wrestled with how to tell her. How, after all, do you describe a miracle? Struck by lightning, but instead of incineration, you reach out and play with the stuff? What kind of craziness was that? And yet, his memory of the night wasn't his only corroborating evidence. He had the testimony of Abe and the preternaturally rapid healing of his wounds. He peeked at her profile in the dusk and girded himself to make the effort.

She noticed and smiled in return. "You feeling up for this? Walking I mean?"

"I've done a little walking in my life." He hesitated. "Seldom with anyone as pretty as you."

Her laughter rang in the dusk, genuine and unaffected. "Does that usually work?" She laughed again, and the white of her teeth looked like a string of pearls. "That may be the worst line I've heard in a loooong time."

"Hah." He kicked a stone down the side of the road. It hopped three, four, five times and then spun off into the grass beside the deep forest. "I honestly don't know. That's the most creative I could be at the moment. I, uh, I got nervous."

Jill smiled and touched him on the arm.

Jack eyed the tree line, the sky, his feet, put his hands into his pockets, then took them back out. For some reason, he felt the urge to start whistling but didn't.

"So," she said. "I make the big, bad marine nervous, huh?"

"Hah!" He laughed. "Yeah, I'll admit you're a little scary."

"Realllly..." Her voice was warm, happy.

Jack felt a sudden warmth himself and realized that there was nowhere in the world that he'd rather be.

"Tell me about the marines," she said.

"What about them? I did my time."

"I mean, how did you end up there? What did you do? Where did you go? Did you like it? All the details, geez."

"Well, that's going to take a while."

"Good. Get started. I plan to get your whole life story. Maybe I'll do a feature on you for the paper."

He kicked another rock down the road. "I doubt your boyfriend will care for you spending that much time with me, probably wouldn't care for you taking this walk with me."

She arched a brow. "My boyfriend doesn't get a say in who I interview and why."

"So you say." He looked at her from the corner of

his eye. "Are you okay being out here in the dark, after—after, you know?"

For a moment, something crossed her face, a shadow of fear. He worried that she might be hurting more than she was letting on, that he might have derailed the conversation with his clumsiness. He didn't want to lose this fine moment with her.

She squared her shoulders and offered him a tight smile. "Yes." She took him by the arm. "I can take care of myself." She gestured out at the darkened forest. "There are bears and wild cats and lions out there, and probably serial killers and used car salesmen, too. I realize that might frighten a city boy like you, but don't worry, I'll protect you."

"Very kind." He chuckled.

"Yes, it is." She looked up at him from under her lashes. "So to entertain me during my constitutional, I want you to tell me your story. Got it?"

He smiled and nodded.

"Good. So get started already."

"All right, the marines?"

"Actually, no. For tonight, tell me how you got here. I want to hear everything eventually, but let's start with how you got here. How did that happen? Why did you come to Arkansas?"

"Uhh." He found himself face to face with the bad thing that had sent him running from San Diego, the trouble that had put him on that bus. Telling her that story was dangerous. "It'd be better if we talked about you. That's what I'm interested in."

"Very gallant." She tilted her head and frowned at him. "Jack, don't hold out on me. Why come to Arkansas? Tell me the story."

They walked a little farther, she glancing at him, a crease resting between her brows. She was beautiful, even when frustrated. He wanted to shape the story to show himself in a favorable light. He couldn't. "There's nothing to tell. I wanted to see Arkansas. How about we talk about the marines?"

"Leon doesn't like you, Jack." She stopped walking and took her arm back. "I'm not sure what to make of you either, to be honest. I appreciate what you did when we got attacked, but I don't know you, and you seem awfully comfortable with violence. My friends, people that I trust, aren't mysteries." Jack took a breath to respond. She interrupted him. "No. Let me finish. To me, you're a homeless drunk with no back story. I heard enough of what Grandpa said to know he wants you to stay. I know he thinks he's got his reasons, but he's getting old, and I don't know how much of what I heard I can actually believe." She shifted her hips and crossed her arms. "But you'd better believe this, Jack: I will not let that man get hurt. Not by you, not by anybody. You not telling me about yourself doesn't make me trust you. Not even a little." Her eyes were hard in the moonlight. "If I don't trust you, we aren't going to be friends. Are you following me, Jack?"

"Yes." He had a sour taste in his mouth.

"You sure?"

"Yes, ma'am." He scowled.

Jill took a step back. "Leon is looking into how you got to Arkansas. I don't know if he told you that, but he told me. Did he? Did he ask you how you got here? Where you're from?"

Jack gave a terse nod and started to walk down the

highway again. He was looking into the distance and wondering if he shouldn't split town. He wondered why he'd thought this place could ever be home. Jill walked beside him, glanced over at him as she spoke.

"Did you tell him the truth, Jack? About how you got here?"

Jack shook his head, no.

Jill sighed. "I was afraid of that. He's going to find out. He's very good at what he does, Jack."

"So."

"So? Is that all you have to say? So?"

"So maybe it's time I moved on." His jaw clenched.

"You could do that. You could. Or..."

"Or what?"

"Or you can take a chance on telling me." Jill touched Jack's shoulder. It brought him to a stop, made him turn to face her. "Leon doesn't like you, but Grandpa does. Grandpa thinks he needs you, Jack. I don't know if that's true, but it doesn't matter. What I *do* think is that I'm a pretty good judge of character, and if you tell me what you're running from, I might help you with Leon. If you're honest, that is. And don't think you can lie to me, Jack. You've seen what I can do." She twiddled her fingers, smiling playfully again.

Jack remembered the ripple of power he'd experienced before, wondered if she told the truth, whether she could tell that he was lying or not. "What's in it for me?"

"Man, you're good at being annoying." She sighed. "I'll give you that. All right, what's in it for you? Well, you seem sad to me, Jack." He looked down, and she stooped to look up into his face. "Sad and, really, really lonely. Aren't you tired of running? Aren't you ready to have a home?"

"Yeah." His voice sounded like gravel. "Yeah."

"Well? Then tell me something. Try to trust someone. Try to make a friend. Tell me what you're running from."

The wind rippled through the trees above. The sound of a semi hectored through the night as it climbed Abe's mountain. He pictured putting a thumb out, hopping on that distant truck's sideboard and riding out of the mountains. Going back on the road, back to working his way from town to town, from bottle to bottle. He sighed and made a decision. "All right." He began walking down the side of the road again. He was certain that, once she heard, she'd see him gone or in jail.

Jill took his arm. He flinched, surprised. She smiled, and he opened his mouth, closed it, then began with a name. "Jill was her name," he began. "I was married, and believe it or not, her name was Jill…"

Chapter 25
Jack

1983: Beirut, Lebanon, San Diego, California

Jack did his best to be honest with Jill, to tell her everything as he remembered it. The words came as he went along. He told her how easy his ex-wife had found it to fall out of love with him.

A week before returning from Beirut with his marine company, Jack had received a magnificent tear-filled *Dear Jack* letter that had made it clear that the relationship was over, and that he was at fault. The upshot was that his constant deployments had "sucked the life from their marriage," his "love affair with alcohol had left her as dry as a desert island," and the "hell of daily worry knowing that he was in a combat zone" had created a "firestorm in her heart that left nothing but the charred vestiges of a youthful passion."

The letter went on and on and on. She closed by telling Jack that she had met another guy and was leaving town. Please, she'd written, don't be mad. He'd been, he told Jill, a little mad. Mad enough that he had to talk to someone, and that someone turned out to be his only friend in-country, his gunnery sergeant, Ray. "She should have her own soap opera, Ray. I swear, if you read this letter… It's like a joke. She was pregnant; did I tell you that?"

"Yes sir, yes sir. You sure did."

"I guess she got rid of it. Without even telling me."

"I guess so, sir. I guess so."

"That," Jack told Jill, "is when I made some bad decisions. I'd been off the sauce for a long time because the ex-wife was always on my ass about it. It'd been almost a year since I'd had a drop. I thought things were getting better, but when I got that letter, I lost all hope of anything. I felt like—like the whole world was as bad as I'd always thought it was, and what was the point anyway. I guess I was depressed or something. I don't know. Maybe I was looking for an excuse."

"I decided that, combat zone or no, it was time to get drunk. Not surprisingly, Ray didn't understand why I thought that was a good idea. I yelled and fussed but agreed to hold off for a week until we were safely on the plane back to the States."

Jack chuckled. "I was a real terror till I got on that plane. I almost got myself in trouble a dozen times. Ray even yelled at me, though I was his boss. He didn't know how the idea of that first drink was riding me. Like I said, I'd been dry for months, even before we'd arrived in Beirut. Not a drop for months. Months. And that was a long time for me, the longest time I'd been without booze since…well, it doesn't matter. You'd think after that much time, I'd have broken the habit, but it didn't work that way. Knowing I was going to have a drink soon was making my teeth itch. It was bad. It was real bad."

A truck, laden with caged chickens rattled by in a cloud of white feathers. Jack watched it until it was out of sight, then continued. "As soon as the plane landed in England, I was out of the bird like a shot. I found a duty-free store and bought two big bottles of Jameson's Irish whiskey and started drinking it down. I passed out by the time they were loading our flight to J.F.K. Ray had to come find me." He grimaced. "He half carried me onto the plane. He wasn't happy. I'll tell you that." He chuckled. "Once I was on the plane, everything might have been okay. Ray was trying to avoid a scene, so he was rationing my drinks. That probably would have worked." Jack shrugged and ran a hand across his mouth, looked embarrassed. "What he didn't know, though, was that I had an extra hip flask hidden in my cargo pocket. I kept taking hits off of that every time he got up to go check on somebody, or to use the head, you know, the, uh, the bathroom." Jill nodded, and Jack continued. "So I got drunker and drunker. You should have seen it. Ray was so damn confused. He kept saying, 'What the hell, sir? You get the long-lasting stuff or what?' " Jack shook his head. "I was pretty calm, though. I wanted to drink, not party. But when I landed in New York. Good God. I fell down the disembarking stairs and threw up three times. All over myself, the pavement, Ray, when he tried to help me. The press was there, and all the families were standing on the tarmac waiting for their marine daddies and husbands. I gave them a real treat. It was…terrible."

He swatted at a night-flying moth. "The CO was going to can me, but Ray told him we'd had some bad *kafta* before leaving Lebanon. I don't think the old man believed him, but he let me off anyway. Probably because he thought Ray would keep me in line, and he knew Jill had split on me."

Jill bumped him with her shoulder. "So the CO wasn't a bad guy?"

Jack shrugged. "Not really." He scowled. "I guess he tried to be fair. Anyway, back in the States there wasn't much to keep me off the sauce. I wasn't facing combat every day, the booze was easy to get." He sighed. "I didn't have the wife around anymore, so nobody was nagging me to keep it out of the house or anything. I figured everything was fine as long as I made it to work and did my job. I *always* made it to work. I was showing up drunk most mornings, but I figured, as long as I stayed away from the CO till lunch, I was all good. I know that sounds insane, but for some reason, I really thought I was doing okay." He grimaced. "That didn't last."

"One morning in PT formation, standing in front of all my marines, I passed out on my feet. Ray told me it gave everyone a big laugh, but he didn't find it funny...at all. He was seriously pissed with me. Not many things make him that angry, but messing with the honor of the Corps is one of them. Still, he tried to defend me again." He paused. "No, defend is the wrong word. He lied for me again. Told the old man that I was a heat casualty. It didn't work this time, though, and it cost Ray some points with the colonel, too. The CO knew I was a drunk, see? He was done with me." Sadness and anger warred within him. "He couldn't kick me out directly; I had to do other things first. Substance abuse counseling, psychiatric referrals, letters of apology, meet with the chaplain like a dozen times. It was pointless, I drank to get through it all, and I was...pissed. At the colonel, the marines, Jill, hell, even Ray. Somehow, I even blamed Ray." He made a disgusted sound. "He took me in after I got booted out. I didn't have anywhere else to go. He did that even though his wife didn't want me around. I promised I'd get a job and move out, but that never…happened."

"What did happen, Jack?"

He sighed. "I got drunk a lot. Ray and I argued. I cursed out his wife, broke some of their furniture. Finally…" He trailed off. He didn't want to go farther but forced himself to finish. "I hit him. He kicked me out."

A soft breeze rustled through the trees. Jack swiped at his eyes.

"I have been a pretty shitty friend."

She squeezed his arm.

He cleared his throat. "After that, I was on the street. I started wandering. Working my way from one small town to another, always moving on. I was pretty good at washing up. The restaurants I was working at didn't care whether I was drunk or sober, so long as I didn't break the dishes." He shrugged. "You get tired working all day and drinking all night. That's how I got on the pills. Some dude gave me some uppers, and I got hooked on them pretty quick. I slept wherever I could, underpasses, shelters, whatever."

"That must have been terrible."

"Eh, sleeping outside isn't too bad. I was used to that, but I didn't like the shelters. Everyone wanted to preach at me. People were too…I don't know. I didn't like it. It doesn't matter. Eventually, it all started to catch up to me. The pills, the sleeping in the weather, the rotgut. It just—it caught up. There's no other way of saying it." He gave her a questioning look. "You're a California girl, right?"

She nodded.

"Have you ever been to Coronado beach? That's

where things started changing for me."

"No."

"It's an ugly beach in some ways. The sand is dark gray, but when you get close, it's amazing. The water is full of millions of flecks of fool's gold. It looks like— like a snow globe or something and it leaves a line of gold flakes all along the shore." He smiled at her. "It's beautiful. Only, I discovered it while I was strung out on pills and booze, and I thought it was real gold. I almost drowned trying to collect the stuff." He chuckled ruefully. "Hell, I did drown. I came to with this lifeguard, a kid, giving me mouth-to-mouth. He'd pulled me ashore.

"Anyway, once I came around, the lifeguard wanted to know why I didn't listen to him when he told me not to go too deep. I didn't know what to tell him." He sighed. "Part of me wanted to say that I didn't hear him, but the truth is, I kinda know that I did. I didn't care at the time. I was chasing the gold and, well… How do you tell a teenage kid that you wished he hadn't saved your life? You know? It doesn't matter, I don't think I answered him anyway. Least not the way he wanted me to."

Jill bumped him to continue. "What did you do?"

Jack squinted. "I, uh, started to hallucinate. I thought the kid was a monster or something. I—I freaked out and hit him. Hard. Knocked him down and broke his nose." He gave a grim chuckle. "That stunt got me a stint in the drunk tank and charges of battery under California penal code 242. The charges got dropped, believe it or not. That lifeguard. His daddy was in the army, and he told my lawyer he couldn't see sending a 'hero' to jail because of one bad trip. Can you believe that? I punched the dude, and he still thought I was a hero. I don't get people. But, man, I don't know. It ate at me. I almost wished he'd sent me to jail. I wouldn't have fought it. He told my lawyer he felt pity for me. That killed me. Absolutely killed me. Some sixteen- or seventeen-year-old feeling pity for me. That... Well, that—that hurt my feelings."

"What happened next?"

"I—" Jack swallowed hard. This was the part of the story that he dreaded. "I made a friend."

Chapter 26
Jack

1983: San Diego, California
1987: Moondust Motor Inn, Arkansas

When Jack encountered Berto for the first time, the kid was starving on an American street corner, somehow managing to freeze his ass off in San Diego, California, average temperature seventy degrees. "Seriously," he told Jill. "The kid was standing there shivering in the middle of the day. It was crazy. Junkie-stuff. He had a proposition for me."

The thirteen-year-old addict had tried to sell Jack an old plug of tobacco, a lint-covered twist of dog turd brown that he tugged from his blue jeans pocket. Jack had never seen a tobacco plug outside of old western movies. Berto tried to trade it to him for the price of a meal, his smile ingratiating and nervous. He had nothing else to offer.

Jack had looked at him hazily. Then hard. He couldn't have weighed more than seventy-five pounds. He was reminded of his own childhood days fending for himself while his mom got up to God-knew-what. In Berto, he saw a familiar desperation and hunger, the same abandoned loneliness. He saw a version of himself.

He had broken his own rules and handed the kid a

few bills, then walked away. He should have known better. Berto had followed him to the shelter that day and followed him out of the shelter the next morning. He hadn't asked anything more of Jack. He had watched Jack with cautious eyes and stayed close to him. With Jack around, Berto wasn't prey anymore. He began to gain some weight, started to smile, and began to talk about the future. He was a rarity. He was honest and smart, loyal and trusting. Jack began to think about the child he had lost and what that kid might have turned out to be. If his aborted child had been allowed to grow up, he wondered, might he have been like Berto?

"I had this idea," Jack continued his story. "I should take care of him and that it would be easy. That I could be a role model or something."

Jack buckled down, managed to stay straight long enough to get a steady job again. He wasn't making a lot of money, but he and Berto were at least eating regularly. They negotiated a cheap room behind Jack's favorite bar. On the wrong side of town, but the price was right, and they knew their way around the neighborhood. It was only a starting point anyway.

He convinced Berto to register for school in the fall. He got him a new wardrobe at the local thrift store, taught him how to cook some basic meals on a second-hand hotplate. Berto checked into a juvenile day-rehab and managed to get off the drugs. They had a feast of carnitas and dulce de leche when he reached his thirtieth day of sobriety. They'd had a good time.

"I was still using, though," he told Jill. "And drinking, drinking, drinking. I felt guilty about it. Berto needed me to be reliable, but I couldn't stop. It must seem like we were a…weird family, just the two of us, and he wasn't my kid by blood or anything, but it felt like a real one. It felt like I had somebody to take care of, and somebody who loved me. It was a family, all right."

It all fell apart. While Jack was elbows-deep in a sink of suds, holding away the shakes and considering how to pay for Berto's school supplies; the kid himself was being shot five and a half times in a back alley behind a 7-Eleven. Five and a half because the sixth bullet had split in two against a fire escape rail. The bigger half had planted itself under Berto's left eye.

Jack looked at Jill. The highway was quiet and so was she. He wasn't seeing her. He was crying.

Bob, Jack's half buddy who worked the bar, had given him the news. He'd watched Jack for a reaction. "No arrests. No one is talking to the cops. Looks like a drug or sex deal gone bad." He'd shrugged. "Berto's street, man. And he's Mexican. Cops ain't gonna lose sleep over it."

"Who?"

"Nancy, they say."

Jack's eyes burned. His voice was hoarse. "I hated that dude."

"Nancy?"

"Yeah, Nancy."

Nancy was a greasy, pink, small-time dealer. He was unpredictable and often stoked on his own product. He was known for picking fights with kids, and for rape. Nancy, Nancy, Nancy. The name fell into Jack's mind and started burning. When he left the storeroom at one o'clock in the morning, he was hopped up on something strong. The exposed muscles on his arms were corded and taut. His teeth were clenched shatteringly tight. He almost vibrated. Bob's Bar didn't attract nervous drinkers, but the room went silent at the crash of the storeroom door, and even the roughest clients made a cautious path for Jack as he crossed the room.

"I had," Jack sneered, "some crazy idea of dragging Nancy in to the cops. I hadn't really thought it out, to be honest. I wasn't…" He trailed off and put his head in his hands. When he started speaking again, his voice had gone rough. "Let's just say, I wasn't thinking real straight."

Jack found Nancy in the early morning, darkness still shrouding the city, somewhere on the south side. He spent some time with him in an abandoned crack house. Nancy fought back, but Jack was no defenseless kid, like Berto. He bounced Nancy off a few walls, and when Nancy pulled his pistol and fired a couple of shots at him, Jack got *personal* with him, took him apart a little and, finally coming down off the junk and rage, wiped down his knife and left the murderer sprawled on a swaybacked and stained, blue suede couch.

"After the fight," Jack continued, "and the—the blood and all. I knew I couldn't bring him in to the cops. I'd go away for a long time. I didn't know what to do."

He didn't know if Nancy was still breathing when he left. He didn't check. He told himself that he didn't care. A hot stone of nausea burned in his gut, and his legs palsied when he pulled the front door shut behind him. He considered killing himself but couldn't quite find the courage. He postponed the decision. From the bus station he called 911 to send an ambulance after

Nancy, hung up, then called Ray and told him he needed help. "Like right now, Gunny." Ray wired him two hundred-and-fifty dollars, no questions asked.

Jack bought a ticket out of San Diego, out of California. Lacking inspiration, or a destination, he'd looked at a map of the USA. He couldn't stomach a return to New York, had to get the hell out of San Diego. He saw a green spot in the middle of the country, a place that his Mom had told him about on one of the rare times she'd been both sober *and* attentive. The place she'd been born. The bus ticket would get him to Arkansas.

"I was in free fall," Jack said. "I couldn't find the bottom. Couldn't even see it anymore. Then...Army of God, Abe...the rest of it." It felt good to reach the end of the story. He crossed his feet before him, tilted his head back to see the moon through the leaves of the giant branches arching over his head and waited for Jill's reaction. They'd doubled back, returned to the grounds of Abe's old motel and reclined under the ancient oak in the center of the circular drive.

"That's a tough story, Jack," she said finally. She lay in the grass beside him, crossed her arms over her chest, like she'd caught a sudden chill. He could see her, shoes discarded on the lawn, flexing her toes in the turf, exploring its texture, luxuriating in the night and nature. "One more question?"

He nodded. He'd told her the worst, one more revelation couldn't hurt.

She ran a slim finger down the scar on his cheek. "Where did this come from? Beirut?"

He blushed. Her touch had been intimate, electric. "No. This came from one of my foster brothers. He was a big fan of knives."

"Seriously? How old were you?"

"Umm." He tilted back on his elbows to look up at the night sky. "Eleven, I think. He was…well, I guess he was about thirteen."

"God. Why?"

"I don't know. Maybe he didn't like how I looked or talked or something. Maybe he didn't like me being in his house. I'm not sure. To be fair, I had a mouth on me, and we fought about everything. I was trying hard to be tough back then. I was pretty scared of the world." He paused to gather his thoughts. "I thought I was a man. I thought I had to be hard—harder than him, anyway. That's funny to think when I say. I was only eleven, but there you go. I had a chip on my shoulder, and I guess he got tired of it."

"What happened to him?"

"I don't know. They moved me to another home after I got out of the hospital." He closed his eyes for a moment, then reopened them. "It happens. It's not a big deal."

Jill gave him a fragile smile. "If you say so." The wind played with the long grass, the hanging leaves. Her hair blew gently across her face, toyed with her lips.

Jack almost reached over to smooth it away, almost. He stopped himself. Looking up through the night and the rustling leaves, he was aware of the vastness of the sky and his own tiny place in it. He was relieved to have told her about San Diego. He felt almost weightless. There could be consequences, but he didn't care. It was out now.

"I love the moon," she said. "I appreciate you

taking me for a walk, but…"

Jack didn't say anything, waited for the hammer to fall.

"I almost forgot." She rolled to her feet and rushed inside the motel.

Here we go. She'll be gone long enough to call Leon, tell him about Nancy, and then it'll all be over.

Jill returned moments later, wincing her way across the gravel. She'd left her sneakers lying in the grass. Despite his fears, Jack couldn't help but grin in the dark. She was carrying a mason jar. Something inside sloshed and slithered around.

"Not again." He groaned when she knelt beside him and offered the jar. The smell made him wince.

"Yes, again. My friends don't ruin their lives, Jack, not without me doing something about it. You've been too sad for too long. Drink up." She pushed the glass toward his mouth.

He pulled the jar away. "Wait. Doesn't anything I said change anything for you?"

A frown crossed her lips. "I don't think so. I think if you're serious about getting clean, then I need to help. It doesn't mean you get a blank check from me. I'm not saying your story doesn't make me cautious of you. I'm not saying you haven't done some bad things and made some wrong decisions, but… I think you deserve a chance. Just don't screw it up."

"What are you smiling at?" she asked.

"I, uh, honestly thought, when you went inside, that you were calling your boyfriend to come pick me up. I guess I'm relieved."

She shrugged self-consciously and placed her hands on her thighs. "I thought about it." She brushed a stray hair away from her face. "One day, you're going to have to find out what happened to Nancy. I think…" A lonely pickup passed down the highway. "I think you're going to have to do the right thing, when you do. But I don't think you're the kind of man that hurts people because he wants to. When the day comes that you have to face up to what you've done, I'll be there to help you. Can we make that agreement? One step at a time, and when it's time, I'll help you. In the meantime, I'll do what I can to keep Leon off of your back."

"He's gonna put my ass in jail. I just know it."

"We'll see. Now drink. We're going to keep you sober." She pushed the jar back to his mouth.

Jack steeled himself and downed it. He grimaced when the anchovy entered his mouth, it crunched between his teeth. "Gah. The anchovy is the worst."

"Oh. I found some minnows at the quick stop. I figured we should do it right, if we were going to do it."

For a quick, nauseating moment, Jack feared it was all coming back up.

"It can't," she continued, "be any worse than drinking the worm out of the bottom of a mescal bottle, and I'm betting you've done that."

Jill braced one hand on her hip and formed the other so that it gripped an imaginary bottle, made glugging motions, and lolled her tongue out of her mouth. The play-acting was so absurd that instead of vomiting he found himself laughing. The first real belly laugh he'd had in years.

"One more thing," she said. "Get those books from Grandpa. We can read them together."

Chapter 27
Leon

1987: Roadways Bus Terminal, LaFayette, Arkansas

"How's your morning, Hal?" Leon asked. The venetian blinds on the bus station door rattled as it shut behind him.

"Oh." The bus station clerk looked up from his books, his white hair stark against his dark skin. He smiled, his lips tight, weathered eyes seeming pleased. "Pretty good, Detective. What brings you round?"

Leon walked across the empty waiting room, sidestepped a yellow cleaning bucket. The floor had been recently mopped and smelled of pine cleaner; the windows were streaked where Hal had wiped them down. "You know, a little of this, a little of that." The detective gave the older man a genuine smile. He liked Hal, always had.

"Yeah?" Hal smiled back. "You catch the game on Sunday?"

"No. I had a thing. Don't tell me about it. I have it recorded on the VCR. I've been trying to stay out of the office, so none of those chuckleheads will ruin it for me."

"Shoo, you done gone this long without hearin' nothing?" Hal chuckled. "You must be lucky or hidin' yourself under a rock somewhere. It was a big game—"

"Don't you say any more, Hal!" Leon raised his hands in mock supplication. "Please, please, don't say any more. I'm supposed to watch it tonight, assuming my girlfriend hasn't got other plans, and praise God, I don't think she does."

"Yeah. You better get her watched quick, man. It's a miracle you ain't heard nothin' yet."

"I will, I will."

Hal smiled again, clicked his teeth, and adjusted his brass nameplate. One of the things Leon liked about Hal, the man was always neat, always professional, always friendly. "Squared away" was the phrase Leon liked to use.

"How's your love life these days?" Leon said lightly, a gentle teasing. No one could call Hal handsome, not with a straight face. Hal was a confirmed bachelor.

"Oh, you know. No kissin' and telling."

"Hah." Leon snorted. "Good one."

Hal blinked at Leon for a moment, then looked down at his desk. A blush spread across his cheeks. He opened one of the wood paneled cabinets behind him. "So I take it you need to know 'bout somebody who might have come through here?"

"Yep." Leon pulled a foot back, kicked his right toe into the freshly mopped floor. It was habitual, tap, tap, tap and it showed in the scuff on the toe of his dress shoe. "That I do, Hal."

"What day?"

"I know it's difficult, but I don't rightly know. Fellow says he's been here about three months, might be around then? Three months ago? Coming into town, not going out. I'm looking for an arrival."

"All right." Hal's hands hovered over the shelves while he hummed to himself. Each of the ledgers rested before him, divided and placed into some system that was a mystery to Leon.

"How's your nephew up at Varner? He doin' the time, or the time doin' him?"

Hal's shoulders slumped, then his hands dipped into the shelves and pulled out three folders, laid them on the desk. "He's doin' all right. He told me you been writing to him. I wanna say, I appreciate you doin' that. He was mighty down for a while. I didn't know if he was gonna make it."

"How much time does he have left?"

"Nine months. Nine months and a week, maybe two. Something like that."

"Yeah? You tell him to hang in there. I always liked Terry. I know he's gonna have a hard time finding work, but if he'll look me up, I'll do what I can to help."

"Man. I sure do appreciate that. I sure do."

"No problem. Drugs are a bitch, man. I hope he's got them whipped this time. I hate what happened last time."

Hal's head went up and down. He adjusted his glasses and focused on the paper in front of him, avoided Leon's eyes. Leon looked out of the streaked window. Some teenagers horsed around in the McDonald's parking lot. Hal's nephew, Terry, hadn't been much older when Leon had arrested him. The empty bus station was filled with a long silence and the glow of the late afternoon sun. Hal had a Polaroid pinned to the notice board behind his counter. It showed a little girl, three or four years old, cute with the huge smile you could only capture on a child's face, a woman in shadowed profile. They looked familiar to Leon, but he couldn't place them. A fly buzzed against one of the sheet glass walls.

Hal stood as if frozen, his restless hands gripping each other. "You couldn't have said that better." Hal broke the silence. "No sir, you couldn't never. What name we looking for?" He tapped his thin fingernail on the opened folders in front of him.

"Diaz, Jack. I hate to waste your time, Hal. He may not have come in with y'all. He claims he hitched."

"Don't worry about it. Ain't nothing happening around here but killing flies. This'll give me something to do. Grab yourself a cup of coffee." He gestured to the silver canister and foam cups at the end of the counter. "I'll go through these real quick, see what I can see."

"You're a prince, Hal."

"Just give me a few minutes."

Leon watched the teenagers through the plate glass. Two of the boys were tussling with each other behind their pickup truck, putting on a show for a couple of girls who sat on the tailgate swinging their feet and smiling, laughing. Pages turned behind him, stopped.

"Got a Johnathon Diaz," Hal said. "That your fellow?" He spun the book for Leon. The entry read:

Johnathon Diaz—One-Way—San Diego, CA— LaFayette, AR—5/15/87

Leon made a clicking noise with his mouth. "Yep. That's my guy. You know, Hal, everybody I deal with at this bus station is a criminal. You must get awfully tired of having to work with scum all damn day. Seems like, anyway."

"No sir." Hal blinked and the flush climbed his cheeks again. "Most folks comin' through this station are as honest as you like. They tight on funds or trying to save for something bigger. Most are hoping for a better life or visitin' people they love. Lots of great stories coming through here. I think anyway. People can change, you know." The older man's eyes were grim. "You in the kind of business where everybody you deal with is in trouble." He pointed a finger at Leon. "And you the man that's usually bringing it."

"You may be right, Hal, but that doesn't change the fact that Mr. Jack Diaz here." He tapped his finger on the journal entry. "He's lying. And if he's lying? It means he's hiding something."

Chapter 28
Jack

1987: Our Lady of the Mountains Shrine, Windsor, Arkansas

"Ease up, Abe," Jack said and took the pot of potato salad from the old man. They'd walked the two miles down the highway to Father Preddy's church. "I'm not getting it yet. It's only been a couple of months." Abe was riding him again about his inability to sense the Wall, to channel the mysterious power that the old man claimed that he should be able to harness.

Abe winced and pressed his hand hard to the side of his stomach. He'd taken the same stance both times that he'd had "to catch his wind" on the walk down. Jack had noticed Abe moving slower, bending over, grimacing more. Something was wrong.

"You going to be all right?" Jack asked.

"I'm just winded."

Jack sighed and scuffed his boot in the gravel shoulder of the highway that ran in front of Our Lady of the Mountains Catholic Shrine. The sky was high and blue, a lighter shade of the chapel's arched entrance door. The day was beautiful, the mountains clear and sharp.

"You gotta get it, Jack," Abe rasped. "The Wall's gettin' weaker again. Already. That last power you give it, it was strong and should have lasted, but it ain't. Maybe you did somethin' different than I do, or maybe it was a different kinda power, maybe something else is goin' on. I don't know, but the Wall's fadin' faster than I thought it would."

Jack inspected the chapel, picturesque against the mountain scenery, pale gray with a vibrant blue door, the building a dressed stone pile, a white statue of the Virgin Mary towered from her raised plinth in the center of the gravel loop. She stood with hands spread in welcome, gazed benevolently on the guests and pickup trucks arriving for the church's monthly fish fry at the detached community center. "Look, I'm doing the best I can. I've got the bird-controlling thing, at least. And the skunks and rabbits and sheep and all. They do what I say."

"Yeah. You do. In fact, you're better at it than Jill or me put together. But I can't *feel* you doin' it, Jack. Whatever you're doin', it ain't the way I'm teaching you."

"I'm trying, Abe."

"You been practicing your prayers? You been doin' the meditatin' I showed you?"

The morning after Jack had agreed to learn, Abe had woken him in the dark, sat with him on the broken-down bench that overlooked the valley, and guided him through clearing his mind, centering his body. The old man called it "opening yourself to God."

"Of course, I have, Abe. You've been waking me up every dam—every morning. You ought to know."

"You falling back asleep?"

Abe was inflexible that Jack not doze off. Jack had pointed out, reasonably, he thought, that if Abe allowed him to meditate at a sane hour of the day, say ten in the morning, he'd be far less likely to doze off.

Jack kicked his boot in the gravel on the side of the Arkansas highway.

"I gotta start sitting with you again?" Abe asked. "I bet you ain't even doing the meditation no more at all, are you?"

Jack scowled and began to gesture, forgetting that his hands were full with a Corningware bowl of potato salad. The thick glass lid jumped and rattled, came close to falling to the pavement. He managed to clamp the lid down before it fell. It was a close thing. "I'm doing it, okay? I'm finding my peace. Every dam— dang morning. Don't I look peaceful?"

"And the prayers?" Abe shook his pipe stem at Jack. "You know the verses? Give me the verse for… Stopping bleedin'."

Jack sighed.

Abe prodded him in the ribs with his pipe. "Come on now."

"And when I saw…" Jack started, stopped when Abe looked like he was going to interrupt. He stepped away from the man to keep from being jabbed with the pipe again. "No, no, wait. I meant… When I passed, when I passed…" He took a breath and started from the beginning. "And when I passed by thee, and saw thee polluted in thine own blood, I said unto thee when thou wast in thy blood, uh…" Jack stopped, blank. A pickup truck door thunked closed. "I know this one. I know this one, Abe."

Abe's lips curled. "Live; yea, I said unto thee when thou wast in thy blood, live. Ezek—"

"Ezekiel, chapter sixteen, verse nine," Jack

147

interrupted.

A crowd milled around the community building, and Jack could smell hot grease and the scent of fried fish in the air. His stomach rumbled. He was hungry.

"Six!" Abe corrected. "Ezekiel, sixteen, six. You need to study more, Jack."

Jack sighed. Some of the guests were shading their eyes and looking out to the highway to see what they were up to, whether they were planning on coming to the meal or not. Jack's stomach rumbled. "I would have remembered it, Abe. I just needed a minute. Can we go eat now?"

"In a minute."

Jack noted that the old man grimaced again and pressed his hand harder against the wall of his stomach.

"I gave you those books," Abe said. "You oughta be studying this stuff."

"Jesus. I am, Abe."

A small man detached himself from the little crowd around the community center and ambled across the grass, headed toward the two men standing by the highway. It was Father Preddy. He wore a shapeless tan fishing hat and overalls with a white shirt.

"Language, young man," Abe snapped. "I done told you."

"Look, I got it, okay?" Jack's eyes were on the little priest. "I know you use peach wood for a water wand. I know buckeyes are good luck and good for rheumatism and lung stuff and for keeping away bad snakes, and I know to watch out for witch women with spirit balls and that flying wrens carry bad news. I know. I know. I know. I've been reading all of your crazy stuff, I swear." He had, he'd worked his way through the newest book once, its pages typed on an old typewriter and bound in a ring binder. Now he was going back through it again. The binder was hundreds of sheets thick and alternated between spells and pieces of lore that Abe called "wisdoms." There were three similar folders that Jack still hadn't had time to do more than scan. None of them mentioned the Wall, sacrifices, or the Fountain.

In addition to the binders of family wisdom and practical magic, there were two older books, both journals. The first of them was marked *Our History.* He and Jill had read through it together, huddled around a lantern after Abe had gone to bed. It turned out to be the history of Jill and Abe's family and their years in the Ozarks, their efforts to keep the Wall going. Other families and their religious practices were mentioned, but only in passing. She was interested, but it wasn't helpful to Jack.

The oldest book, bound in leather and thick with dried rough paper, was written in archaic Spanish. Abe claimed to have never read it. It was fragile. The words, handwritten like Jill's book of genealogy, were looped and faded. Jill kept pushing Jack to translate it, but he was reluctant. He was afraid of it. The old journal radiated sadness and darkness. He was frightened of what he might learn.

"Meditating, reading, praying, the whole thing," Jack said. "I can't sense anything, that's all. I can feel some...power, but I can't hold it." He could feel the power even now, though he didn't tell the old man. It coiled deep inside him, glowing with life and energy. It was slippery. He couldn't grasp it. "I can't control it. I don't even know when it will be there and when it won't. I don't sense any Wall. Look…" He pointed at Preddy, hoping to end the discussion before the priest could overhear them.

Abe ignored him. "You know what your problem is? Your problem is, you don't believe in nothin'. That's your problem."

"He doesn't believe in what, Abe?" Preddy asked.

Abe turned, a look of surprise on his face. "Just—" He snatched his hand away from his stomach and rubbed his brow. "Just stuff, Father. How're you doin'?"

"Oh," Preddy replied. "All right, I guess. This wouldn't be a God problem, would it? I've got a little experience along those lines. You might say it's my love, my life, and my vocation." He chuckled.

"It ain't nothing to do with Mary and the saints, Father," Abe growled. "I'll let ya know if I need help with polishing a statue or somethin'." He took the potato salad from Jack and stalked off toward the community center.

Father Preddy and Jack stood bemused by the side of the road.

Preddy grinned. "Abe is a hard man to like sometimes."

"You don't have any idea."

"Oh. I might have an idea." He laughed. "Forgive me. We priests are supposed to reserve judgment on our flock, but I say: Why let God have all of the fun?" His eyes flashed with good humor.

"You remember me?" Jack squinted at the priest.

"Jack. Of course I do. I'm the one that suggested you to Abe. Robert didn't tell you that when he introduced you two?"

"He did. I thought, you know, you must run into a lot of people, and it's been a while."

"I understand, Jack, I do, but I don't forget. I'm pretty good at remembering folks."

There was a moment of silence between the two men. Jack didn't quite know what to say. He was flattered that the man remembered him. He'd assumed that he was another in a long line of drunks the priest had dealt with.

"Say," Preddy asked. "I don't suppose you know anything about fixing cars, do you?"

"Maybe a little."

"Come with me, you may be an answer from God."

Jack looked forlornly at the group of people eating and followed the little priest as he led him to the parsonage.

Chapter 29
Jack

1987: Our Lady of the Mountains Shrine, Windsor, Arkansas

Jack ignored his grumbling stomach and followed the little priest toward the small white clergy house separated from the Our Lady chapel by a smooth stretch of grass. Three cars huddled under a lean-to that slanted off the side of Preddy's home. The vehicles lurked there, nose to nose like inquisitive dogs. Their hoods were up

"This is my pet project," Preddy said. "I'm trying to get these beauties running." He laughed. "Again! You mind taking a look?" He patted the flank of a long, low, and rusted Chevy station wagon, early seventies model if Jack was any judge. The front window was cracked and hazed, the interior sun-faded, seats torn. The engine was in pieces and scattered around, parts lying on cardboard sheets under the lean-to. The other two cars didn't look much better, though the orange Ford Pinto at least had all of its engine parts mounted.

Preddy patted the Chevy again. "This old Townsman, I know what's wrong with her, and I don't have what I need, but maybe you could look at the Pinto for me?"

"Well…" Jack pushed the hair out his eyes. "You

restoring them for a—for a show, or something?"

"A show?" Preddy laughed. "Oh goodness, no." He turned the Pinto's ignition key. The engine gave a painful grinding sound, like teeth clashing. "I'm trying to keep them running in case folks around here need them. There are a lot of poor people in this community, you know. Good people! But poor. Some of them…well, some of them need some help. I don't have much money." He shrugged as if that were of little consequence. "Sometimes people donate cars or parts, and I…" He shrugged again.

"Which one is yours?"

"None of them, son. They're all the Lord's. I don't have a driver's license. I used to, but—and you're not going to believe this—I forgot to renew it, and I just never…" He gestured helplessly. "Well, I've been busy."

"Really? How do you get around?"

"My deacon, Paul—remind me to introduce you later—he doesn't mind driving me when I need him to, and people around here aren't averse to picking me up. I like being a passenger. It gives me a chance to talk to folks when they're relaxed, and their minds are on something else. People are usually more open when they're a little distracted. You ever notice that?" He turned the key again. *Grindddd*. "Any idea what that might be?"

"Sounds like a starter." Jack leaned over the motor; his hunger forgotten. "Turn it again?"

Grinddd.

Jack began moving through the engine, moving belts, twisting his hands between parts to dig deeper into the motor. The familiar smell of oil and old metal caught in the back of his nose.

Preddy watched over his shoulder. "How's Abe treating you?"

"Oh." Jack threaded his hand farther down into the engine. "Pretty well. He's not paying much, but…" He winced as his knuckles got caught between two hard pieces of metal.

"How long have you been sober now?"

Jack stared at Preddy, surprised. He snagged the edge of his hand; his skin tore. He brought his knuckles to his mouth and sucked his teeth. "How'd you know I quit?"

"Just a guess. You look good, Jack. Your eyes aren't bloodshot anymore, and your skin looks healthier. You look like you've put on a little weight." He made cautioning gestures with his hands. "The good kind of weight, the good kind."

"Huh. Well, that's good to hear, I guess. You're right. I quit drinking, ohhh…" He turned back to the engine. "A couple of months ago, I guess. You have some tools?"

"Sure do." Preddy pointed him to a rolling tool chest huddled against the house. "That's amazing news. The Lord works miracles." He paused. "I guess Abe has been good for you. Just goes to show, the Lord uses everything to his purpose. Even Abe."

There was something in his voice that sounded off to Jack, a hesitation. "Why wouldn't the Lord use Abe?"

"Of course, he would. I was talking out of the side of my face. God can use anybody. It's just that Abe believes some…how do I put this?"

"Weird shit."

"Hah, yes! Exactly! Though I would have probably said unorthodox. He's told you what he believes in?"

Jack nodded. He doubted Father Preddy knew the half of what Abe believed.

"His beliefs don't bother you?" Preddy asked.

"What beliefs exactly should I be bothered about?"

"His refusal to worship in a church? And did you know he won't trust any Bible but the one his grandmother gave him? I mean, that specific Bible, I'm not talking about the translation but the actual physical Bible. It's falling apart, it's so old. I asked if I could look at it, but he refused." He gave Jack a small, embarrassed smile. "And then there's... Well, he's got some interesting beliefs about weather forecasting and healing and so on."

Jack smiled. "Yeah. I didn't know about the Bible thing, but I know about that other stuff. It doesn't bother me. To each his own, I guess."

"Nothing he believes in bothers you?"

Jack went through the tool drawers, looking for wrenches, sockets. The chest was a disorganized mess. "No. Why should it?"

"Abe seem okay to you?"

"Seems so." Jack faced the little priest. The man had a troubled look on his face that turned into a disarming smile when he saw Jack looking. "Why?"

"I don't know. He's been, well... He's been very strange lately. Stranger than usual, I mean."

"Oh." If what Abe had been telling him about the Fountain and the Wall was true, the old man had had plenty of reason for concern. If not, well... He turned his attention back to the toolbox, found the wrench he needed, flipped open a few more drawers. "They were attacked by those criminals from Oklahoma, you know."

"Oh no, Jack. I mean before that. Way before that. He had been visiting me, you know."

Jack turned with the tools he needed, shrugged, a question.

"Abe," Preddy continued, "may have told you that he doesn't like me very much."

"I'm not answering that one, Father." Jack grinned and bent under the Pinto's hood again. "So why was he visiting you?"

"I don't know. I truly don't. He came up here several times to have long theological discussions. I thought, maybe, that he was having a spiritual breakthrough, but he only ever wanted to talk about one thing."

"Yeah?" Jack tightened some bolts, grunting with the effort. "What's that?"

"About the 'korban.' It, uh, it means the animal used in sacrificial rituals. It's a specific word, it means a kosher beast, as in a bull or sheep. And the sacrificial rites in general. That kind of thing. He wanted to know how the whole Jewish tabernacle system worked, very specific things. I told him that I wasn't an expert. I'm Catholic, not Jewish. Very strange stuff."

"Hmm. Well, you know Abe raises his own stock. Maybe it was a matter of, I don't know, professional curiosity or something. You said it yourself, Abe's a weird duck." Jack pushed himself out from under the hood. "Give her another go." He wiped the back of his hand across his forehead, left a black smudge.

"I said unorthodox, not weird, don't put words in my mouth." The priest turned the key, and the engine turned over with a cough and rumbled. It didn't sound good, but it was running. "Hey, hey! That's excellent. Thank you, Jack."

"Don't mention it, Father." He smiled in return. "Consider it a favor repaid. I appreciate you going to Abe to get me a job. I don't know where I'd be right now if you hadn't."

Preddy looked uncomfortable. "I didn't actually go to Abe. He came to me. He asked if I knew anyone at the Army of God who might need a place to be. He was looking for... Well, I hate to say it."

"Looking for what?"

"Well... he said he was looking for someone who was hopeless. I, uh, I told him about you."

"Hopeless, huh?" Jack's mouth twisted.

Preddy handed him a rag for his hands and some mechanic's soap. "Don't take it that way. I didn't think you were hopeless. I knew you weren't doing so great at the Army of God. I didn't want to see you back on the street."

"Yeah. I get it."

"Anyway, it was an odd request. Abe's never looked for help before, and with his other questions, I thought I'd see if he was... Well, you know."

"What did he want to know about the sacrifice thing?" Jack cleaned his hands. The soap turned a foamy black, dripped from his fingers.

"Pretty specific stuff. He wanted to know about the six stages of the qorbanot offering."

Jack gave him a quizzical look.

"Sorry," the priest explained. "The qorbanot was the Jewish sacrifice. He wanted to know about the ritual animals that they used, you know, sheep, goats, cattle, etc., and the different kinds of offerings, the use of the blood. He wasn't interested in any of the non-blood sacrifices, which I thought was strange. I tried to tell him about the grain and the fruit offerings, but he kept telling me they didn't matter. We talked a little about Abraham and Isaac. He had questions about a lot of things that aren't actually in the Bible. It made me curious where he was getting his information from, but he wouldn't tell me. He said, 'here and there.' "

"Hmm." Jack was afraid to say more. Obviously, Abe didn't want the little priest to know about his sacrificial ceremonies. Jack didn't want to betray Abe's confidence, but he was troubled that Abe still hadn't shared anything with him about the sacrifice ritual. The old man was hiding something.

"I was a tad worried," Preddy went on, "that he was thinking about going into the sacrificial business himself. I realize that sounds ridiculous, but for some reason, it didn't feel ridiculous when I was talking to him. I don't know. I get carried away. He never actually said he was going to start sacrificing, but he had this look, this tone of voice… I decided I had to dissuade him somehow." Preddy shrugged. "Gently, of course. Abe doesn't like to be told what to do. You haven't seen him doing any…sacrifices, have you, Jack?" The little priest searched his face.

Jack shook his head, no. It was the truth, after all, he hadn't been witness to anything of the sort, not yet anyway.

"Hah, silly of me," Preddy said. "Anyway, I tried to explain to him that the Biblical prophets disliked the blood offerings and that they felt it distracted from the true worship of God. Most of them, anyway. Micah,

Amos, and Jeremiah, for example, didn't seem to care for the practice very much." The priest sighed. "Abe disagreed, as he usually does. He argued that Ezekiel was pro-sacrifice and that, in the Old Testament, God called for blood atonement and even for human sacrifice sometimes. He was right, of course. We wrestled our way to a standstill on that one. I reminded him that the Jews haven't really gone in for blood sacrifice since the destruction of the Temple. He didn't care about that, so I reminded him that, as Christians, Jesus was *our* blood sacrifice. Sacrifices aren't necessary anymore." Preddy swatted at a fly trying to land on his nose. "He was interested in that, but not the remission of sins part. He was more enthused about the idea of Jesus being a blood sacrifice. I don't think he'd thought of that before. That seemed to spark something for him."

"Did he tell you why the subject was bothering him? Had something happened to make him want to talk about it?"

"Not really." Preddy spread his hands. "He said he was curious was all."

"That must have been a pretty long discussion."

"Like I said, it was over several visits and several weeks. I've had some odd conversations with some of these hill folk, but seldom do I have a discussion as odd as that one and with someone so obviously well-versed on the topic. I mean, he had very specific questions, Jack. Very specific. He knew, for instance, a lot of the original Jewish words used in the rituals. I must admit, I had to refer to seminary notes and reference books in between our meetings so that I could keep up with him. In the end, I doubt I helped him much, and he hasn't been back until today. Maybe it was a phase or something?"

"Maybe."

"And he seems all right to you? I don't mean to pry. It's…" The little man offered Jack an embarrassed smile. "I guess I was worried."

"Seems so."

Preddy rubbed his hands together, his mouth pursed.

Jack scrubbed the last of the black from his fingers. "I don't mean to be rude, but I'm hungry, Father. Do you mind if…"

"Of course! Of course! I shouldn't have been so selfish. Let's go get you something to eat."

Jack draped the rag over the front of the Pinto and slapped the orange hood. It felt good to fix something. Together, the two men walked toward the community center.

"I should have asked, Jack. I overheard Abe say that you were struggling with faith when I walked up on you fellows. I'm sorry, I got caught up in my own concerns." He glanced up at Jack. "Are you struggling with God?"

"That's part of it."

Preddy gestured for him to continue.

"I…" Jack hesitated, "can't seem to believe, Father. I'm willing to, but I can't force it, you know? Abe wants me to say that I do. Believe, I mean. But if you don't believe and say you do, wouldn't that, well… wouldn't that be the worst kind of lying? To say you believe in something that you don't? And how do you make yourself believe? Do you understand what I'm saying? I can't figure out how to decide something like that. Because if I *do* decide, it's not really belief, is it? I don't know, I get all twisted up. I don't mean to offend. I just…can't seem to get there, and I don't want to fake it."

"Hm." Preddy put his hands behind his back while he walked. "I understand what you mean, my son, and I'm glad you're taking it seriously. It's a serious topic, and you are correct. It has to be a sincere belief, not something that you fake. Have you considered trying a church?" He pointed to his little chapel and grinned. "I happen to know of one with a pretty good pastor."

"Eh." Jack laughed. "Maybe sometime, Father."

"But not likely, huh?"

"Not just yet. I think I need to come to grips with some stuff before I try to—to, I don't know, fit into the whole…ritual structure, I guess? Does that make sense?"

Preddy made a noncommittal half shrug, half nod.

The two men turned the corner of the little gray chapel. The crowd of mountain folk sat on the grass at the picnic tables under the community center's awning. They chatted, laughed.

Abe sat off by himself, eating fried fish from a paper plate and ignoring the others. A small middle-aged woman waved at Father Preddy. She was pretty, though worn, as if life hadn't been kind to her. Her smile was nice, and she looked happy to see the priest.

Preddy smiled, mouthed: "Hi, Sue." Preddy scanned the rest of his parishioners. "Do you see the tall dark-haired man there in the back?" The man he pointed to was middle-aged, not as old as Preddy or Abe but older than Jack. His face was lined, hair marked with gray at the temples. He was hovering over a young woman wearing a threadbare sundress. She was pretty in a bruised sort of way, resembled the middle-aged woman who had waved at Preddy, maybe the woman's daughter. She had a baby on her hip and was ignoring the dark-haired man while she conversed with another teenage girl. She was too young to be a mother.

Preddy looked upset for the first time. His eyes were on the tall man, and his jaw was set with anger.

"Yeah," Jack replied. "I see him, Father. Is everything all right?"

Father Preddy smoothed the expression from his face. "Of course. Of course."

Jack didn't believe him.

"That is my deacon, Paul. He's, um, how do I say this. He's, uh, one of you guys. You and Abe, I mean. Paul struggled with alcohol a lot when he was younger. He's been sober for a lot of years now, though."

"Jesus. Is everyone around here a drunk?"

"Hah. Seems that way sometimes, doesn't it? No, not everyone, Jack, but a fair amount are. More than some other places, I suspect. I don't know if it's because the mountains draw people who need or want to drop out of society or whether it's in the nature of the folks who are already in the mountains or whether it's something else entirely, but there are a lot of folks who struggle with addiction in this community. Alcohol, drugs…other things." He shrugged. "We get different kinds of folks out here. We've got the old hill folk like Abe. We've got end-of-the-world preppers, back-to-nature hippies, highly educated and underemployed marijuana farmers, millionaires looking for a place to disappear for a while, cults. We get them all. Lots of them happen to be drunks, too."

"So what about Paul, then? So, he's a drunk. Why does that matter to me?"

"Well, his sobriety group, the place he goes to help himself stay sober... You understand. They don't worry so much about the traditional religions. They try to focus more on the spirituality of the thing and let the religion come later or not at all. Paul says it helps people find their way to God. Maybe you'd find that more...palatable?"

"Maybe." He doubted it.

"From what you're telling me, what you're trying isn't working. You're wrestling with belief, correct?"

Jack nodded.

"If what you're doing isn't working, something else might. Paul's group might work. Or coming to church might. Try something different. Just think about it, Jack, okay?" Preddy winked at him and turned as some children skipped out of the crowd, each competing for his attention. "And remember, I'm here if you need to talk. Oh, do me one more favor? Please keep an eye on you-know-who." The priest nodded in Abe's direction. "Let me know if you need help."

"I will, Father."

Father Preddy smiled and walked into his congregation.

Jack looked back at the tall dark-haired man, Preddy's Deacon Paul. The man still shadowed the younger woman. She had to move around Paul, he was hovering so close. Jack didn't like the look of him. He looked hungry, predatory. *Preddy is a good man, but maybe not such a good judge of character*.

Jack thought that he might take Father Preddy up

on his offer to talk about faith, but that he would avoid Deacon Paul. Paul looked sick to Jack. Sick in all the wrong ways.

Chapter 30
Diario del P. Johan Pablo Ortiz, 1540

1540: Translated by Jack Diaz

This day, I Johan Pablo Ortiz, poor man of God and priest of his Holy Name, take my life into my own hands and depart into Florida with the honorable and terrible Governor Hernando de Soto.

I was with the people of the village of Masaqui, a native tribe who knew nothing of our Lord. I had done much work in the sight of God and for my fellow man bringing the savages to salvation. I brought God's Holy Word unto the people, and they repaid me with their trust, their food, and their homes. I have found them kind and most wonderfully intelligent.

Yesterday, word came of a strong force of men moving through the forest. The chieftain's son, who has made great progress in his faith, described the soldiers as wrapped in iron clothing. By this, I knew it to be fellow Spaniards and not another tribe of Indians making war. I knew that the Spaniards came to despoil the village. Upon seeing the governor's flag, I knew that it was he, Hernando de Soto, and that it would be far worse than I had feared. He has a reputation for cruelty.

I instructed the women to hide themselves for fear of the soldiers' harassment and hastened to speak with

165

the governor before he reached the village. I insisted on going alone and ran all the way down the hill. I feared that he would have his crossbowmen shoot me before I could speak, but he recognized my wooden cross and forbore to have me slain.

When I recovered my breath. I greeted the men with prayer and argued most strongly that the governor and his forces turn aside. I pretended to be most miserable and thanked him for rescuing me from death. I told him that the Masaqui were an impoverished people and much given to a strange disease that rotted the flesh, that it attacked the genitals first and spread over the whole body. God forgive me for my lies.

I swore to de Soto, before God, that the natives knew nothing of gold or treasures and warned that any man entering the village would likely die, not of violence but of pestilence. The common soldiers were most upset and feared to go forward. The governor threatened to kill them, but still the men would not go forward. I repeated to de Soto that there was no gold or treasure. The men grumbled more and looked frightened. I feared de Soto would have me beaten or slain as well. He did not. (For which I thank God.) The governor turned aside. He insisted that I accompany him as his interpreter. It was the price that I had to pay to protect the village, and it allowed the man to save face in front of his troops. He is proud. Oh, he is proud.

The governor (de Soto) is a strong man and handsome in his way. The soldiers say that he is rich and ambitious. He recently turned forty and has an air of command. It seems that his men do not like him very much, but they are very afraid of him.

I believe God wishes me to bring these soldiers to

salvation and to be a holy influence upon them. These men, though they are my countrymen, are little more than beasts. They care for nothing but the riches of the world and pay scant attention to their heavenly Father or their eternal reward. These men speak of nothing but gold and slaves. Gold and slaves.

Chapter 31
Jill

1987: Moondust Motor Inn, Windsor, Arkansas

"Thanks for helping me with this." Jill ran her scraper down the motel's window frame. Thick red chips of peeling paint flaked and fell onto the sheet of plastic she and Jack had spread over the grass. The leaves falling from the trees matched the paint on the wood, red and glowing in the early October sun. She'd been meaning to get to this all summer, but with one thing or another, it'd had to wait.

"No problem." Jack smiled down at her from his ladder. He had paint chips in his hair, on his overalls. "Summer's over. If we're going to get this thing repainted, this is the time to do it."

"Yeah." She grinned. "Isn't that what *I* told you?"

"You're right, you're right. Maybe, since you know everything, I should let you finish the job on your own."

"Don't you dare. Aren't you supposed to be the handyman around here or something?"

"Yep, but Abe told me, this was your mess, and that I should let you clean it up yourself."

"Did he?"

It wasn't atypical for Abe to say things like that when he felt a lesson was in order. He'd say it, but then help anyway. Odd that her grandfather had meddled. That was strange, belligerent behavior. It worried her. He had been distant, snappish and sullen.

Abe's good mood had faded over the summer as the Wall had faded and Jack's power failed to reassert itself. Jill wasn't supposed to know about that, but she did. She was itching to get involved, to help somehow, but was frustrated by her grandfather's desire to protect her. How could she help when she wasn't supposed to know about the Wall? She was trying to respect Abe's wishes and Jack's, but it was becoming annoying. The Wall was weakening by the day now. Now that she knew it existed, she could feel it.

The Wall's weakening was already affecting peoples' behavior. She'd begun sensing a pulsing malevolence, oily and insidious, radiating up from the valley. The people she rubbed shoulders with in West Port were feeling the effects. Hadn't Walt, the newspaper's owner, yelled at his oldest reporter, Pearl, on the phone the other day? Those two were practically brother and sister, and she'd never heard a cross word from either of them about the other. Then there was that Harry Peterson that killed all of his neighbors' dogs because they wouldn't stop barking. Twelve dogs shot and stacked on his front porch, all in the stretch of an hour. No one could tell her that was normal behavior. People were more argumentative, from the grocery check-out line to the horns honking at the single stoplight in town. In her experience, no one in West Port had ever used their horn for anything but a friendly greeting.

She worried. She felt it herself. Maintaining patience with her grandfather's paternalistic behavior was growing difficult. She was equally frustrated with Jack for supporting him. She'd been hoping that Abe would come to his senses and bring her into the discussion. She had power. She could help. So far that had not happened, but she'd promised herself that, if Jack didn't figure it out, if Abe didn't talk to her, if, indeed, her grandfather didn't stop walking around like a bear with a sore tooth, she was going to confront him and bring the whole thing out into the open. *These men and their stupid ideas about women.* "Then why are you helping me, if Abe told you not to?"

"Because." Jill could hear the smile in his voice. "Abe's down in Fort Smith for the day, and I figured if I wanted it done right, I'd better do it myself."

"Oh, really?" He was kidding, but the joke still set her teeth on edge.

"Of course."

"They teach you house painting in the marines?"

"Well, no. But, really, how hard can it be?"

She glared at him. He was stretched out precariously, painting far from the top of the ladder. "You better watch it." She considered throwing her scraper at him. Between her grandfather and Leon, Jill wasn't in the mood for another chauvinist. She went back to scraping instead. *This isn't like me. Why am I so angry all of the sudden?*

"Nah," Jack continued, oblivious. "I wanted to help, and I figured it would give us some time to talk. Honestly, I never lived anyplace long enough to paint anything. I would have made the same mistake. It doesn't make any sense to me that you'd have to peel stuff off before you paint it. Still, like I said, I'm glad to hang out...you know. Abe gets pretty weird about…well…he worries about you, I guess."

The Fountain. That's why I was so ready to fight. It's the Fountain. She centered her mind, closed her eyes, and put her hands together in a pose of supplication. When she'd achieved an inner state of serenity, she spoke a verse of calming. Her anger dissipated. She took a deep breath, relieved, and smiled at the man helping her. He was doing the best he could to walk a narrow path, telling her things and still mollifying Abe. "I know. Sometimes, I wish he was a little less worried about me is all."

The early fall wind scattered the chips as they fell from the eaves, rustled the leaves on the grass of the browning lawn. A smell of woodsmoke lurked in the air. Winter's cool rose from the depths of the valley, cool enough to need flannel shirts over their tees. It left a shivery feeling in her bones, a feeling of urgent desire, but for what she couldn't say. It felt delicious and needsome. "How are you coming on the translation?"

The ladder clattered against the fascia as Jack walked it down the side of the building. He refused to come down to move it along, choosing instead to perform an awkward ladder shuffle along the edge of the roof. Her heart froze a little every time he performed the maneuver, certain that he would plummet into the flower bed. She pursed her lips and kept her silence.

"Well," he said. "I don't know."

"What do you mean?"

"I mean, I don't really know." He was looking up at the sky, his hair falling down his back in a loose ponytail. "It's a journal written by a man named Johan

Ortiz."

"Well, it sounds like you know *something*, at least."

"I guess. But the thing is, it's slow going, and I don't know if I should keep working on it or not. I don't know if it's worth the effort."

"Why? I thought we agreed it was important?"

"It's all about Hernando de Soto. Do you remember him? The Spanish conquistador? He wandered all over Central and South America, then he, apparently, explored Florida." He pointed into the valley. "I don't see what it has to do with that valley or the Fountain."

A gust of cool wind sent oak leaves skirling around Jill like a benediction. "De Soto?" She caught a falling leaf in her hand. "That's strange. What's it saying about him?" It was a rusty red and mottled yellow. She released it to spin to the ground. It made her wistful. *Some fall days should never be allowed to end.* "You know he came through here, right? He came right through Arkansas?"

"What?" He stopped scraping, looked down on her. His hair fell in a sun-limned curtain around his sharp-edged features.

Jill found herself staring.

"Seriously?" he asked. "De Soto was here? Well, I didn't know that. I thought it was all about Florida. The book hasn't mentioned anything about Arkansas. I guess I haven't gotten to that part yet."

"Who's this Johan guy?"

"Johan Ortiz. He was a priest. His writing style is hard to follow, and I had a hell of a time at the beginning. The early parts are all about de Soto's travels in Mexico and how he became the governor-general of Florida. It's a kind of biography. Mostly it's about his behavior and official actions." Jack gave a low breathy whistle. "Let me tell you, he was a real piece of work. Seriously, he was a real bad dude. Anyway, the story changes and becomes more like a journal when Ortiz and de Soto meet. That's as far as I've gotten. Strange meeting, though."

"How so?"

Jack climbed down the ladder backwards, crouched beside her in the flowerbed, and offered her a cigarette. Jill refused. "De Soto landed in Florida and attacked one tribe of natives after another. He developed a reputation for turning the dogs on his captives. He let them be killed that way, the captives I mean. I guess because they were natives—Indians, nobody much cared." Jack's mouth twisted with distaste. "He started all the torture stuff down in Peru, but according to some of the folks in this book, he didn't get real good at it until he landed in Florida. I guess you could say he tried to make an art form out of it." Jack cleared his throat. "Seriously, Jill, he'd actually let the dogs eat people— to death. He, uh, he enjoyed it enough that he'd save some of them to be eaten while he was having a meal. It was like dinner theater to this guy. If he wasn't setting the dogs on folks, he'd... This is pretty rough; do you want me to tell you?"

Jill nodded. What could be worse than being torn limb from limb by dogs?

"All right. It's on your head if you get nightmares. It sure gave me a few. He'd, uh—he liked to string a bunch of natives up from a long tree limb and light fires under them. He'd have their hands and feet tied and then put a noose around their necks, so that they were on tiptoe. Then he'd have wood stacked around their feet and light it on fire." Jack wiped a hand across his brow. "He didn't just do it to the warriors, Jill. Not even just the adults. He'd do the same to children, women. One entry in the journal says that his victims' cries were 'the most piteous thing under heaven.'" He paused. "That's not even the worst. He, well… It says he'd feed babies to his dogs as well. The way the journal reports it, de Soto did all this stuff trying to find gold, to get the natives to do what he wanted, but I think he was just…"

"Evil," Jill finished. Picturing small children, little girls and boys, frightened, attacked, and eaten by dogs while grown men watched and laughed made her sick to her stomach.

"Yeah. He was evil all right. I think we'd call him a serial killer if he was running around today." Jack took a drag on his cigarette.

Jill shuddered and went back to scraping. "How did Ortiz feel about it?"

"I don't know. I haven't gotten that far yet. I get the impression that Ortiz doesn't like de Soto much, but I'd really have to read more."

"So how did they meet?"

"De Soto went to attack a native village. He was convinced that someone was hiding gold or could show him how to find gold or something. He was going to kill them all, or at least, Ortiz thought he was. Anyway, Ortiz was living with the natives in that village. He says he was trying to convert them to Christianity. He doesn't say whether he was successful or not, but according to him, when de Soto and his troops showed up, he knew things were about to go really bad. So, Ortiz ran down the hill and convinced de Soto to stop the attack. And de Soto actually did…stop the attack, I mean. And, I have to say; that's really weird." Jack's voice was puzzled. "From what I've read so far, it would have been much more like him to listen to the priest and then burn the village and the Indians anyway. Ortiz must have been a pretty persuasive guy. That or he distracted de Soto somehow. I don't know." Jack paused to stub his cigarette out in the flower bed. Jill noticed with approval that he put the butt into his pocket. He began speaking again. "Then there was another weird thing…"

Jill paused her scraping and looked at him, waiting. For a moment, their eyes locked. He looked away.

"So this guy," she asked. "He was…already there?"

"Yeah." Jack climbed the ladder again. "The book doesn't say how long or how he got there, just that he was there, that he stopped de Soto from destroying the village, and that he started traveling with him after that. That's it, no mention—" Jack went silent as Leon's low-slung, gray Cougar roared off the highway and into the circle drive in front of the Moondust. "Well, crap, this doesn't look good."

Jill cursed to herself. She hadn't seen Leon in more than a week, and their last meeting hadn't been a good one. He'd tried to persuade her to stop going to Abe's because of Jack's presence. When she'd demurred, he'd commanded that she stop. That, of course, had led to a big argument, and her boyfriend had left her house in a heated rush. Jill had been letting the situation cool since then. This was becoming the new pattern for their relationship, Leon's controlling nature butting up against her intense desire to make her own decisions. Seeing Jill working with Jack wasn't going to do anything to improve the situation. "Don't worry. Leon just drives like that." She hoped Jack didn't hear how nervous she was. Jill stuck her scraper in her back pocket.

The car's driver's side door swung open, and Leon stepped out onto the gravel loop. His face was stiff and emotionless, but Jill saw the warning signs already. His color was high.

Leon was moving with purpose but froze when he saw Jill standing at the base of the ladder, Jack at the top. Jill could tell that he was surprised to see her, that somehow it altered his plans. He went white in the face. She braced herself.

"Jill!" Leon shouted. "Can I speak to you for a moment?"

Jill didn't like the tone of his voice, proprietary and angry. She considered turning her back on him, but remembered her promise to Jack, her intention to keep him out of trouble with Leon. It seemed the lesser of two evils to try to diffuse the situation. She told Jack to keep working, she'd be back, and walked out to the car where her boyfriend waited.

His arms were crossed, and a deep frown marred his dark, handsome face. For a moment she was tempted to wade into the fight, to ask him why he thought he could boss her around, but then remembered that she was trying to bring peace to the situation, not make it worse. She smoothed the worry lines from her face, put on a false smile, attempted to hug him. "Hi, Leon. What brings you out here?" She felt false and, what's more, she felt that he knew she was being false.

"Jill." He grabbed her by the arm and pulled her around the back of his car. "I thought I told you it was a bad idea to be hanging out with that guy."

"You did." Jill tried to wrest her arm from his painful grip.

Jack had stopped working, watched over his shoulder.

"Obviously you didn't listen!" Leon shoved her against the trunk of the car, not hard, but enough to start a slow fuse burning in Jill's brain.

"Of course I listened. I didn't happen to agree."

Jack took a step, then two, down the ladder.

She wished he'd get back to work. Him watching, she suspected, only made things worse.

"What does that have to do with it?" Leon asked, taken aback. "What the hell does that mean?"

She waved at Jack behind Leon's back, waved him back to work. The man frowned but went back up the ladder and resumed scraping, though slowly. The doubtful look the handyman gave her fed her exasperation, and she snapped at Leon. "It means I can think for myself. I don't need you telling me what to do. Go find some criminals to boss around if you need to feel like a big man. I'm not interested." *So much for keeping the peace.*

Leon's mouth opened and closed like a fish, his face growing redder, and the muscles in his neck tensed. His lips snaked back to reveal teeth clenched with sudden hate. She frowned, her worry increasing. Leon was spiraling out of control. Too late, Jill remembered the Fountain's influence. What had started as a normal lover's quarrel was, in Leon, burning like a fire. This was getting too heated, too fast. If she didn't do something to get him away from this scene, away from the valley, something bad was going to happen. "You're right." She laid her hand on his shoulder. "You're right. I should have had the discussion with you earlier. Let's go somewhere and talk, okay?" She tried to pull him away, got him turned toward the car and moving to the open door, but Leon's eyes passed over Jack again. He grunted like a buck in rut.

He shook Jill off and slammed the door of his car. She had to jump away to avoid being hit, but he didn't notice; he was rushing down the drive, face contorted. "Diaz!"

Jack looked at him, sullen but silent.

Jack, Jill thought, hurrying after, *stay cool. Please stay cool.*

"Detective." Jack nodded, his eyes cautious.

"Get yourself down here, Diaz!" Leon shouted from the base of the ladder. "Right now! I want to know why you lied to me!" He had his jacket pulled back, displaying gun and badge. There was a set to his shoulders that told Jill he was winding himself up to fight.

Jack climbed down the ladder.

As he turned to face Leon, the shorter man shoved him hard, and Jack fell back against the old wooden ladder. "What are you hiding, you lying son-of-a-bitch?" Leon shoved him again. The ladder rattled and slid down the roof line.

Jack fell with a crash into the brittle bushes. Brown and yellow leaves showered the ground. He yelped.

Jill rushed forward, trying to close the distance and running through a list of possible verses, spells, something, anything to calm the situation, to get Leon settled down. She settled on a verse in Matthew and began subvocalizing it, exerting some force of will. "Blessed are the peace—" she began.

Leon flinched at her unexpected, rushing arrival. His arm went up and back; his elbow caught her across the face. It was a hard blow, and her lips splayed across her teeth, the sharp edges tearing the inside of her tender mouth. It hurt. She fell, verse interrupted.

His eyes went wide when he saw what he'd done, her lip split and bleeding, and reached out to her.

She pulled away.

His eyes went fierce again as the rejection settled under his skin. He turned back to Jack. "See what you did—"

But Jack was on his feet already and moving fast. He rose from the dirt with a clenched fist that caught Leon a blow to the head. It sounded like meat smacking a tabletop. Leon's eyes went vague, his legs rubbery, and he staggered back, his nose flowing with crimson, the blood smearing across his teeth and dripping from his pendulous lip. His hand went to his waist, to his pistol, as Jack stepped forward to finish him.

"Jack!" Jill screamed. "No!"

She began vocalizing a different verse, no longer worrying about keeping it quiet. It came from the book of John. She rattled through the words, applying a will bolstered by fear. "His disciples replied!"

Jack pressed forward, going after the man, and Leon, eyes still shocked, fumbled with his pistol. Going backwards, he yanked the weapon from its holster and pointed it at Jack. His breath came hard and quick.

"Lord, if he sleeps…" she rushed on.

Leon had the drop on Jack now. As if in slow motion, Jack's hands went up, his eyes going flat with the expectation of death. Leon's pistol was dead center on his chest, his eyes like an animal's, pain-filled and alien. She saw the decision to shoot settle on her boyfriend's face. His mouth clenched like a fist. His shoulders tensed, and Jill screamed the end of the spell at the top of her voice, imbuing it with all of her power. "...he will get better!"

She had panicked and put too much of herself into the spell. She didn't know what the effect would be. The air quivered with the release, and Leon and Jack both took a step back, shook their heads muzzily, then dropped to the ground. Leon's pistol fell to the gravel beside him, forgotten, his head drooped onto his arm, his eyes fell closed, and he was out. She'd put him to sleep.

Jack nodded for a moment, his eyes gone distant, his face slack, and Jill thought he was going out as well, but he shook it off. Comprehension dawned on his face. "What—" He pulled himself to his feet, then helped her up. "What did you do?"

"I—I put him to sleep."

"And me?"

"You were caught in the edge of it."

"Good God, that was the edge? Everything went dark. I've never felt more—more exhausted in my life." He pinched the bridge of his nose. "Is he going to wake up? Is he going to be all right?"

"Yes." She hoped. "He'll have a nap, a real deep one, then he'll wake up, and he should be fine. Everything is going to be fine." A rising panic circled in her chest, made her breathy. She'd never applied that particular prayer before, and never had she aimed her power at another person. Even the little cowboy had only gotten a generalized bad luck, not a direct intervention like this. Her grandfather had been particular about that. He'd always said that doing what she'd done was the path from Witchmastering to pure Witching, that it was a step toward evil. *Dear God, please let everything be fine.* "It was the Fountain, you know." She felt that if she kept talking, she could keep the situation from falling apart. "It wasn't Leon, Jack. It was the Fountain. It was the Fountain. Leon wouldn't do this."

"Hell," Jack growled and pulled away from her. "You don't believe that. Leon hates my guts, and we both know it. You heard what he said. He knows I lied to him. When he wakes up…"

Jill tried to master her nerves. "When he wakes up, you're not going to be here to get him going again, and he and I are going to have a talk about my being a witness to police brutality. I saw him start it, and I've got a busted lip to prove that he was out of control. Leon's a lot of things, Jack, but he's not dishonest; he'd never lie to get out of something. He'll leave you alone."

"He'll never forgive you for that."

"Probably not." She quivered on the inside; she wanted to cry. Jack was right. She was choosing sides, and Leon would see it as her having chosen Jack's.

Jack rubbed a hand across the back of his head.

Jill remembered the fear she had felt, searched Jack's face for any sign that he had shared the feeling. She wanted for someone to hug her, to hold onto her and tell her it was going to be all right. She maintained her distance, so did Jack. *It's just shock. I'll get over it.*

Jack looked like he might understand how costly her solution was. He sighed. "Okay. What do you want me to do?"

"Go—go see Father Preddy. See if you can help him with one of his cars or something. Help him clean the chapel. I don't care. Just stay there and out of sight. I'll come get you when Leon is gone."

"All right." He grimaced. "I'm sorry…."

"What's done is done." She repeated one of Abe's favorite phrases. "Go."

He went.

Jill arranged Leon more comfortably, brought a pillow for his head, and covered him with a light blanket. After that, she prayed and prayed that he would wake normally. As the sun set in the west, he did.

"Why the hell am I lying in the driveway?" He sat up in the gravel and blinked the sleep from his eyes. For a moment, he looked like a bewildered child, and Jill's heart broke a little. He was so confused and his face, freshly woken, looked innocent and fearful. The fall of his dark hair across his brow and his beseeching eyes reminded her of all that they had been, still were, to each other.

Jill shrugged uncomfortably and managed to keep the tears inside. She had no answers for him. She'd wracked her mind trying to find a way to explain it away but had come up with nothing. Nothing convincing anyway. Better not to explain.

When Leon saw her lip, split and swollen, his face went slack with despair. He claimed not to remember what had happened.

She nodded once, tersely, when he asked if he was

responsible for her pain.

When Leon asked where Jack was, Jill took a deep breath, made her heart a stone, and delivered her ultimatum, the whole thing—police brutality, witnesses, all of it. As she'd predicted, Leon agreed to leave Jack alone in return for her silence, and as Jack had predicted, Jill didn't think Leon would ever get over it. Her threat had pierced him like a poisoned barb. The hurt spread through his system, and then, for the first time ever, she saw Leon cry. It was for that, perhaps, that she felt the worst. He was less likely to forgive her for having seen his tears than for defending Jack.

"So." He looked at her with a horrible wonder, as at a stranger. "We are…" He pointed back and forth from her to himself. "This is over. This is really over."

"It doesn't have to be." She heard herself saying.

"Yes, it does. You won't tell me what you did to me, and you've chosen that…criminal." The words were angry, but his tone was not.

Jill would have preferred the anger; this defeated, flat man was not the Leon that she knew. "I haven't…"

"Yes." Anger crept back into his voice. "Yes, you have. You're protecting a man that you know nothing about. You've chosen an addict. An addict! Do you know he lied to me? Who knows what he's hiding? And you are threatening me. Me! To protect this—this, I don't even know. Do you know what you're doing?"

Jill took a deep breath. "I think I do."

Leon searched her eyes, looking for an explanation. "I hope so, Jill. I surely hope so." He stared at her for a moment more; his lips quivered, then firmed. He yanked his car door open, looked down the highway each way.

Jill thought he was looking for a sign of Jack in the darkening twilight. "Leon…" The tears welled from her eyes, spilled down her cheeks. It wasn't that she loved him; she didn't think she did. It was that it was ending and ending badly, weighted with guilt and secrets. It came hard.

He held up his hand to stop her speaking, started the car's engine, mashed the pedal to make the motor roar, and was gone in a shower of gravel and dust.

Jill sank to the ground and sat there until the sun had set and the night insects had begun their music. Bats and moths swooped around the single fluorescent light in front of the motel's guest lobby. Later, she went inside, made herself a cup of coffee, wiped the tear tracks from her eyes, and went to get Jack.

It was a quiet ride home. She didn't tell him what had happened with Leon. He was wise enough not to ask. He rested his hand on her shoulder. She kept her eyes on the road.

Chapter 32
Ronnie (Pilgrim)

1987: The Valley of the Fountain

The shadowman rode inside of Ronnie now. It gave him guidance, ideas. Ideas that felt right. Even better, his invisible passenger gave him the strength to carry those ideas out. He and the spirit had become one. Ronnie had taken to calling it Pilgrim. He had always liked it when John Wayne called people Pilgrim. The name suggested to him that this thing in his brain was traveling with him temporarily and that soon he would be free again. He hoped so, anyway. Sometimes, Pilgrim scared him.

Ronnie didn't know what Pilgrim was, only that it gave him power and company and burned with a hatred for the living that frightened him if he let himself think about it. But, the spirit didn't seem to want much of him outside of the ability to ride along as he traveled the valley, that and to offer the occasional idea.

Sometimes, Pilgrim gave him commands instead of ideas, and that was scarier still, but it was a small price to pay for life, healing, and power at his fingertips in return for a little loss of control. Cocaine, he justified, wasn't much different, and the Fountain "high" lasted a lot longer.

His eyesight was sharper, his hearing more

sensitive. His body, much abused in his short life, was renewed and refreshed. He was remade. He was the best Ronnie that he could be. His muscles were tight and crackled with power, his lungs open and seemingly bottomless, his heart pounded along slowly no matter how hard he pushed himself. He found that he could go without food. The water of the Fountain was enough to sustain him, enough to make him whole.

As time passed, Ronnie came to understand that Pilgrim and the Fountain were not one and the same, though they *were* linked in some obscure way. The Fountain, wonderful as it was, had no intelligence that Ronnie could comprehend. It simply was. Pilgrim, however, had a delightful and malicious sense of humor. He nurtured long, slow thoughts of revenge. The miraculous Fountain was a source of life, endless and powerful, nothing more. Pilgrim, though, Pilgrim was something else.

The spirit in his mind gave him knowledge, whispered dark secrets to him, and showed him things, things that he could not have seen with his own eyes. Pilgrim taught him how to concentrate his hatred, how to focus it and to nurture it. Pilgrim taught him how to plan and to work ahead. Pilgrim was like a father to Ronnie.

Sometimes, Pilgrim's fierceness would take hold of him, a feeling of bubbling rage that brought a savage joy. He'd break things then, pull branches from trees, and stomp through mushroom patches, like a spoilt child. The fury would last for hours before he was spent, before he'd done enough damage. He'd fall exhausted beside the Fountain and pant while Pilgrim growled and circled in his mind, only partially requited.

Later, destroying mere things wasn't enough to satisfy his passenger.

One day Ronnie found a nest of baby rabbits, hairless and sleeping nose to nose. They lay hidden in the deep grass. He plucked one from its nest while Pilgrim watched through his eyes. He stroked the smooth form while it squirmed blindly in his palm. He held it up to his face, smelled of its skin, and traced the tiny bumps of its spine along its bare back. Pilgrim was silent in his brain, waiting. Ronnie twisted the little creature in his fingers, cracking the bones and tearing the flesh with his fingers. It brought an unexpected smile to his face as Pilgrim flooded his brain with glee. He did the first few that way until realizing that, more than killing them, what would please Pilgrim was to own them, to dominate them.

Ronnie decided to eat them.

The little rabbits crunched between his teeth, wriggling and mewling with their pain. The taste of their fear and the hot blood in his mouth released a tempest of elation from Pilgrim that brought Ronnie to his knees. The primal pleasure was orgasmic. Pilgrim gibbered its approval in the back of Ronnie's mind, and he grinned. The rabbits' blood ran unnoticed down his chin.

He became a predator that day, traveling the valley floor, killing and eating when he wanted the taste of something in his mouth, torturing and violating when he did not. He found many ways to cause pain and realized that the more he caused, the more fulfilled he felt, the more connected he was to Pilgrim. He craved the power he received.

He'd been moving up and down the valley for

months now, climbing its slopes, scrambling back down into its deeps. His clothing was shredded, hair grown long and matted, and his skin darkened by living in the outdoors. He'd tried to leave the valley but found himself trapped.

There was a great invisible Wall around the valley that kept him in, kept turning him around. At first it infuriated him, made him fearful that he would be forever imprisoned, but Pilgrim had whispered comfort to him, had told him to wait, that his time would come. Ronnie came to understand that he and Pilgrim were eroding the Wall, that his muscle and bone and human brain melded and strengthened by Pilgrim's supernatural rage was enough to bring the whole thing down. It was only a matter of time.

When he'd reached the peak of his strength and mastered the necessary killing skills, Pilgrim led him to the edge of a small clearing on the valley side. Standing on the valley side of the bone spirit fence, Ronnie got as close to the Wall as he could. A great notched stone hunkered in the clearing. He examined the spirit staves, the skulls hanging in the air, the feathers twisting in the wind.

Pilgrim suggested that he try to break through. Ronnie pushed hard against the Wall but to no avail. He struggled until he was gasping on the ground.

Pilgrim delivered a thought that arrived like the edge of a slicing knife. *The old man uses blood to keep the Wall up.*

Ronnie pushed back from the Wall on all fours and rose to his feet. He knew who Pilgrim was talking about. The old dude from the motel. *Pilgrim, are you saying that I can use blood to bring it down?*

Yes, came the reply.

He didn't question. He hunted through the forest until, above him in the trees, a squirrel chittered to its mate. He knocked it from the tree with a stone and carried it, stunned but still breathing, to the base of the spirit fence. He placed it as close to the wall as he could and with a sharpened piece of flint skinned it alive. The blood dripped from his fingers and stained the dried bones of the fence. He splayed the small body, ripped its organs out and smeared them against the ground. He wasted the animal, destroyed it.

When he was finished, he rocked back on his heels and licked his fingers. The small creature was little more than smashed bones and shredded meat. He tested the Wall again and, sure enough, it was weaker than it had been. Still strong enough to keep him in the valley, but weaker.

He crowed with happiness and felt an echo of joy from Pilgrim.

He returned to killing.

Chapter 33
Jack

December 22, 1987: The Isaac Stone, Moondust Motor Inn, Windsor, Arkansas

The Isaac Stone was frosted in the early morning light. December had locked the mountains in a winter embrace. Snow hid in the cracks and seams of the hillside. The cloud cover was low and gray, and the rising sun glowed in the east like an angry smear on the distant mountains. Christmas was three days away. It was the morning of the winter solstice.

Jack's breath clouded when he exhaled. His eyes were swollen and red after a long, sleepless night under the claustrophobic sky. He bore a willow basket filled with mistletoe in one hand, and carried a long oak stick in the other. Both hands had been scrubbed with cold water and lye soap. They'd been clasped roughly and prayed over by an obstinate Abe.

Abe had insisted that he and Jack maintain an overnight vigil on the mountainside, that they wash ceremonially and dress in fresh linens. They must, he said, be clean vessels before the Lord or their offering would not be accepted. They were to pray, meditate, and wait for the dawning sun before sacrificing the young lamb that bleated pitifully on the end of the lead that Abe held. It was one of the two late winter lambs born to his flock and an important part, he said, of the sacrifice ritual. This was to be a burnt offering, a giving of blood and a burning of the korban's meat. No man would eat of the flesh of this beast. God would consume the lamb. With the Wall growing dangerously weak, Abe was taking no chances.

It gave Jack the creeps.

Abe adjusted his sacrifice garment, a long shirt that reached to his calves, bleached white and buttoned tight around his neck and wrists. He measured the angle of the sun above the eastern mountains with his hand. It had risen three fingers over the horizon. He pulled a long knife, narrow from years of sharpening and looked to make sure that Jack was tending the fire.

Jack couldn't meet Abe's eyes.

The lamb tugged at the end of its lead and cried for its mother.

Jack poked the pyramid of beech logs with his staff and sent a cloud of sparks swirling into the sky. His stomach was rolling with an acidy discontent. This did not feel right, not even a little bit.

Abe approached the stone, bent, and pulled the lamb into his arms. Its spindly legs waved wildly. It cried and bucked in his grip. He turned to face the stone, the sun. He held the struggling lamb across his body and raised the knife to the glowing eastern sky. He stood silent for a moment, then spoke. "Lord. Take this our most earnest sacrifice. It is a pure creature, Lord, never shorn nor harmed. I've fed it good and cared for it since its birth." The lamb jerked again and rammed its head into the bottom of Abe's chin. He grunted and struggled with the tiny creature for a moment, then raised the knife again. "You know, oh

Lord, that what I do here is important, and I ask you, please, that the blood of this innocent contain the evil in the valley below. I am not a good man, Lord, but I have sought to do thy will. I am not a rich man, Lord, but I am wealthy in your love. I am not a humble man, Lord, but I prostrate myself before thee. May this sacrifice be good in your sight." He lay the lamb on the stone and held it flat with one hand splayed across its body. It kicked and cried, terrified.

Jack covered his eyes with his hands, queasy. *Jesus, what am I doing?*

Abe raised the knife over the supine creature. "Yea. Though I walk through the valley of the shadow of death, I will fear no evil: for thou art with me; thy rod and thy staff, they comfort me. Forever and ever. Amen." He tensed to bring the knife down.

"Abe!" Jack put his hands out in front of him, pleading. "Come on, man. We can't do this. It's one thing when it's for food but this—this is wrong."

Abe whirled, his face a mask of outrage. "I told you not to interrupt. I've only got this one chance." His voice was weak and wavery, with panic or old age, Jack couldn't tell. The old man pled with him, though his words were harsh.

"Please, Abe." Jack reached for the knife. "There's got to be another way."

Abe snarled and swept the knife back and forth. The blade bit into the pad of Jack's thumb. He sucked air through his teeth and jerked his hand to him. Blood flowed into his palm and the thumb pulsed with pain. "Dammit, Abe." He held his bloody hand out to the old man. "This is crazy."

The rising sun cast Abe's face in shadow. His gray

beard bristled its way down the front of his makeshift cassock, the whites of his eyes exposed in a desperate glare. "I wouldn't have to do this, if you'd get yourself together and do what you did before. But you haven't done that, now, have you?" There was an edge to his voice, a quaver of hysteria.

Jack gave a small shake of his head, no. Try as he might, he couldn't recapture the power he'd experienced on the night of the storm. Even now, it coiled inside of him, ever restless, ever moving, and unattainable. "What does killing a defenseless animal have to do with protecting people, Abe?" The blood fell from his outstretched hand, pattered on the frosted earth. "It doesn't make any sense. What kind of God requires that kind of thing? Didn't you tell me your power came from within anyway? Why do we need to do this? Come on, man, let's think about this first."

"You shut up!" Abe jabbed his blade at the air to punctuate his sentences. "I ain't got no time to mess around with no unbeliever. That sun is risin', and it's the shortest day of the year." He pointed at the eastern sky where the fiery fingerprint of the sun rose higher over the mountains. "I don't have time to wait for you. Not anymore, Jack. I've tried to be patient with you. God knows, I hoped you'd figure it out, but we're past that now. I been doing this for years." He pointed the knife at the lamb. "It's what's gotta be done. If you ain't got the guts to follow through with me, then just you shut up! And if you can't shut up, then you get out of here. I got a job of work to do. Shame on you for bein' a coward."

Jack made a gesture of surrender with his hands. *If this is faith, count me out.*

Abe turned back to the lamb and looked to the sun to see that it hadn't risen too high in the sky. He nodded and bent his head to pray.

Jack added a few logs to the fire, prodded them into place with his oak staff, and watched miserably as Abe raised the knife again.

The blade flashed down. The little white form cried out and went limp on the stone. The blood drained in a channel, fell from the side of the Isaac stone, and collected in an old farm bucket that Abe had brought for the purpose. Abe cut the skin away from the corpse, pulling it down the torso and then yanking it by degrees off each leg. He used a meat cleaver to dissect the lamb and returned to the ceremonial knife for the final small cuts. He stacked the meaty parts on the lamb's bloodied skin and wrapped it into a tight parcel. The bones he stacked to the side with threads of bloody tendon still attached. Abe carried the bundled skin to the fire, raised his face to the sky and spoke. "See this, see this, Lord! Your servant does your will." He dropped the remains on the center of the fire. The weight of the corpse tumbled the beech logs and sent ash and sparks climbing into the sky. Smoke swirled around the two men and brought tears to Jack's eyes.

Abe returned to the stone and splashed the bucket of blood liberally on all four corners of the rock so that it sheeted down into the dirt. He took the last few drops and applied them to the base of each of the beast poles. He bowed his head at each totem and spoke some quiet words that Jack was unable to hear. He stopped under the pole topped with a human skull and fell to his knees, the front of his white shirt and beard dyed red by the little lamb's blood. The old man raised his arms to the sky. "Take this, oh Lord! See thy will done! Rescue me, thy servant, oh Lord. Let your protection and bounty be upon this land!" Abe lowered his blood-drenched arms, placed his palms in the dirt, and rested his forehead on the backs of his hands. He lay like that for a long time.

Jack waited as the lamb, skin, muscle, and offal burned. Greasy black smoke climbed into the sky, making a pillar straight up to the lowering clouds. Abe remained prostrate. Jack stood beside the pyre, thirty minutes, an hour, he wasn't sure. He waited until the beech logs had burned down, and the smoke had begun to thin. When the coals were mere whitened glows, Jack did as instructed and tossed the mistletoe on top. It curled and burned away. With his staff, he struck the Isaac stone three measured blows. The knocks echoed back from the walls of the valley and were a sign to Abe that the ritual was finished.

The old man rose to his feet and staggered. He steadied himself on the skull pole and grimaced. His hand went to his side, and he bent at the waist with a groan. His face went white.

Jack rushed down the hill to take him by the arm, afraid that Abe would fall. "Are you okay?"

Abe's lips moved, but no sound came, and, when he looked up at Jack, his eyes were frightened.

Jack wrapped his arm around his shoulders and held him up, gave him his other hand to hold on to. "Do you need a doctor?"

Abe shook his head no, vehemently. "No—no. I'll be okay. It's just—just wind, is all." He was able to straighten in Jack's grip. He took a full breath and eased it out. His voice, when he spoke, was thin. "I need to get to bed for a little while. Just need to rest my head. That's all. I'm tired, Jack. I'm real tired."

"What about the bones?" The little sheep's grisly remains were still stacked haphazardly on the stone.

"Spread them out. They—they gotta dry before they go on the fence."

Jack grimaced but did what Abe asked. The small bones were still warm under his fingers. He arrayed them the best he could and wiped his hands off on his own ceremonial garment. If that pissed off Abe, Jack didn't care.

Abe swayed, hunched over the staff. His knuckles looked like knotted rope. His face was gray and long, the wrinkles deep and vertical. His eyes had an out-rushing look to them, as if he was fighting to stay conscious. Jack rushed back to him and took him by the arm.

Abe gestured weakly up the hill.

Jack guided him up the valley slope, held him by his elbow, then wrapped him with his free arm when Abe looked to fall. Together they proceeded, Jack stepping up, then Abe, one step at a time. They stopped often for Abe to rest, the old man leaning on Jack. Jack offered to get the tractor. Abe nodded agreement, his eyes on the toes of his blood-splashed boots.

Jack found him semi-comatose when he returned. He wrestled him off the ground and checked his pulse. Thready, but there.

Abe rode back up the hill on the flatbed trailer. Jack tried to keep the ride smooth. Abe cried out on the harshest bumps.

He saw him into his kitchen and to his small table. Abe's hands trembled on the Formica surface. He saw

Jack looking and pulled his quivering fingers into his lap. He gave the younger man a fierce scowl. Jack warmed up some coffee and gave it to him. Abe took sips of the hot, stale drink and sighed.

"Are you sure…" Jack began.

"No. No doctor."

"That's not wind, Abe. There's something else going on. Isn't there?"

Abe glared at him.

Jack wanted to shake him, to yell at him. He wanted Abe to tell the truth, for once, to tell the whole truth. To Jack's surprise, the old man's eyes lost their ferocity, and he nodded.

"What is it?"

"I dunno. It just happens sometimes. Not very often."

"You sure I can't talk you into the doctor? Or maybe Jill can do something?"

"Don't—" Abe took a deep breath. "Don't worry Jill. I gotta cure for it. No need to get Jill involved. I forgot to take my treatment this mornin', and I put a lot of myself into the ritual. Almost all of myself. That's all. Long night. I ain't as young as I used to be. That's the truth of it. I don't like admitting it, but that's how it is."

Jack tried to determine if Abe were telling the truth. The man had been working hard for the last twenty-four hours, making trips up and down the mountain, daylight and dark, and it was true that he was no spring chicken. Jack was tired himself. He could only imagine how tired Abe must be. Jack poured himself a cup of coffee and sat across from him at the table.

"You gonna let it alone?" Abe asked and now his voice sounded stronger, more like the irritable hill man that Jack had grown to know.

Jack took a sip. "Yeah. I guess. If you say you're okay, what can I do about it? It's not like I can drag you to the hospital."

"That's right."

Jack shrugged. "All right."

A little relief entered the old man's face. "No tellin' Jill."

Jack nodded noncommittally. He'd make that decision later. He was tired of keeping secrets. Abe could make an issue out of it if he wanted to. "Did the ritual work?"

Abe's fierce glare softened into sadness, and he looked down at his hands. He raised them from the table, clasped them together as if praying. Thick veins roped the backs of his forearms; his fingernails were still caked with dried blood. They were the hands of a man who had spent his life fighting. He looked up at Jack, and his faded blue eyes were bleak.

Chapter 34
Diario del P. Johan Pablo Ortiz, 1540

1540: Translated by Jack Diaz

Tragedy. This morning, on Governor de Soto's orders, Captain Rogelia Sacillo went with thirty foot soldiers to a village nearby. The soldiers sought gold and slaves. The natives scattered at the Spaniard's approach, and Captain Sacillo managed to capture but two women, one most old and the other very young. They bound the women and began to return to the main body of Spaniards but were followed for many leagues. The natives are like ghosts and can move through the forest at will. They hide behind trees and brush; sometimes they appear out of the very air. It is as if they can disappear behind the smallest object, and though they do not bear steel, they are very deadly with their bows.

One Christian was killed, and two others wounded. The captain and his small group lost the two women during their flight. De Soto believes that Sacillo's soldiers released the captives. He accuses Sacillo of cowardice. Captain Sacillo denies this strongly and states that he was greatly outnumbered. Governor de Soto beat Sacillo terribly and called him a liar in front of the men.

Though we had crossbows, the men of the tribes

are agile and fight as bravely as those that can be found anywhere in the world. They can be most fierce. I try to convince the governor to take the word of God to the tribesmen, instead of the sword, but the governor speaks only of gold and does not think of God like me. He thinks instead of blood. He orders that the soldiers never separate but remain in one body. Together, our superior arms are more than a match for the tribesmen. So the governor believes.

Governor de Soto has developed a habit of killing the Indians. He says he must do so to instill fear in them and thus to avoid attack, but I believe that he enjoys hearing their cries and screams. It is said that he learned this sport from military expeditions with Governor Pedrarias Dávila and Francisco Pizarro in the provinces of Castilla del Oro and Nicaragua, and that they served him well in those places. He speaks often of how he was enriched in the capture of Prince Atahualpa, the last of the Inca kings. He laughs loudly when he speaks of the Prince's murder. He says that natives must be met with treachery and violence and that they do not respect kindness or the word of God. His eyes go dark when he speaks so, and I fear to disagree with him.

Governor de Soto captured a group of natives this day. They were all women and children, as well as a few elderly men, useless to defend their people. He was very angry because there was no gold in their village despite the promises of one of our native guides. De Soto grew most furious, and I saw the blackness in his eyes. The governor had the guide captured and thrown in chains. He ordered a soldier to remove the guide's hands, nose, and feet. The man's cries were very pitiful, but, blessed God, Governor de Soto allowed him to die instead of burning the wounds to staunch the blood flow as he had done with the previous prisoners. The children died horribly. I shall never forget their screams.

What kind of devil is this? The soldiers seem accustomed to his brutality, and I begin to despair of bringing God's peace to any of them. There is one soldier, though, who seems to have the love of God in his heart and is becoming my friend. (For which, I thank God.) He is a young soldier named Remero Diaz, whom I hope to tempt to serve Christ.

Chapter 35
Jack

December 24, 1987: Moondust Motor Inn, Windsor, Arkansas

Two days after the sacrificial ritual, Abe was still recuperating. He had informed Jack, the morning after, that things were bad but that the Wall was a little stronger than it had been, not enough, but some. He'd paused then, and Jack saw the black mood return. "Not nearly strong enough." Jack suspected that Abe wanted to blame him for the failure of the ceremony, but he hadn't. He'd squeezed Jack's shoulder. It felt paternal. Abe was listless after, sleeping late and often drifting off in his chair behind the desk or by the fire in his small study. Jack attributed Abe's weariness to the old man's outpouring of power during the ceremony or the long cold night without sleep. Neither of those things explained the weakness of the old man's grip.

Jill drove up through a picturesque snowfall on Christmas Eve and settled into the newly repainted section of the motel. Jack had labored most of the day, ensuring that the gas heaters were lit and collecting firewood to stock each of the fireplaces in both her room and Abe's living quarters. He hoped that, perhaps, she would have some method of remedying Abe's listlessness.

The three had a cozy dinner of chicken and dumplings, courtesy of Jack. Abe had taken a few uninterested bites and let the rest of the doughy dumplings cool and congeal on his plate. Jill questioned his lack of appetite. Abe told her that he'd had a rough night's sleep and that all would be well after he'd slept. Jack didn't contradict him. After dinner, Abe settled into his chair in the study and fell asleep, his face wan and thin in the firelight.

Jack and Jill moved to the kitchen to prep the turkey for the Christmas meal. They were oddly shy of speaking and clumsy. They bumped into each other while trying to stay out of the other's way. She found her grandmother's apron and dropped it over her head to protect her red cashmere sweater. Jack found the combination of the older woman's checked apron and Jill's soft sweater oddly attractive. Jill's cheeks were flushed in the warm kitchen, her eyes alive and reflective.

Jack had no idea what he was doing with the fresh-plucked bird and had been hoping that Jill would. It turned out, she had no idea either. Together they read the instructions in one of her grandmother's yellowed cookbooks, slathered everything with butter, salt, pepper, and sage, and crossed their fingers. They moved on to the side dishes, Jack reading and rereading the stuffing recipe, Jill wrestling with Abe's cardboard box of homegrown squash.

Jack was happy in the kitchen. "It reminds me," he told Jill, "of the few times I helped my mom cook." He watched her out of the corner of his eye. She hummed along to the sound of Bing Crosby's "I'll Be Home for Christmas" emerging from Abe's small kitchen radio.

She had a small smile on her face and her hair pulled back into a ponytail. Her clever fingers shone with melted butter and from the water she'd used for washing. He found her beautiful.

Jack set the oven to four hundred degrees and poured flour, cornmeal, sugar, salt, and baking powder into the largest mixing bowl he could find. Like everything else in Abe's kitchen, the bowl was old and green.

Jill stopped what she was doing to check on Abe through the kitchen door.

"How's he doing?" Jack asked.

"He's still asleep." She brushed a lock of hair out of her eyes. "I've never seen him this tired. You fellows must have been up to a lot of work lately."

"Yeah." His voice hitched. "He's been pretty…wore out, I guess."

A worry line appeared on Jill's forehead. "Has something happened, Jack?"

Jack shrugged, remembering Abe's admonition to keep Jill in the dark. He felt stuck between one set of secrets and another.

Jill turned away from the baking tray, crossed her arms across her chest. "Something did happen. Didn't it, Jack? What's going on? What aren't you telling me?"

"Abe told me not to."

"Jack," she warned.

"I'll tell you. I didn't promise to keep it quiet. I wanted you to know that he's going to be upset when he finds out that I did."

The stern look disappeared from Jill's face. She turned back to the squash on the baking sheet. "What happened?"

"There's something wrong with him. I don't know what. He's been doing this thing. He kind of holds onto his side." Jack mimicked Abe's actions, placing his right hand against the wall of his stomach, bending over sharply at the waist, and gasping. "You haven't seen him do that?"

The worry was back on Jill's face. "Once or twice. Not that bad. He always said it was wind."

"It's been happening a lot. I mean, a lot. And it seems to be getting worse." He cleared his throat, glanced at Jill to see how she was taking it. She was looking out of the small kitchen window, and Jack could see her troubled eyes reflected in the night-darkened glass. "A lot worse," he continued. "Two days ago, he had a real bad episode, and uh, he's been recuperating ever since."

"How bad was it?"

Jack tilted his head. He weighed the severity of Abe's illness before speaking. "I was worried. I had to get the tractor to get him back up the mountain. I've never had to do that; Abe's part mountain goat. He almost passed out, I think. He lost his color. His face went all white. I, uh, I really wanted to take him to the hospital, but you know Abe. He… Well, he wasn't having any of that."

Jill went to stand by the door to Abe's study, the squash forgotten. "Why didn't you call me?"

Jack sighed. "He told me not to worry you. I should have, though. I realize that now. He didn't seem to be in danger after I got him back to the kitchen. I checked on him while he was napping, and I've been making sure he eats and all, since. He's been sleeping a lot. I thought that might help. And I knew you were going to be here for Christmas, so… I guess, I figured we'd talk about it when you got here. I wanted to see if you noticed a difference or whether I was overreacting. I didn't mean to leave you out or to scare you, I promise. I'm really, really sorry."

"It's okay, Jack." She placed her hand on his shoulder. "I'm sure you did what you thought was best. You've been a good friend to him." Her words were kind, but there was worry in her eyes. He doubted she was seeing him at all.

He liked this woman. Too much maybe. He patted her hand, conscious of her touch. He went back to cooking, pouring the cornbread mixture from the mixing bowl into the long metal bread pan. "I never knew my father. Abe's kind of—I don't know. Kind of like the grumpy old man I never had."

Jill laughed and returned to her pan of squash. "The Wall is weaker. A lot weaker. I'm having to constantly hold myself in check. I imagine it's wearing on Abe living this close to it all of the time."

"Yes. He's been…edgy, I guess."

"And it still doesn't affect you?"

"No. Doesn't seem to."

"And you can't feel it, not at all?"

"No. I wish I could." He shrugged.

She sighed. "I think it's time."

Jack didn't need to ask for clarification. Jill intended to confront her grandfather, force her way into the situation. "You may be right. Can you, uh, wait?"

She looked at him questioningly.

"Not long," he said. "I've got something to show you first. After we get done here, I mean." He gestured to the food spread out on the kitchen counters. "I, uh, I don't want Abe to know that I've been showing you the books. You know."

She smiled. "Sure, let's finish this up, then we can meet, uh, back in my—my room after we see Abe to bed." She cleared her throat, a small uncertain sound and placed her hand on his chest. "Is that okay?" Her voice had gone low and hesitant. She took her hand away and turned back to the counter, to spreading brown sugar on the squash. Jack suspected that she was blushing.

His heart pounded in his chest. He hoped against hope that she was suggesting more. He slid the tray of cornbread into the oven and told himself to get real. He didn't have anything this woman wanted. He stood and stretched, cracked his neck in an effort to release the tension. He looked over at her and, when their eyes met, he smiled. "Yeah." He tried to sound casual, though his heart thumped in his chest. "That would be perfect."

Chapter 36
Jack

December 24, 1987: Moondust Motor Inn, Windsor, Arkansas

Abe woke. The snow fell heavy now, and the wind had picked up. It made a mournful howl around the old motel building, and the fire glowed red in his study. Jill had a single end-table lamp lit, and the antique shade issued a muted glow. She'd set up a Christmas tree in the corner of the room and had strung multicolor lights on it. The air smelled of burning oak and fresh pine. It was cozy and too warm.

He insisted on reading from his family Bible, a huge leather-bound book that filled his lap. Jack saw handwritten notes, messages left for the living by the dead, on the Bible's pages. He expected Abe to read the Christmas story, but instead, he read from Genesis. His voice was thin and slow. He stopped often to think or to run his finger over a verse which he repeated to himself under his breath. Jill cocked her head and frowned. Jack shrugged when she gave him a questioning look. They listened as Abe recounted the story of Abraham and his covenant with God, his travels and travails.

Abe lingered over the story of Abraham's attempt to sacrifice his son Isaac on Mount Moriah. He frowned as he read: "After these things God tested Abraham and said to him, "Abraham!" And Abraham said, "Here I am." God said, "Take your son, your only son Isaac, whom you love, and go to the land of Moriah, and offer him there as a burnt offering on one of the mountains of which I shall tell you." So Abraham rose early in the morning, saddled his donkey, and took two of his young men with him, and his son Isaac." Abe sat back and closed his eyes; his lips writhed with an inner struggle. After a moment, he leaned forward and ran his fingers over the text, then continued reading. "And Abraham took the wood of the burnt offering and laid it on Isaac his son. And he took in his hand the fire and the knife. So they went both of them together. And Isaac said to his father Abraham, "My father!" And he said, "Here I am, my son." Isaac said, "Behold, the fire and the wood, but where is the lamb for a burnt offering?" Abraham replied, "God will provide for himself the lamb for a burnt offering, my son." Abe paused. The silence in the room was oppressive.

Jack looked at Jill out of the corner of his eye. She had her chin in the palm of her hand and gave him a small shrug when she noticed him looking.

Abe read again. "Abraham bound his son and laid him on the stone for sacrifice, but the angel of the Lord called to him from heaven and said, "Abraham, Abraham!" And Abraham said, "Here I am." The angel said, "Do not lay your hand on the boy or do anything to him, for now I know that you fear God, seeing you have not withheld your son, your only son, from me." And Abraham lifted up his eyes and looked, and behold, behind him was a ram, caught in a thicket by his horns. And Abraham went and took the ram and offered it up as a burnt offering instead of his son." Abe ran his fingers over the text again and repeated. "Bound his son and laid him on the stone…" His voice trailed away, and silence reclaimed the room. He seemed to have forgotten that Jack and Jill were present.

Jack leaned forward in his chair and clasped his hands together.

Jill cleared her throat and stood up. "Well, Grandpa, that's not very cheerful Christmas reading. Why don't I get us some eggnog, and we can sing some Christmas carols or pop some popcorn or something? What do you think?"

Abe came back to himself and spoke to his granddaughter in a faded but friendly sort of way. "Okay, but—but not for long. I'm…awful tired."

She brought the radio in from the kitchen. Christmas music filled the study while Jill popped corn over the kitchen's gas stove. Jack and Abe were left alone.

Jack sipped his eggnog. He grimaced. He'd never liked it. He glanced at Abe. It had been hard to speak to him since the failed sacrifice. A distance had developed between them. He wracked his mind to come up with something now. "I can't believe Abraham tried to sacrifice his own son."

Abe blinked and looked around the room, focused on the Bible in front of him, and closed it. The old man's eyes regained some of their ferocity. "That's the difference between you and me, Jack. I understand Abraham pretty good. He was doing what God tol' him to do. He knew, see, that as much as he loved that boy, that nothin', but nothin' mattered, nohow, if he didn't have God on his side."

"But the cruelty of it. He'd been trying to have a

son his whole life, and then, God… What kind of God orders someone to murder a kid?"

"God's ways ain't our ways. Might seem cruel to you. Might be it seems cruel to me, but God always knows best. That's all. And it ain't murder. It ain't a crime if God tells you to do it. Aint' nothin' God says is a crime. You just remember that. There's some laws higher than man's laws."

"If you say so. I don't get it, I guess. What was the point? Especially since God stopped the whole thing. Surely God knew Abraham was willing. He knows everything anyway."

Abe glared at him for a moment, then his face softened into reflection. "I don't know about that neither. My grandma said it was 'cause it wasn't *for* God. It was for Abraham and for Isaac."

"How so?"

"'Cause Abraham had to understand that he was capable of it, she said, and 'cause Isaac needed to know how important God was to his daddy, and that way God would be important to him, too." He looked into the fire. "And also as a message to the rest of us that sometimes God needs us to do things that we really don't wanna do, even terrible things. I reckon Abraham was lucky God didn't make him go through with it."

"I guess. I just can't imagine anybody being willing to do that. Sacrifice another human being, I mean, especially a son or daughter."

"Yeah," Abe murmured. "It's hard to imagine." The old man put his pipe in his mouth and lit it with long practice. Jill returned with the popcorn, and they listened to the Christmas music. Jill tried to get the men to sing along, but Jack was self-conscious, Abe too withdrawn. She suggested a game. Jack was willing, Abe uninterested.

The long silence stretched, and Abe's eyes began to droop. Jill rousted him from his chair with Jack's help and ushered the old man into his bedroom. Jack could hear Abe complaining that he didn't need any assistance, that he'd been putting himself to bed for years.

Jack waited until Jill stepped back into the hall and gestured for him to leave, that she would follow soon. He darted out to his trailer to get her gift. He had little money, so after much thought, he had translated the first half of Johan Ortiz' journal, writing the text as clearly as he could with a calligraphy pen that he'd borrowed from Father Preddy. The priest had loaned him some pencils and watercolors as well, and with those tools, Jack had illustrated the strange priest's story. He had always liked painting and, though out of practice, knew that he was pretty good. He enjoyed the work, and since it was for Jill, he took his time with it. The result was personal and, because of that, he hoped, beautiful. When he'd finished, he'd wrapped the manuscript in red paper that he'd found in one of Abe's kitchen cabinets and tied a bow around it.

Jack returned from his trailer, package in hand. He saw the slim shadow of Jill moving in Abe's room, saw her adjusting the curtains against the light, and then saw the old man's table lamp go out. He waited on the front porch of her motel room. The snow had stopped falling, the wind had settled, and the small outdoor lanterns made paths and tracks of golden light across the hummocked white fall. Icicles dangled from the thick branches of the oak in the center of the gravel drive, its frozen limbs spread like the arms of a skeletal cross. The sky was clear now, and the stars shone a crystalline white against the endless blackness, beautiful and cold. He huddled into his secondhand sweater and rubbed his hands together for warmth. The kitchen door slammed. She was coming. He cleared his throat and breathed warmth into his fingers.

Jill rounded the corner of the building, looking down as she walked. Her brilliant red sweater stood out against the flawless snow. Jack moved uncertainly, and the snow crunched under his feet.

She stopped when she saw him waiting for her. The moonlight turned her hair into a silver stream as she pulled a strand back from her face. She pursed her lips, looked uncertain. Jack froze as well, afraid that if he moved, she would startle and run.

They stared at each other, the cold forgotten, their fears and worries suspended in the moment. He searched the curve of her cheek, the flush of her lips, and the sudden liquid excitement in her eye. This was the woman he wanted.

Then, between one moment and the next, she was in his arms and their lips met.

Her hair smelled of jasmine, and their bodies fit into each other like puzzle pieces. Her hands clutched like she was reaching for salvation, and for a hot moment, Jack lost his place in the world, in life. She pulled away from him, gasping. He looked at her with delight and wonder, smiled and kissed her again. He laughed low in his throat and fumbled with the brass handle till the door swung open, and together they fell into her room.

His handmade gift rested on her end table

unopened, for a while at least.

Chapter 37
Jack

December 25, 1987: Moondust Motor Inn, Windsor, Arkansas, The Isaac Stone

Jack woke early, his skin pebbled with goose pimples. The fire in Jill's chimney had died in the night, and the room was cold. He pulled the blankets up to keep her warm, pulled on socks and blue jeans and the new sheepskin coat that she had given him for Christmas. The gas heater was turned off. He depressed the knob and gave the starter a single long-practiced push. The heater whoomphed back to life, its blue flames marching across the burner in a glowing line of heat. The room began to warm. He slipped on his boots and cast around for his discarded shirt and sweater.

Jill sighed, and the sheets rustled as she rolled over in the bed, a long, smooth leg appeared from under the blankets. Jack froze. The woman's green eyes opened, and she took him in standing at the end of the bed. She smiled. "You look like you were trying to sneak out on me." She stretched her arms over her head and wrapped her fingers around the top of the headboard, looked up at him through her lashes.

Jack blushed. "And you are beautiful in the morning. I didn't think it was possible for anyone to wake up that pretty."

She gave a low laugh and sat up, pulled the blankets above her breasts. "Oh, please. Where were you going?"

He bent and kissed her. "I thought it might be better if Abe didn't find me here."

"Uh-huh." She poked at him playfully. "He may be my grandfather, but he doesn't get to tell me what to do, you know."

He leaned forward to kiss her on the brow. "I'm just an employee, and Abe *does* get to tell me what to do."

She laughed and put her hand on the back of his neck, drew him in for another long kiss. "You're right. Christmas is better without a fight. We can break it to him later. Let me get up and—"

"No. You stay right where you are until the room warms up. Just relax. I'll go check on Abe and make us some coffee. Okay?"

She smiled and pulled his translation of the Juan Ortiz journal into her lap. "What a beautiful gift." She opened the book and ran her finger along the edge of the first page. She touched her finger to the watercolor painting of the Spanish man-o'-war landing on the coast of Florida that he'd illuminated on the first page. "You go on. I'll stay here and read for a little while." She wagged a finger at him. "You're getting your other Christmas gift later, though."

"Other gift?"

"A haircut. I don't date guys with ponytails. Too macho for my taste."

Jack laughed. "All right. Join me in the kitchen when you're done lolling around? I'll have some breakfast and coffee ready." He peeked through the window blinds. "It looks like the snow stopped. Maybe we can go for a walk later."

"Sounds good. Now get going before my grandpa shoots you or something."

Jack took one more quick kiss and exited the motel room. He didn't feel the frigid wind. He was glowing on the inside.

****

Abe was asleep when Jack checked on him and still asleep after Jill and he had finished their breakfast. She insisted on turning on the small Christmas tree in Abe's study and switching his radio to KERA West Port for Christmas music before she would agree to go on the walk. Jack found it amusing that she was treating her grandfather like a child, trying to get him into the Christmas spirit. He loved her reaction to his gift, as well; she'd teared up and whispered, her lips close to his ear: "No one has ever painted anything for me before, Jack. It's beautiful."

Abe slept on, oblivious. They went for their walk.

At the edge of the highway, Jill balked, looking north and south down the pristine sheet of white. "It's so pretty. It seems a shame to mess it up."

Jack shrugged and agreed, then asked her what she wanted to do.

Jill turned away from the highway and fixed her gaze down the long slope into the valley of the Fountain. A small frown line appeared between her eyes. "You said Abe's sacrificial...place or whatever is down there?"

Jack blanched. He hadn't expected mention of the ceremony this morning. Memory of the bloody ritual clashed in his mind with the Christmas morning he'd been experiencing. "Yes. Uh, he calls it the Isaac Stone."

"Let's walk there."

"It's not exactly…Christmassy to go to a…well, you know."

"Come on, Jack. I've heard about it. I haven't seen it. If we go now, Abe won't know. I want to see it. Will you take me?" She put her arm through his and tugged at him. "You can tell me more about Ortiz's journal on the way. How does that sound?"

He looked at the high blue sky and then the ground, covered in a three-inch blanket of snow. Surely, under this sky and buried under that pristine white, the Isaac Stone would look less like an abattoir than when he'd last seen it. "Okay." The morning was beautiful, one of those rare winter days that are jewel-like in precision, when the static in the air brings a current of electricity to the world. The edges of the trees were sharp, like glass. Jack was happy, truly happy.

They passed Abe's outbuildings, the chicken coops, and the small winter sheep pen. He looked for the twin of the lamb that Abe had slaughtered, but it was not in sight. He'd taken to checking on it since the morning of the sacrifice. His new sheepskin coat was warm and soft, the sun sparkled on the trees and bushes, and the snow blazed with morning light. Jill bundled and walking beside him was another reason to enjoy the moment. "How far did you get in the book?"

"Not very far. I couldn't focus on the reading. Your paintings were so beautiful, I got lost in looking at them for a while."

Jack laughed and squeezed her arm against his body. "You really like it?"

"I really do. Can you tell me what you've gotten out of it? I promise I'll read it on my own, but I'm curious."

"I haven't gotten all the way through it, yet. I guess I could have read it all and then gone back and translated, but I'm having to slow down and figure out the words and sentences anyway, so I figured I might as well be writing it out as I go."

She nodded understanding, and Jack continued. "There are some surprises in the journal. At least, there were some things that surprised *me*."

"Like what?"

"First." He gestured to encompass all of the mountains, the territory, the land for as far as they could see in the winter morning. "From here to the tip of the Florida Keys, the Spanish called it all Florida, even up into Missouri."

"That's interesting. Sure doesn't feel like Florida this morning." She slipped a little as they negotiated a tricky part of Abe's small winding trail.

Jack steadied her with his arm. "The second thing: de Soto traveled all over the place. I mean, those guys wandered a *lot,* and I got to thinking, how did he fight his way through all of this stuff?" Jack pointed at the thick underbrush on both sides of the trail. "I was thinking it would be hard because I was picturing the whole country as an empty wilderness, you know?"

"But it wasn't that way."

"Exactly. There were native tribes all over the country, and they had trade routes and paths and river stations and just…you know, civilization. There were ways of getting around and moving through the land. There were probably dirt trails all over the place. Hell,

I'd bet some of them were as wide as highways. I looked it up at the library. Some of the tribes were mound builders. Some even built raised roadways, bridges, all kinds of things that we think started when the white folks showed up. It probably wasn't that hard to get around…if you knew what you were doing and where you were going."

"But, surely, de Soto didn't know where he was going?"

"He didn't. He knew what he wanted, sure. He wanted gold. But you're right, he didn't know how to find his way around. So he got some native guides and they led him from tribe to tribe."

"That makes sense."

"I can't figure out why they helped him, though. I mean the guy was a killer, and no one could ever tell when he'd snap. Maybe they were hoping to move him on. You know? Get rid of him. Or maybe they were hoping that they could sic him on their neighbors or something. Power politics, I guess, could be part of it. I don't know." He took a swipe at a low-hanging branch with his hand. Ice and snow fell to the ground. "He only had a few hundred guys. That was a surprise, too. It was just a small group of guys, killing and torturing their way across the country." He stepped over a fallen limb and waited for her to join him. They'd reached the snow-lined stock tank. It looked like a rounded eye staring at heaven. They worked their way around the pond, and Jack pulled away the deadfall that hid Abe's secret path to the Isaac Stone. He swore under his breath when he realized that he'd forgotten the key to the new padlock that Abe had placed on the fence.

Jill laughed at his consternation and climbed over

the gate, waiting for him on the far side.

He laughed as well, short and sharp, and followed her over. "Anyway, there had to be some kind of intertribal rivalry, or something like that because, even with European technology, the Indians could've whipped de Soto and his men pretty easily. It seems so to me, anyway. According to Ortiz, they did sometimes. There are a couple of stories in there that sound a whole lot like de Soto and team had to run away. I say sounds like because Ortiz didn't come right out and say it."

"So," she replied. "Some of the tribes helped him. You never can tell why. That was too far back. Maybe they were terrified of him. Maybe they were inherently peaceful. You said he was a bad guy.Maybe he was holding hostages or something. You're thinking too much like a soldier. No one knows what anyone was thinking back then. How would you react if…" She laughed. "Never mind. I know how you'd react." She shrugged. "I'm just saying, it almost sounds like you're saying the natives were, were… I don't know, responsible for their own destruction or something. I don't believe that, Jack."

He thought hard before he responded. "I don't. I really don't. I'm just trying really hard to understand."

"I don't see why any of that matters to the Wall and Fountain."

He grinned. "You're the one who said we should go ahead and translate the journal. I told you it didn't look like it had much to do with anything. I'm just telling you what I found."

She laughed. "I stand corrected. Have I mentioned that I hate history, by the way? Too many old men telling us how things happened. Most of them weren't even there to see it."

"The last thing." He found himself embarrassed to mention it but couldn't help himself. "Father Ortiz made a friend with one of de Soto's common soldiers. The guy wasn't an officer or anything. I don't think, anyway. Ortiz describes him as a simple man. Anyway, Ortiz was hoping to convert the guy into a priest. He said he had a real gentle heart and all that."

"Okay…"

"His friend's name was Remero Díaz." He gave her a look, shy but delighted that this long-ago soldier and he shared the same last name. "Remero Díaz, Jack Diaz. Isn't that crazy?"

"You think it was one of your ancestors?"

"No." He shook his head. "There are so many Diazes in the world it would be an incredible coincidence if it was. Still… It's pretty cool, no?"

"Yes." She had a thoughtful look on her face.

They were coming close to the stone now. Jack craned his head to see if he could spot the clearing around the next bend. "I don't want to ruin it for you, but Remero had a love interest. It's the last part I translated for you. He met an Indian woman named Sikena—Sahkenna, something like that. She was a chieftain's daughter, and she was acting as a translator for the Spaniards. Father Ortiz was seriously bummed out that Remero had traded the idea of the priesthood for the mere charms of a woman."

Jill's eyes sparkled. Her cheeks were flushed with the walk. Jack felt an overwhelming desire to take her in his arms and kiss her.

The clearing came into view. The smile dropped from her face.

The stench rolled over them first. It smelled like a charnel house. The forest around the clearing was draped in the same snow and ice as the rest of the mountain, but the cleared area itself was dry as a bone and open like a wound to the sky. A miasma of humidity and sweaty heat hung over the ceremonial plot, and the stink was a clawing thing at the back of Jack's throat. The stone stood bare of snow in the center of the small clearing, still tumbled with fresh bones and streaked with the lamb's lifeblood. Likewise, the spirit poles stood unencumbered by ice or frost. The human skull on the center leered at them against the high blue sky. Flies buzzed over the stone, lighting in the still wet blood.

"Oh, God, Jack." Jill put her hand to her mouth. "I wasn't—I wasn't expecting this. I don't know what I expected but...not this. This is magic, but...it's gone wrong. This isn't natural."

Jack released her arm and moved around the clearing, viewing the stone from all angles as if it would jump at him. The blood was still fresh on the rock. He saw it through Jill's eyes. "It's, uh..." He started but couldn't finish, ashamed that he'd been involved in the ritual. His fear grew the longer he remained in the circle.

"Terrible," she cried. "It's so barbaric, Jack. And where did he get a human skull?"

The skull's jaw hung open. It looked hungry. "I don't know. Abe told me it was before his time."

"So," she said, and Jack could tell that she was trying to talk herself down. "So it's not Abe's?"

"He didn't put it there. He says he didn't put any of them there. He just maintains them."

Tears ran down her face. Her fists were clenched, jaw locked. The sadness and hurt in her eyes made Jack's heart lurch in his chest. He moved back to her side and put his arm around her waist. "I'm sorry." It was inadequate, and he knew it.

"I heard him say it. I heard him tell you about sacrifice, and I thought I understood but... Jack, this isn't right. This is the exact opposite of everything he's ever taught me. This feels evil. What else has he been hiding from me? I feel—I feel like I've been punched in the stomach. It's such a—a—"

Betrayal. Jack knew the feeling. He'd had it when he realized that his mother wasn't coming back to get him at his final foster home. The understanding that someone you loved wasn't the person that you thought they were. He hugged Jill tighter; and she turned in his arms, put her face to his chest, and wept. He held her and looked out into the valley. Something moved in the corner of his eye, a shape in the deep forest. It looked like a man moving on all fours or a bear shambling along behind the bone spirit fence, flitting from one tree to another, hiding. Jack tensed.

Jill pulled away from him. He felt rather than saw the question in her eyes. Jack put his hand on her shoulder and guided her behind him.

"Wha—?" she asked.

Jack raised a finger to his lips, signaling silence. He walked across the clearing, giving the Isaac Stone a wide berth. He searched the thick winter forest for the intruder.

"Jack?" Jill asked.

"Hush!" He moved closer to the spirit fence, looked deeper into the forest. The scent of death and corruption grew stronger. He couldn't see anything. Whatever it was, was out of his view. He walked backwards a few steps, keeping his eye on the woods, then took Jill by the hand. "Can you still feel the Wall?"

"Yes." She wiped tears from her eyes. "It's weak. Very weak, but I can feel it. Only…" Her face had gone porcelain. "There is—There is something out there." She pointed past Jack and into the forest. "Something evil. I can feel it. It feels like a cancer in my head." Her hands took in the blood-soaked stone, the grinning skulls. "It makes all of this feel like nothing."

"What is it?"

"I don't know, but it means us harm. It…hates us."

Jack looked across the spirit fence into the forest. Nothing moved, a crow called out harsh against the winter air. Clouds streamed in from the west. The bright winter day began to darken, and the clearing was covered in shadow. "Let's get out of here."

****

They were silent on the way back to the motel. The thing he'd seen in the woods looked like a man. He was almost positive that it was a man, but it had moved with the liquid grace of an animal. *Maybe I imagined it.*

He knew that he hadn't.

Jill didn't speak as they wound their way up the valley-side. She held onto his arm, but her brow was furrowed and her mouth twisted with anger and fear. Jack had a feeling that she was on the edge of doing something drastic and irrevocable. "What are you thinking?" he asked.

She glanced up at him and then back down at the footprints that they had left in the snow on the way down. Her blonde hair fell forward and shadowed her face. "I'm thinking that it's time that I confronted Grandpa. I've had enough of the secrets."

His stomach knotted up. As he'd feared, things were about to get ugly. Worse, once Abe found out that Jack had shared his secrets with his granddaughter, all hell would break loose. "Why? What good is that going to do? You know he's just going to get angry."

"I don't care, Jack!" She pulled away from him. "He's been doing that for years." She pointed back down the hill. "That's bad enough. He's been hiding that. From me!"

"Maybe he knew you wouldn't approve. Maybe he was trying to protect you."

"That's such bullshit. How is it protecting me to not tell me that everything is falling apart? How is that protecting me? I'm a part of all of this whether I know about it or not, and I might add, I actually have some means to do something about it. You men and your patriarchal bullshit. He was protecting himself. He knew I wouldn't approve. He knew he didn't know what he was doing, and he didn't have the courage to tell me. Enough is enough."

Jack looked up at the now leaden sky. Dark clouds rolled over themselves, moving fast over the mountains. The day was growing darker, the wind picking up. "What purpose does it serve? You can see he's not feeling well. Let him get to feeling better, at least?"

"Look, Jack. I get it. I really get it. You don't want Grandpa mad at you."

His face tightened.

"Yes!" she shouted. "That's exactly it. You don't want Abe upset with you. It's all about you. It's always about you. You men, it's always the same. Grandpa,

Leon, you. All you men ever want is what's going to make you happy. Deny it! Just try and deny it again." She made an angry motion with her hand, sweeping away his objections before he'd had a chance to offer them.

He slumped. She was right. He *was* afraid, afraid of being kicked out, afraid that he couldn't solve the problem himself.

"Jesus!" she screamed. "The whole damned Wall is coming down, and Grandpa wants to hide it from me. He thinks you're going to fix it, but you can't seem to do a damned thing about it, either. His damn blood rituals aren't working. Something is down there now. Something that's going to make all of this worse. Worse than Grandpa thinks it can be. I know it." She stopped to take a deep breath and stepped farther away from him.

He could feel the gulf between them growing, their recent closeness becoming a thing of the past. She began to walk away. It made him desperate. "I'm trying to figure it out…"

"I have power!" She whirled to face him. "I do, Jack. Me! You two men are still playing around, and I'm right here. I've got all this power, and that old man won't teach me what I need to know. And neither you nor him is getting it done. Enough is enough. If you can't face it, if he's got you that scared, the bus station is in LaFayette; I'll deal with this on my own."

Chapter 38
Ronnie

December 25, 1987: The Valley of the Fountain, Arkansas

Ronnie checked on the status of the Wall. The snow made his progress slow, but the cold didn't bother him, despite the tattered rags he wore. The air was still and the forest quiet. The clearing around the sacrificial stone looked different. Blood was splashed around the rock and the skull poles and warmth bled through the Wall. Someone had been busy. The scent of the blood made him smile.

He'd brought a live rabbit with him and got down to business. He smashed its brains out with a rock at the base of the bone spirit fence. He grinned when it shrieked. He ripped into its belly with his hands and tore its limbs off with his fingers. He scattered the bits and pieces of the viscera on the soil at the base of the fence. The Wall's presence diminished.

He was still on his knees in the snow, about to rise, when Pilgrim halted him with an urgent warning. A man and a woman entered the clearing. The tall man that had killed Chuck and Barry and the hot little bitch that he'd come so close to getting a piece of. Ronnie rose to peek over the top of the bones.

The couple was talking, oblivious to his presence.

He hugged himself. His muscles quivered. He was itching to get at them, to kill the man, to have his way with the woman. Pilgrim damped him down, held him in check, reminded him that the Wall separated him from his victims. He cursed under his breath and dragged his fingers through the blood-soaked snow. He clawed and clawed until his fingers raked into the forest floor, until his nails split and tore, and his fingers ran red with blood. Pilgrim chuckled in his brain. He didn't care. He was focused on the man and the woman.

The tall man walked around the clearing. His long hair swung down his back in a knotted ponytail. He looked bigger, more muscular than Ronnie remembered him. He had a guilty look on his angular face, and he glanced back at the woman often. The young woman said something to the man, pointing at the sacrifice stone and the skull-topped poles before putting her face into her hands and beginning to cry. The tall dude grimaced and looked at the ground, rubbed his hand across the bridge of his great angular nose. Yeah, he was feeling bad all right. It gave Ronnie a sense of satisfaction.

The tall guy put his arms around her, attempted to comfort her, then looked Ronnie's way. He ducked too fast. His daddy had always told him to move slow when you didn't want to be spotted by your prey. He stayed frozen for a moment, but unable to see what the couple was doing, he began to worry that he might have been spotted, that they might be approaching him while he lay in the dirt like a helpless baby rabbit. Pilgrim tried to soothe him, but panic settled into his brain and he ignored the spirit's orders to stay where he was. He dashed through the snow, ducked behind a large trunk, and then rolled under an icy bush. A shower of ice crystals fell onto the back of his neck, melted, and ran down the back of his spine. He lay there facedown, gasping with fear.

Pilgrim was displeased with him. He could sense the presence growling at him, telling him that he'd been spotted. Ronnie raised his head. He'd been seen, all right. The tall man was pointing into the woods now and talking urgently to the woman. They stood at the far side of the clearing searching the forest with their eyes.

The panic returned, sending his heart leaping in his chest. He tensed his limbs to rise and make a run for it. Pilgrim laid hold of Ronnie's body, forced him flat in the snow. He struggled to breathe with the soft snow powder jammed into his nostrils. He tried to get his hands under him, to lift his mouth and nose from the choking ice, to roll to the left or the right. He moaned with fear. He could not move. Pilgrim owned him. Ronnie hadn't known the spirit was capable of doing such a thing. Incredulity turned to terror as his body, still stubbornly unresponsive, begged for oxygen. His vision started to go black.

Please! He begged, his panic rising. *Please. You're killing me! Please, please, please!*

The spirit allowed him to lift his head. The snow melting on his skin mixed with the hot tears running down his cheeks and chin. He took a great breath and shuddered with relief. He felt the urge to jerk himself to his feet and to run down the mountainside, to flap his arms around, to roll his neck or chatter his teeth, anything to prove that he was once again in charge, that his body was his own. He did not. He could sense

Pilgrim lurking, ready and waiting to seize control again.

Ronnie blinked and raised his head a little more. He was able to see the clearing through the latticed limbs of the bush. The tall man pointed into the woods but was no longer pointing in Ronnie's direction. The man and his companion weren't certain what they'd seen, and in any case, they didn't seem to have any idea where he'd ended up.

Pilgrim, watching through Ronnie's eyes, moved farther back in his head, released its control, and relaxed its vigilance.

Ronnie stayed where he was. He was afraid to move.

He didn't know how he could stop the creature from doing what it'd done, and that thought, the understanding that he was no longer his own, was frightening. There was an engine of anxiety running in his chest, and he didn't know how to switch it off. He understood, now, that Pilgrim could do with him whatever it wanted, whenever it wanted. He'd thought they were friends, partners. He suspected, now, that he might be more of a pet.

He didn't want to believe that. He told himself that Pilgrim had only controlled him to protect him. He repeated it to himself, ran it through his mind over and over, until he almost believed it. Pilgrim didn't interrupt his thoughts, didn't try to influence him one way or the other, though Ronnie sensed amusement from his passenger and chose to overlook it.

The man and woman spoke a little longer. Toward the end, the woman flailed her arms and screamed at the tall man, something about power that Ronnie didn't understand. Her raw emotion called to him, and he felt a violent surge of lust as she left the clearing. Unthinking, he leapt to his feet and charged up the hill. He wanted to be on them, to rend them, to smash them.

Pilgrim didn't try to stop him this time. The spirit watched and grinned in the little cowboy's mind.

He was moving fast when he hit the invisible Wall. His nose snapped, splayed across his face, and he was thrown onto the forest floor. He lay in the snow stunned, his head ringing and his thoughts circling like buzzards. He rolled over with a snarl and wiped away the blood trickling from his nose. The fury returned, and he kicked the snow, the dirt, punched trees, snapped branches and beat them to pieces against the stones and the bones of the spirit fence. The rage passed, and when it did, he sat beside the Wall drawing in great ragged breaths. *I've gotta get to them. I've gotta fuckin' kill them.*

He thought on the problem of the Wall. His small animal mutilations were working, draining the Wall a little at a time. The process was slow, though, too slow for Ronnie's taste. He wondered what would happen if he brought something larger. Would more blood cause the Wall to fail faster? He thought about it for a while, and then, careful not to encourage his passenger to take control again, he sent questioning thoughts in Pilgrim's direction.

The spirit's approval was immediate, its pleasure obvious.

Ronnie smiled to himself, convinced that he and the spirit were back on even footing. "See, Pilgrim," he spoke aloud. "I ain't stupid."

He turned from the spirit fence and worked his way

down the mountainside. He was thinking hard as he walked, unconsciously avoiding the deadfall trunks and the reaching brambles. His hands moved automatically, reaching to grasp the rough-barked trees when the grade became too steep, breaking limbs and twisting aside branches that got in his way.

I haven't caught a deer. He was fast enough now and strong enough that overmastering a doe might be within his abilities. He thought about the creatures' bounding agility, and his mouth turned down. *Maybe not.* But then: *A rock might do it.* He had a good arm now. He'd been practicing all summer. If he got close enough and caught a deer in the head with a baseball sized rock? *That could work.* He stopped and turned back to look in the direction of the Wall. *Time to get serious. Time to bring this fucker down.*

He turned back to the valley and began moving in a great lope, bounding four and five feet at a time as he fell down the slope like a whirring partridge. He was hunting again. His fangs were out, and his feet were sure. This time he'd kill something big.

Chapter 39
Diario del P. Johan Pablo Ortiz, 1540

1540: Translated by Jack Diaz

After many weeks of continuing north, the governor ordered his troops to march on a large hill town named Oçita. The governor had heard that the people of this place gathered there for protection, and he thought it good to destroy them in one setting. On arriving, we found the people departed. The governor burned the village and threw an Indian named Tepuac to the dogs. The savage had been a guide to the Spaniards and a friend of mine. Truly, as I write this, I begin to wonder who are the real savages.

It is terrible to see the jaws of the governor's hounds red with the blood of men, to find human body parts lying between the dogs' paws. There is so much meat on a man that the hounds scatter it around the camp. De Soto liked Tepuac's screams very much and, taking a child from its native mother, cast it to the hounds as well. Many of the men laughed at the sport, as did de Soto. Remero, thank God, did not. He is as sickened by the governor's behavior as I.

****

Governor de Soto and his men talk about gold constantly, but I no longer think he expects to find treasure. The men were very excited last week about the

234

pearls that they found in the nearby river, and for many days, they worked the riverbed. Their joy has turned to despair. The pearls are not of the quality to make these men rich. The men's grumbles increase. We have lost more Christians over the months. The terrain and the weather are harsh, and the constant battle brings its own cost in blood.

Governor de Soto must find something to justify the death of men, since he has lost a fourth of them and the mood among ordinary soldiers is low. I believe that if something does not improve, there will be a mutiny against Hernando de Soto and his officers. The Indians have many reasons to hate us, and, if we turn against ourselves, I cannot believe they will take pity on us. They will certainly kill us all. The governor does not wish to speak of this with me.

****

Today, as we traveled into the unknown west, we came to a great river. One of our guides, a woman of the Aquixo, named Sikena, told us that the river's name was Meaot Massipi, which means Father of the Waters. Sikena is said to be a great princess of a holy tribe to the far north and to the west, though she will not speak of it herself. They say that she is from a great valley in the mountains that we have not yet reached. Why she has come east, no one knows. The other native guides pay her the greatest respect and take her words as wisdom. They believe her to have holy powers and consult her on many things. The natives are most perplexing in their behavior toward their women. A woman must know her place, and these savages, though honorable in many ways, do not seem to understand this.

235

Upon reaching the eastern bank of the Meaot Massipi, we saw a great congregation of natives on the far western shore. They were a tribe unknown to us. The warriors put up a great cry upon our arrival and got aboard their many long canoes. These are great trees, laid on their sides, and carved out, so that many warriors can sit in them from front to back. They use branches and wicker paddles to move the boats through the water.

The Indians crossed the river to meet us. We were afraid, but I saw many of the Indians smiling as if to welcome us. They appeared most wonderful and fierce in their headdresses. There were two hundred canoes, each canoe holding many warriors. The greatest of the canoes was covered by a canopy and was most grandly designed with feathers and beads interwoven. It was a beautiful sight. By this, we knew the man under the canopy to be the tribal chief, or cacique, as Sikena has told us to call him.

The chief brought to us gifts of fish and plum loaves. They were piled high in the front of the canoes and would have been most welcome as we had been many days without fresh food, but Governor de Soto did not trust their intentions and had his soldiers shoot the chief and his attendants before they reached our shore. The waters of the Meaot Massipi ran red with the natives' blood, and the air was dark with our arrows. Oh, the mistrust and hatred in this man.

The natives, though they outnumbered us, withdrew in confusion and fear. Sikena, the Indian princess who guided us, warned Governor de Soto that the gifts of food were from an even greater cacique, and that, by slaying this minor chief, the governor had declared war against the natives of the entire land. The governor, upon hearing this, became enraged that a woman had spoken to him and hit her against the ground and cursed her like a dog. I had to restrain my friend Remero for he is certainly in love with the poor savage. I had hoped to make him a priest but have begun to despair because of his growing love for the woman. Remero may never make a soldier of God, but he is still my friend and a good man, and I did not want to see Governor de Soto execute him for bad behavior.

****

We have crossed the Meaot Massipi and spent many days on foot traveling ever west. We are less than four hundred men, though we numbered seven hundred at the start. War and constant deprivation have killed many of us. Most go on foot now as we have eaten many of our horses and even our mules. It is as if the earth itself has turned against us and wishes to see us dead. We have spent many days in a large swamp, and the men constantly murmur. They no longer talk of gold but of going home to Spain. If it were not for their great fear of the war nation who live in these forests, I think the soldiers would have killed Hernando de Soto.

Governor de Soto is very silent these days and keeps to himself. When he acts, he does so with great fury. The soldiers fear that he loses his mind, as do I. Although only two years have passed, he seems to be a man in his later years. He is drawn and brittle like a dry stick, and his fury is great. He speaks of nothing but gold, but even he no longer seems to believe in its existence.

****

It has become very bitter. De Soto has dedicated

himself to torturing many of the Indians we encounter, more than ever. He asks them about gold, gold, gold. This morning, a cacique, bound over a fire and being skinned alive, told the governor in desperation of a water of superior power that he called the Nee-Ooh-Lassah. The man said that it had many strange powers, and that it was holy. He did not say more because Sikena put the man out of his misery with a quick stab to the heart. The governor was most wroth with her, and I thought he would have her tortured in the chief's place. The other native guides grew restless at de Soto's threats, and he released her.

I am certain that the mention of these wonderful waters were but the ravings of a man being tortured over the flames. Since we have come to this land, we have heard many strange tales. I have heard legends of whole tribes disappearing into caves and of a dragon that coils under the great mounds on the plain. Savages often tell such tales, but no proper Christian takes heed of such lies. Governor de Soto, however, has become very excited and speaks much of Johan Ponce de Leon. I think this is not good for us.

My friend Remero Díaz is very excited as well. Sikena is pregnant with his child. Praise God for his blessings even in difficult times. I have tried to warn the man and his woman that she must not interfere with the governor again for I fear de Soto's tolerance will not last forever. I do not know if they have taken me at my word. Sikena is a strangely stubborn creature for a female. At least they are no longer in sin. I, poor instrument of God, made the marriage of my friend, and although his fellows do not know it, he and Sikena are in the good graces of our heavenly Father. I doubt that

Sikena took the ceremony seriously, but Remero did, and it is now his responsibility to see to her soul.

I do not know how the marriage will last, as we must return to Spain. I am certain that the governor will not allow Sikena aboard one of our ships, and if there is a mutiny, I do not know if any of us will survive to see our homeland again. However, it is better to marry before the eyes of God for a short time than to be overwhelmed by sin forever.

Chapter 40
Jill

December 25, 1987: Moondust Motor Inn, Windsor, Arkansas

Jill and Jack found that Abe had placed a wire dog kennel in the center of the kitchen's linoleum floor. The sacrificial lamb's twin lay in the center of the cage. The smell of fresh coffee and roasting turkey hung in the air. Banging and shuffling sounds came from the rear of her grandfather's residence. It sounded like Abe was moving boxes around. He must be feeling better.

Jack got himself a cup of coffee and walked into Abe's study.

The tinny sound of "Silent Night" came from the little radio that she'd left on. She reached her fingers through the kennel's wire mesh. The little lamb butted its head against her fingers, and she stroked the edge of its muzzle. She had an awful feeling that she knew why Abe had brought the creature into the house.

She went to the coffee pot to get a cup but found it empty. Jack had gotten the last cup. A sharp spike of Fountain-inspired annoyance made her want to put her fist through the counter-top, but she restrained herself, closed her eyes, and breathed deeply until the last vestiges of her argument with Jack were mere cobwebs blown out of her mind. She released the tension in her shoulders and clenched fists. She sagged against the counter and resolved to make peace with Jack.

She fished out the coffee grounds, poured them into the percolator's basket, filled the pot with water, and set it over the stove's ring of blue flames. Now that the emotion had been curbed, she found comfort in the oft-repeated ritual. The water heated, and the percolator grew hot enough to make the strange sucking and gurgling sound that proved it was working. Satisfied, she leaned against the edge of the sink and stared into space.

Abe's rituals weren't working. That was obvious to her, and what's more, she didn't believe the ceremonies were necessary. Every part of her soul rejected the idea that destroying the life of an innocent creature could achieve a good ending. She was no vegetarian. She understood that animals were killed to provide her with hamburgers or fried chicken. She wasn't a fool. Death itself did not disturb her. The nature of the lamb's death, the sheer wastefulness of it, offended her. The idea, tenuous and hard to define, that the sacrifice ritual, rather than building something good, venerated fear and violence shook her. It felt evil. She'd listened in, all of those months ago, while her grandfather told Jack about the rituals. At the time, she'd thought that she understood. Seeing the aftereffects of the magic proved to her that she had not. More important, though, she remembered Abe telling Jack that the natives, who had been keeping the Wall in place before her ancestors, managed to do so without the blood. They hadn't needed to despoil, to destroy in this way. *If they did it without blood, then I can too.*

The problem was she'd been through all of Abe's

books, and none of them mentioned how the natives had managed it or, in fact, how to do the blood rituals that Abe performed. He had to have that stuff written down somewhere. Jill didn't believe that her family, even with as many secrets as they had, would risk losing the knowledge necessary to keep the Wall strong. She toyed with the idea that the two men, together, might be hiding something from her. Her resentment began to return. She quickly dismissed the thought. Jack was being honest with her.

Jill poured herself a cup of coffee and walked into the study. Jack watched her warily from his recliner and stopped rocking, took a sip from his coffee mug. She glanced down the hallway. The attic door stood open. "Silent Night" had become "The Little Drummer Boy," and the lights of the Christmas tree twinkled in the shadowed room. Abe's blanket and Bible rested on his recliner where he'd left them. Her present to Abe, wrapped with care in shiny green paper with a blood red ribbon, looked lonely under the tree. It stood in stark contrast to the big Christmases she'd experienced growing up.

Jill sat in the rocking chair across the room from Jack. Weariness settled on her like a woolen shawl. She rocked and began to relax. The heat in the room made her head feel stuffed with cotton. The grandmother clock on the wall over Jack's head tick-tocked, and the fire crackled on its grate. Jill drifted a little, nostalgic. She found that she missed her father this morning. She resolved to call him later. Not too late or he'd be off to the country club. She wondered whether Leon was having a good Christmas. Now that she was ensconced in Abe's den, watching the flames lick up the side of the fireplace, the shock of the Isaac Stone and the weakening of the Wall seemed a little less urgent. She decided that the confrontation with her grandfather could wait.

Jill cleared her throat, and Jack looked up from examining his hands. His face was drawn tight. He looked frustrated and fearful. She realized that whatever anger she'd felt toward him was gone. She did like him. Maybe he reminded her a little too much of Abe sometimes. Maybe he was a tad too protective of her, but he was earnest and gentle and kind. No one had ever made her a gift so beautiful and so personal as the manuscript he'd given her the night before. Jack was flawed, yes, but precious to her, nonetheless. She smiled at him. The worry lines faded from his brow. "Tomorrow," she said.

Jack tilted his head then, understanding that she meant to hold off one more day for the confrontation with Abe. He nodded.

Chapter 41
Abe

December 25, 1987: Moondust Motor Inn, Windsor, Arkansas

"You look good with a man's haircut, Jack." Abe stood in the kitchen doorway. He rocked forward and backward on his feet. He felt good, better, at least. Yesterday's deep weariness had passed, and the pain that had become almost constant was, for the moment, gone.

Jill brushed the last of the fresh cut hair from the back of Jack's neck. The short hair suited his angular face and tight-muscled frame. The kid even carried himself differently, as if his spine had stiffened. He looked more complete rather than less. Abe could see the marine in him, and it looked good, natural.

"Hah," Jack said. "Thanks, and Merry Christmas." His head was down, looking at the floor between his boots, while Jill ran the stiff brush down the back of his ears.

"Merry Christmas," Abe replied.

Someone had let the lamb out of its kennel. The little, white animal was nosing in a bowl of feed, one of the good bowls no less. He suspected Jill. Maybe Jack, but probably Jill.

"That little critter is gonna do his business all over

my house, you know."

"Don't worry," Jill replied. "I'll clean it up if he does." Her voice was light, but to Abe, she seemed tense. He searched her face for a hint as to why.

She didn't make eye contact. "Why did you bring him in the house?"

Jack gave her a warning look. That was odd.

Abe shrugged. "The rooster. He was fluffing up something fierce this morning. We got another big storm coming in. Judging by the sky, I'd say ice this time. I figured this little fellow might do better out of the weather."

There was doubt in Jack's eyes, worry. Abe frowned. *You think I'm gonna sacrifice another, don't you, Jack.* Some of Abe's good mood disappeared. He'd told the truth about the lamb. There wasn't any need to sacrifice this one; the last hadn't worked.

Jill was giving him the same look, though, and Abe began to wonder where the two had gotten off to this morning, what Jill knew. Jack and his granddaughter had gone down the hill. He knew that. He'd seen them returning, and they hadn't looked happy. He began to worry about how far down they'd gone. Surely, Jack hadn't taken her to the Isaac Stone? The silence stretched until it was uncomfortable. Abe broke it by shuffling his feet. "Turkey smells good."

Jack smiled, and the moment of strangeness passed. "I hope so. I'm damn hungry."

"Language," Abe and Jill said simultaneously, and all three of them laughed.

Jill took the towel from around Jack's neck with a flourish. Blond hair whipped into the air and floated to the green linoleum. "You're all done. Go get a shower, or you'll itch to death."

Jack ran his hand through his hair and grinned at her. "Whatever you say, dear." He turned a bright smile on her, and she blushed. The look they shared went on longer than Abe thought necessary. The quiet kitchen was full of crackling feeling. He clenched his pipe tight between his teeth. Jack had feelings for his granddaughter. That was obvious. He cursed himself for failing to see it coming on. Why hadn't he recognized it in time to stop it? The way Jill returned Jack's look told Abe everything that he needed to know. His Sarah had looked at him the same way once. That wasn't good.

Not good at all.

****

Abe gave Jack a new Bowie knife for Christmas, eleven inches long and wickedly sharp. He'd carried the blade when he was younger, had gotten it from his father. He had meant to give it to his own son in the distant past, but he and David had had their falling out before he could. It seemed appropriate to him that Jack have it. Judging by the delight in his eyes, he figured he'd been right.

Jack gave Abe a felt slouch hat that he'd picked up at one of Preddy's infrequent fundraisers. The kid's face reddened with embarrassment. "It's not nearly as nice as the knife, Abe…"

"Way better than a knife." He dropped the hat onto his head. "This'll keep my brains from bein' cooked. That old knife ain't gonna be nothing but hours of work for you. Keepin' it sharp." He smiled to take the sting out of his words.

Jack smiled in return and rested a hand on his

shoulder. "Thanks for everything, Abe."

Abe cleared his throat and loaded his pipe. His chest was heavy with guilt. He'd never meant to let himself get close to Jack. God had a way of playing tricks on you like that. The silence stretched long, and when he looked up Jill was staring at Jack, her eyes bright with unshed tears and, perhaps, love.

Jack wore a new sheepskin jacket this morning. Abe wondered aloud where he'd gotten it. Jack blushed and confirmed Abe's suspicions. He didn't ask when and how Jack and Jill had done their gift swap. He wasn't sure he wanted to know.

Jill's eyes lit with joy when Abe gave her the gift that he'd been looking for in his attic. The flat leather box glowed with the oil he'd rubbed into it this morning. The gold monogram letters SW shone against the rich brown surface. A strand of pearls snaked across the velvet inside. SW for Sarah Woodley. Jill hugged him tight, thanking him, and when she pulled away, tears ran down her cheeks.

Abe cleared his throat. Christmas had grown more complicated now that he had a family again. "They were your grandma's. I bought them in Kansas City in, oh, 1957, I think. I bought her some earrings, too, but I ain't seem them since she died." Jill knelt at his feet and rested her hand on his knee. She was beautiful. She reminded him of Sarah and of David. Seeing two such different people in this young woman that he loved was strange. Abe smiled. "She gave me a piece of her mind when I give these to her. They cost more than I want to admit, but...I was in love. She said..." Abe could feel his eyes pricking with tears. "She said they was a ridiculous gift and that I was a wasteful fool." He laughed. "She told me there weren't no need for a mountain woman to be wearin' pearls, but, I'll tell you this, she wore 'em every chance she got. She was the most beautiful woman in the world. It was a long time ago."

Jill plucked the strand of pearls from the old leather jewel box and, putting her hands behind her neck, struggled to work the clasp. Jack got out of his chair to help her and then guided her over to the mirror on the wall. She stood transfixed for a long time. He hovered behind her as if mesmerized. Abe watched helplessly.

After gifts, they ate the meal that Jill and Jack had prepared. Abe ate little. The pain was returning and worried at him. It was growing worse.

As the meal came to an end, a gentle rattling on the windows of the motel announced that the ice storm had started. It had come before he'd expected. He touched his hand to his stomach and grimaced. The pain was building. He hoped the storm wasn't too bad; he worried what might happen between the two young people if they were iced in together.

Jack insisted on cleaning up.

Abe smoked his pipe and gritted his teeth as the pain rolled around in his belly. It came in waves when it came, building and then receding, each succeeding rise in pain sharper and longer than the last. He resigned himself to riding out the agony as it came and went. He locked his teeth around his pipe stem and tried to keep his face still. His forehead tingled and broke into a sweat. He prayed that God give him the strength to finish what he'd set out to do.

He didn't look forward to his duty. In fact, he'd hoped that the burden had passed, but the Wall was weaker now than he'd ever seen it. A faint humming in the back of his mind was all that remained of it, and sometimes, if he failed to concentrate hard enough, it disappeared from his consciousness. He was doing his best to protect himself and Jill from the harmful influences of the Fountain emanating through the weakened barrier, but that, in itself, was wearing his strength away.

He relit his pipe and took the cool smoke into his mouth. He sent it out through his nostrils in puffs. He was grateful for the pipe. Despite his wife's and granddaughter's best efforts, he'd never given it up and never would. When all else failed, the pipe gave him space to think. He needed to think.

Jill settled into the recliner across the room from him. She had a book of some kind in her hands. He hadn't seen it before, but from where he was sitting the text looked handwritten. Jack had claimed a chair at the kitchen table and was poring over the little Spanish book that he had given him. The kid held the text open with one hand and wrote on a legal pad with the other. Abe found it amusing that Jack spent so much time in that old journal. He had never read it. Interesting the book may be, but interesting was not the same as important.

Abe opened the family Bible to the book of Revelation. The animal sacrifice instructions were written in the margins of Genesis. Other, darker things had been recorded in the final book. The Genesis notes were in a neat orderly hand. The Revelation writing was near indecipherable, as if written in an extreme of emotion. He'd planned on sharing this book with Jack, once the young man had proven himself. That didn't look like it was going to happen now. He hadn't taken to the sacrifice well. He had, in fact, ruined it.

Abe pursed his lips as a new wave of pain crashed over him. He grunted and fought the desire to curl up around the hot feeling flowering in his gut. Slowly it passed, and he turned back to the Bible. His lips moved as he read. He wasn't reading the verses. He was focused on the notes. Abe's great-grandfather Jephthah had written these scrawling instructions. He was the last Woodley to be called upon by God, like his biblical namesake, to sacrifice a human. The man had lost everything because of it, his family, his community standing, and, finally, his life, but it had worked. No one had ever denied that it had worked.

Abe dreaded following in his ancestor's footsteps, but he didn't have a choice. And like Abraham told Isaac he would, God had provided Abe with the korban that he needed. He watched Jack in the kitchen and felt a deep sadness. He'd grown to love the kid, but, sometimes, you did what you had to, not what you wanted.

He looked at his granddaughter where she read. Her hand strayed unconsciously to the pearl necklace around her neck. The biblical Jephthah had foolishly promised the Lord that he would sacrifice the first thing that met him when he returned home, if only God would give him victory over the Ammonites. To Jephthah's horror, he had won the battle and then been met by his only daughter when he arrived home. The girl had sealed her fate by throwing her arms around her father in the doorway. Abe shuddered. He couldn't imagine the strength of will that God had required of the man. At least, he wasn't Jephthah. Such a sacrifice would drive him mad.

KERA West Port interrupted its Christmas programming to give an evening news report. Joe Jordan reported two fires in West Port that night, a stabbing, and an attempted rape. That was a lot for a town of four thousand people. Things were coming apart down there. The ice storm in progress made the fire department slow to respond, and both of the burning properties were reduced to smoldering wrecks. Two people dead. A myriad of smaller violences were happening as well. Things, Abe knew, that weren't being reported. Jack shrugged it all off as coincidence, but Abe knew that it was the influence of the Fountain. He knew what he had to do. *After Jill leaves. Tomorrow. Before I get too sick to do what needs to be done. Tomorrow.*

That night he cried out in his sleep and woke once again to the pain in his gut. It receded, and he lay panting in his bed. Ice tinkled on the roof of the hotel and pinged on the glass of the window. Tree branches cracked in the night, breaking under the weight of the accumulation. The roads would be impassable.

They were trapped.

Chapter 42
Leon

December 26, 1987, 11:14 a.m.: Radisson Hotel, Chicago, Illinois

"Detective Fratelli," Leon said into the phone. His head pounded, and his eyes burned. He'd been dragged from sleep by the ringing of the damned cell phone.

"Yeah?" The voice came back. It sounded weak over the large squarish receiver that Leon held in his hand. "This is Detective Peter Finch, San Diego PD."

Leon inched his way up in the unfamiliar hotel bed, so that he was half sitting, half lying propped against the pillows. He'd had too much to drink at his cousin's house the night before. Facing Christmas in Arkansas without Jill had been an impossibility. Karl had been nagging him to visit Chicago for years, and on a last-minute impulse he had taken him up on it. "I'm sorry." He yawned. "Who is this?"

"Detective Peter Finch, San Di—"

"Right, right. I got it. It's early here, man. What can I do for you? "He glanced at the bedside clock. It was 11:14 a.m. He grimaced as the line went quiet. Apparently, it wasn't that early. He looked out the window. The winter sun shone through the cloud cover over Lake Michigan. *Oh, well. It's early somewhere.* He pulled a pillow over his eyes to block the glare. Karl and his Flaming Dr Pepper. *Any drink that's on fire has got to be a bad idea.*

"Hey, Fratelli. I'm just calling you back, man. You don't wanna talk, that's fine with me. I'm trying to catch up on paperwork. I don't particularly want to be sitting in the office the day after Christmas. You got me?"

"You're calling *me* back?"

"I gotta note here. Says you called a couple of months ago looking for information on..." Leon imagined him flipping through papers on his desk. "Diaz," the San Diego cop continued. "Johnathon Diaz. That right?"

Leon considered his promise to Jill. He'd sworn that he wouldn't follow up on this, and he hadn't. In fact, he'd forgotten that he'd made the information request. "Nah. That didn't turn out to be anything."

"All right," the distant cop said, and Leon could hear him shuffling the papers again. "You, uh, hang tight a minute, okay?"

"All right, man." He got out of the bed and walked across the hotel room floor in his underwear. He'd only been here three days, but, somehow, he'd managed to scatter the entire contents of his suitcase across the room. He flipped on the bathroom light and fished around in his overnight case looking for and finding his travel-sized Tylenol. He took four. A slow heartburn built in his diaphragm, and he belched acidly, tasted once again the 151-proof rum from the night before.

"You still there, Fratelli?"

"Yep. Look, man. I really don't need to talk to you about this guy. That was just a thing. All's good over here, and I had a really rough night. You mind if I..."

"Yeah, yeah." Finch's voice had become urgent. "I gotta quick question for you."

Leon sighed. "All right, go ahead."

"You know where to find this guy? We've got questions for him about a murder in San Diego."

The words blew the last of the cobwebs from Leon's mind. He left the bathroom and sat on the edge of his bed. "Murder?"

"Yeah. A young guy over here. They found him all cut up. Diaz is wanted for questioning."

Jill was up on the mountain. She always went up for Christmas. She was with Jack and the old man. She was alone with a murderer. "Look, Detective. You're reaching me in Chicago. I'm not back in Arkansas. I've got one of those new cell phones."

"Oh yeah? You like it?"

"…Yeah, yeah, I guess." Leon ran a hand over his face. "This Diaz guy, he a suspect or witness or what?"

"He looks good for it, man. Only reason we hadn't followed up earlier is caseload. The victim was a pusher, not exactly high priority around here. If you could lay your hands on him, we'd be pretty grateful. Not even junkies deserve what this guy did to him."

Leon's stomach roiled, and he fought the urge to vomit. "I don't got him right now, but I'm gonna go get a hold of him. I'll call you back in…" He looked at the clock again. "Forty-eight hours. Okay?"

"Sure. You really got him? I figured he probably drifted on by now."

"Yeah, man. I know right where he is. Forty-eight hours, okay? You got a phone number?" Leon yanked open the end table drawer and pulled out some hotel stationary.

"Yeah, it's six-one-nine, five-three-one, two thousand. Ask for Finch in narcotics. Got that?"

Leon wrote the number down. "Finch. Narcotics, right?"

"Right."

"Listen. How sure are you about this guy? You think he did it?"

"That's the word on the street. Guy was found all cut up with a couple bullet holes in his head. Knife wounds wouldn't have killed him, but the bullets sure as hell did. Some guys saw Diaz all hopped up and pissed off earlier in the night. They said he was looking for the victim. Word was the guy might've killed Diaz's little Mexican boyfriend, but we're not sure. Diaz might've killed the Mexican kid, too. We got matching ballistics on both bullets."

"You think he killed two guys?" Fear settled deeper in Leon's stomach.

"Yeah, maybe. That's what it says here. I been out for a while. I just got this case, but the last guy working it thought so."

"All right, give me forty-eight hours. I'll call you back."

"You bet."

"Later." Leon shoved his clothes into his suitcase as fast as he could. He had to return to the bathroom twice. Once to vomit, once to gather his forgotten overnight bag. On the way out of the hotel, he called his cousin from his cell phone. "Hey, Karl. I gotta get back to Arkansas. Got something bad happenin' over there."

"Haven't you been payin' attention to the news? Winter storm from here to Oklahoma, man. Arkansas is gettin' hammered. Ice storm. You ain't gonna make it."

Leon stopped under the hotel's portico. "How bad?"

"They're saying three to four inches, man. They're calling it the winter storm of the century."

"Shit."

"Might as well stay here, man."

"Much as I love your Flaming Dr Peppers, Karl. I gotta go. I really gotta go. Wish me luck, cuz."

"Luck."

The valet pulled Leon's Cougar up in front of the hotel. He threw his suitcase in the trunk, started the engine, and punched a number into the cell phone, a friend from Kansas City, Missouri. "Hey, Bobby," he said into the receiver. "I'm heading back to Arkansas. I need to borrow your four-wheel drive. You got snow chains?"

He listened to the man's reply, said: "Good, I'm on my way." He slammed the car into first gear and pulled out of the hotel. At the stoplight, he pointed the hood of the car south, waited impatiently for the light to change, then, head pounding and anxiety rolling in his belly, he drove.

Chapter 43
Jack

December 26, 1987, 8:00 a.m.: Moondust Motor Inn, Windsor, Arkansas

The ice clung thick to the branches of the oak in the courtyard. Its lower limbs touched the ground in a circle around the main trunk. Some of the higher had split and fallen in the night. The overnight ice storm had left a two-inch thick layer of ice on top of the existing snow and more fell from the sky, rattled on the roof of Jack's camper. The storm was not over.

He snugged into his sheepskin jacket, stomped through the snow and up the hill to Abe's kitchen. The door stuck under his hand, and he had to yank it hard to break the ice seal holding it shut.

Abe and Jill sat at the small Formica table. They glared at each other over their untouched coffee. Jack could see the family resemblance. Abe's face was white, his mouth knotted like a bruised knuckle. Jill's color was up. She leaned across the table, her fists clenched tight with anger. Jack sensed that he had interrupted hot words. The tension floated in the air.

Abe's glare switched from Jill to Jack. "You told her. You son of a bitch. You told her."

Abe cursing was more frightening than Abe glaring.

"I told you he didn't, Grandpa," Jill snapped. "I eavesdropped."

The old man pounded the table with his fist. "Is that s'posed to make it better? I ain't forgivin' you for sneaking around, but he ain't no better. He's been telling you everything I said ever since, hasn't he? Every little thing I trusted him with, he's been telling you. All the time lettin' me think that he was keepin' my secrets. Isn't that what you said?"

"Look, Grandpa, if you think—" Jill threw the words like they were stones.

Abe looked ready to give as good as he got.

Jack interrupted before things got out of hand. "You're right, Abe." He shut the kitchen door behind him, a little too hard. Abe and Jill stared at him, their eyes defensive and waiting. Now that the confrontation he'd been dreading was here, Jack found that he was ready for it. He turned and faced the old man squarely, as he'd done with his marine CO every time the colonel had called him on the carpet. He took a deep breath and pointed at Jill but spoke to Abe. "She needed to know. She needed to know, man." Jack drummed out the words with his finger on the table. "You damn well know it."

"Don't you curse at me you—you useless drunk! I was the only fellow that treated you right around here. Everybody done give up on you and what'd I do? I took you in, I fed you, I helped you get sober, and I give you a purpose, a roof over your head. All I asked was that you leave her out of it. And this is how you repay me?"

Jill opened her mouth to jump into the conversation, but Jack cut her off. "Shut up, old man!"

Abe sat back in his chair, his brow knitted. Jill's

mouth fell open, her eyes wide.

"You're right. You've done some of that stuff, but it wasn't because you were looking out for me. You needed someone who didn't matter to you. Do you remember what you said to me when I got here? You told me we weren't going to be friends, Abe. That was one of the very first things you said to me. You basically told me that you didn't give a shit about me."

Abe looked down at his hands.

"And if that's not enough"—Jack pressed on—"Father Preddy told me what you thought of me when you took me in. He said you wanted somebody that was hopeless. Hopeless, Abe! You remember telling him that? He made it real clear to me."

Abe's already pale face went paler. His lips trembled. Jill was staring at her grandfather, like he was a stranger.

Jack continued. "You wanted somebody you could push around. If you hadn't been deluded enough to think that I had some kind of power, who knows how long you would've kept me around? You wanted a loser you could get to do a bunch of shit work for no money, and I was just the sucker you needed. So don't give me some sob story about how you were looking out for me. You were looking out for you."

"Deluded?" Abe asked quietly. "You think I'm deluded?"

"Hell, I don't know. Sometimes I believe everything you say and sometimes I think you're off your rocker, but I do know this. I know you're a sick man, and you need help. Definitely physical help, maybe mental. I know you think you're doing something important, but here's the problem. I can't tell

259

what it is that you're trying to do. I can't help you. You keep telling me that you can sense it. Hell, Jill tells me that she can sense it. I can't. No matter how I try, I can't feel the Wall, I don't feel the...vibe or whatever it is you two say drives you half crazy, but she..." He pointed at Jill. "I may not trust you, Abe, but I trust her. She tells me it's real. I tend to believe her. But here's the biggest thing: She can sense it and I can't! She can do all of that and more. And didn't you tell me that only a woman could teach a man, and only a man could teach a woman? Back and forth like that, you said. So why the hell did you think it would work for you to teach me in the first place? If the things that you're telling me are true, why the hell aren't you asking for her help? It's madness."

Abe ran a quivering hand across his mouth. His whiskers rasped under his fingers.

Jill placed her hand on his arm. "Grandpa, you know I love you. I know you think you're protecting me, but I can feel the Wall, too. It's almost gone now. We don't have time for this anymore." His hand trembled on the tabletop. She slid her hand down his forearm and took his wrinkled fingers in her own. He laid his other hand over hers and looked at her with pain in his eyes.

"I can help," she continued. "I really can help."

Tears flowed down Abe's face. They left shining tracks on his weathered skin. He blinked and nodded. "I hear you. I hear you." He patted her hand. "You know everything near as I can tell. What do you want me to tell you?" He looked at Jack, and his eyes hardened.

He may have forgiven her, but he hasn't forgiven me. Not yet, anyway.

"Tell me," Jill replied. "Please tell me. What is the Fountain?"

Abe stared at her with his faded blue eyes. "I don't know." He was hoarse. "My grandma didn't know. Sam didn't know. I don't know if anybody ever knew. I've got ideas. My grandma thought it was the devil's work. Sam thought it was something natural, but they didn't really know, and I don't either."

Jack took a seat at the table. "It's called the Nee-ooh-lassah." He placed Johan Ortiz's old journal in the center of the table. "I couldn't sleep last night. I didn't have time to finish writing it out, but with everything going on, I thought it was important to get to the end. I tried my damnedest, and I got through almost all of it. The priest says that it's called the Nee-ooh-lassah. It's an Indian word. I don't know what it means."

Jill picked up the book and turned it over in her hands. The leather cover was ragged and sweat-stained. The pages were yellowed and brittle and smelled of old cinnamon. Hand-written Spanish covered each page.

"What—" Abe said, confusion in his eyes. "What do you mean? That book—you're saying that book is about…" He turned his eyes on the valley below.

"Yes, Abe." Jack nodded. "It is. Didn't you suspect that? I mean it was with all of the other old books. Didn't anyone ever tell you that it was important?"

The hardness was gone from Abe's eyes. He looked strange, ashamed. "Nah. I thought it was—I don't know, an antique handed down by the family. I don't know nobody who ever read it. I had the other books, and I had the family B—" He stopped speaking and placed his hand over his mouth. "I didn't know."

"What does Nee-ooh-lassah—what does it mean?"

261

Jill asked.

"Ortiz didn't know," Jack replied. "Not the literal translation, anyway."

"Then what?"

"Do you remember the Indian woman I told you about? Sikena? The one that the soldier Remero Diaz wanted to marry?"

"Yes."

"She told Ortiz about the Fountain and about the Nee-ooh-lassah. She told him it was powerful water, that it healed people, made people live a long time, maybe forever. She also said it was dangerous."

"Live forever?" Jill said. "That almost sounds like…"

"The fountain of youth," Jack finished. "That's what de Soto decided it was."

"Seriously?"

Abe gave Jack a doubtful look. He didn't let that stop him. It was Abe's turn to see if he could believe the unbelievable. "Yes." He pointed his finger at him. "You don't have to believe it, Abe, but that book says that de Soto came up here looking for gold. He never found it. His soldiers were dying off. He'd been wandering around the Mississippi river for, oh, at least two years when he overheard Sikena talking about the Nee-ooh-lassah. He'd found no gold. His men were mutinous. By that point, all of the Indians wanted to kill him because he'd been torturing and murdering folks for years, and his slaves kept escaping or dying. The way I see it, the man had to be grasping at straws by then. All of his hopes of returning home wealthy and powerful must have seemed like they were collapsing around his ears. Hell, he must have been desperate. And when he heard about the Fountain, he must have remembered Ponce de Leon's stories." Jack took an already opened pack of cigarettes from his jacket pocket, shook one out, and lit it. Jill didn't try to stop him. "It didn't occur to me when I started reading the book, but de Soto took over the governorship of Florida from de Leon. De Soto would have heard lots about the fountain of youth. Ponce de Leon couldn't shut up about it. You remember learning about him in school, Jill? Ponce de Leon, I mean?"

"Vaguely."

"Governor de Leon spent his career and his fortune searching for the fountain of youth," Jack continued. "The native tribespeople told him it was a real thing but never could take him to it. They kept sending de Leon and his soldiers from one place to another. He went all over the state, tracked through swamps, slept in the wild. He was obsessed. He never found it." He took a drag on his cigarette and blew the smoke at the ceiling. It swirled around the glass globe of the light fixture. "By the time de Leon died, his contemporaries thought he was a madman or a fool. I remember thinking, when I was a kid, that he was the clown of the conquistadors. Kind of like a real-life Don Quixote. I thought the Indians were probably laughing at him the whole time. Turns out I was wrong about that." Jack went to the kitchen counter for an ashtray. He returned to his seat and knocked the ash off the end of his cigarette. "The Fountain is real. Somebody in your family must have known that at some time. Otherwise they would never have called it the Fountain in the first place. Makes sense, doesn't it?"

Jill blinked, and the old man's face took on a

thoughtful look.

"Maybe I should say that the Nee-ooh-lassah is real," Jack corrected himself. "According to Ortiz, Governor Hernando de Soto, actually found it...and it drove him mad."

"The fountain of youth," Jill said. "It's evil?"

Abe looked from Jill to Jack. "Of course, it's evil." He crossed his arms. "If it's the same Fountain that I know, then it's evil."

"Not evil." Jack made a hold-on motion when Abe looked like he wanted to argue. "It's dangerous. Dangerous isn't the same as evil. Just like a lion or a rattlesnake. Both dangerous, but neither is evil. You understand?"

Jill nodded, but Abe still looked dubious.

"Ortiz," Jack continued, "claimed that there was a spirit of the fountain that merged with people, but that it wasn't evil. He didn't say what the effects of that merging was, just that it happened. It may be evil now, though. In fact, I think it's definitely evil *now*, but it wasn't then is my point. De Soto did something. He, uh, corrupted it or something."

"How did he do that?" Jill asked.

"Sikena didn't want to take de Soto to the Nee-ooh-lassah, so she and Remero Diaz ran away. Ortiz said that Remero loved the woman, and that she was pregnant with his child. She was also Remero's wife, at this point; Ortiz had married them secretly. Ortiz writes that Remero was worried for Sikena's safety. He knew that de Soto would do whatever it took to get what he wanted, including torturing the woman he loved, so Remero took his wife and...split." Jack tapped his cigarette. "I guess, if you look at it from de Soto's point of view, Remero was a deserter. He was a soldier and under orders." He shrugged. "Honestly though, I don't think it would have mattered. De Soto wanted that water, and he wasn't the kind of man to let something he wanted get away from him."

"So de Soto went after them?" Jill asked.

"Yeah. He split his forces and took off after them. He brought Ortiz along to translate. The priest wasn't real happy about it. De Soto followed Remero and Sikena all the way from somewhere down near Fort Smith to your valley. De Soto and his men caught the couple down there."

"How do you know it was down there?" Abe asked.

"Had to be. It's where the Fountain is. If everything else the priest says is true, that has to be where de Soto found them."

"Why?" Jill asked. "Why did Sikena go there? Didn't they know they were being followed? It doesn't make any sense to lead the man to the thing he was looking for in the first place."

"I don't know," Jack answered slowly. "I guess, maybe they thought they'd escaped and they were safe. Or maybe her family was from this area, and she thought her tribe would protect her and Remero." Jack popped his hand on the table. "That actually makes sense! I never thought of that before. That would also explain how she knew where the Fountain was. What if her people lived here the whole time? What if it were her…tribe or whatever that guarded the Fountain? What if it was that same tribe, the descendants of Sikena's people that still guarded the Fountain when your ancestors got here, Abe? I bet that's what it was. In fact,

I know it is. It has to be." Jack looked at Jill, then Abe. The old man seemed to be struggling with all of the new information. Jack slumped a little and shrugged. "Maybe all of that's wrong. I just don't know."

"It sounds…right," Jill said.

Jack reached out to put his hand on her shoulder, remembered that Abe was present, and let it drop. "What I do know is that de Soto caught up with them and tortured Remero until Sikena agreed to guide the Spaniards the rest of the way to the Nee-ooh-lassah. That whole section of the journal was very jumbled and the handwriting was terrible. Father Ortiz must have been really messed up when he wrote it. I don't mean drunk. I mean stressed or…I don't know." Jack tapped his finger on the old book. "All I know is that Remero, Sikena, de Soto, and Ortiz all ended up at the Fountain together, and that's where things went really wrong." He went to the counter, poured some coffee into a mug, and returned to his seat. Abe looked ill again. Ill and weary.

"De Soto," Jack continued. "He's gotten to the Fountain now. He's gotten everything he wanted. He's got Remero in chains. He's got the fountain of youth. But that's not enough for the governor. No, he wanted to punish Remero. And that is how de Soto corrupted the Fountain."

"What did he do?" Jill asked.

"Forgive me," Jack said. "It's not a pleasant story, so I'm just going to come out and say it."

Jill nodded. Abe gestured with his pipe for Jack to continue. "De Soto had his soldiers stake Remero to a tree in the clearing of the Nee-ooh-lassah. Remember, they'd already tortured him once, so I don't know what kind of shape he was in when they got there. De Soto's soldiers used their daggers and crucified him."

Jill looked as if she'd taken a blow to the stomach.

Jack placed a hand over hers and squeezed gently. "He had several of his soldiers rape Sikena."

Abe's head came up, his jaw clenched.

"Then," Jack continued, "he had Remero tortured, for the second time. Ortiz said they 'visited terrible brutalities upon his body,' worse than he'd ever seen." Jack paused to swallow the words that had gotten caught in his throat. "After all of the horrible stuff Ortiz had seen de Soto do to innocent men, women, and children over a two-year period, I can't imagine what qualifies as terrible brutalities. I just can't imagine. It's clear that they castrated the soldier. I'm not sure I want to imagine the rest of it." He cleared his throat. "Anyway, the Spaniards finally killed Remero, or he just died, I don't know. Somehow in all of the...torturing, Sikena stabbed de Soto, but he didn't die. Sikena escaped, and Remero, well... They chopped off his head and threw it and his body into the Fountain when they were through with him."

Jill blinked, fighting back tears.

"That," Jack said, "is what corrupted the Nee-ooh-lassah."

Chapter 44
Diario del P. Johan Pablo Ortiz, 1540

1540: Translated by Jack Diaz

Governor de Soto, who all thought near death, for there was much blood from the wound that the woman had given him, drank from the waters and became immediately healthy. His proud features, lined with the scars of battle and age, smoothed, and he became the fresh face of youth. His wound, which was very serious, joined before our eyes. He moves now with the grace of a much younger man, though his eyes seem to be only black now. A sure sign that evil has won him over. I was overcome and fell to my knees and prayed to God for his deliverance.

I reject the water in the pool. The Nee-Ooh-Lassah is the cause of great evil this day. Nothing stained by the blood of a murdered man can lead to good.

May God accompany you, my friend Remero Díaz. Your beloved Sikena escaped and perhaps your memory will live on through your future child, be it son or daughter. Perhaps.

Tonight, we leave the valley and the Nee-Ooh-Lassah, though the governor says that he will return. The soldiers say that they see native warriors sneaking in the trees, but try though I might, I see nothing. I think of Sikena's family who is said to live on the heights over the valley and the great vengeance that she owes to the governor. Perhaps they have come to exact justice.

I hope that I will see the morning sun rise in the east.

Chapter 45
Jack

December 26, 1987, 8:00 a.m.: Moondust Motor Inn, Windsor, Arkansas

Abe's chair scraped across the kitchen floor as he pushed back from the table and walked to the kitchen counter. Jack's description of Remero Diaz's torture and murder still hung heavy over the conversation.

"Jack," Jill said. "I've been thinking."

"Yeah?"

Abe glanced at her, then away. He looked like he was chewing on something he didn't like the taste of.

"Remero Diaz…"

Jack gave her a questioning look.

"I think, Jack," she continued. "I know it sounds crazy. I know you thought it was just a coincidence, but I think, he's your great-great-great-something-grandfather, Jack."

Jack waved her words away.

Abe turned, a look of surprise and speculation on his face.

"No," she said. "Think about it. I know it's a crazy coincidence, but if what I'm saying is true, you'd be the descendent of both Remero and of Sikena. Correct?"

Jack nodded slowly.

"And you've got a power, Jack," she continued.

"Some power that Abe and I can't sense. Sikena had power, too. Right? And you've told me that you can't do a lot of the stuff that Abe's been trying to teach you, right?"

"Right."

"You also said Sikena knew about the Fountain, the Nee—nee-ooh—whatever, right? And that her family was from this area."

Jack nodded again.

"Grandpa." She turned to Abe. "I overheard you telling Jack." Her cheeks pinked with embarrassment. "There was a special tribe or something keeping the Wall in place before our ancestors got here, right?"

Abe nodded.

"You also said that most of them were run off," she continued. "Now, Jack, your mother said your family was from this area and that you've got Native American blood." She waited a moment for that to sink in. "You have a power. Sikena's tribe was the group holding the Fountain in check, and you're from this area. It all makes sense. Maybe you're the key to everything, Jack. Maybe…I don't know. Maybe the ghost of your ancestor is haunting this valley or something. Maybe Remero Diaz is down there right now, looking for revenge? I know it sounds stupid, but maybe that's why the Fountain is radiating evil like it does."

Jack shook his head. "I can't believe that some long dead…spirit or something is doing this. Everything Abe has told us is about the Fountain, not some bogeyman."

Abe had a thoughtful look on his face. "She could be right. I ain't told you, 'cause I didn't think it mattered, but I've seen a dark thing walking around down there many a time. My whole family seen it, one time or another. It's in the shape of a man, walks like a man, but it ain't got no face or nothin'. It's like a shadowman that comes up to the Wall sometimes. Usually when things is real bad. Heckfire, it was there the night you got struck by lightnin'. Clear as day on the other side of the Wall. It was watching you."

Jack frowned. *Do I remember that?*

"We—I," Abe continued, "always thought it was the Fountain itself. The spirit of it and all. Maybe we were wrong. I didn't think it was that important."

"Dammit, Abe," Jack said. "There's a lot you never thought was important. You should have told me. How could that not be important, man?"

Abe's eyes lit with anger. "It don't matter, no how. It's a good story, and it might even be true, but it don't have nothin' to do with what's goin' on right now." Abe pointed his pipe toward the valley. "Unless you got any ideas on how to fix the Wall, none of that matters."

"Look, Abe," Jack began, "knowing this means that there might be a way to—"

"It don't mean nothin'!" Abe's face closed like a fist. "I ain't got time to waste on fairy tales and—and family reunions. I don't care if it is your great-great grandpappy hauntin' the place. What needs to be done, needs to be done."

"What is it that needs to be done, Grandpa?" Jill asked. "What is it that needs to be done? The sacrifices aren't working. Jack told me so, and so did you. You slaughtered that poor beast, and it did no good. It. Did. No. Good. At. All." She jabbed her finger at him. "At least let's talk about it. Maybe there's another way." She hefted the journal in her hand, "Maybe this book offers some clues."

Abe placed his hand against the side of his stomach and lurched back to the table with a groan. Jill placed a hand on his shoulder to steady him. He pulled away from her. His cheeks were white and planed like carved wood. "It didn't work. Because it was interrupted by that man!" He pointed his pipe at Jack. His hand shook. "I ain't lettin' that happen again. This time I'm gonna do it right."

"You're not killing that lamb!" Jill cried. "It's barbaric. I won't let you."

He stared at her, his eyes gone cold and distant. He sneered, stomped into his study, and dropped into his recliner with a stifled groan. Jack had never seen Abe so hard, so alien.

Jill began to go after but hesitated. "I shouldn't have yelled at him. He's so frustrating, but...he's in pain."

"He needs a doctor," Jack whispered. "Something is really wrong, Jill." He could see the emotions warring on her face. Anger at her grandfather, distress over the Fountain, worry over Abe's health.

"People are doing bad things, Jack. Right now, all over, people are starting to lose control." She pulled a strand of hair away from her face. "We both know that's true, don't we?"

Jack had had his doubts, but like he'd told Abe, he trusted Jill. *If she believes... What is faith but a decision?* "Yes, I think you're right." She went to the back door, opened it, and looked out onto the icy landscape. The freezing rain pattered on the ground. The susurration was soothing, like the whisper of angels. He peeked into the study. The lamb was asleep in its kennel. Abe was asleep as well, his head rolled back in his recliner, his Bible in his lap.

"I don't know what to do, Jack," she said. "Abe says he won't go to the hospital until the Wall is fixed."

Jack wrapped his arms around her from behind and looked through the door. She covered his arms with hers and tilted her head back against his chest. "There's no way my Beetle can drive in this stuff. Grandpa's truck can't do it, either. It's two-wheel drive, and the back end will just slide right out from under us. Maybe I should call emergency services?" She turned in Jack's arms and looked up at him. "What do you think?"

"I don't know. He's been a little better since last night. He had enough energy to argue with you. I don't know. How long do these storms last?"

"They don't usually last *this* long. The problem's not the storm, though. It's the roads. They're going to be really slick, and everything is downhill from here. I've seen people get *up* the mountain during ice storms. They're fools for trying, I think, but if they've got a four-wheel drive, they go slow, and if they're lucky, sometimes it can be done. Getting back down the mountain, though. That's super dangerous. Once you start sliding…" She mimicked a car going over the side of a cliff. "You've had it."

"Can't—can't you do something for him?"

She pulled away. "Don't you think I would if I could?"

"I'm sorry. I thought…"

She paced the kitchen floor, her hands in constant motion as if acting out her frustration and powerlessness. "I tried this morning, before we argued. I'm sorry, I shouldn't have snapped. It didn't work.

That's what started the argument. I can sense the problem. I prayed over him like I'm supposed to. I anointed his forehead with oil. I applied the power." She spread her fingers and made a pushing motion. "It didn't work." She wrung her hands. "Abe said I didn't have enough faith."

"Is that the problem?"

She looked up at him, two slow tears tracked down her cheeks. "I don't know. I just don't know. I can sense something big in there. Growing. He's got a tumor, Jack, and it's cancerous. I don't know how I know, but I know. I've healed bad stuff before, but this time…something is pushing back."

"What do you mean? Pushing back?"

"It's—it's like it doesn't want to be healed. I think, well, I think he's doing this to himself."

"Abe is?"

She nodded. "I don't know if it's the sacrifices or the stress he's been carrying or—or some guilt or something else entirely. It's like his body has turned the magic against himself. It's like some part of him has decided to die. I can't budge it. I don't think he even knows he's doing it, but he's killing himself. I don't see how I can fix that. He needs a doctor. He needs surgery."

Jack wrapped his arms around her again. "It's going to be all right."

"You don't know that."

He didn't say anything, hugged her tighter, and listened to the soft rattle of the rain freezing them in. The lights in the kitchen flickered, once, twice, then went off. The refrigerator's condenser stopped, and in the sudden silence, Jack could hear the ticking of Abe's grandmother clock chopping away the seconds in the study. The quiet rustling of the ice storm filled the silence with an all-encompassing sibilance that made Jack think of snakes crawling through the grass. "What happened?"

Jill's expression was bleak. "The power is out, probably the phone, too. It happens."

Jack closed his eyes and rubbed the bridge of his nose. *When it rains, it pours.*

Chapter 46
Leon

December 27, 1987, 2:15 a.m.: Bella Vista,
Arkansas

The farther south Leon drove, the worse the
weather got. The roads decayed, and by the time he
reached the Arkansas border, he was doing forty-five
miles an hour despite having swapped to his buddy's
International Scout.

He couldn't explain the sense of urgency that was
driving him or why the feeling was growing rather than
receding the closer he got to home. He'd been trying to
call Abe's motel ever since leaving the hotel. A black
fear had settled on his mind when he hadn't been able
to get through. Desperate, he'd tried calling friends of
his in the sheriff's department. He'd gotten the same
result. The phone lines, he realized, must be down.
Which meant that the storm was bad where Jill was. It
also meant that Jill couldn't call for help.

The state of the roads on the Arkansas side of
Highway 71 made him curse the highway department,
the weather, the governor, his own luck, and then the
highway department again. Missouri's roads had been
bad, but the salt trucks were out and fighting the falling
ice. No one fought the storm on the Arkansas side. His
speed dropped to thirty, then twenty-five, then to a

virtual crawl.

The roads were deserted, the traffic lights and businesses darkened. He suspected a power outage. He pulled over at a gas station. A CLOSED sign rested in the window. He cursed. He'd been hoping for coffee. He *needed* coffee.

For the next thirty minutes, he fought to put the snow chains on the big truck's tires. By the time he'd finished, he'd lost the feeling in his fingertips. He rubbed his hands together and breathed on them, then climbed back into the truck's warm cabin. His fingers burned as circulation returned. When he could once again make a fist, he put the old orange 4x4 in low and pulled out of the gas station.

The chains made an odd rattling sound on the icy road, and the vehicle wandered a little as he applied the gas. He found that he couldn't get above fifteen miles per hour without the rig sliding out of control. At this rate, he wouldn't be there for hours yet. Leon crossed himself, prayed that he would make it on time, and ran his hand over the inside of the windshield to clear the fog away.

Please, Lord, please keep her safe.

Chapter 47
Ronnie

December 26, 1987, 5:32 p.m.: The Isaac Stone

Ronnie had done it. It had taken him most of two days, but with Pilgrim's help, he'd managed to track and, with a well-thrown rock, stun a small deer on the far side of the valley. He had torn strips from his shirt and bound the creature. He'd hefted the beast onto his shoulders and begun the miles-long journey through the icy valley and up the long mountain slope to arrive back at the Isaac Stone.

By the time he'd arrived, his shoulders were on fire and his legs jelly, his mind scattered, and thoughts slow. He staggered and almost fell when the spirit fence hove into view. He dropped the struggling animal to the ground with a crash and sagged to the snow beside the pile of bones. He almost went out then, the exhaustion of two days physical exertion dragging his eyes down. Pilgrim, however, wasn't finished.

The spirit snatched him out of sleep and prodded him to crawl over to the deer on his hands and knees. He whined, but his passenger was unrelenting. He found a large, jagged rock. Stone in hand, he crawled back to the deer, and raised the primitive hammer above his head with quivering arms. The frightened deer's eye rolled in its head, and it bleated and lurched in the snow. He waited for it to exhaust itself, drawing energy from its distress, then, when it had stilled, bashed the doe's head in with a succession of soggy blows.

The Wall collapsed.

Ronnie knelt stupidly in the snow, his mouth hanging open. Pilgrim's laughter racketed around in his mind, and the spirit's exultation flooded his punch-drunk brain. Confused but joyful, he howled in triumph, staggered to his feet and crossed the spirit fence for the first time. He almost fell when he entered the clearing. He lay a hand on the Isaac stone to steady himself. Its warmth was seductive, and the blood smeared across its surface stuck to his hands like syrup. He grinned at the scattered little bones that someone had arranged on the top of the great rock. A small pulse of energy rose through the stone and up his arm.

He rolled onto the altar and lay looking up at the night sky. The totem poles arched over him. The human skull's mouth hung open as if to speak. He wondered dimly who the skull belonged to, whether it was a man or a woman, how old it was. His brain felt fuzzy. He stopped thinking about it. "I'm tired, Pilgrim. I cain't go no farther. I cain't do it."

Pilgrim was quiet in his head, patient.

He chuckled to himself. "Don't you worry, though, Pilgrim. I can feel her up there. She's right up there waitin' for me. I just need some shut-eye. When I catch her, man… You ain't even gonna believe it. I'm gonna give it to her like she ain't never got it before. I'm gonna tear her clean apart. I got plans, man. I been thinking about that woman for months, and I'm awful, awful hungry. I'm getting' hard just thinkin' about it. Just you wait, Pilgrim. You'll see." He groaned and stretched out on the stone. The warmth oozed into his wasted muscles. Pilgrim embraced him with comforting words.

Finally, I'm free.

The thought had strange harmonics, and Ronnie was uncertain whether it was his or his passenger's. No matter, they were both pleased. The rock was warm, the blood sticky under his bare back. His aching limbs dragged him down into the darkness.

He drifted off with a smile on his lips.

Chapter 48
Jill

December 26, 1987, 5:32 p.m.: Moondust Motor Inn

Jill cried out. Her fingers spasmed, dropping the dish that she had been drying. The plate shattered and sent shards of glass skittering across the kitchen floor. The Wall was down. The sudden silence in her head, where before there had been the constant buzzing presence of the magical barrier, left her stunned. The Fountain's maddening influence streamed unchecked through her mind.

Abe rushed into the kitchen, his pipe clenched between his teeth, his eyes wild with panic. "It's down!" His hands were reaching and grasping the empty air like he wanted, needed to do something, touch something, fix something, but there was nothing to do or fix.

Jack came to the kitchen door and leaned into the room. He'd been lighting candles and lanterns against the encroaching twilight. His face was grim. "The Wall?"

Jill didn't respond. She was rubbing her hands down the front of her apron in ragged, jerking motions. She'd barely registered that he'd spoken. She was battling for her mind. She ran through prayers of protection, walling off her emotions, drawing her fear down and down, smaller and smaller, making her horrors manageable, and then tucking them away in safe corners of her mind. Her lips and cheeks twitched as she fought to bring herself under control.

Abe staggered to the table and fell into a chair. He pressed hard against his belly. His face was ashen. His lips moved as he spoke the spells necessary to keep himself under control; his shoulders and arms twitched and jumped. Fear and fury chased each other across his face.

"He that is slow to anger," Jill quavered, "is better than the mighty…" She moved, as one feeling her way, over to the table and took her grandfather's hand. It shook badly, the palsy had taken his entire body. His mouth hung open, his breath coming in short, sharp gasps. The look of gratitude and panic on his face shook her confidence. She'd never seen Abe unable to deal with a situation. "Say it with me," she said. "He that is slow to anger," she began, and Abe joined her, his words tumbling out between gasped breaths. Together they continued the verse, "Is better than the mighty, and he that ruleth his spirit, than he that taketh a city." She exerted her will and visualized the power creating a shield around her mind and spirit. Simultaneously, she tried to extend the protection to Abe through their linked hands. A weak bloom of power rose from her grandfather in return, and he settled a little. His breathing calmed. She nodded and smiled at him and started a new verse.

"And the peace of God," she said, and, once again Abe joined in, his voice grown more confident. "Which passeth all understanding." They stared into each other's eyes and nodded, saying the words in unison. "Shall keep your hearts and minds through Christ Jesus." When they finished, she applied her power again, and this time the echo from Abe, while not strong, was strong enough. They'd built a small Wall around themselves.

Abe sighed, and his shoulders dropped. He nodded at her. She released his hand and patted him on the arm. "Thank you," he rasped.

"You're welcome." It had been a close thing.

Abe rose from the table, and, though his face was lined with pain, he was in control of his emotions. "That's the end." His voice sounded like burnt hopes.

Jack dropped his arms from the doorway and walked the rest of the way into the kitchen. "Maybe— maybe it won't be that bad."

Abe glared at the young man. "You've got no idea what you've done." He turned away.

Jill reached out with her hand and power to calm her grandfather.

He shook her off. "No idea," he repeated.

"What I've done?" Jack asked.

"If you hadn't messed up the sacrifice, the Wall would still be up. All of the blood, all of the destruction and death that is coming... There's a lot of people gonna die now, Jack. Men, women, kids. A lot of people. All their deaths are on you. Because you got squeamish over an animal! All the blood, all the pain. It's your fault. Your fault." There was no anger in his voice now, only a cruel certainty.

Jack opened his mouth, and Jill thought for one hot moment that he would tell Abe that he was crazy, that he would argue. He didn't. He dropped his head in defeat. Jill's heart ached. "You—you don't know that, Grandpa. You're not being fair."

The old man turned his cold gaze upon her and spoke with finality. "Yes, I do." He walked out of the kitchen, his hand dug into the side of his stomach.

Jill turned to Jack, moved to take him in her arms, Abe's concerns be damned. She could feel the pain radiating from Jack, could see the look of baffled guilt on his face. Her grandfather was wrong. Jill's heart told her so. Jack didn't deserve the way Abe had spoken to him. He didn't deserve all of the responsibility for the Wall's failure. So she reached out, tried to offer comfort.

It was not to be. He sidestepped her embrace and rushed out of the back door, down the hill. Jill stood in the kitchen, her empty arms held out to hold the man with whom she was falling in love. Hot tears spilled over her cheeks. Everything was falling apart.

****

Jill put batteries in Abe's little radio, and she and he tuned in to KERA that night. Jack stayed gone. The radio station had suspended all of its music programming, had dedicated itself to reporting the strange happenings in the local area.

They sat and listened as the reports came in, as Abe's predictions came true. The DJ, Joe Garrick, reported dozens of house fires in West Port. Initial reports said the fire department had them under control. They were stretched, but covering it. Later, the reports grew less hopeful. Fights between firefighters and homeowners were called in. More reports of the fire, now unchecked, spreading until whole neighborhoods were engulfed. Still it went unfought. Fire trucks were abandoned, their volunteer crews disappeared to God knew where. The hungry conflagration continued to grow until it had marched all the way to downtown West Port. Businesses and city administration offices were now in jeopardy. Jill listened anxiously for word of the *West Port Partisan* but didn't get any.

"Who the hell," Joe raved over the radio, "is doing this shit?"

The sheriff's department and highway patrol were responding to multi-car collisions on the interstate, some of which sounded intentional. Reports came in of gunplay between a deputy and a trooper.

Jill looked at Abe unbelievingly. "The police are shooting each other?"

Abe's eyes cinched closed. Tears built at the corner of his lids.

"That'll teach those state guys!" Joe crowed.

The ERs in LaFayette warned that they were filling up with gunshot wounds, accidents. A young woman had been picked up naked on the side of the road. She'd had a four- or five-year-old girl in her arms and blood smeared all over her face. She'd bitten a man named Hal to death. She claimed she'd been kept captive for almost a year.

"Bitten to death," Joe shouted into the mic, the last vestiges of self-control gone. "Holy shit! That's awesome!"

Abe sank lower and lower in his recliner.

Jill touched his forehead. He was hot to the touch and dry.

Her grandfather shook her off. "I told you. I told you." He scowled and went to the bathroom.

Jill put a glass of water beside his chair and, when

he returned, asked him to drink it. They listened on into the night, growing more and more hopeless as the reports grew worse

Around 9:30 p.m., Joe the DJ and his soundman got into a heated argument over whether it was okay to say "fuck" on the air in a crisis situation. Joe claimed that it was entirely appropriate, and, in order to drown out his coworker's complaints, he began repeating the curse word louder and louder until he was shrieking into his mic. That didn't last long. Joe's shouted "fucks" were interrupted by a long, loud shriek of rage and a metallic clank as something, maybe Joe, hit the studio microphone.

Jill raised her eyebrows at Abe.

He shook his head.

The last sounds coming through the radio were a crashing and screaming from the control room. The argument had progressed from words to fists. Soon after, the station went to static.

Jill dialed the band up and down looking for other stations and, finding only white noise, finally turned the unit off. "What do we do now, Grandpa?"

He grunted, rose unsteadily from his recliner, and laid his Bible on the end table. "Pray." He left the study, bracing himself against the walls as he went. He stopped at his bedroom door, his back bent and a grimace of pain on his face. "Pray." The door shut behind him.

Jill debated with herself. Go find Jack and talk to him? Or check on her grandfather, push him for a solution?

The lamb moved around in the kennel. She could try to sacrifice it. She didn't want to, but surely a human life was more important than an animal's. If sacrificing the little thing would get the Wall back up, if it would stop the craziness, wasn't that worth trying? The idea of killing the creature made her sick. She stood in the study, turning first to the hall, then to the kitchen, then back to the lamb. She didn't know what to do. Jack had made it clear he wanted to be left alone, her grandfather was in no mood to offer comfort, and even if she was willing to do the sacrifice, she didn't know how. *God, what do I do?*

If God answered, she didn't hear.

Chapter 49
Jack

December 27, 1987, 2:13 a.m.: Moondust Motor Inn

Jack's trailer rocked as someone entered. He woke, startled and muzzy. A bottle of Abe's shine clinked and rolled across the floor of the camper, kicked by the intruder. The small space smelled of alcohol. He had come close to drinking, had agonized over it, had twisted off the lid, and held it to his nose. It smelled like oblivion, like liquid forgiveness. It smelled delicious. He'd tilted it to his lips, felt the liquid touch his lips and stopped.

For a moment it was touch and go, Jack frozen with the bottle to his lips while, inside, he fought one of the toughest battles of his life. In the end, shaking, he'd cast the bottle to the floor and thrown himself onto the bed that took up most of the trailer's single room. He'd wept then, and later, he'd slept.

He blinked to clear the sleep from his eyes. A small dark shape stood outlined against the trailer's louvered windows. The intruder's arm was raised and there was something in its hand, bat or stick, bar or...something. Before he could react, before he could raise a hand in his own defense, the intruder's arm came down. The weapon cracked against his temple.

Christopher Farris

Jack fell back into the darkness.

Chapter 50
Leon

December 27, 1987, 5:01 a.m.: Highway 71, West Port, Arkansas

West Port was chaos. Even in the dark, Leon could see the smudges of smoke rising over the small town. Fires dotted the hillsides up and down the surrounding mountains. Blue and red lights strobed and cycled around every curve of the highway and in the town's neighborhoods. Cars and trucks scattered the streets, heaped up in angular collisions, bleeding their oil and fuel onto the pavement. He didn't care. He had to get up the mountain. He had to. He navigated the big International around the vehicles that blocked his progress.

Police officers, troopers, and deputies patrolled the community. Fire truck sirens wailed in the dark. Several times, Leon had to floor it and swerve around state troopers who tried to flag him down. He'd stopped for the first guy, but the trooper had threatened to arrest him on the spot and then tried to break his window to drag him out of the vehicle. He had elbowed the man in the face and driven away. Since then, he'd avoided the other lawmen.

Somewhere inside of him, he was shocked at their behavior, at his own and at the hellish state of anarchy that he was seeing through the truck's windows. But that small sane part of his mind was a tiny voice drowning in a sea of rising emotion. His fear and anger climbed fast the farther south he drove. He itched, like he was going to jump out of his skin. The exhaustion and stress had grown and evolved into a raging impatience that ran through his limbs, like acid. He almost hoped another trooper tried to stop him.

Leon wanted to hurt someone.

****

The big International's snow-chained tires clattered to a stop on the bridge that spanned West Port's Grey River. Leon groaned. The road was blocked. After fighting his way through town, circling wide around the burning neighborhoods, avoiding rampaging gangs of teens and the police officers chasing them, it was maddening to be stopped at the edge of the mountains.

The traffic jam was caused by a group of sheriff's department deputies. They pushed, shoved, and in some cases, kicked a milling crowd of citizens into the back of an Adams County prisoner transport. The prisoners shrieked and raised their fists; their faces doughy and bruised in his headlights, like deep-sea creatures dragged gasping to the surface. They were in various states of dress, some bundled up for the cold, others still in their pajamas or less. A red-bearded middle-aged man, incongruously clothed in flannel shirt and boxer shorts, refused to be herded. He backed up two steps, bent forward at the waist and screamed his fury at the deputies. Leon could see the veins standing out in the man's neck, the corded muscles in his clenched fists. His rounded belly protruded between the panels of his torn-open shirt. His nose had sheeted blood down his beard and onto his pale white chest. He looked like a Viking on a rampage. The deputies moved forward as a group, cutting the man out of the crowd.

Red Beard's fellow prisoners milled about, pushing and shoving, hollering at each other. Leon knew what was coming next; he could feel it, almost wanted it. He recognized some of the deputies now. Big Charlie, Leon's sometime partner, an obese detective with a penchant for Reuben sandwiches and beer and Leroy Fuller, eleven years in the Adams County Sheriff's Department. Leroy lunged and cracked the red-headed fellow in the head with his nightstick. He hit him hard. Viking guy dropped to the pavement, like a bag of raw meat. Leroy kicked and kicked and kicked the unconscious man. Other deputies rushed the nervous crowd, and Leon saw their sticks going up and down as the prisoners wailed. Big Charlie waded into the citizens as well. He shoved a middle-aged woman hard. She fell. Charlie grabbed her nightgown to drag her back to her feet, and it ripped from her back. She shrieked and clawed at his arms with her fingernails. He kicked her then and struck her naked breasts with his nightstick. She rolled over and lay still.

Charlie stepped over her prone body and shaded his eyes against Leon's headlights. The fat detective snarled and walked down the bridge toward him.

I don't have time for this shit. Leon hunched over the truck's steering wheel and revved the engine. The big truck roared and the heads of the crowd, prisoners, and deputies, snapped around. Big Charlie's face was a mere blob in his windshield. A thin deputy walked up to flank the fat man, shining his flashlight in the windshield of the truck. Leon couldn't identify him

293

behind the glow. A nasty joy washed through him. He meant to go around the men, sure, but if one of those dudes was too stupid to get out of the way? If big, fat Charlie fell under Leon's big, fat tires? Well...so be it. Big Charlie was a loser, always had been. Leon popped the clutch.

The International leapt forward, its tire chains clanking and scattering the salt on the bridge. The unidentified deputy flanking Charlie threw up his hands. Big Charlie, smarter or luckier, lurched out of the International's path.

Leon suddenly recognized the man in his headlights, Danny Banks, nineteen-year-old recent graduate of the police academy. Leon liked Danny. The kid's face was a long smudge of terror. He slammed on the brakes, and the truck went into a lurching slide. Danny bounced off the truck's front grate with a sickening thud. The truck shuddered to a halt. The motor rumbled, like it was hungry.

The prisoners took advantage of the confusion, leapt off the far end of the bridge and scattered along the riverbank, east and west. Leroy and the rest of the deputies took off after them.

Leon scrubbed his face with his fists. Sweat rolled down his forehead and cheeks. He needed to deal with Danny. He needed to see if he was alive. He tried to clear his mind and wiped the tears from his eyes.

Big Charlie propped himself on the bridge bannister. The man's distended potbelly swung ridiculously as he tried to find his footing. He staggered away from Leon's truck, his hand on his chest, looked back at the International once, hitched up his pants, and lumbered after his fellow deputies.

Leon crossed himself. He swung the truck's door open and walked to the front of the truck, prepared to see the kid's body shattered on the ground.

Danny sat on the pavement, cradling his right arm in his left, and bawling like a baby. He let out a wail of outraged horror and fear when he saw Leon. *Broken arm.* That was it. *Broken arm. Hurt but alive.* Danny spit at him. "You broke my arm! You assho—"

Leon snatched him by his uninjured arm and dragged him across the pavement to the bridge's railing and tossed him against it. Danny howled and spit curses at him, tried to go for his gun but the movement twisted his outraged arm. He shrieked. Leon back-handed him, stripped him of his pistol and dropped it into the river below.

"What the hell are you doin', man?" Danny yelled and, despite the pain, flopped over the railing to go after his weapon.

Leon caught him, pulled him back and pushed him hard against the barrier. His anger was building again. He needed to be on his way, and this idiot kept slowing him down. He turned to leave, and Danny lurched after him, grabbed at the pistol on Leon's belt. Leon slapped him, back and forth, back and forth. He had to force himself to stop. He bent down and put his finger into the kid's face. "Stay here!" He ordered the deputy. "Stay here, asshole! You got me? Stay!" He kicked Danny in the side. Danny howled but stayed put.

Leon climbed back into the International and put it into first. Big Charlie climbed the slope at the end of the bridge, returning from the riverside, his pistol dangling in his fist. *Just what I need, this asshole again.* Leon hammered the gas, and Big Charlie watched, his fat mouth gaping, like a fish as the truck blasted by him. It was a disappointment not to run him down.

Then the bridge was behind Leon, and he began the long climb up to Windsor, to the Moondust Motor Inn, and to Jill. *God help you, Jack, if you've hurt her.*

Chapter 51
Abe

December 27, 1987, 3:45 a.m.: Moondust Motor Inn, Windsor, Arkansas

Jack was alive, though there was a walnut-sized knot on his forehead where he had been struck. Abe dropped the hickory stick and grabbed him by the legs. The kid was dead weight. He pulled hard to get his unconscious body across the floor, then out the door. Jack's head struck both metal steps on the way down. Outside, the ground was uneven, and Abe had to bend over farther. His stomach was grinding again, the weakness returning. He struggled with Jack, pulled with all of his might and got him twenty feet before he admitted defeat. He'd have to get the tractor.

He checked Jack's pulse before leaving him. Still breathing. His face looked like marble in the moonlight, eagle-nosed and proud, but also young and... For a moment, Abe wavered in his determination.

He'd had a lot of hopes for Jack. They'd come close to solving this thing without bloodshed, and they'd spent a lot of months together, him teaching, Jack learning. The kid's insistence on getting sober, and the way his granddaughter had looked at Jack last night weighed on Abe. Jill would never forgive him for what he was about to do. Tears squeezed between his lids and spilled hot down his cheeks. He wiped them away with roughened knuckles.

He didn't have time for this. He hardened his heart. He was going to have to do much worse than hit the kid on the head. He was going to have to sacrifice him. God had made that clear. Abe was out of options. Jack was his korban. God had provided the sacrifice when the moment came. It was time for him to do his duty, and time to get the Wall back up.

Abe hurried to the tractor. The ground was slick. The pain gnawed away at him. When he reached his barn, he rested against the tractor, took deep breaths, and tried to center himself. The ache passed. He climbed into the elevated seat and pressed the ignition button. The starter whirred and whirred in the cold and finally caught with a cough and a rumble. Abe flipped on the single light, drove back up the hill to where he'd left Jack lying in the snow.

A second wave of pain rolled through him as he levered Jack onto the trailer. This agony took him to his knees and made black spots dance around the edges of his vision. He was slow getting back to his feet. He held onto the cold steel of the tractor with tight fingers and gritted his teeth against the desire to scream. The pain was fierce, fiercer than ever. *Please, Lord, give me the strength to do thy will. Please, Lord. Please, Lord.* With a mighty effort, he planted his butt in the driver seat. He had to rest then, settled his head on the top of his forearms and gripped the steering wheel hard. He focused on breathing until the pain receded. "Thank you, Lord."

He put the tractor in gear and gave it some gas. The engine stuttered, stuttered, then, with a metallic lurch, backfired. The report echoed up and down the mountainside. Abe jerked in the driver's seat and his stomach clenched up. The pain whiplashed through him and ripped at his guts, like a chainsaw. He curled into a tight ball of agony. His foot slipped from the clutch, and the tractor rolled forward. Abe didn't notice. He'd forgotten where he was, forgotten everything but the glowing world of pain that centered in his gut. The tractor hit the barn at fifteen miles an hour. Its heavy nose split the weathered pine-siding with a terminal crunch. He flew over the steering wheel and crashed to the ground. His arm snapped. He screamed and blacked out.

The tractor lurched, and chuffed, and then, choked out by the lack of fuel, died. Silence returned to the night.

The old man lay, like a broken bird, in snow as cold as the stars overhead.

The ice storm was over.

Chapter 52
Jill

December 27, 1987, 4:15 a.m.: Moondust Motor Inn, Windsor, Arkansas

Jill woke from a fitful sleep. She was in her grandfather's recliner. She'd been poring over his books of magic, looking for anything that might help her to solve the problem of the Fountain and the Wall. She'd read until her eyes were sticky, and her head was pounding. She hadn't found anything.

The fire in the grate was almost out. She tested the end table lamp, clicked it on and off. Nothing. The power hadn't been restored. She picked up her grandfather's chunky black telephone, held it to her ear to listen for a dial tone. Nothing.

She got out of her chair and stretched, tried to rub the kinks out of her neck. She hated sleeping sitting up. Nothing felt right after that. She checked Abe's grandmother clock and cursed under her breath. It was four in the morning. Four in the morning, and the whole world was falling apart. She walked into the kitchen.

She picked the percolator off the stove but fumbled it on the way to the sink. It fell to the floor and shattered sending shards of glass dancing across the linoleum. She choked back a scream of frustration and stood before the sink with her eyes closed, repeating the spell to reinforce her protective barrier. When she'd finished, and no longer wanted to throw the pot across the room, she forced herself to calmly set the ruined coffee-maker in the sink. *Nothing is ever easy.*

She found an old blue camp percolator in Abe's hunting closet. She took it back to the kitchen and filled the canister with water, added the grounds to the top basket, and set it to heat.

She cracked Abe's door and peeked in on him. A thin beam of moonlight streamed across the foot of his bed. *He's still asleep.*

She went on to the bathroom, sat on the toilet, and rubbed her temples. It occurred to her that with her grandfather asleep she might have better luck at treating his ailment. Maybe she'd face less resistance from his own magic.

She stepped into his room. She felt along the bed, trying to find Abe's body with her hands. She found nothing. The bed was empty. Her grandfather wasn't there.

****

She searched the motel office first. On finding it empty, she checked the attic. Nothing. Her anxiety rising, she swept the grounds near the motel. No new footprints going out to the highway, both vehicles, her Beetle and her grandfather's truck, accounted for. She checked her motel room. Nothing. She went to Jack's trailer. The door was open.

The little camper was unoccupied and cold, the bed in disarray. An empty liquor bottle lay on the floor. Abe's hickory stick lay beside it. Fear clenched her heart, squeezed until she thought it would burst.

The Isaac Stone.

She rushed back to Abe's hunting closet. She'd need a flashlight and heavy jacket. She found them and, having equipped herself, went out of the kitchen door in a rush. She hurried down the hill, slipping in the icy snow.

The tractor stood halfway through the wall of the barn.

She found her grandfather unresponsive, splayed in the snow. He wore a strange long-sleeved white shirt. It almost looked like a dressing gown. The old man's snowy hair matched the ice on the ground, his skin and the gown. She felt for a pulse, ragged, but there. He was still alive.

A sling bag lay beside him. It looked familiar. She picked it up. Something clanked inside, but she ignored it. She rolled Abe onto his back. His arm moved wrong, and he cried out, though he didn't wake. His bicep felt lumpy under her fingers.

Jill exerted her healing power without preparation or thought. She laid it on her grandfather, like an intricate quilt, and wrapped his limbs and his outraged torso in her power. She tried to drive health into his bones. The old man's arm knit. The lumps smoothed out. His fingers twitched, and the pain lines ravaging his cheeks smoothed. She sighed, relieved, until she became aware of the great festering blackness in Abe's stomach. She pulled her hands back with a cry. It had grown.

The tumor was a deep pit that absorbed anything that she pushed at it, a poisonous canker that writhed and decayed in his belly. She focused herself and tried again, tried a different spell, pulled power from the deepest part of her soul and rammed it into the evil thing that was killing him.

It ate it.

She couldn't fix this. "Dammit, Grandpa! Dammit."

She clambered to her feet, stumbled to the back of the tractor and found Jack laid out on the trailer. She played her flashlight over his still form. He looked dead, his face yellowed bone. He wore blue jeans. His chest was bare. Her heart dropped in her chest, and the tears threatened to burn her up. She rushed to his side, knelt, and tested his pulse. He was cold to the touch. She felt the thin skin of his wrist for a heartbeat and pried back his eyelids. The pupils were mismatched and failed to track the light of her flashlight. A huge purple lump rose from his forehead, and the young man's breathing was shallow, almost imperceptible. The flesh under the lump gave suspiciously under her fingers. If Abe had hit Jack, as she suspected, he'd hit him hard.

She called Jack's name, chafed his wrists. She called louder and shook him gently, then hard. No response. She focused her flagging healing energies. She'd put a lot into Abe. She was terrified that she didn't have enough left to give, that Jack would slip deeper into his comatose state, would disappear. *I can't lose them both. Please God.*

She ran the prayer of healing through her mind. She didn't even think about the words, she rattled off what she'd been taught, one verse after another, and pushed the remainder of her magic, her love, her hope and fear, all of it, she forced into the man who lay before her and willed with all of her heart that he be healed. Tears ran unnoticed down her face and fell onto her hands where she rested them on Jack's forehead. Jill spoke the final verse. "Bless the Lord, O my soul, and forget none of His benefits: Who pardons all your iniquities, Who heals all your diseases," and as the final words fell from her tongue, all of the magic and the belief exploded from her body, rippling the air and juddering down her fingers and into Jack.

Something inside of him responded, and for a moment, she sensed Jack's power, twisting and spiraling, like a shoot of golden growth in the depths of his spirit. It bloomed and spread like the petals of a rose. Her power was magnified by his, changed and shaped, became something wild. It flowed back into her, giving her life and hope. The feeling was indescribable, like sunlight and honey pouring into her soul. She gasped with wonder.

Jack hitched in a breath, held it for a long moment, then convulsed and gasped, hitched in another, froze, then relaxed and breathed deeply, his chest rising and falling smoothly. His face regained its normal color.

She slumped back on her heels and wept with relief. She rested her palm on his bare chest. Touching him helped. His skin was warming now. He opened his eyes, sat up and focused on her, ran his fingers down her cheek, capturing her tears.

She wrapped her arms around his neck and hugged him tight. She couldn't stop crying. Tentatively, he returned her embrace. She fought to control her hitching sobs. "I—I—" She gulped. "I need help. I—I need your help to carry Grandpa."

Jack pulled away from her but didn't let her go. He rubbed his hand up and down her arm while he took in the trailer, the barn, the tractor halfway through the wall. He traced the tracks in the snow going up the hill to his camper. When he spotted Abe lying on the ground, he rose from the trailer and walked over to the old man, knelt beside him, and checked his pulse. "Did Abe bring me out here?" He fingered Abe's white gown. "He was going to sacrifice me, wasn't he?"

Jill's breath caught in her throat. She knelt by her grandfather. She considered lying. She considered telling him that it was a misunderstanding. She couldn't. Not to Jack. She nodded.

He pulled Abe's bag to him and went through the contents. He pulled out a long knife, thin from much sharpening and the family Bible. He flipped it open and ruffled through the pages. He ran his finger down the edge of the text. His face grew harder. His eyes were as cold as the frozen sky. He snapped the book shut and put the items back in the bag. "We found the instructions for the sacrifice ritual." He would not meet her eyes.

"Please, Jack."

"He was going to sacrifice me." His face looked hatchet-like and cruel. The veins in his forearms stood stark against his sun-tanned flesh, his fists clenched and shaking with repressed violence. He closed his eyes and held his arms tight to his sides. He shook.

Jill waited as he tried to find his way out of the hurt. Moments stretched to minutes as he stood like a statue in the winter night. Finally, he took a deep breath and released it. Without opening his eyes, he took her by the hand and squeezed. His fingers were warm, his touch gentle, and her hopes rose. He opened his eyes and looked at her. He wasn't all the way back, she could still see a deep hurt there, but the rage that she'd feared had receded. Jack was calm. He pulled her to her feet. "We need to get him out of the cold."

She squeezed his hand in return and blinked, trying to keep the tears from returning. "Thank you, Jack."

Together, they lifted the old man and carried him back to the motel, back to his bed. Jack stripped Abe of his sodden clothing and got him into his thin nightclothes. He didn't wake.

Jill tucked the blankets around her grandfather while Jack added logs to the fire in the study. She checked Abe's temperature. He was cold, so cold. Jack entered the bedroom, stood by the bed, two cups of steaming coffee in his hands. "He's dying."

She dropped her head and swallowed. There was a knot of tears in her throat.

He set the cups down and took her hand. "The phone is out."

She nodded, not trusting herself to speak.

"I'm going to go down to Our Lady," he said. "I'm going to see if Preddy's phone is working. Maybe they can get an ambulance up here. Maybe they have a helicopter. I don't know."

Jill wanted to argue. She was afraid to be left alone with Abe, afraid to watch him die. The mountain felt like a dangerous place tonight, a place of emptiness and blood. Part of her wanted to curse Jack for a coward, for using the old man's illness as an excuse to run, but she couldn't. He might be right. There was a slim chance Preddy's phone worked.

"I'll hurry."

She nodded.

Jack took her in his arms and kissed her on the forehead, smoothed the hair from her face. He tilted her chin up with a finger and looked her in the eyes and kissed her once more on the mouth. His lips were dry and hot against hers, his arm strong around her waist. She was conscious of his body against hers, not in a sexual way, but as a comfort, as a strength and a support that she needed.

"I love you," he said.

Jill searched his face, this strange contradiction of strength and weakness, this man with the proud, kind eyes. She said nothing.

He drew her into a slow, deep kiss, then released her and walked out.

She raised her fingers to her lips to hold onto the feeling of his mouth upon hers. Things were happening too fast.

Chapter 53
Jack

December 27, 1987, 6:00 a.m.: Our Lady of the Mountains, Windsor, Arkansas

The walk to Our Lady was longer in the dark and cold. Jack huddled into his sheepskin coat. The night was eerie and still now that the storm was over. He felt the reassuring weight of the big Bowie knife in his pocket. Limbs broke and groaned under the weight of the ice. Some of them, arm-thick, had fallen and speared into the soil like nails driven home by the hand of God. He didn't want to be under a breaking limb when that happened. He stuck to the middle of the highway.

It took him forty minutes to reach Our Lady. No lights shone in the chapel or in the parsonage. If the power was out, the phone was likely out as well. Jack had been hoping against hope that the little priest might have some kind of bat-phone or shortwave radio that let him communicate with the authorities, but now that he was here, that seemed a foolish thought.

He swept his flashlight over the highway as he approached the turn-off to the little church. Tire tracks marred the snow. They had been made before the ice fell. He didn't think anyone had been here since. He worried that the priest might not be home. If the man had been in LaFayette or West Port when the ice storm hit, he could be trapped down there. He debated with himself what he would do if the parsonage was empty. Considering Abe's condition, he decided that he'd have to break in and take his chances.

He trudged onto the gravel drive. He pointed the flashlight over the lean-to attached to the parsonage. The broken-down vehicles' taillights reflected like cat's eyes in his beam. He twitched the flashlight around the grounds looking for signs of visitors. His light crossed the statue of the Virgin Mary. She leapt brilliantly white from the night. Her starry crown glowed in the flashlight beam. A dark shape lay draped around the bottom of her pristine white robes, the shape of a man.

Jack took an uncertain step back. It was Father Preddy. His white-haired head slumped forward over the pedestal. His hands had been bound with sisal rope in front of the Virgin's bare toes. The priest was kneeling, the knees of his thick pajama pants deep in the snow. He wore an old, ragged Scottish hunting coat. His cheek rested against the side of Mary's gown as if in adoration. The front of his jacket was soaked a deep red and his limp fingers dangled bloody icicles. His blood had run down Mary's skirts, run down the marble pedestal and into the snow at the base.

Jack crouched, conscious of the silence of the still-dark morning, the crunch of his boots in the snow. He flashed his light around the church property again, ran it across the front of the chapel, the parsonage, the community center. Nothing moved in the night. He shined the light directly on Father Preddy. He had taken a terrific battering. Both of his eyes were purpled and swollen shut, nose smeared across his face, his lips split, teeth shattered. His throat had been cut.

Jack backed away from the statue, his heart pounding. Mother Mary's face changed as the light receded. Her eyes became deep shadows. Her mouth curved down in a hungry sneer. Her arms, once a symbol of benediction, of hope, seemed to Jack to represent something else now. A threat, a hunger, as if her hands, thrown wide, were reaching to snatch the world, to take it. She looked ravenous, yet oddly satisfied, as if the dead man at her feet was a suitable offering. As if she were happy that someone had finally figured out what God wanted, that he wanted blood, blood, blood. He closed his eyes and took a deep breath, shook his head. *She's a statue, just a statue.*

He looked down at the boot marks he was leaving behind. They were distinct in the fresh snow. He saw a stranger's footprints as well. They looked older, blurred and scuffed. The lugs from Jack's combat boots were clear. He dragged his boots back and forth through his footprints. He did the same to each of the footprints he'd left as he worked his way back across the lawn. When he finished, Jack didn't think anyone would be able to identify his boot tracks. He hoped not, anyway. He turned at the edge of the highway and groaned in dismay. The trail he'd left coming from the Moondust was clear, all two miles of it. There was no hiding that. He put his face into his hands and breathed deeply. *I'm screwed.*

He was afraid to break into the parsonage now. His fingerprints on a broken door or window would sign his death warrant. He couldn't unsee the dark shape wrapped around the statue's feet.

He hated the idea of leaving Preddy propped up

like that, like a trophy. He turned back to take the priest down from the obscene display but halfway across the lawn he thought better of it. The cops would want to see it as it was, and if they found that Jack had manipulated the body, it would make things worse for him. He returned to the side of the highway. His options were few and shrinking. He studied the long line of his footprints again. The only pair going all of the way to the Moondust. No way to hide that. No way.

He stomped a big circle out on the road so that he could tell the police that he hadn't approached any closer than that. He finished and then realized that it was stupid. *I must be in shock.* He put his face in his hands and forced his brain to work. *As soon as the telephones start working, I'll call the cops and report the murder.* He hesitated. *What do I do if someone else reports it first? What if somebody already has?* He couldn't do anything about that, except to make the call as early as he could and to offer whatever information he might have. Maybe, with a little luck, the roads would melt, and he and Jill could get Abe off the mountain before the phones came back. *I could report it in person.* He could face it head-on. *I can face Leon head-on.* He grimaced. The detective would make it hard. No amount of Jill's help would keep Leon from investigating him. If Leon talked to San Diego and put that whole scene with Nancy together with what had happened to Preddy? It didn't take a genius to know the man would want to put it all on Jack. Cops, in his experience, always took the easy solution. *Well, I can't do anything about that, either.* "Dammit, Preddy," he said and wiped a tear.

He was surprised to find himself crying. He'd liked

the man. Father Preddy was one of the few kind people that Jack had met. "Why did you have to go and let Paul do this to you?"

Deacon Paul was the murderer. It was obvious. The tire tracks in the snow, Deacon Paul often drove for Father Preddy. The young mother that Paul had been so obsessed with, Preddy had been furious when he'd seen. Jack flashed the light back at the statue. *You confronted Paul, didn't you, Father?* Preddy's corpse huddled at Mary's feet, his hands seeming to beg Jack for help. *This is what he did to you, isn't it?* Jill and Abe would say it was the Wall coming down, that the Fountain was pushing people, that it had pushed Paul, that it had driven the man to murder. Perhaps they would defend the deacon. Other people lived up and down the mountain, and they were also under the Fountain's influence. Preddy could have been murdered by any one of those people or by a random traveler. It could've been anybody, anybody hopped up on anger, or drugs, fueled by the Fountain and their own bad decisions. Who knew? It didn't have to be Paul, but Jack knew a carnivore when he saw one. *Paul's the guy.* Say what anyone might; Paul was the killer.

Jack began the long walk back to the Moondust. He would load Abe and Jill into the old Ford truck and take his chances getting down the mountain. After that, the police station, the inevitable phone calls to San Diego, the questions about Nancy, questions about why he was at Preddy's and why he had lied about this, and this, and this, and all the rest. Then, probably, he'd go to jail. He clenched his teeth, hunched himself deeper into his coat and pushed forward into the wind.

What was coming felt inevitable, like a great wave

towering over him, ready to crash down on his head, a wave made up of the evil he'd done and the broken lives he'd left behind, the rules he'd broken, the people he'd hurt, all of the small selfish decisions he'd made. It was finally catching up to him. All of that bad karma, that whole wave of lingering consequences, was coming. It was almost here, and it would use Preddy's murder to make him pay.

Jack knew it.

Chapter 54
Ronnie

December 27, 1987, 5:15 a.m.: Moondust Motor Inn, Windsor, Arkansas

Pilgrim warned Ronnie of the motel before it came into view. Over a little rise, the telltale skeletal structure of an old rocket-shaped metal swing set rose into Ronnie's view. He'd reached the motel. He dropped to a cautious walk while Pilgrim watched the scene with invisible eyes. Neither saw anyone on the grounds.

There was an old barn to Ronnie's left. He went to it and opened the door. Inside the space was dusty and cobwebby. The far wall had the front end of a tractor through it. He wondered if it had been the sound of the crash that had woken him. Judging by the smell of exhaust lingering in the air, the accident hadn't happened that long ago. Farming implements and grounds-keeping tools hung from pegs along the beams of the barn. He moved his way down the chaotic collection of utensils, running his hand over hoes and shovels, fingering hammers and an old wood saw that brought a smile to his face. He stopped at a pickaxe, fallen to the floor. He ran his fingers over the grip, smooth with many years of use. The pick end was nicked up, the axe blade notched, but the tool was clean and made a satisfying weight in his hands.

He bounced it up and down in his palm and grinned. He swung it in a short savage arc, and the pick head embedded itself in one of the barn's beams with a solid thunk. He pulled and twisted until it came free and smiled again. He felt the rounded point with his fingers and pressed it against his thigh. He tried to picture how it would feel to have the steel driven into your muscle, to feel it tearing its way through your skin, to puncture your bone. It gave him a delicious, vicious feeling that made him dizzy with desire. The pickaxe felt right in his hands.

He found a pair of abandoned work boots in the corner, an old pair of coveralls hanging above them. The boots were curled over on themselves and entombed in spiderwebs. He kicked off his knackered cowboy boots, stripped out of his mildewed jeans. His daddy would have said they were more hole than pants. He slipped the faded orange coverall on over his shirt and zipped it all the way up. It sagged in the butt and at the elbows, but was far, far better than the clothing he'd been wearing for months. He pulled the old boots out of their spidery hole and slid them onto his feet. They were stiff from long outdoor storage. He shrugged. They'd loosen up.

He left the barn and moved up the hill. The shape of the motel's roof rose against the western sky. Pilgrim slowed him and guided him to the right, to the rear of the office. A candle flickered in a window on the back side, right next to a small stoop and a closed back door. *Kitchen door, I bet*. He ducked under the window, then raised himself so that he could see into the room, a kitchen, small and green. *Bingo*. It was empty. Candles burned on the small table and along the countertops.

More small flames glowed in an empty room on the other side of the kitchen's only arched doorway. The room beyond looked like a small sitting area or study. Pilgrim sent him an assurance that one, two, three people were inside, two males and a female. Ronnie sighed with relief. They were here, all three of them. He'd been worried that he'd come all this way to find the place abandoned.

His heart went into a slow, rhythmic pounding that rocked his chest and filled his ears with the rushing of excited blood. His eyes went tight and sharp. *I've got the power now.* He developed an erection. *All of it.* He choked up on the pickaxe and crouched in the flowerbed. He liked sneaking around in the dark, liked seeing into others' lives without being seen. He liked knowing that he held their lives in his hands. In his mind, he was already running through the rooms, putting his pick through the chest of the men as he found them, laying them out bloody and dead, and then—then bringing the woman to see what he'd done. Oh, how she would scream. He hungered to slam the door open and then smash and smash and smash with the pickaxe until the walls ran red with blood. Pilgrim warned him to wait.

Ronnie shook off the spirit's influence. He put his hand on the door's handle and looked through the glass. Still no movement inside.

Pilgrim's displeasure grew.

Ronnie ignored it. He grasped the door handle, ready to swing it wide and charge through the kitchen. He felt Pilgrim's spike of anger as his muscles locked. Ronnie whimpered. His arms trembled against the spirit's control.

The spirit made his hand release the handle.

Ronnie struggled harder, and his hand moved back toward the door. He sensed Pilgrim losing his patience, and then his head went white-hot with pain as his passenger punished him for his disobedience. He wanted to cry out, to scream in agony, but Pilgrim had locked his jaw and stilled his tongue. Ronnie's lips writhed and sweat popped out on his forehead. The spirit released him, body and mind, and Ronnie sagged against the kitchen door, his lips popped open, and he dragged great breaths between his teeth. He raised a trembling hand to his brow and sobbed. "Okay, okay. I'm sorry. Okay. I'm sorry."

Pilgrim wasn't telling him no. He was telling him, not yet.

He needs me to be smart. He's trying to protect me. I can't afford to screw it up.

To his relief, the spirit smiled on him and suggested that putting off the pleasure only served to make the outcome sweeter, that he'd get everything he ever wanted.

"Thank you." Ronnie ducked his head. "You're right. You're right. I gotta be smart." He received a sudden wave of affection and pride from his passenger. The spirit nudged him to continue, and Ronnie's excitement began to rise again. He grinned to himself. Pilgrim was right: This feeling of power, this anticipation, was too sweet to waste on a moment's wild bloodletting. He needed to snoop around a little more, peek through some windows. See what he could see.

He worked his way around to the front of the motel, careful to avoid the rustling dried bushes and dormant plants in the flowerbeds. He rose and peeked in windows as he went. The rooms on the south side of the motel were dark. He peeked in anyway. One window opened onto a bedroom, but he couldn't tell whether it was occupied. The next was a bathroom, empty.

Ronnie reached the next corner and peeked around to the motel's center courtyard. He didn't see any movement. Two windows glowed on this side of the building.

He slid along the wall, watching the courtyard to see if an early riser was out walking the grounds. He scanned the other motel buildings. They were both dark and unoccupied. The snow of the courtyard appeared undisturbed. Still no movement beyond a crow that winged itself from the great oak down to the forest below.

An old Ford truck, glistening under a sheath of ice, poked its nose out of the carport at the end of the building. A VW Beetle made a curved snowy shape on the gravel loop. Its headlights, round like the eyes of a happy baby, showed under its icy blanket. Vehicles were good. It meant he had a means of escape. He'd take the truck if it was running. Beetles were chick cars. He chuckled to himself and clenched the pickaxe. Excitement had his heart thumping in his chest. He felt it in his joints and veins, felt the blood coursing through his body. He hefted the pickaxe in his hand. He wanted to smash something. No, he *needed* to smash something.

He walked down to the first window. His boots crunched in the icy leaves of the flowerbed. The sound was sharp against the winter silence. His heart beat in the base of his spine. He crouched below the lintel and raised himself to peek over the sill. Candlelight cast shadows on the thin curtains. Two people stood inside. One tall, the other shorter. He pressed his ear to the windowpane and heard the deep voice of a man and then the higher voice of a woman. They came together in an embrace. The man spoke again and then turned and left the room.

They were here. He'd found them. The woman wasn't but four feet away. He could smash through the window and be on her before she even knew he was there. His thoughts went white-hot and stupid. He wanted her, wanted to hurt her, to take her. He raised the pickaxe to smash it through the glass pane and froze as Pilgrim locked him up again. The door to the motel office rattled once, twice, and then opened into the courtyard. Pilgrim threw Ronnie to his knees and then face-first onto the dirt behind a bare-branched bush.

The little man gasped with terror, of being seen and of Pilgrim's growing level of control. He lay still, breathing in the scent of ice and stale mulch. After a moment, Pilgrim released his body back to him. He raised his head to see who had come outside.

It was the tall man. The one who had killed Barry and Chuck. He stepped from the office and stopped on the concrete stoop, buttoned his heavy sheepskin coat. He had a long Bowie knife in his hand. He pulled it from its sheath and inspected it in the light of the moon. Ronnie frowned as the dude wiped the blade down both sides of his jacket sleeve and held it up to inspect it once again. He slid it back into its sheath, then into his jacket pocket and looked around the yard. Ronnie turned so that the white of his face wouldn't show in

Christopher Farris

the night. The tall man's eyes passed over his hiding spot without seeing him, and that was good. That knife, though… He cursed to himself. Instead of risking being locked down by Pilgrim again, he sent the spirit a question. Charge the man or wait?

A cold trickle of fear ran down his spine as he waited for Pilgrim's answer. He was afraid to attack. He eyed the Bowie in the man's pocket. That was a damned big knife. He measured the distance between them. He couldn't cover the ground between without being seen, without giving the dude time to pull that knife, time to fight back. He remembered this asshole moving around the motel office, like a ghost. Every time he had had a bead on him, the dude was somewhere else. He'd never fought anyone so fast before. There was no doubt, the guy was dangerous, and he didn't want to take any chances. To his relief, Pilgrim told him to wait, to see if the man went back inside.

But the tall man didn't go back inside. He stood on the stoop and looked out to the highway then back into the motel office. He was hesitating, rubbing his hands on his pants like he was considering returning to the motel. The man flipped up the collar of his coat, shoved his hands in his pockets, and walked out toward the highway.

Pilgrim told Ronnie to follow.

He worked his way from shrubbery to shrubbery, careful to make as little noise as possible and making use of what cover he could find. When he reached the highway's verge, he crouched in a low bush. The road was a pure white strip running between the frosted trees of the mountaintop. The moon sparkled from the smooth surface like the stars had descended from heaven. The tall dude was ruining it, of course, tromping his big ass boots through the snow as he walked away from the motel.

What now? Ronnie asked Pilgrim. Ronnie could sense fear in his passenger as well as indecisiveness. The idea that the supernatural being was capable of fear made him feel both a little better and a little worse. The tall man continued walking down the road, away from Ronnie. If Ronnie was going to get at him, he'd have to run down the open highway in order to catch up. There was no way he'd go unseen or unheard. He was pretty sure he could take the tall dude in a fair fight, but he wasn't positive. In the end, he settled on his haunches behind a pine tree's trunk and waited and waited for Pilgrim's orders. His quarry walked into the winter night.

Pilgrim instructed him to let the dude go.

It was for the best. It allowed him to focus on the old man and the girl. He hefted the pickaxe and returned to the motel.

Time to have some fun.

Chapter 55
Jill

December 27, 1987, 5:50 a.m.: Moondust Motor Inn, Windsor, Arkansas

How like a man to tell you that he loves you, then leave you to deal with reality while he went off on an adventure. It was maddening.

Jill sat by Abe's bedside. His face was gray and splotchy in the candlelight, deep pain lines etched his brow. She put a hand on his forehead, touched his fish-white chest where it showed through his nightshirt. She'd been worried that the chill he'd taken would linger. He had a fever now. She went to the bathroom and ran some cool water over a cloth, brought it back, and wiped his face, his hands. She folded the cloth and draped it over his forehead. He sighed, and his brow smoothed. She prayed for God's guidance while tears ran down her face. God didn't offer any immediate answers, so she pulled Abe's tattered Bible from his satchel.

The sacrifice knife fell to the floor. She picked it up. It felt wicked in her hands. It was old, its handle deeply etched with pictograms of animals and men. She shuddered. The knife had been marked with its intended victims. The grip was stained with the sweat of many generations, the blade narrow, like a sliver. It looked hungry. She laid it on Abe's end table.

She opened the Bible. The pages of the book were thinned with age and crackled as she turned them. They'd yellowed, darker at the edges than at the center. Handwritten notes filled the margins, simple spells, instructions for planting, even some kitchen recipes. Much of the writings were in blocky angular scripts that she assumed were male, some in looping feminine hands. She wondered how many generations of work she held in her hands. She read, not the verses, but the notes left by her ancestors.

Jack was right. All of the ritual sacrifices had been recorded in the book. Abe had added, in his child-like scrawl, the record of the lamb's sacrifice at the bottom of a long list. The Old Testament book of Genesis contained scrawled instructions on animal sacrifices, the book of Revelation, human. Her stomach flipped and flipped as she tried to read them. She hadn't believed it, hadn't been able to grasp that ritual murder was a part of her heritage. She pictured Jack on the Isaac Stone, Abe standing over him with his wicked knife. She snapped the book closed and took deep calming breaths.

When she reopened it, she did so on the *Members of Our Family* page. Abe had recorded his own small family there, Sarah Woodley, his wife; David Woodley, his son. He had used a red ballpoint pen to slash a furious X through David's name, evidence of their feud writ large. Under her father's name was her own. Abe had underlined it twice, as if with glee.

She flipped to the section on sacrifices and tried to read. She gave up. *It's not right*. She closed the book and let it lay on her lap. She couldn't sacrifice the lamb.

None of the magic that Abe had taught her required suffering as an ingredient. She'd healed, she'd communed with animals, she'd refreshed spoiling food, and encouraged plants to grow. She knew the methods to adjust luck, positive and negative. She could protect her mind from influences like the Fountain. In a pinch, she knew the ingredients for a number of love spells and potions. She could predict the weather with a fair degree of certainty and, sometimes, tell how someone was feeling when they were close to her. All of these things and more, she had learned to do, but not one of them, not one, called for the spilling of blood. All of those spells, all of those adjustments to reality came, not from pain, but from her own power and, perhaps, from her belief in the God that hovered always in the back of her thoughts. This blood worship of her ancestors was evil. *No wonder Abe is dying.*

These rituals didn't fit the gentle man that she loved. They weren't Abe. Performing them, he must have been doing violence to himself. All of these years, practicing these dark acts out of fear and, all the time, watching things get worse. He must have blamed himself. He must have doubted the rituals, and those doubts had led him to believe that he was responsible for the Wall's failure. Using that knife had been like plunging it into his own soul. That great, black tumor was a sort of psychic scar tissue. She knew it. No wonder his power had turned against him. He'd been trapped by his ancestors, warped by their stunted beliefs. His parents had sacrificed him to their faith, and he'd let them. Could it be that Abe had tried to pass the burden on to his son and that David Woodley had fled? That would explain her grandfather and father's falling-out. Perhaps it was an awareness of how wrong the practices were that had kept Abe from telling her the whole truth. Maybe that was why he'd tried to keep her out? She didn't know, but the enormity of the burden that Abe had been carrying, all of the guilt, the isolation, and the sin came home to her, and she pitied him. The tears came then, and she let them. They made tracks down her cheeks and pooled in her palms when she cupped her eyes. Abe deserved to be cried over. She held his creased palm and wept. He was her grandfather, and she loved him.

The tears stopped. She sniffled a little, dried her eyes, and checked his temperature again. He was warmer. She returned to the bathroom with the washcloth, turned on the faucet. Nothing came. "You've got to be kidding me." Burst pipe or failed water pump at the well, she didn't know. It was one more thing. She searched the fridge. No water in there, either. She groaned. Where would she get water?

An idea sailed in from the darkness with a smooth, liquid simplicity. *The Fountain. It's full of water. The Wall is down. I can go get it. I can bring it back. I can heal him!* She looked down the slope into the dark of the valley. Her excitement grew. *What about the curse?* She fished her parka out of the closet, found the gloves in the pockets and pulled them on. *Jack said they threw the man's body in the water. He said that that was what caused the curse. If I get the skeleton out, the curse will be lifted. The spirit, or whatever it is, will be exorcised. I can undo what de Soto did. I can fix two things at once.* "I know that's it. I know it. That's the solution." She thought about the enormity of what she was proposing. To enter the valley, to go to the bottom, and to fish a long-dead man's remains from the Fountain. To seek out, to get closer to the source of so much evil. It seemed too much. It seemed insane. It was freezing outside, and who knew if the storm would return. She wrestled with herself. She didn't believe in calling a man to solve her problems, but she honestly didn't know if she could do what she proposed without help. *I should wait for Jack*. She returned to Abe's room and checked his forehead again. He was on fire. She cursed. "Jack, where are you?"

She moved into the study, poked the fire, and added a few more logs. She sat in Abe's recliner and waited for Jack. The little lamb butted its head against the cage and bleated. She ignored it, thinking. Jack might not be back for hours. If the phone at Preddy's worked, if an ambulance was dispatched, the dispatcher would ask that Jack wait at Our Lady. They'd want to be able to reach someone if the ambulance got lost. Jack would hate that she didn't know what was happening, but he wouldn't have a choice. He'd have to wait until they arrived. She checked Abe's grandmother clock, counted the hours till daylight. One, one and half. Not long at all.

She jumped to her feet and paced the carpet in front of the fireplace. She wanted to go to the Fountain; she needed to. *It's dangerous*. If she waited for Jack, it might be too late for Abe. That fever was out of control. She stopped and looked at the clock again. He might die before help arrived, or even if the ambulance made it, Abe could be too far gone.

She looked down at Jack's translation of Johan Ortiz's story of the Fountain and spoke aloud. "Somebody has to fix this, Jill. Somebody's got to do *something* about the Fountain. Grandpa is dying, and innocent people are hurting each other while you're trying to make up your mind."

The grandmother clock sliced away the seconds.

"If I go to the Fountain, I can solve both problems at the same time." She pulled her winter gear back on and rushed into the kitchen, wrote a quick note and put it on the table, slipped it under one of her grandmother's kissing-fish salt-and-pepper shakers. She went through her pockets, patted herself down to see if she'd forgotten anything, returned to Abe's closet for the flashlight, and then, finally, went out the kitchen door.

Outside, she collected a tin pail from the stoop. She'd need it to carry the Fountain's water. She looked at the night sky. Soon the cool winter sun would rise over the eastern mountains. Daylight should arrive by the time she made it to the bottom of the valley. She had no idea what to expect down there, didn't know exactly where the Fountain was. The light could only help. *Are you sure you want to do this?* She hesitated. *Are you sure this is a good idea?* She stood on the stoop for a moment longer, looked into the candlelit kitchen, warm and full of good memories and then back to the frozen valley below. She pulled her stocking cap down over her ears and headed down the mountainside.

I have to.

Chapter 56
Ronnie

December 27, 1987, 5:50 a.m.: Moondust Motor Inn, Windsor, Arkansas

Ronnie opened the motel office's door. The hinges squealed. He winced and crouched behind the reception desk. He listened, sweating. No one came. He hugged the pickaxe to his chest and counted to a hundred. Still no footsteps or raised voices. He rose and walked on tiptoe to the other door in the room. He pushed it gently, holding his breath. It rotated open without a sound. He exhaled.

He entered the candlelit kitchen on the other side. The room was chilly, the sink full of dishes. His stomach growled. The scent of roast turkey lingered in the air. He crept across the linoleum and peeked around the door frame into the study, empty but for a small lamb, visible by the light of the fire burning in the fireplace. It saw him and butted its head against the wire door of its cage, rustled in the straw. Ronnie froze. It bleated plaintively, then lay down with a snort. Silence returned. No one came to investigate.

He entered the room, his heart hammering with a mixture of fear and excitement. He could sense Pilgrim watching through his eyes, sharing his excitement. Ronnie scanned the room. No sign of guns.

Unfortunate, a rifle or pistol would have made his job easier. He moved to the picture window that opened onto the courtyard and looked as far toward the highway as he could see. No sign of the tall dude returning. He turned from the window. The pickaxe, forgotten in his hand, struck an end table lamp and sent it plunging to the floor. It smashed with a bright and terrifying crash. His heart froze in his chest. There was no way anyone could sleep through that. He crouched and raised the pickaxe, waiting to see who would come. No one did.

He frowned. Somebody *must* have heard that. They must have. Maybe they were trying to arm themselves before they came to see what was wrong. He checked with Pilgrim. The spirit didn't answer, simply urged him on, its earlier caution gone. Ronnie rushed down the hall. He stopped at the open door on the right. The bedroom glowed in the light of a hurricane lantern. The old man lay in his bed, covers pulled up. Somehow, despite the racket, he was still asleep. His face was white, his eyes lined with red. He didn't look good.

Ronnie grinned. *Got you, asshole. But first...*

He moved down the hall opening doors. Closet. Bathroom. Bedroom. With each room, his anger increased. Empty, empty, empty. The guest bed hadn't even been slept in.

He checked with Pilgrim, but the spirit gave him no response other than to point him back to the old man. *Kill the man, kill the Wall. Kill the man, kill the Wall.* Waves of the spirit's fury spilled into Ronnie's mind. He stomped back down the hall, frustrated and careless of the noise he made. He leaned over the old man in his bed and popped him on the cheek with his fingers. He didn't wake. He slapped him again, this time harder. "Wake up, asshole! Wake up!" Then again and again, until the old innkeeper's head rocked on his pillow; his sunken eyes opened, and his gray lips shuddered. He raised his hands in a weak bid to protect himself.

Pilgrim chuckled. He was enjoying this.

"Wake up!" Ronnie slapped the man a final time.

"Wha…?" The innkeeper's voice was full of sand, raspy and rough. He blinked his watery, blue eyes trying to focus on Ronnie.

Ronnie slapped him once more for the fun of it. "It's me, y'old bastard. You remember me? Heh. Bet you thought I was dead. Didn't ya?"

Recognition dawned on the old guy's face. "I—I—" He got an arm under him and pushed, then cried out in pain and fell back against his pillow. His hands moved to his stomach.

Pilgrim watched from Ronnie's mind, like a vulture perched on a fence.

"Something hurtin' ya, old man?" Ronnie popped his hand on the man's belly. The old guy lurched and cried out again. Ronnie laughed. He sensed Pilgrim's approval. He liked it. "Oh, boy." He poked the man's stomach again, laughed harder when he lurched and screamed. Two fat tears streamed down the side of the innkeeper's face. "I guess you don't like that much, do ya? Huh? Huh?" Ronnie prodded him twice more in the belly. The old guy gasped. His tongue looked like a sea creature darting in and out between his dried-up lips. He made no effort to hide his tears. Ronnie backed away from the bed and waited for him to regain his breath. He bounced the pickaxe in his hands and looked around the room. Typical old guy place, lots of knick-knack garbage from the fifties and sixties, some from before then, stupid porcelain owls and calendars from hardware stores, little bowls full of peppermints and penknives, odd string, and safety pins, a painting of a man praying over a half loaf of bread. Garbage.

He turned back to the old man in the bed. "Where's the girl?"

The old man shook his head and licked his lips. His eyes looked feverish, his skin sallow.

"Come on, old man." Ronnie improvised a lie. "I ain't gonna hurt her. I mean to get off this mountain without the cops catchin' me. I just gotta know where everybody is before I do. Don't want no surprises. I'm just gonna take your ol' truck—she runs right?"

The old man nodded, and a little cautious hope bloomed in his face.

Pilgrim pressed forward then, insisting that Ronnie end it, end it now.

Ronnie shuddered and pushed back, won a reprieve. "Good, good," Ronnie continued when he could speak again. "So I'm just gonna take the truck and hit the road. I don't want nobody calling the cops or tryin' to chase after me. Ain't nobody need to be a hero. So I just gotta find ever'body and make sure they're all in the same place. You know what I mean?"

The old guy nodded again. Small.

"So, where's the girl?"

The old man licked his lips and spoke in a raspy voice. "Pho—phone's out. Keys are in the wooden bowl…" He had to stop to catch his breath. "In the—in the kitchen. Nobody's gonna call nobody."

Pilgrim prodded harder, tried to take control of

Ronnie's hands.

Fear and rage swept through Ronnie. "That ain't what I asked!" He smashed the pickaxe through the headboard of the innkeeper's bed. "That ain't what I asked!" He struck again. The blade smashed through the portrait of the praying man, the glass shattered and scattered like flame-lit stars over the old man cowering in his bed. "That. Ain't. What. I. Asked!" He swung a final time. The picture frame fell and struck the old man a glancing blow to his head. A trickle of blood started under the innkeeper's thin white hair and ran down his forehead. "Where's the girl!" Ronnie raised the pickaxe as if to strike.

The old man stared at him. The hope died in his eyes, and it seemed that his life-light faded with it. He shook his head, no, clenched his jaw.

"Dammit!" Ronnie shook the pickaxe at the man. "Tell me! Tell me! Tell me!"

Again, the old man shook his head. No.

Ronnie's head pounded with frustration. Pilgrim gibbered his bloodlust in the back of his head. All of this time, and now he was to be cheated of the woman. He shook with rage and lust. He tried to think, tried to come up with a way to make the man speak. There must be a trick or something, something that would get him what he wanted, but thinking was hard. Pilgrim was pounding Ronnie's emotions, and his rage was spiraling. "Tell me!" he shrieked. The old man closed his eyes, refusing. Ronnie surrendered to Pilgrim's wishes. He drove the pickaxe's long steel spike through the old man's stomach and into the mattress.

The innkeeper screamed.

Ronnie dragged and twisted the pick from the

man's body, careless of the blood spattering his face, his overalls. He swung again and again and again until the old man was no longer moving, until the corpse's mid-section was a torn mess of gore, until Pilgrim was laughing with joy in his head and Ronnie's arms were quivering with exhaustion. He gave one final great swing of the axe, and this time the spike went straight through the man, the mattress, and into the wooden bedframe. He twisted and pulled to free it but could not. It was fully stuck. He released the handle and stepped back, wiped the blood from his eyes. He panted with exertion and frustration. *Dammit! Dammit! Dammit!* The old man's watery blue eyes fixed on him in death. Ronnie snarled and twisted away.

Pilgrim radiated satisfaction. The spirit rode a cushion of ecstasy, savoring the innkeeper's violent end. *Set the dogs on him.* The spectral voice echoed in Ronnie's head.

"Gawdammit!" Ronnie shouted. Even in death, the old man hadn't given him what he wanted. He screamed and yanked on the handle of the pickaxe again. It was no good. It wasn't coming out. He stalked around the bed, stomping his feet on the yellow-carpeted floor, picking up knick-knacks and throwing them against the walls. Anything to smash, to break. He destroyed things until he calmed, then tried extracting the pickaxe once more, no good. He needed a weapon. He came back around the bed and spotted a long, thin blade on the old man's end table. It was old and beautiful. He hefted it in his hand. The carved haft fit his palm like it was made for it.

He sat on the edge of the bed. *The car is here. The truck is here. I wasn't watching the tall dude that long*... He moved the thin blade through the air, swiveled the tip in small figure eights. "She's around here somewhere. She's around here." He walked back down the hall and checked the bedroom again. The closets were empty, no one under the bed. No one hid behind the bathroom curtain. He wandered back into the kitchen, opened the fridge, grabbed the milk jug, and turned it up. The cool liquid splashed into his mouth and down his chin. Out of the corner of his eye, he spotted a piece of yellow paper on the table. He picked it up and read it. She was going to the Fountain. To the Fountain. He whooped with joy and rushed out of the back door of the kitchen. The door swung partially closed behind him.

He ran as fast as he could, slipping in the icy snow as he went. His heart pounded in his chest, and the ground flew by beneath his feet. Finally, finally, it was happening. He was going to catch her. He was going to catch her good. God have mercy on her when he did, because Ronnie sure as hell wouldn't.

Chapter 57
Jack

December 27, 1987, 7:10 a.m.: Moondust Motor Inn, Windsor, Arkansas

Jack was weary and dejected when he arrived back at the motel. He found the truck keys in the kitchen, fished them out of the wooden bowl and checked to see if there was any coffee left. He swore to himself. Someone had left the back door open, and the coffee was gone, the blue camp percolator washed and top-down in the sink. He closed the back door and considered firing up the percolator again but decided against it. He needed to get the three of them on the road to the hospital. Abe needed help, and Jack wanted to report Preddy's murder. "Jill?" He walked toward Abe's sitting room. No response. "Jill," he repeated and walked down the hall. "We're going to have to take him in the truck, there's…" Abe's room was a blood-drenched mess. Jack's eyes couldn't seem to stay fixed on one thing., They jumped and jumped and jumped from Abe's face, to his feet, to the holes in the wall, to the blood, the blood, the blood. His eyes were open and filmed gray, his innards and blankets forever intertwined and sopping wet with blood and ordure. The red stuff was in the carpet, on the walls, on the ceiling. The blood was under Jack's feet and splashed on the curtains. The blood. He vomited. "Jill!" he screamed when he had finished. "Jill!" He ran down the hall, throwing open one door after another. Empty, empty, empty.

He hurried back to the kitchen, berating himself for failing to see the bloody footprints in the yellow pile carpet. How had Paul done this? Why? What did Preddy's deacon have against the old man? How had the guy managed to get back to the motel without Jack seeing him? Without seeing his footprints on the highway? It didn't make sense. He picked up the wall phone. The line was still dead. "Dammit!" He slammed the phone back into its cradle. It fell from the wall and clattered on the kitchen floor. Jack spun in place, panicking. *Oh God, oh God, oh God. Where is she?* His eyes fell on a red-smeared scrap of yellow paper lying under the kitchen table. He pounced on it and uncurled the paper in his fingers. He read with disbelief and fear. *She's alive.* He tore open the kitchen door and ran down the mountainside.

He had to get to Jill before Paul did.

Chapter 58
Leon

December 27, 1987, 7:05 a.m.: Moondust Motor Inn, Windsor, Arkansas

The International's headlights shone on Father Preddy's corpse as Our Lady came into Leon's view. He let the vehicle coast to a stop, so that he could be sure of what he was seeing. He trained binoculars on the feet of the statue. Preddy's face leapt into view. *Diaz.* Fear took him, and he slammed the gas pedal to the floor. He had to get to Jill. Preddy was dead; he couldn't help him. He had to save Jill.

The International swung wide on the final turn to the Moondust and slid in a graceful and unstoppable arc. Leon's stomach knotted up as he waited for the inevitable. The truck came to a jolting halt in the ditch beside the highway and rolled onto its side. His door was pinned under the weight of the vehicle. Leon cursed and slammed his fist on the steering wheel. He killed the engine and turned off the old truck's lights. The engine ticked, ticked, ticked as it cooled. "Dammit!" He pounded the steering wheel. "Dammit! Dammit!" He climbed up through the truck, got his flailing hand on the passenger side door release, scrambled out and onto the snowy shoulder. His boots slipped on the ice, and he went down, rolling into the ditch. "Dammit!" His shoulder hurt, but no permanent damage. He climbed to his feet and checked for his service weapon. It was still there, riding in its holster. *I've gotta find Jill. Stop Diaz.* Beyond that, he had no plans. Fear and anger were in control. He thought of only one thing. Find and stop Jack Diaz. By any means possible. He ran, slipping and sliding, the last hundred yards to the Moondust.

A door slammed as he entered the motel's circle drive. He sprinted the last few feet to the motel's office. He pulled his pistol and ran into the motel. There was a right way to do this, a procedure, but he couldn't make himself slow down. He couldn't. He was going to make Diaz pay for the priest, for the lies, for Jill, for all of it. He was going to make him pay. "By any means possible."

He went through the office, the kitchen, the den. He stopped at the first bedroom he came to. He took in the wreck of the old man, the pick through his stomach, the blood on the walls. Everything he had feared was true. Leon turned back to the kitchen, to the back door that he'd seen partially open on his first pass. He prayed he wasn't too late to save Jill, to stop Jack.

Chapter 59
Jill

December 27, 1987, 7:05 a.m.: The Isaac Stone, Windsor, Arkansas

Jill stopped at the Isaac Stone. She was glad to hear feet pounding down the trail behind her. It meant Jack had made it back and found her note. It was a relief that he'd caught up with her. She'd had time to rethink her impulsive decision a thousand times. Jack's presence gave her a renewed feeling of confidence. "Jack," she called and shifted the bucket from one hand to the other.

A figure darted between the trees, coming her way. The man that burst into the clearing wasn't Jack. She was stunned. The cowboy, the rapist, his face splattered in red and lips drawn back in a feral grin, stood at the bottom of the trail. He wore a pair of Abe's old orange coveralls. Jill stuttered. "You're—you're dead." The man's arm went back and back, a slow-motion wind-up. She turned to run. Her feet tangled. The world skipped on her, and she stumbled against the Isaac Stone. She looked back at the rapist. His arm shot forward. The thrown rock exploded against her temple. The world went dark.

Chapter 60
Ronnie

December 27, 1987, 7:06 a.m.: The Isaac Stone, Windsor, Arkansas

Ronnie placed the girl on the stone. It pleased him that all of those months' practice hunting with a rock was what he needed to bring her down. He rolled her onto her back and adjusted her to his liking, first with her arms by her side, then splayed out like a starfish.

Pilgrim watched, amused, but content to let Ronnie get after it.

He pulled the stocking cap from her head to free her hair. A large lump stood out on her brow. It marred her beauty, but he didn't care about that. He wanted her body. Besides, if he tilted her head a little, he couldn't see the wound. He yanked her hair out of its ponytail and spread it around her face. He adjusted a strand here and there, tugging it into place or tucking it away. He unzipped her jacket to expose her brilliant, red sweater and chuckled with delight at the shape of her breasts. He grasped the cashmere at the neck and yanked it hard to tear it open. The material was too strong.

The woman mumbled something, her eyelids moving back and forth. She was coming around. Ronnie smiled. That made it more fun. He gave up on tearing the sweater and pulled out the knife he'd found.

It felt right in his hand, hungry, like him. He tested the blade against the bottom of the cashmere. It cut. He ran the blade up the material, and it fell away from her chest. Her skin was creamy white and dimpled in the cold moonlight. He took a hitching breath and ran his palm across her stomach. It was smooth and warm. He licked his lips, cupped her breast in his hand. *Hell, yeah.* The material of her bra was lacy and rough.

Pilgrim chuckled in his mind.

Ronnie curled his index finger under the cup of her bra. Her eyes opened. He grinned at her and rested the point of the blade on her belly-button. "Look at you, Sunshine. You woke up just in time." He ran his finger up under the bra, felt the bulge of her breast. Her lips quivered, a tear ran down her cheek. He prodded her in the stomach with the tip of the long knife and ran it over her stomach, so that she could feel the edge.

She took a quick in-drawn breath.

"Don't you move now." Ronnie chuckled. "I don't expect you to do nothin' but lay there. I'm gonna make it easy on ya. I'm gonna do all the work." He pushed her bra up so that her breasts were exposed to the winter air. "Damn. I tol' ya she was a hot one," he told Pilgrim.

The woman shuddered, and her lips began to move. She was whispering something, something low, but that was okay. He didn't care. She could cry and holler. She could even sing, for all he cared.

Pilgrim's interest changed, became wary.

Ronnie didn't care about that, either. He held the knife blade against the woman's stomach and fumbled with the front of his coveralls. He had to shimmy to unzip them far enough to reach his member and to keep the knife under control.

The woman opened her eyes wide, and Ronnie, standing there with his penis in his hand, froze. He saw rage, not fear in the set of her face. Purpose, not hesitation. She was doing something, something strange. She was speaking aloud, and her voice rose so that Ronnie could hear.

"...curse of the Lord is in the house of the wi—" the woman said, her voice growing stronger as she spoke.

He felt a sudden stab of fear from Pilgrim, bright and powerful. The spirit seized control of Ronnie's hands and plunged the long knife into the woman's stomach, again and again, jabbing and tearing, ripping her apart. She screamed and screamed as the steel tore through her. Ronnie felt Pilgrim's emotions climbing and climbing, changing from fear to frenzy. It sliced the woman's throat, stabbed her in the breasts, then the belly again. Ronnie's shrieks were trapped in his head. The creature's thrill washed over him, a carnal wave of ecstasy. His body grunted and groaned in the grips of Pilgrim's raging pleasure, then bucked as, against Ronnie's will, it achieved a soul-scraping orgasm. He cried out, horrified, as his spent seed ran down the inside of his coveralls. Pilgrim, sated, plunged the knife home in the woman's stomach and stepped away from the stone.

Ronnie sagged as his body returned to his control. "No!" He bawled and fell to his knees. "No! No! No!" Tears poured from his eyes. He scrubbed at his wet coveralls, trying to wipe away what had happened, trying to wipe away his shame. He pulled the knife from her belly and tried to push her skin back together, tried to undo what Pilgrim had done. There was no fixing it. She was shredded. He screamed and plunged the knife into the dirt. He threw himself onto the ground and beat his fists and head on the soil, tried to batter the memories from his skull. Anything, anything to erase the last few minutes. He wanted to take it all back, to force Pilgrim to undo what he'd done. He howled. The woman he'd been dreaming about all of this time, the woman he'd almost had, his woman, was ruined. Ruined and wasted and dead. Dead. Dead. Dead. Ronnie had nothing left.

Pilgrim watched his pet's tantrum. It didn't care. The witch woman had been dangerous. Dangerous, as Sikena had been dangerous. He let the little cowboy vent his disappointment a little longer before sending the small man to hide in the woods. The tall man was coming, Pilgrim wanted to be ready.

Chapter 61
Jack

December 27, 1987, 7:22 a.m.: The Isaac Stone, Windsor, Arkansas

There was something on the Isaac Stone, something pale and white in the center of a red pool that ran down all four sides of the rough rock. *Oh, God, don't let it be.* But it was. "No!" Jack cried and ran to the stone. The skull grinned at him from its post as if sharing some lewd joke. "No!" He bent over her body and shook her by the shoulders, willing himself not to see the red ruin of her torso, the great gaping slash across her smooth white throat. "Please, Jill! Please, please!" Tears streamed down his face unnoticed. He kept shaking her, shaking her, hoping that she would wake, though he could see with his own eyes that she'd taken a terrible amount of damage, that her eyes were fogged with death. He fell to his knees at the side of the Isaac Stone and grasped one of her cold hands in his own. "Oh, God, why? Why?"

He exerted himself then, in desperation, reached deep for whatever power he had and tried to force it out. He begged it to come, whatever it was that had run through him on the night of the storm, whatever his ancestor Sikena had left in his body or spirit, he pleaded for it to come forth, to heal this woman that he loved.

For one moment, one silver moment, something stirred, some building vibration or energy, some curling of liquid electricity that snapped and curled in his veins, but, when he reached for it, it disappeared. He tried again and again, but it was slippery in his mind. He could not compel it. The more he grasped at it, the farther it fled from him. He lay his head on the stone then and wept, heartbroken and a failure. Once again, a failure.

The blow landed at the base of his skull. The pain was sharp and instant. Jack cried out and rolled away from the Isaac Stone. A baseball-sized rock rested on the ground between his feet, and a small shape in an orange jumpsuit was charging across the clearing with Abe's sacrificial knife in his hand. The cowboy.

Jack back-pedaled and put the stone between himself and his attacker. The cowboy jabbed the knife across the stone, trying to get at him. His face was red-lined with Jill's blood, his teeth exposed in a snarl. He growled like an animal and lunged. The blade sliced through Jack's stomach.

He felt blood sheet down his groin. He fumbled in his coat pocket, trying to get his Bowie knife out. His fingers felt like sausages, his pocket a puzzle that he couldn't solve. The murderer danced around the Isaac Stone, and, as he moved, Jack saw the shadowman that possessed him. The large black shape enveloped the orange jump-suited cowboy and rode him like a bad dream. It was the thing that Abe had described, Jack's ancient ancestor Remero Diaz, intent on mayhem and revenge.

Jack stumbled out of reach, and the Bowie came free. It turned in his fingers, and he dropped both knife and sheath into the dirt. He cursed and brought his fist around fast, striking the cowboy a glancing blow to the jaw. It had been a lucky hit. The cowboy was fast, inhumanly fast.

The cowboy fell backwards against the Isaac Stone and shook his head muzzily. He ran a blood-drenched hand across his mouth and grinned at Jack. "Damn. You hit like a girl."

Jack crouched and picked up his Bowie, unsheathed it.

The two men faced each other.

The cowboy's breath came heavy, and his face was splotchy with blood, some dried, some fresh. Jack wasn't paying attention to him. He was watching the shadow riding the little man's body, the way that it moved over his limbs with a greasy and repellant intimacy. He was certain that the cowboy's strength came from the spirit. "Remero! Remero Diaz!" Jack called. He backed away, put his hands up.

"I ain't no Remero. I'm Ronnie, asshole." His face writhed with anger and, then, sudden fear. His body twitched as if he were trying to move, to attack, but could not.

The shadowman lurked over Ronnie's small frame. It appeared to be studying Jack.

Jack continued. "I know, Remero. I know what happened to you. I read the journal of Johan Ortiz. I am—I am your descendant. Your great, great—It doesn't matter!"

Ronnie whined and his lips writhed, but still he stood frozen while the shadowman listened.

"I can put your spirit to rest," Jack said. He lowered his knife, and Ronnie twitched. The veins in the murderer's neck stood out as he wrestled against the shadowman that held him in place. Jack smothered the urge to kill him where he stood, to make him pay for what he'd done. *Dispel the evil first, then deal with the piece of shit left behind.* "I will give your remains a proper burial. I promise. Please give over your revenge. Sikena lived, Remero! Your descendants live! I will make it right." Jack placed his open palm on the shoulder of the shadowman. The spirit reached back, seeking Jack's consciousness. He let it. He wanted to break through, to find some connection with this ghost of Remero Diaz.

It was like stepping into sewage, the aura of the shadowman ran through Jack's soul like a scouring pollution. Jack gasped and began to pull away. Something was wrong. This was no ancestor of his. This was a ravening beast, a creature of hunger and evil.

"Pilgrim says," Ronnie snarled, "that he's glad that he has the chance to kill Remero's grandson, too." Abe's knife plunged into Jack's side.

Jack gasped and twisted, as the hot tip slid around in the muscle of his stomach wall. This wasn't his ancestor. This wasn't Remero Diaz. This wasn't some confused and hurting spirit. This creature, this thing, was some dark sink of sin, depredation, violence, and evil. It didn't seek revenge; it enjoyed the evil that it did. *De Soto.* Jack stared at the shadowman. He knew, now. De Soto never lived to make it out of the valley. Sikena's ancestors had gotten their revenge, after all. The Fountain hadn't been corrupted by Remero Diaz's murder; it had been haunted by the ghost of this evil man. De Soto was the source of all the pain and the suffering that had happened since. De Soto had been the evil that Abe and his ancestors had been holding at bay.

The shadowman flowed between Jack and Ronnie, enveloped Jack in a black embrace. The spirit's touch brought madness. The pain in his stomach was forgotten, the anger and grief gone. Jack fought to hold on to who he was while the ghost of Hernando de Soto tried to eat his soul. He was losing.

Ronnie twitched, and the blade, tearing Jack's skin, slicing through muscle, snapped him out of it. He screamed to his power, and uncontrolled, it rose to repulse de Soto. Jack swung a backhanded fist at Ronnie, knocked him and the shadowman back against the stone. The murderer's eyes wobbled. Jack struck once more, and Ronnie's legs failed him. He fell back across Jill's splayed corpse. Jack planted a hand on his shoulder and stabbed his Bowie knife down to finish him.

The knife didn't land.

A hammering bullet took Jack in the shoulder and spun him away from the Isaac Stone. He staggered down the hill a step, two, knife hanging forgotten in his hand. He blinked and blinked, his eyes gone fuzzy with shock. There was a man in the tree line, a man pointing something at him. Leon. Jack heard another report. The hammering bullet struck him high in the chest and knocked him flat on the ground. Jack stared stupidly at the red bloom on his jacket. He fought and rolled on to his side.

"Stay down!" Leon shrieked and ran to him. His breath came in chunks, ragged and vicious. "Stay down!"

"He—" Jack tried to protest, but something

obstructed his airway. He coughed and blood splattered onto his chin. He couldn't breathe. He was being constricted in a great vise. He lifted a shaking hand to his mouth, and it came away red. "He…"

Ronnie rose from the stone to meet Leon.

"Get the fuck out of the way." Leon commanded. He struck Ronnie with a backhand, knocking him to the ground. Leon's face was tight with bottled madness. His eyes, lined with red strain, were fixed on Jack. He shrieked with rage and agony. His pistol wavered, and he turned to Jill.

"Wha—what'd'ya do that for?" Ronnie ran a hand over his swollen lips. He clenched his jaw and fumbled for his knife. Leon didn't notice.

"Why did you do it?" Leon shrieked at Jack. The policeman beat his hands against the side of his forehead, then bent with a wail, as if to vomit. He clenched one hand in a fist against his thigh and pointed the pistol in Jack's direction. He took two, then three, hitching steps. He made *hurk*, *hurk*, *hurk*ing sounds in his throat and spewed his last meal onto the ground.

Ronnie circled behind Leon and raised his knife.

Jack tried to cry out but couldn't catch a breath. He hitched himself up and coughed. Blood splattered the ground. He waved to get Leon's attention, to get the man to turn and face Ronnie.

Leon ran his fist across his eyes, wiping away tears. He aimed his pistol at Jack. "Stay down, Diaz!" His words came out frayed. Rage battled its way across his face. The pistol shook in his hand.

"I—I didn't. Do. This…" Jack lifted a trembling finger and pointed at the little cowboy who had gone low, was moving up behind Leon, but Leon wouldn't turn away, wouldn't listen. Jack lunged forward and grasped the policeman's ankle. "Please!" A black wave of pain rolled through his body, leaving him gasping and on the bare edge of consciousness.

Leon struck him in the temple with his pistol. Lights flashed in Jack's skull, and he collapsed onto his back. The world washed in and out of focus. He groaned and looked up at Leon, outlined against the morning sky.

Leon's pistol was in Jack's face. His lips were drawn back, a rictus of pain and hate. "You piece of shit. You complete piece of shit. Why did you have to kill her?" His finger tightened on the trigger.

Ronnie jabbed his blade into Leon's back, once, twice, three times. He was all over him, stabbing and stabbing. Leon shrieked and fell to the ground. The pistol went off. The wild bullet caromed off the sacrifice stone and whined into the sky. Ronnie laughed and laughed, delighted with his work. He spat on Leon. "Fuckin' pig. Gonna let you bleed out, brother. Like a stuck pig. Get it? Huh? Pig!" He kicked the policeman in the side, twice and hard, then turned away.

He set Abe's knife on the sacrifice stone and bent to pick up the dropped pistol. "Who you think you gonna hit?" He rapped Leon on the forehead with the pistol. He popped the clip, pulled the slide, and looked for the round inside, then reversed the action, clicked the safety to off. "Jesus, man. Nine mils are pieces of shit. Why don'tcha get a real gun, huh?"

Leon's breath came hard. His face was losing color as he drained blood onto the floor of the clearing. He had his hands over his belly, trying to keep his guts from spilling out. His lips moved as if he would speak.

He caught Jack's eyes. The two men stared at each other while their lives drained away.

Ronnie turned to Jack, pistol in hand. "Your name, Diaz, huh?"

Jack didn't answer.

"Pilgrim said it was," Ronnie continued, "and then old Porkchop." He waved at Leon. "He said your name, too. Funny world, huh? Pilgrim done killed your great, great-grandpa, and now I get to help him kill *you*. Sucks to be you, buddy." He squatted. He smelled of sweat and blood. He poked the wound in Jack's chest with the pistol and smiled when Jack screamed. He leaned back on his heels, chuckling. The shadowman lurked over Ronnie's features, watched Jack with curiosity and pleasure. "That your girl?" He asked. He pointed at the stone.

Jack drew in a hard breath., It bubbled in his chest.

"I swear, buddy," Ronnie continued. "She was a sweet piece. I didn't get none of her, though. I tried. Boy howdy, I tried, but it didn't work out. She was trying some magic mumbo-jumbo, and we had to kill her off." He sighed. "Pilgrim tells me he'll get me some more, though. Anyone I want really." He seemed to cheer. "You almost had me. I swear you're a tough son of a bitch." He poked Jack's wound again.

Jack groaned.

Ronnie chuckled again. He pointed the gun at Jack's face, ran its muzzle in small circles, around and around, tapped Jack's left brow, then his right, then his chin, then pulled back to sit on his haunches, the gun still pointed casually in Jack's direction. "I'm tougher, hombre."

Please, Jack begged his hidden power, *please. You*

did something before. Please... He could feel it. It trembled like an unfolding flower at the base of his spine. It spun and churned in his blood. When he reached for it, it slipped away. "Ronnie. You—you've got a demon riding on your shoulder," Jack ground out. "Did you—did you know?"

Ronnie's smile was cocky, but his eyes told a story of fear. "Who? Pilgrim? Pilgrim's my buddy. He helps me out, Diaz."

Jack could see de Soto's spirit sliding in and out of Ronnie's body, moving up and down through his skin, running into his mouth and ears. He understood now why they called it possession. Pilgrim owned Ronnie, even if Ronnie didn't want to admit it.

Jack reached for the power. It slipped away. He could feel it, feel it pumping through him. It was strong, but he couldn't use it, couldn't send it where he wanted. "I don't know, Ronnie..." He was growing dizzy and sagged over his arm, trying to keep the cowboy talking, trying to buy time for his power to manifest. De Soto's spirit watched him.

"What are you doing?" Ronnie asked, frowning. "Pilgrim don't like it."

Jack ignored the question. "Some—something like Pilgrim," he slurred, "will eat you up."

"Nah. He's my friend." He waved the gun around the clearing. "He helped me do all this, ya know? Ya'll left me for dead down in that valley. Hell, ya'll were probably glad I was dead." He spat on the ground.

Jack could hear the man speaking, but his body was growing cold, cold, colder. The power pumping through him didn't seem to touch any part of him. He was losing the will to struggle with it. He was dying.

The thought didn't bring tears to his eyes. He'd spent those on Jill. The worst had come. Everything was over. All the fighting, all the struggles. They were done. He was beaten. Whatever happened next was going to be all right. It had to be, because the worst thing he could imagine had already come to pass. He'd lost Jill. His life was nothing in comparison.

Ronnie droned on, but Jack wasn't listening. He was floating in a peaceful space inside of his own head. He embraced the pain, let it flow, let it be. Let it all, let everything…be.

"You went and killed my buddies," Ronnie accused Jack. "Then I got my beautiful car wrecked. Assholes like you and that old man, you're always ruining things for people like me. I ain't never had nothin' or nobody to give a shit about me. Pilgrim cares." Ronnie banged the pistol hard against Jack's forehead and repeated himself. "Pilgrim cares."

Jack saw the pistol aimed at his face again. He smiled to himself. This was becoming a habit. Ronnie's eyes were tight with hate. De Soto crouched over the man's skin. He would never know which of them pulled the trigger, the man or the spirit. He chuckled from his closed-off world and let his eyes drop closed.

Ronnie snarled. He didn't like, Jack thought, that he wasn't begging for his life. *Too bad for him.*

The power twisted inside of him. He wished it a final farewell. *You're going to have to take it from here. I've got nothing left.* The power rose in response, a silver flood that sprang from the base of Jack's spine, twined around his backbone, flowed through Jack, a searing heat. The light built and built and, somehow, offered to take it all away, the pain, the fear, the sorrow, everything. If only he'd stop fighting.

Jack let go. He let it all go.

The power jolted through him with a sudden burst of electric heat. It cascaded along his limbs, bloomed in his mind with a liquid eruption of joy and life. His gunshot wounds knit; his belly screamed as the edges of his wound closed. A new energy suffused his body. Jack threw back his head and screamed in ecstasy and pain. A part of him was dying. The black and despairing part of his psyche, the part that had hated and feared, the part that had been selfish and self-absorbed, burned away. It blackened and curled up like cauterized tissue, vaporized and disappeared. He was washed in a stream of cleansing force. He kept a thin grasp on consciousness but no longer knew what he was, only that he was alive. *I am.... I am...* The power streamed from his head, his shoulders. It reached for de Soto's spirit.

Jack didn't hear the gun go off or Ronnie's screams as his mind was shredded by the struggling spirit. De Soto fled his pet's mind, leaving a ruined hulk.

The power flowed now, unconstrained, and unguided. It whipped through Jack's body. *I am...* His mind snapped back, whole and clean. *Jack.* He opened his eyes. Light streamed from his body, swirling and furling through the air like a flock of starlings changing direction in beautiful and natural concert. The power built glowing patterns in the air, stacked them higher and higher, and then curled and swooped to wrap Ronnie and de Soto in a blanket of light and life. It snubbed the man up tight. The shadowman, de Soto, shrank, compressed, and constricted like a tallow candle squeezed in a tight fist. It twisted in the power's grip but could not escape the fire.

De Soto shrieked, high and on the edge of Jack's hearing. The shadowman was falling apart, shredding in front of his eyes. It was dying. The darkness, all of the sin that the spirit represented, was being eaten up, swallowed in chunks by the power roaring through Jack's body. He felt the spirit's intelligence, torn down and absorbed into his own. The power fed de Soto into Jack's mind and, like an alloy, in the blending the spirit became something else, an amalgam of iron hatred and silver life, of resolute vengeance and striving hope. Like the melding of carbon and iron into steel, Jack became harder and stronger. He became more.

Ronnie's screams were frantic now. He yipped as the power, cleansing him of evil, burned his mind away. He was left no more than a hurting animal. He curled around himself in the dirt and hugged his knees to his chest.

It was over, the spirit, the shadowman, de Soto, consumed. Ronnie burned out, mindless.

Jack's power swirled free and triumphant in the winter morning light. It moved through the soil and the stone, cleaning the land of the accumulated sins of blood and sacrifice that Abe and his ancestors had visited on the site. It flowed through the trees around the clearing, destroyed the ancient skull-topped totems in bursts of bright fire.

Jack watched in wonder. He rose to his feet and walked to where Leon lay on the ground. Each step was a jubilation, a celebration of life. The dirt sprouted fresh grass under the soles of his feet. It spread and the smell of spring graced the morning air. Leon's chest rose and fell weakly. His face whitened.

Jack looked down on the man, then turned to look at Jill. He placed a gentle hand on the woman's forehead. The power surged through his body again, reassuring him that all would be well. The last of his grief burned away. A rising certainty replaced it.

Leon's eyes were on Jack. He looked afraid.

Chapter 62
Leon

December 27, 1987, 7:22 a.m.: The Isaac Stone, Windsor, Arkansas

The rising sun limned Jack's form in golden light, and a hot ball of pain clawed the inside of Leon's gut. He squinted into the light. Jack stood over him, his angular face smooth and full of a beautiful serenity.

Leon coughed; something inside of his chest shifted. Jack's coat was blood-drenched, his hands coated in dried blood. He couldn't understand how he was breathing, let alone standing. Leon propped himself on an elbow, but the pain was too great. He cried out and fell back to the blood-soaked patch of dirt. Jack pointed at him and a burst of heat passed through his body. Like a swarm of bees, it rushed down his limbs and through his outraged belly and back. It brought a thousand sharp stabs of pain and a bursting vibration that took his breath before he could scream. It passed. He was whole. The pain was gone, and Jack stood in the same place he had before, his face peaceful.

Leon warily climbed to his feet. "What…" He ran his hands over his belly, looking for punctures and not finding any. "What did you do?"

Jack held his hands apart in a gesture that looked like surrender.

"Why don't you answer me?"

Jack moved to the stone and bent to touch Jill's hair. Leon scowled and tears came to his eyes. How could this man be so calm? Jill was dead. *He must be crazy.*

He edged his way around Jack, moving slow to avoid catching his attention. Fresh spring grass now filled the clearing. Small flowers of red and white populated the area around the great stone that held Jill's corpse. Leon took it in, the forest frozen and winter-dead, this clearing alive and sparkling with life. He couldn't understand it. He shoved the thought aside and focused on what he knew. He bent down by the little man in the orange coveralls. Jill's murderer, most likely Abe's, almost his own.

The creep was no longer weeping. He had his knees hugged to his chest, his face, tanned and lined from long exposure to the sun, was empty of emotion or thought. He looked blank as a baby.

Leon crouched to pick up his pistol. It smelled of burnt gunpowder and was reassuring in his hand. In a world gone off-kilter, the weapon was a bit of reality. He had to tug to pull it from the fresh grass grown around the blued steel. He turned back.

Jack no longer bent over the stone. He stood, feet planted solidly in the blooming clearing and gazed at Leon. He bore Jill in his arms, held like a baby with her forehead against his shoulder, her arms and legs dangling limp and lifeless. The stone shone red in the new dawn light. The blood reflecting back the sun looked innocent, as if it weren't the very life of the woman he'd loved, splattered and wasted on the surface of the mountain.

"What are you doing?" he asked.

Jack took a step down the slope, cradling Jill.

Leon raised his pistol uncertainly, pointed it at Jack. "Where are you going? Put her back, Jack. Put her back where she was." He sounded like a child to himself, scared and petulant.

Jack kept walking until he stood within arm's reach of Leon.

Leon put both hands on his gun to keep it from shaking. He pointed the weapon at Jack's face. He couldn't bear the thought of putting a bullet through Jill's body. "Jack." He tried to be reasonable, tried to master his own emotions. "I know you've been through a lot. I know, man. But you can't take her." The glow around Jack hadn't been a trick of the sun. He radiated a pure white light in the dawn. His face was so peaceful, so calm, that Leon was certain that something had broken in the man. "Put her down, Jack," Leon motioned at the stone.

Jack ignored him.

Leon scowled. "Put her back on the stone." He gestured with the pistol again.

Jack looked at the stone. It made a great cracking noise and crumbled into a hundred, a thousand pieces of small red rock. It rolled and tumbled into a pile and scattered in the fresh grass.

Leon's mouth fell open. He stared at Jack and realized that he didn't know what to do.

"I'm leaving now," Jack said, as if dredging the words up from deep in his memory. He walked around him.

Leon turned. Jack, carrying Jill, climbed the low fence of sun-whitened bones. He placed his feet and walked as if he was scaling the side of a small and gentle slope.

"Where are you going?" Leon asked.

Jack didn't answer.

"Stop!" Leon heard the desperation in his voice. "Please don't take her. Please don't!" The tears flowed from his eyes, left scorching tracks down his cheeks. He lowered the gun and begged. "Please don't take her."

Jack turned, and his expression changed. The tall man's lips turned down and his eyes softened. "I have to. I'm sorry, Leon. I have to."

Leon wailed until it knotted in his throat. A sudden weakness washed through his body. He fell to his knees and dropped the gun. "Take me? Please? Take me?"

Jack shook his head, no.

Leon wiped his eyes, felt the grass under his other hand, smelled the fresh flowers and the spring-like air. He remembered how it had felt when his life was draining away, the knowledge that his insides had been slashed beyond repair. Then he remembered the scouring and cleaning healing power that had righted what was beyond fixing. "Can you—Can you...heal her? Can you bring her back?"

Jack smiled at him, looked at the girl, looked down into the valley for a long moment, as if searching for something, and then back at Leon. "Me? No. Not me..." His voice rose at the end, as if there were more to say. He stood for a moment, looked like he would finish, would explain that there was hope, but he didn't. "Goodbye, Leon." He descended the bone fence into the valley, Jill in his arms.

Leon darted forward to follow the man into the

valley. He could not cross the fence of bones. He watched, helpless, as Jack descended the valley wall.

Jill's limp arm came up and around Jack's neck, like a sleepy child, as if holding on.

Leon shook his head. It was impossible.

He watched until they disappeared. He sat on the fresh grass, wet with the morning dew and tried to understand. The sun broke free of the mountain across the valley. Understanding was beyond him. He holstered his pistol and pulled the little orange-clad man to his feet. The murderer offered no resistance, took his hand with innocent eyes. Leon led him up the mountainside.

Things needed to be done. Things needed to be explained. Citizens needed help.

As he climbed, the sunlight flooded the mountainside like a benediction, lighting the frozen trees with a million diamond flashes. Leon, tears unnoticed on his face, felt an unaccustomed wonder. He hoped that what he'd seen hadn't been an illusion or a hope-driven fantasy. He prayed that Jack had found a way and that Jill lived. He locked that hope away in his mind, a promise that the woman he loved still graced the world.

One day, he resolved, he'd see her again.

A word about the author...

Christopher Farris is a veteran of both the United States Air Force and the United States Army National Guard, a former IT executive, and a family man. After many years and a few life-changing experiences, he has returned to his first love—literature.

He and his wife live in a small house built in 1921 (1,000 square feet) nestled in an equally small town buried deep in a valley of the Boston Mountains of Northwest Arkansas. Together, they try to coax life out of their reluctant roses and manage their three crazy dogs.

He has short stories published by Fairlight Books, Proud to be: Writing by America's Warriors, Military Experience and the *Arts and Coffin Bell Journal*. *The Fountain* is his first novel.

Visit him at:

https://cmfarris.wixsite.com/ozarkgothic

Thank you for purchasing
this publication of The Wild Rose Press, Inc.

For questions or more information
contact us at
info@thewildrosepress.com.

The Wild Rose Press, Inc.
www.thewildrosepress.com